The Flying Yorkshireman

The
Flying Yorkshireman

NOVELLAS

ERIC KNIGHT · HELEN HULL · ALBERT MALTZ

RACHEL MADDUX · I. J. KAPSTEIN

With a Note by WHIT BURNETT *and* MARTHA FOLEY

HARPER & BROTHERS PUBLISHERS
New York and London
1938

A STORY PRESS BOOK

To

Thérèse Heilner Simon

TABLE OF CONTENTS

The Flying Yorkshireman

BY

Eric Knight

The Flying Yorkshireman

THE CONVICTION that he could fly didn't come over Sam Small gradually. It just hit him all of a sudden.

That night he and Mully had been down to Los Angeles to hear Sister Minnie Tekel Upharsin Smith at the Temple. First off Sam hadn't wanted to go, but before it was over even he agreed that it was quite a bit of a do, and Mully had as rare a time as she'd had in all her born days.

Sister Minnie sang a hymn she had written herself, which started:

Won't you buy my violetsss—m'dam?

When that was over she had all the people who were from California stand up and turn round and shake hands with the people who were sitting and who weren't from California, and say: "God Bless you, Brother or Sister," as the case was.

Sam felt right funny what with a stranger pumping his hand, but Mully began to warm up to the whole thing; so that when Sister Minnie asked the people from foreign lands to get up and say where they were from, Mully kept nudging Sam to stand on his legs like a man and put their ha'porth in. But Sam wasn't having any. People got up and shouted that they were from Germany and Italy and China and Hawaii and Mexico and Canada. There was even one chap from India.

Finally Mully couldn't stand it any longer, so she tied her bonnet tight under her chin and got up and shouted at the top of her lungs:

"Mr. and Mrs. Sammywell Small, Powki'thorpe Brig, near Huddersfield, Yorksha', England."

Then she sat down with her face all flushed, while everybody applauded and the woman next to her, who was from the city of Ioway, struck up acquaintance with her, and Mully decided that California was the right nicest and friendliest place they'd struck since they'd started on that trip around the world.

Sam tried to make out as if he didn't think much to it all, but even he got interested when Sister Minnie tore into her sermon.

It was entitled: "Faith Will Move Mountains," and a rare champion thing it was, too, all full of quotations and rhetoric and little halts to give the people chance to applaud, and big halts where everyone sang the chorus of a hymn and clapped their hands to keep time. During these long pauses Sister Minnie would work up another store of energy and come out for the next round fresh as a daisy.

Everything depended on Faith, she said, and for her part she believed in it so much that she just *knew* that if the 5000 or so Brothers and Sisters present tonight, Praise be to God, were to head right out of that Blessed Temple and drive down to San Bernardino, she would bet you right now that if they would have Faith together they could make Mount Baldy shift ten feet toward the sea. The only thing that stopped her from putting it all into execution, she said, was that her legal advisers had told her it would cause too many possible suits for damages; because naturally, if you moved a mountain ten feet there was going to be a lot of disturbance. There'd be a ten-foot gap on one side, like as not running down through a lot of good real estate developments, and on the other side there'd be a churning and a whortling of the earth that wouldn't be too good for California. People with spiteful tongues were ready enough to talk about earthquakes anyhow, even when you could call up the Chamber of Commerce and find out it was never a thing at all but the Battle Fleet off San Diego in firing practise that was making the ornaments on the mantelpiece sound like Fred Astaire in the introduction part of the Packard hour on the radio.

But nevertheless, as she was saying, Faith was a very, very wonderful thing, in fact, a marvelous thing, and if the Sisters and Brothers believed in our Dear Lord Jesus and believed in the power of Faith, there was nothing they couldn't do. Nothing!

That was the sermon on Faith, and everybody applauded and clapped their hands in rhythm, being not only pleased with Sister Minnie's faith, but her evident faith in their faith, and her clever explanation of why they were not going to have to drive ninety miles on a chilly evening to do anything about demonstrating it.

That was about the end of the do. They closed up with some more hymns, one half the audience singing and then the other half to see who could be loudest; then the women singing and after them the men all by themselves, to see who could be loudest. And then it was over and everybody streaked for the doors.

Mully had had a good time, and there was no two ways about that. When she and Sam had pushed out through the crowd and were standing on the corner, waiting for the Wilshire Boulevard bus, she got enough words together to say:

"Well, Ah don't knaw how tha feels about it, Sammywell, but Ah've had a rare good time, and Ah think this is the right nicest place us has struck in all our travels."

Sam didn't doubt that she'd enjoyed it, but he knew, too, her remark was all part of the campaign to keep him in California. Neither Mully nor Lavinia, their daughter, ever missed a chance to put in a good word about Southern California. Vinnie wanted to stay so's she could have a bit of a dab at becoming one of these cinema stars; and Mully wanted to stay partly because of Vinnie and partly because she could never get over it that palm trees really grew in a white man's land. On top of that, there was no doubt about it that Sam had given the women quite a turn with the bad attack of bronchitis he'd had when they were visiting Vancouver.

So, of course, they never missed any opportunity now to keep after Sam about how good California was for his chest, and how that since he now was retired and a chap of independent means as you might say, there was no use leaving this sunshine to go dashing right back to England.

Now Sam knew all about the way the women were working on him, and he knew why they were doing it. He knew, too, that it wasn't over sensible to battle with them because probably they'd wear him down in the end. But still and all, a chap can't help putting his ha'porth in once in a while. So he blew his nose and said:

"Aye, taking the rough with the smooth, this ain't a bad place—for Yankeeland, o'course. But still and all, Ah'd give ten quid, Ah would, reight now, to be sitting back hoam i' t' Spread Eagle wi' ma chums on either side o' me and a good pint o' Guinness's in front o' me and a nice gert big coal fire to warm ma behind on."

Mully snorted.

"Sammywell," she said. "Didn't Ah tell thee to put a clean henker-cha' in thy pocket afore tha coomed out toneight?"

Sam knew he was licked if he got drawn away from the subject into any minor skirmishes. Everyone's cock on their own midden tip, and he wasn't off to argue about handkerchiefs, where Mully was on her own ground. So he just jammed his shameful bandana into his pants pocket and kept quiet. Mully kept on giving him a little bit of hell— the way a woman will; and finally Sam stopped listening to her—the way a man will.

And while she barneyed on, his mind went floating away in a hazy sort of a manner and settled on two things. First he began wishing the bus would hurry up and come so Mully would stop talking; second he got to thinking about Sister Minnie's sermon. He began wondering if there was anything to it all—this Faith business. He began wonder-ing if a whole bunch of people, all having Faith together with a sort of yo-heave-oh effect, really could move a mountain—if only for a mat-ter of an inch or two.

He thought about it a long time, and decided that if a chap was going to do anything with Faith, he'd be smart if he picked on some-thing rather easy at first and progressed gently to stubborn things like mountains.

Now all the time Sam had been thinking that, he'd been standing there waiting for the bus—and it gets rare chilly in California when the sun goes down. And that was what put the bus idea in his head. He said to himself that if a chap decided to try moving things by Faith a bus would be a champion thing to begin on—it having wheels which, as you might say, would aid the whole proposition.

It was no sooner thought than done, because, as Sam said to him-self, it doesn't cost a chap a ha'penny to have Faith. Even if it doesn't work out, what have you lost?

So Sam shut his eyes and said to himself: "Ah have Faith that by t' time Ah open ma ee's that so-and-so bus will have arrived."

And by gum, he had no sooner said it than Mully was poking him in the short ribs and saying:

"Wakken up, gormless!"

And he opened his eyes, and there was the bus standing there.

Now naturally Sam was both surprised and pleased. As he said to himself, it might have been just a bit of coincidence, but still and all, it fair gave a chap something to think about. The best thing to do about it, he decided, was to give it a good thinking over. So when he got himself settled nicely on the bus he started putting his mind to thinking about Faith, and kept at it all the way home, being only interrupted once as the bus went past the Beverley-Wilshire and Mully said she saw Nelson Eddy coming out of the Brown Derby.

After that Sam got back to his thinking and kept right at it until they got to the end of the line. Then he and Mully got off right by the statue of Santa Monica on the Beach Drive palisade, and walked slowly and wearily along the palisade toward their boardinghouse.

They were both quite a bit played out after their exciting evening, and they went along slowly, arm in arm. Mully always liked that good night walk along the alameda, because it was peaceful and romantic and so tropical. Bordering the gravel walks there are no less than *three* kinds of palms: date palms, royal palms and palmettoes. Then, too, it's on a cliff high up over the shore, and as you walk along you can look out over the rustic wood railing and see far out to the ocean, or you can look straight down on the shore and see all the beach castles of the movie stars. They are all very splendid and big, but the biggest and most splendid one belongs to Marion Davies. It is such a sight that the tourist buses always stop by that palisade and all the sightseers get out and have a five minute stop to look down on the very home that Marion Davies lives in sometimes.

Mully never tired of looking down from that palisade. She never liked to go to bed without a sort of good night look at it; because she always thought that some night she might see a light in an upstairs window, and that would be Marion Davies going to bed, perhaps.

So when Sam and Mully got up by Marion Davies' house, they stopped and looked over the rail. There was Mully, full up of the awe of standing underneath a real palm tree and looking at a real cinema star's palace, and never aware of what Sam was thinking. For Sam, now he'd stopped walking, was able to think again. He had his pipe going good, and there he stood, looking far out over the ocean to where the fifty-cent all-night fishing barge lay, lit up and festooned with lights so that it looked like a twinkling diamond brooch of a ship.

And it was there and at that moment, that he first got his amazing conviction. Perhaps it came from being so high up, together with the sermon and the upsetting episode of the bus coming by Faith. No matter what it was, he got the conviction as surely as ever a man had one.

What he felt was that he could fly. That was the conviction he had. He had it so strongly that he couldn't keep quiet about it.

"Mully," he said. "Tha knaws, sometimes Ah hev a feeling that a chap could put out his arms and launch himself off of here and fly—if he nobbut hed Faith."

"Aye. If!" Mully retorted. "And if thy aunt hed of hed you-know-whats she'd ha' been thy uncle."

In spite of her determination to live up to the position of wife of a rich retired man, Mully could be quite Yorkshire at times. And her last remark wasn't calculated to help a chap who wanted to talk things over. Not things like Faith and really moving mountains.

It really made Sam a bit mawngy. But there's one thing about a Yorkshireman. The madder you make him, the more determined he gets. And as Sam got undressed that night he couldn't help feeling stubborn.

"Well, at that," he said to himself, "Ah'll bet a chap *could* do it—if he hed Faith enow."

He kept thinking that after he got into bed. He felt he'd like to fly, just to show Mully that she wasn't right all the time. And as he lay there, he had Faith, and had Faith, and then his hair almost stood on end. For he could feel his body lifting, and lifting, until it was completely clear of the bed beneath him.

IT WAS SO AMAZING that he could hardly believe it himself. So, cautiously, he passed his hand under his body. It was true! As far as he could reach, he was free of the bed. It was so staggering that he had to drop back into bed to think it over. He must have been quite clear of the bed, because when he dropped back the mattress squeaked, and Mully said, snippily:

"Ba gum, Sammywell, if tha doesn't stop jiggling this bed Ah'm bahn to get up and sleep on t' sofa."

But Sam hardly heard her. He was too upset at his discovery. He decided to wait until Mully was surely asleep and try it again, but unfortunately he fell asleep himself.

In the morning when he woke, his first thought was to tell Mully of his wonderful discovery. But, somehow, it didn't seem too easy in the daylight, sitting there at the breakfast table, with the California sunshine spanking down on the tablecloth and on the tea pot and muffins and marmalade and porridge and eggs and a little rasher of ham and cold steak-and-kidney pie and two or three nice bloaters that Mully had bought down in a Scotch bakery and grocery shop she'd run across down by the Santa Monica pier.

Moreover, Lavinia came in to breakfast, and it's hard for a chap to talk about imaginative things like flying of his own accord when right across the table there's his own daughter with her face all cold cream and her body wearing silk lounging pajamas that start a chap wondering if she's really brazen enough to be walking around without her corsets on, even if it is your own daughter.

So all Sam said was:

"Tha knaws, it's funny, Mully; but Ah dreamt last neight Ah were really flying around. Ah were floating i' t' air like one o' them bloody Zeppelins what come ovver i' t' wartime."

"Hmmm," said Mully. "What was it that tourist office lad said we maun ax for in this country when us wants brimstone and treacle?"

"Sulphur and molasses, mother," Lavinia said.

"Nay now, it ent ma blood that's off," Sam protested. "This were a varry real and onusual dream, so much so Ah still think Ah were awake."

"Oh, fawther," Lavinia said. "There's nothing unusual about it at all."

"Nowt onusual abaht a chap believes he were flying?"

"Of course not. It's one of the most common of dreams. It's a pre-natal memory that's left from the time when you were a foetus swimming and floating in fluid inside your mother's womb."

"Here, here, young lady," Mully said. "What kind o' talk is that to be using at the breakfast table? If Ah hear thee speak like that ony more, cinema star or no cinema star, Ah'll smack thy bare backside for thee. The idea! And of your Pa's own Ma, too; dead though she may be. Now thee eat thy breakfast and hurry about it, too. We've got to see t' casting director at Selznick International i' Coolver City by ten o'clock."

Sam said nothing more about flying; but he determined that the minute he was alone he would try it again. He had quite a wait, because the minute Mully and Lavinia were gone, the maid came in to clean up the apartment. There was the maid, dusting and sweeping and humming to herself in a come-day, go-day, God-send-Sunday sort of California way, and Sam thought she'd never be through.

But at last she was. Sam shut the door, tapped out his pipe and got ready. He lay on the sofa and willed and willed, and almost before he could catch his breath there he was floating in the air with the greatest of ease. For a while he just lay there, suspended in space, and amazed at this wonderful new power. He turned his head and looked down. He was fully a foot above the sofa. Very gently he floated to one side, where he was a good three feet above the floor. There could be no mistake about it. Amazed at himself he floated back to the sofa.

"Well, Ah'll be a monkey's ooncle!" he breathed to himself. "That Ah will indeed! Why even Ah can scarcely believe it's so."

To prove it to himself he tried it again. This time he floated up in the air, then drifted out clean into the middle of the room. He felt quite uncomfortable, somehow, but he thought that only natural.

Then he turned over to look down at the floor. Very slowly he began revolving his body. And the minute he did that all feeling of awkwardness left him. Once he was face-down toward the floor, a new and tremendous feeling of security and power seized him.

"Why, of course," he said to himself. "Ah were upside down—like a burd trying to fly on its back. This maun be the right way up!"

So now, imbued with a new and very great confidence, he stretched out his arms and zoomed down toward the sofa. A foot from it, he banked with his palms, brought his body upright, and lit on his feet as gently as a thrush.

"Well, if this ain't a do!" he breathed.

He spread his arms again, pushed gently with the tips of his toes, and took off again. He soared along like a glider, making a complete circle of the room about a foot below the ceiling. As he did so he was seized with a tremendous exhilaration. All hesitation now was gone, and he used his new power with a fierce joy. He found flying took almost no physical effort whatsoever. Nor did he need any conscious mental effort in controlling himself; that is to say, he did not have to *think* how to do things. When he came to a corner the muscles of his body and the delicate distribution of his weight adjusted themselves by some instinct so that he banked perfectly.

The world became a new place to Sam Small. To us who merely walk, the world is a two-dimensional place; but to Sam it was now three-dimensional.

The room in which he flew thus took on aspects unknown to us who could only know it from a monotonous five-foot eye-level. He could see the tops of doors and of cupboards and could get a bird's-eye view of the chairs and table—which looked very silly pieces of furniture indeed from that angle. He noted, too, that while the room might be clean down below, it certainly wasn't up where he was. There were cobwebs over a closet and dust galore atop every door.

"Ah'll just hev Mully give that maid a good talking-to," he resolved.

Then he gave himself over to the beautiful pure joy of flowing and effortless flying. He swooped around the room, landing lightly as a feather where he would, taking off again with the merest preliminary drive of his toes. He practised landings in awkward corners, to test the range of his new abilities.

Unfortunately he was so occupied that he didn't hear Mully and Lavinia come back; and when they walked into the room, there he happened to be, perched atop a highboy.

"Well, Ah'll goa to Helifax," Mully snorted. "Sammywell Small! What in the name o' God is ta laiking up theer for? Coom dahn here afore tha breaks thy bloody neck!"

Sam was so surprised and upset by being discovered that he forgot about flying and jumped down in quite an ordinary, mortal sort of way. He landed with a horrible crash that nearly drove his spine up into his back teeth, and of course there was quite a bit of a do about it. Mully rubbed Sam's back with a little Elliman's Embrocation and sailed into him so hard that Sam got stubborn and wouldn't have told her about his new accomplishment even if he had got a chance to get a word in edgewise.

"Sammywell Small," Mully said. "Heavens knaws Ah've swallered a lot o' things since Ah married thee; but this caps the bloody climax, it does. Ba gum, lad, if tha goas on like this, folk'll begin to think tha's balmy i' t' crumpet. Eigh, sometimes Ah rue the day we took out a license."

"Aye?" Sam came back. "Well, it cost me seven and sixpence. Ah could ha' got a dog license for t' same price."

"Aye, and there's soom days Ah wish tha'd bowt a dog," Mully rebutted. "And today's one on 'em."

FOR SEVERAL DAYS after that Sam did nothing about flying. For one thing, he was quite jarred up from his jump off the highboy. For another, Mully gave him no chance to be alone.

But one night Sam woke up, and there was Mully sleeping as sound
as an Egyptian mummy. So Sam tiptoed out of bed in his nightshirt
and took off. For a couple of hours he flew around in the living room,
zooming and volplaning and banking to his heart's content. It was
quite a sight, for Sam was steady as an albatross in flight. Just one lift
of a palm, and he was banking; a slight bend of his knees and he
zoomed. It all came natural to him and he flew and flew with a sort of
wild ecstasy.

After that, night after night, when Mully was abed, he would swoop
around the house, having great fun cutting capers and corners, sailing
through doorways, swooping within an inch of the carpet and then
banking swiftly upward again.

He began to set himself difficult tasks. For, curiously enough, although all the movements that a bird makes normally in flight came
natural to him, he had to learn of his own accord the evolutions that
an airplane can achieve. He taught himself to loop the loop and do
the barrel-roll, the wingover, the falling leaf, the tail-spin. Finally he
became very proficient in this sort of thing. But it was his desire to
emulate not only a bird, but a machine, that got Sam into a bit of
trouble.

He was soaring about in the dining room one night, concentrating
on his latest stunt, the Immelman turn (which is a sort of mixture
of a half inside loop and a barrel-roll, bringing you to the top of the
loop the right side up). For the first time that night Sam managed to
do it right nicely. The surging thrill of this new evolution intoxicated
him, and he sailed about the room, wildly doing Immelman turns.
Unfortunately, in the dark, he forgot about the fine cut glass chandelier right over the dining room table, and crash! He went into it head
first!

Sam, all tangled up in cut glass chandelier, came down with a jangle
and a thump that would have wakened Lazarus himself.

When Mully came charging in there was a pretty sight to be seen
indeed. She switched on the light, and there she saw Sam in his nightshirt, sitting in a welter of bits of cut glass and blood and wire and
bursted electric light bulbs.

"Eigh, bless ma heart and soul! What's tha been oop to now?"
Mully snorted wearily.

Sam was as dizzy as a goat in spring, for he'd taken a crack on his head that had laid about four inches of scalp open, and likely would have split the skull of anyone else but a Yorkshireman.

"It were a forced landing," he said. "Help ma oop out o' here."

"Help thee oop! Ah should think soa! And a pretty picture indeed tha is, ligging there in thy nightgown and showing all tha's got! A man o' thy age, too!"

Sam did his best to make himself decent, for just then Lavinia came walking in, and the girl started giggling fit to die. At this Mully turned and caught the lass a skelp over her backside that lifted her nearly a foot in the air.

For no matter what Sam had done, Mully was determined that Lavinia should grow up with the decent respect for parents that any good girl should have—Hollywood or no Hollywood.

"That'll teach thee, my fine young lady, to watch thy P's and Q's," Mully said. "Now off tha goas back to bed. Ah'll stand no sauce from thee."

She was that put out she gave Lavinia an extra clip on the lug for good luck. Then she pulled Sam out and got him to bed, and got a doctor on the telephone who came over and put six stitches in Sam's head. What with one thing and another Mully had a right eventful night.

FOR A COUPLE OF DAYS Sam was in bed and Mully said never a word about the goings-on. But Sam could see by the way she held her lips tight together that she was just saving it all up. And the day Sam got up, Mully hustled Lavinia out of the house, and sat Sam on the sofa, and had her say.

"Now Sam," she said, "Ah want thee to bear in mind that Ah'm quite remindful of the fact that, after all, tha did turn out to be an inventor, what with thy self-doffing spindle and all. But what Ah say is this, there's limits to what a man can do, even an inventor, in a manner of speaking.

"But this much Ah will tell thee. When a chap of thy age starts gating up in t' middle o' t' neight, and swinging in his shirt-tail from the chandeliers like a hoorang-ootang, well, all Ah gate to say is, if tha keeps it up they'll be sending for thee from Menston yet.

"Now Ah wean't say no moar about it, but enow's enow, so pull thysen together, lad. And if tha wean't do it for me; at least remember tha hes a daughter what's gate her life and career before her, as you might say."

Then Mully jumped up and went and locked herself in the kitchen and had a champion good cry. After that she made a nice pot of tea and fixed up a tray for Sam with a duck egg and a little bit of ham and some brown bread and butter, and a few odds and ends of pickelets and toasted muffins and scones and a couple of curd-lemon-cheese tarts and a little pot of Stilton cheese—just the things that Sam liked especially well. And they sat down and had tea and never a word more was said about the chandelier.

Of course, after that tea, Sam was contrite, just as Mully had known he would be, and he resolved to behave himself.

"Ah'm that sorry, Mully," he said. "It were just that Ah been a little funny-like i' this land. Let's goa hoam to Yorksha."

"Now Sammywell, tha knows our Vinnie's right on the varry brink and threshold of a cinema career. Why can'ta stay here?"

"Well, could Ah hev a tyke, then—happen just a bit of a tarrier?"

"Nay Sammywell, lad. Tha knaws t' landlady wean't have no doags i' this house. Ah doan't see why tha can't goa out and mak friends. Goodness knaws there's plenty of well-to-do chaps like thee that manages to find this place interesting."

"Them? Eigh Mully, they're nowt but a lot o' mawngy owd toffs—sitting on the park benches each day waiting for t' undertakker to coom along and measure 'em. Ah can't mak friends wi' the like o' yon. Why, they got such a bloody funny accent Ah gate nobbut one word i' ten o' what they're yammering abaht. Now, if Ah nobbut hed a dog. . . ."

"Tha can't hev noa dog!" Mully stated. And that ended it.

SAM really did put up a terrifically hard battle to keep from flying again. But, naturally, it was too much for him. If you yourself were suddenly faced by the fact that you were the first man in the history of the whole world who had developed the power to fly by your own efforts, you would not be able to dismiss the matter lightly. And neither could Sam.

In the days that followed, as he sat in the sunshine on the Ocean Drive, or walked along the paths under the palm trees, he would watch the sea gulls, lifting and soaring in the magnificent air currents. He never got tired of watching them. Now he was, as you might say, practically a bird himself, Sam found himself thinking like a bird, and thinking and knowing things that the ordinary man never gets in his head. Mostly he sensed and felt about air currents.

There would be days when he sat there and he would be greatly troubled, for the air currents were short and choppy—what Sam called "wivvery." He didn't know where he got the word, but that explained it. On those days his body would be almost torn by a sort of anguish, and he would sit there watching the gulls fight and turn and twist and make myriad delicate readjustments of their bodies every second as they flew. Sam himself could feel those currents, and as each gull went by he would squirm and twist his own body as if to help it along in its battle, just as a crowd of people at the tense moment of a championship golf match will twist their bodies and strain when they see an important putt going an inch to one side of the cup, as if their straining would bend the ball toward the cup.

After such a day Sam would go home, weary and irritable, and would only half-listen to Mully chattering on about how their Vinnie was right on the verge now of being given a screen test by an important company.

But then there would be other days when the air currents would be broad and untroubled—great anthems of sweeping simplicity that came chanting in from the Pacific. Then Sam felt at peace, for the magnificent breezes would move in from the sea and, meeting the face of the great earthwall, would shoot up untroubled to great heights. Especially was this so in the late afternoons when the seldom-failing sea breeze came powerfully to the land.

It was exactly like music, only instead of a vibration that could be heard, it was a music that Sam could feel on the skin of his face, thrumming and tingling so beautifully that he forgot the earth-bound world. Then, in spirit, he was with the gulls who would come over from feeding at the fishing boats by the breakwater. Those gulls would pick up the air column that ran along the face of the Santa Monica pier, volplane over the sand and then, reaching the great upcurrent at the cliff, would go screaming away on the moving tower. Up their bodies would shoot, high—high! Then, quartering to the current, they would go sailing along up the coast, over his head, all the way up to Malibu. There they flicked their bodies and quartering the other way, came sailing back on the lifting breeze, never moving a wing, but merely playing with their pinions on the ecstatic air that vibrated beneath them.

Sam would sit there, and the sun would sink ruddy up the coast as the gulls played in the evening breeze. For they did play. Sam could tell that they were flying, not for food, but just for the pure joy they found in that unheard music of soaring.

For it was soaring rather than flying that gripped Sam's mind. He himself, it must be understood, never used a "wing-beat" of any kind. His propulsion through the air came rather from a dynamic play of air currents beneath him as he passed over. Although he could float, merely by a lightness of his body, if he wished, he got little pleasure from this. His great ecstasy came from the swift passing of his body over air currents, as a soaring bird does.

He had little real interest in the swift-winging birds like the hell-divers. He found a great deal more to his liking in the pelicans, who were extraordinarily clever in petty currents: as going trickily over the sea about a foot above the water so that they could catch the minute upshoots that came as the wind drove at the back of a shore-coming breaker. They were very clever at this, following along the line of the wave as they went up the coast, balancing precariously on the narrow, moving sheet of air. And, too, he gave the pelicans top score in their ability to utilize the air currents left by another bird. That's why the pelicans flew in formation, like a squadron of seaplanes. The leading bird would use a vagrant, lifting current to soar for a while, the bird behind would take advantage of the eddying air that the first bird left, the third pelican would use the vibrating tangles left by the first two, and so on.

Yes, Sam had a certain admiration for the pelicans, but, after all, they were only the smalltime gamblers of the airways. His heart really was with the gulls, plunging boldly into the great sundown air columns. He would watch them rocketing up, borne high into the sky, there to scream at the setting sun. And Sam would sit there, his heart lifting with the birds far above, until Mully would come along the path.

"Eigh-oop, lad," she'd call. "Time to coom hoam afore it gates too chilly."

They would walk home and she would tell him of Lavinia's progress, and Sam would say aye and nay at appropriate places; but he never really listened. His mind was half a mile up in the air.

SAM really meant to keep his promise to Mully and behave himself. Though each day, on the palm-covered walk high up above the shore road, his senses and muscles cried to be sporting up on the air currents, he did no flying.

For one thing, Sam's Yorkshire practicality overcame him. As he said to himself, it would look right queer now, if a chap were to suddenly go sailing up and down in the air with the sea gulls in front of all those people, sitting there on the benches and taking the nice California sunshine. Everyone would be that capped, and likely as not there'd be all sorts of bother afterward.

No, Sam held himself well in hand; but he couldn't help his senses feeling as they did. The delicious play of the harmonious air currents on his face, this new soundless music that he alone could feel, drew him in spite of himself. And one day, he could not help leaving his bench and walking to the edge of the palisade. There, far down below him, was the shore road and the sands and the movie stars' beach palaces; and the wind came thrumming up that cliffside like a great harp struck in sweeping chords.

Sam drew nearer and nearer to the edge. He wasn't going to fly, mind you. He only wanted to feel more awarely the heavenly play of the air. Before he knew it, he was over the fence. No one was in sight. With a sigh of pleasure, like a tobacco-starved man with his first cigarette in weeks, he leaned against the upshooting current. He did not let his feet leave the ground. He merely leaned forward on the column of air, letting it play and vibrate about his intoxicated body.

And then he was grasped rudely. All his delicate balance was destroyed as he was yanked over the fence, and found himself wriggling in the hands of a policeman.

"You dizzy old—" the cop yelled. "What the hell's the idea?"

"Hey up, lad," Sam protested. "Ah weren't dewing nowt."

He struggled and struggled, but the cop held on grimly. There was no escape.

"You'd better come along with me," the cop said.

So, of course, Mully heard about the whole thing. When she got home that afternoon the landlady rushed up with the news that the police had telephoned for her.

"For me?" Mully said, a little alarmed despite her free conscience. "What in the name o' goodness would they want wi' me?"

"Well, it seems sort of like they've got your mister down there."

"Ma Sammywell! Ooooah, fer the luv of Heaven! What in t' name o' God hez he been up to now!"

So hardly knowing whether she was standing on her head or her feet, Mully dashed around and got her best black gloves, and they put her in a taxicab and off she dashed for the City Hall at Fourth and Santa Monica Boulevard, all the time stewing and fuming and covered with shame as she pictured Sam a criminal and either locked up behind the bars or else sitting in a room with a white light in his face and six detectives with their hats on and cigars in their teeth giving him the Yankee third degree. By the time she reached the station she was about ready to write to the British Embassy and get the Grand Fleet over to California to see that a good British subject had his rights defended.

She was in such a stew that it made her as mad as a setting hen when she walked in and found Sam sitting calmly in the station house, puffing on his pipe.

"You scallywag," she cried. "And what's ta been up to now?"

"Now Mully," Sam said. "Now, now!"

"Doan't thee now-now me," she said. "What's ta been up to?"

Sam shut up in a regular stubborn Yorkshire way and wouldn't say anything, so the police lieutenant, who turned out to be a very affable sort of a lad, took Mully aside and explained that Sam had tried to commit suicide by jumping off the Ocean Drive cliff.

"Suicide?" Mully said. And then the big tears began rolling down her face and she dabbed and dabbed away.

"Now," the Lieutenant said to Sam, "aren't you ashamed of yourself? Causing all this grief to your wife there! Aren't you ashamed!"

"Eigh, doan't scold him, mister," Mully begged. "Properly it's all ma fault. He's been feeling poorly ever since he had a touch of bronchitis i' Vancouver, and Ah hevn't been a good wife and takken care on him like Ah should."

"Now Mully," Sam comforted. "Doan't thee tak on. Tha hez been a good wife—barring one or two little bits o' things, Ah couldn't ha' wished for no better wife."

"Well, what's tha want to goa and commit suicide for?" Mully wailed.

She was so overcome that the Lieutenant invited them into his private office and sat down and wrote on a lot of papers. Then he frowned at Sam.

"Now, Mr. Small," he said, sternly. "I want to tell you something. Underneath this building we've got six cellars. And the further down you go the darker it gets. And in each cellar there's sixty cells. And the further along you go the smaller the cells get.

"Now by rights I ought to take you down into the very bottom cellar, and take you right to the very last cell, and lock you in there, and then come up here and throw the key away! That's what I ought to do!"

"Oh, please," Mully begged. "Doan't do that. He's gate a tarrible poor chest. All his side of the family has. He'd dee o' pneumonia. Oh, please, just lock him oop in a varry nice cell where he can see a little daylight, in a manner o' speaking."

At this the Lieutenant tapped his teeth with his pen, and looked at Mully and then scowled at Sam, and finally he said:

"Mrs. Small, I'm moved to compassion by your evident love for your husband. And don't think I'd do this if it wasn't for her," he snapped at Sam. "But just in this case, I'm going to take a chance. I shouldn't do it by rights, because I should put him away where the sun can't shine on him, but I'll take a chance and release him in your custody."

"Oh no," Mully said. "Ah wouldn't want to connive at owt wrong. If the law says he's got to go behind the bars, then tha'd better do that."

"No, I'll take the responsibility," the Lieutenant said.

"Nay, now. Th' law's th' law," Mully insisted. "Hard on us as it may be, we maun observe it."

"Now, Mully," Sam said. "If t' policeman is off to let me goa, doan't thee upset t' applecart."

"Th' law's th' law," Mully said, stubbornly.

It took quite a while for the two of them to get Mully to give in, but finally she did.

"I'll take care of the law; you just take care of your husband," the Lieutenant said. "Now remember," he said to Sam, "you're being released in her custody—and any more monkey business! The *very last cell* in the *very lowest cellar*! Now go home and behave yourself."

"Ah'll see he does," Mully said, wiping her eyes. "Coom on Sammywell. And just wait till Ah gate thee hoam!"

Of course, for the next week or so Sam never heard the end of it. Mully kept her eye on him every minute of the waking day. He couldn't even take a walk alone. Naturally, he got very fed up with this.

"Ah'm no owd codger that can't tak a walk alone," he would complain.

"That so be as it may," Mully would sniff. "But just the same, Ah'm off to keep an ee on thee."

This, of course, meant that she had to let Lavinia make the rounds of the studios alone. But, just to show how strange things happen, Lavinia seemed to get along much better, and before a week was up she really had a screen test at G-M-G Pictures, and it looked as if the cinema was going to be interested in her after all.

The only thing, she said, that she thought was holding her back was what she called background.

"Tha means tha's ashamed o' me and thy feyther?" Mully challenged.

"Oh no. Nothing of the sort, Mother. I mean this place here."

"What's wrong wi' this place?" Mully asked. "Ah'm sewer there's no Lord or Duke or belted Earl in all England's gate a kitchen that's any bonnier looking. Indeed, Ah nivver thowt Ah'd live to t' day when a hed me a kitchen wi' yaller, black and white tiles coovering ivvery blessed inch o' t' walls."

"I know, Mother, but it's so small—and in what a neighborhood! We ought to have a home, not an apartment—a place where I could have a party and receive guests—and have a cocktail party and meet influential people and make contacts with directors and producers."

"Now I read that for two hundred and fifty dollars a month . . ."

"How much is that i' pounds?" Sam asked.

"Fifty pounds a month," Lavinia calculated.

"Well, Ah'll be a moonkey's ooncle," Sam gasped.

"Sitha, ma fine lady," Mully added. "That's moor 'n us ivver paid in us lives for a whole year in a house. And if tha thinks that we got brass to chuck away on thy fancy ideas, well tha just gate another think cooming."

At this Lavinia burst out bawling.

"Well, I don't know what you want to do with the rest of your lives, but I know what I want to do," she sobbed. "I don't know what Father ever wanted to invent the Small Self-Doffing Spindle for, and make a fortune out of it, if he just wants to go right on living like a mill-worker."

"We're not bahn to move," Mully stated flatly.

"Well, Mother, you might just look at the house I saw. It's not too grand. And it's got a beautiful garden where . . ."

"Tha heeard what thy mother said!" said Sam. "We're not off to move."

"Well, there's no need to bark at t' lass like that," Mully said, turning on him. "Heavens knows she nobbut made a bit of a suggestion."

"Ah didn't bark at her," Sam said.

"Why tha did, fit to snap her yead off. Just because t' lass hes a desire to improve hersen . . ."

"Hey, whose side is tha on i' this argument?" Sam demanded.

"Well, if tha's on one side Ah'm on t' other, for Ah nivver knew thee o' t' reight side i' ma life," Mully came back.

"And onyhow, this place hez a gardin, and happen it'd dew thee good to do a bit o' digging. Tha could put in reddishes an' a few swedes and some leeks and a nice row or two o' lettis."

"Ooh drat ma blasted buttons," Sam said. "Ah wish Ah were back hoam i' Yorksha'—that's what Ah dew!"

And, of course, the upshot was, Mully and Lavinia got the nice big house.

It was up on Pacific Palisades, just beyond where Vicki Baum and Elissa Landi live, and it had orange trees and an avocado grove and a patio with a fountain and an automatic, self-sprinkling lawn all complete. It was quite a mansion.

Lavinia gave a party complete with stuffed celery and influential people, and as luck would have it the conversation turned to flying. A transport plane had just crashed in San Francisco bay killing all the people aboard and everyone at Lavinia's party had a new idea about why it had happened.

"Nay, ye're all wrang," Sam put in. "Like as not the reason he crashed was because the air was wivvery."

"It was what?" asked a young woman with a cut-glass voice.

"It were wivvery," Sam said.

Everyone stopped talking and Sam, seeing he had his audience, expanded.

"It's ma own word," he said, "but Ah'll explain it to ye. Now sometimes the air is all nice and flat as you may wish . . ."

"Oh Father," Lavinia cut in, "wouldn't you like to put up the ping pong net for us?"

"I' just a minute," Sam said. "Now there's other times, when it gets all reyther in mucky little bits, like. And that's what Ah calls wivvery. See now, supposing Ah'm an airyoplane."

He spreads his arms to show them. Everyone looked very amused, and truth to tell, Sam did look a bit of a comic figure, what with his arms spread and his gray head cocked on one side.

Mully saw them smiling, and she began to boil over. She walked over and gave Sam a nudge that nearly buckled in a couple of ribs.

"Time for t' ping pong net, lad," she said with emphasis, like a villain in the cinematographic pictures.

So Sam put up the net on the table in the patio, and all the influential people began batting the little ball around. For a while he watched the game, then he wandered uselessly round his fine big house. He was feeling a bit sorry for himself, when one of the guests, a tall, likely-looking lad, came up.

"Mr. Small," he said. "My name's Harry Hanks."

"Ah'm that pleased to meet you," Sam said, dolefully.

"Mr. Small, I was interested in what you were saying about wivvery air. You were interrupted."

"Well," Sam said. "It's this way."

He began to stretch his arms again, but then he looked round to see if Mully was in sight.

"Come i' t' kitchen, lad," Sam said. "We're not so liable to be disturbed."

They got in the kitchen and Sam explained all about how the air got wivvery at times, and how of course a bird managed to stand it pretty well because its wings and feathers were pliable.

"But an airyoplane wings, tha sees, hes got no give to 'em," Sam explained. "Well, there tha is, lad. There's bits of air pushing up, and bits of it pushing dahn, and there's no give to the wing."

"Very interesting," the young man said. "Go on."

Encouraged by such a good listener Sam went on, pointing out how the wivvery air condition was especially bad some days right where the ocean air met the land air, and it was always worst of all about 4:30 in the afternoon when the shore breeze was setting in.

"Now we got this," Sam went on, marshalling his argument. "It were soa wivvery fower days agoa that the sea gulls was flying like they had the ague.

"The warst place to be is reight where the sea air meets the land air.

"The warst time to be there is about fower-thutty when the breeze changes.

"And that's the day, the place and the time that this poor chap's plane drops smack i' t' ocean, ain't it?"

"Say, you're right at that," the young man said.

"Well, well," Sam smiled. "Here, it's dry wark talking. How abaht a nice bottle o' beer?"

The party was all over before Mully thought to look for Sam in the kitchen. The young man said he had to dash. Mully pursed her lips and waited till he'd gone. Then she stared at the six empty beer bottles.

"So! Up to thy owd tricks again," she began.

Sam knew his Mully, so he escaped, and stayed away until dinner time. He had to go down for his meal, so he ate quietly while Mully and Lavinia sniffed and ignored him in the way women will when a man's in disgrace.

Finally Lavinia broke into tears.

"Now, let's have noan o' that," Sam begged, wearily.

"How can the lass help it?" Mully started, glad to get into battle. "Goodness knaws we try and try to mak' summat on us-selves, and tha upsets t' applecart ivvery time. Showing off abaht things tha knaws nowt abaht—and salming up beer i' t' kitchen."

"Now, now. We nobbut hed two-three bottles apiece. And it's Yankee beer at that—wi' no body nor goa to it, as you might say."

"Tha hed ivveryone laughing at thee," Mully prodded.

"Well, that's their bad manners then," Sam observed. "Ma faith, Ah doan't talk nonsense when Ah dew talk. The lads at the Spread Eagle were allus varry interested in ma observations on owt that were current."

"That bunch!" Mully snorted.

"This isn't the Spread Eagle, Father," Lavinia sobbed. "This is Hollywood. And you go and take Mr. Hanks in the kitchen."

Sam began to lose his temper.

"Well, the lad were interested," Sam stormed. "All we did was sit there and tak' a little beer, and Ah explained to him a few things about flying."

At this Lavinia gave a yowl and covered her face with her hands.

"Now what hev Ah done?" Sam moaned.

"What hesn't ta done?" Mully retorted. "This Mr. Harry Hanks is nobbut one o' t' biggest producers i' Hollywood, who were off to sign up our Vinnie. And on top o' that he's nobbut the avvyator that howds all t' records for speed and height and distance. That's all he is. And so thee, Mister Bighead, Sam Small, Esquire, hez to sit down and tell *him* all abaht flying."

"And now you've ruined my chance of getting a contract," Lavinia said. "He'll think I come from a family that's mad."

"Now, Mr. Smart Sam Small, tha sees what tha's done!" Mully picked up.

What with Mully and Vinnie going in relays, poor Sam had quite a time. It was getting worse and worse, until he stood up.

"Now hev done!" he thundered. "And that's an end to it."

He stared at Mully and Vinnie, and they were quiet. For Sam used that tone of voice about once a year, and when he did, it was time to keep your nose clean, as Mully would say.

And, after all, what was the use of being married to a man if you couldn't harry and chivvy him a little every day? But by the same token, who would want to be married to a man who didn't show a woman who was boss a couple of times a year?

So Mully and Vinnie sat quiet as mice and Sam stared at them.

"Now then," he said. "Ah'm off out for a walk—and what is more, Ah'm off to walk alone wi' no one wetching ma."

He waited, but there was no contradiction. So out he stalked and clapped on his best derby hat, and away he went. Without knowing it exactly, he headed for the seashore. He strode to the palisade beneath the three kinds of palms and stared away out, high over the movie stars' shore palaces and the breaking waters half-seen in the twilight. He looked up the highway to where the lights shine at the Lighthouse Café. Then he turned, placed his hat neatly on the bench, walked back to the edge, and took off.

Out he plunged into the gentle updraught by the cliff face, and then with a swoop he soared high, high above the Santa Monica cañon.

With the wild music of the air currents playing on his face, he zoomed and quartered, feeling the first ecstasy of outdoor flight.

He forgot the original angriness that had sent him to the shore. Everything was gone except that glorious four-dimensional thrill of powerless flying. For heretofore Sam had only flown in the still, stagnant air of his room. This was altogether a different thing. Here were vagrant drafts and petty currents, all surging in a Wagnerian movement of air. The muscles of Sam's outstretched arms, the position of his body, made myriad minute and lightning adjustments to the play of the air.

He dove down into the cañon above its blaze of neon lights where the hot dog stands and service stations clustered. The drive of his weight shot him over to the opposite mesa where he again picked up the lofting air on the cliff face. He quartered and tilted one arm and shot obliquely on the air column, up the beach toward Malibu. Below him he could see the tiny lights of the automobiles crawling up the shore road. The puny size of them and their snail-like pace filled him with amused pity.

Poor, earthbound people!

At Malibu, where the cliff face ends and the hills are rolling, he hovered, balancing gently on the breeze. Then, suddenly depressing his feet, he plunged down, toward the lights, felt the earth rush at him gloriously as he headed toward it in an outside loop, felt his body race keenly through the screaming air as he began the up-part of the loop, and shot high, high, up, up, into the dark again—until he stalled. Then doing a lazy wing-over he soared calmly away inland, flirting on the multiple currents over the broken land, until he was high over the highest mountain.

Now, far beyond him he could see the twinkling iridescence of Van Nuys and San Fernando. To his right was the brilliant blaze of Los Angeles, Hollywood, Beverly Hills. And there, further toward the shore, glowing and dancing like strings of fire-pearls, were the towns of the sea front with their petty bijous of illuminated roads and piers and amusement concessions, all their lights vibrating in the arc that swept around the great bay to the heights of Palos Verdes.

The shimmering beauty of lights when seen down through the layers of air, instead of laterally through but one layer, moved Sam to a half-formed state of pity and compassion.

He did not think of Mully and feel sorry for her. Rather he was touched by a mood that enveloped all Mullys and all women who love and suffer and bicker for a man. And with this feeling coloring every fibre, he rocked over on his side, and then glided slowly through the darkness, back to the Santa Monica palisade. He turned his arms and brought himself to a tiptoe landing beside the bench. He picked up his hat again, and walked quietly home, through the street darkness where the night-blooming jasmine sent out its perfume to tell a man that nothing in that land was real.

THE WILD EXHILARATION of Sam's first outdoor flight remained with his memory, but the ineffable sadness of the mood it had produced clothed his spirit and filled him with lonesomeness. And Sam didn't want to feel lonesome. Above all else he loved gregarious pleasure.

For Sam was not a philosopher who would find warmth in feeling that he had discovered the puny ridiculousness of man and his works. He was a very ordinary sort of chap who wanted nothing quite so much as a good skinful of fish-and-taties from Hobson's shop, or a mug of ale before him at the Spread Eagle and a few of the lads beside him to go thoroughly into some such subject as the Grand National or Stanley Baldwin or the football results.

His gift of flying, however, was unique, and he was made as lonesome by it as the last of the one-time billions of passenger pigeons, which lived three years in captivity, there to coo and call to a mate that would never come. And Sam didn't want to feel lonesome.

Apathetic and useless, he wandered about the streets each day, walking for mile after mile, and discovering only greater lonesomeness in that strange land of palm trees and neon lights and blue mountains and people who all spoke with a funny accent.

It was that desire to find someone like himself that made him stop one day in Beverly Hills as he saw a sign. It said: "How About That Canine's Washing and Stripping." Underneath was a big question mark. And under that it said: "Dick Hogglethwaite. Thirty Years' Experience in England and America."

"Happen it's a dog Ah want," Sam said to himself. "And who would be a better chap to talk to than someone who's had experience in England? And even if Mully wouldn't let me have no tyke, there'd be

noa harm i' talking to the chap, like, to see what prices they get
ovver here."

So Sam ducked under a low-hanging palm frond and pushed open
the screen door. There inside he saw a little chap stripping a wirehair.
Sam watched him work a while, then the chap looked up and said:

"Well, whet can Ah dew for tha?"

"Eigh, how long's ta been away fro' Huddersfield?" Sam asked.

The chap stopped his work.

"How did ta knaw Ah were fro' Huddersfield?" he asked.

"By thy bloody accent, o' course."

"Well, Ah'll goa to hell," the chap said, surprised. "Ah been here
going on thutty year, and Ah thowt Ah'd lost ma accent."

"Eigh, tha does talk a bit like a Yankee," Sam agreed, "but there's
enow left soa a chap could tell. Ah'm fro' near Huddersfield mysen."

"Soa Ah could tell," the chap said. "Here, owd this booger's chops a
minute. The mawngy little bastard, he's spoiled."

He gave the terrier a slap on the nose to show him who was boss,
and Sam held on a while as he trimmed up the tail.

"Now ye booger, ye," the chap said as he finished, "tak' a run for
thysen."

The terrier bounded down from the bench.

"Well, it lewks a bit moar like a tyke now," Sam said, approvingly.

"Aye, fair to middling. But ye doan't see too many good dogs here.
The boogers wouldn't know what to do wi' a good 'un if they had it."

"Aye, it's a bloody foonny coontry," Sam agreed.

"Well, a lad can addle a nice bit o' brass here," the other said.
"These movie stars all have a few dogs, but they don't know nowt
about 'em. Ah tell 'em off proper, Ah do. No beating around the bush
wi' me."

"Well, tha's Yorksha," Sam reminded.

"That's reight. Here, grab that tarrier and coom i' t' back room. Ah
gate to wash a Sealy."

They went in the back room where a regulation bathtub sat amid
the tiered cages and kennels.

"Aye," the chap said, as he soaped up the Sealyham. "They don't
know owt about dogs here."

He cocked his head.

"Eigh, owd this Sealy a minute. There's someone out front."

Sam stripped off his coat and rolled up his sleeves. Since a chap shouldn't be idle when there's work to do, he nearly had the Sealy finished when the kennel chap came back. He was carrying a miserable bundle under his arm.

"In the name o' Helifax," Sam breathed. "And what is that?"

"Th' woman just browt it in," the other said. "And she sez, she sez: 'Can you do owt wi' my dog?' And Ah sez, 'What in the name o' God is it?' And she sez, 'It's my Yorksha tarrier—Ah give him a bath and Ah can't get him combed out ony more.' "

He held up the poor tangled mite, that looked like a tarred and feathered Chihuahua, for Sam to see. And Sam started to laugh. It was the best laugh he'd had since he'd left England.

"Eigh, ba gum. Ah nivver thowt Ah'd live to the day when Ah gate to a land what's soa dumb the people tries to wash a Yorksha tarrier," Sam gurgled.

"Didn't Ah tell thee, lad?" the other said.

He held up the poor bedraggled dog, and the men lay back and laughed till they could hear nothing but their own laughter. Washing a Yorkshire terrier was the funniest thing Sam had ever heard.

"It'll tak thee a month o' Sundays to get it combed out again, lad," Sam would say. He'd wipe the tears from his eyes, but then he would be able to see the terrier again, and that would start him off laughing again.

FROM THAT DAY ON Sam's days were full, and thoughts of flying again were far from his mind. His waking hours were spent with Dickie Hogglethwaite in the little dog shop, where they would wash and pluck dogs, clip a few dew claws and stand aghast at the ignorance of Americans where dogs were concerned. For Sam, like every Yorkshire-man, was born with a fully-fledged omniscience in all things canine.

With the aid of Dickie Hogglethwaite he picked up a collie bitch that didn't have a thing wrong with her—beyond a bit of a gay tail and a touch of a prick ear. But as Hogglethwaite pointed out, there wasn't a thing off with her that couldn't be corrected with a judicious amount of coping—and anyhow, she would make a fine mother.

So when she came in season they pinched a breeding for her from a grand champion collie that a millionaire had sent in to be bathed, and all in all they had a fine time. They washed dogs and talked and made a few bets on the Santa Anita races—for this Dickie Hoggle-thwaite was by the way of being a bit of a sporting chap.

In fact, they might have gone on indefinitely as they were if it hadn't been for a boarding Pekingese that squeezed through the fence.

Sam and Dick were in the back yard letting the boarders out for exercise when Dick gave a yelp that shook the blobs off the acacia trees.

"Cop that bloody Peke," he yelled. "She's i' heat and she'll run to hell and gone."

Sam made a grab, but he was too late. All he got was two whiskers off the Peke's tail as it went through the hole in the fence.

The minute he saw it Dick started out through the front shop, and he was moving fast, because before his eyes was a picture of that Peke disappearing up into the hills and meeting a Siluki or a Keeshond, or even maybe a great Dane—and then he'd have a hell of a job explaining a fine litter of mongrel puppies to the Peke's owner, who was a movie director, and dizzy enough as it stood.

So Dick did record time out through the shop and around into the back lot. And when he got there, there was Sam with the Peke tucked under his arm.

"Well, Ah'll be boogered," Dick said. "How did tha get out here?"

"Joomped ovver t' fence, lad," Sam grinned. "Here, wetch!"

So just taking off from tiptoe, he sailed over the fence. Then he landed, turned, and jumped back again. That is, it looked as if he were jumping, but of course, it was the merest, simplest little bit of flying for Sam.

"Eigh, lad," Dick said. "That's a varry special gift tha's gate there."

"It is, that," Sam replied.

They went back into the shop.

"That were a champion jump," Dick went on. "That there fence is all of seven foot if it's an inch. And tha did it wi' a Peke bitch under thy arm, too. Why didn'ta tell me tha were a champion athalete?"

"Nay, Ah nivver done no athletics in ma life beyond knocking a bit o' knerr and spell," Sam said.

"You don't mean to tell me," Dick ruminated. Then he fumbled in a drawer and found a tape measure and measured the fence. It was seven feet two inches.

"Eigh," he said to Sam. "We got to dew summat about this. Here tha can jump seven foot two, and offhand Ah think the world's record is nobbut six foot eight or summat like that. Ba gum, lad, Ah gate an idea we could clean up a pretty penny on this."

BECAUSE this Dickie Hogglethwaite was a sporting sort of lad, his mind, of course, ran in that direction. And his big idea was to enter Sam in the Veterans Relief Games at the Victor McLaglen stadium.

"Here, dost'a think it all reight for ma to goa capering around at ma time o' life?" Sam asked.

"Ah doan't knaw," Dickie said. "But Ah do knaw there's nowt wrang wi' taking a little brass of these here blooming Yankees. They been winning t' Olympics that long it's time a ruddy good Britisher showed 'em up, and won a few pounds doing so."

"Aye, there'd be nowt wrang wi' winning a honest bet," Sam agreed.

So Sam went into training. Dickie was the manager and after watching Sam work out in the dog-run for a week, he entered his man in the running high jump, broad jump and pole vault. He fed Sam a diet of raw eggs and sherry and toast, and gave him massages with his very special embrocation, which he had invented for massaging hurt dogs, and which was made of alcohol, camphor and vinegar.

All in all he did everything a serious trainer could do.

"Now Sam, lad," he said on the day of the meet, "ah've gate thee in as fine a shape as ivver a man o' thy age could be got. Ah've done ma part. Now thee do thine."

Off they went to the stadium in a taxi, and Dickie went out and placed his bets. When he came back to the dressing room, his face was lit with a religious glow.

"Ah gate five dollars at five to one on thee for each of the three events," he said. "And Ah gate a bet of two dollars against a hundred that tha tak's all three."

"That sounds like a lot," Sam said slowly. "How much is that i' pounds?"

"Now nivver thee mind that. Us hes gate it i' t' bloody bag, as these Yankees say. Now just thee relax."

So Dickie gave Sam a final rubdown, and then helped him pull on a sweat shirt and a long pair of sweat pants. Then he wrapped a dressing gown round him and out they went to the stadium.

"Now doan't worry," Dickie said. "Ah know full sure tha can do it."

"If tha feels like that, Ah'm all reight."

The high jump was first on the schedule of Sam's events. Dick stood there and passed up the jumps until it got to five feet ten. Then he pulled off Sam's robe.

"We passed up jumps, so that maun do it first time, lad," he said. "Now tha can do it easy."

Sam said nothing. He felt a little nervous. But he felt Dick's faith behind him, so he trotted up to the bar and sailed over. There were three other lads, and two of them made it.

The bar went up to five eleven. Sam made it, but one of the other lads dropped out.

That left only Sam and one more competitor, and they jumped and jumped, the bar going up a bit at a time, until the loud speaking arrangement in the grandstand began to say:

"Equalling the outdoor Olympic record in the running high jump. The high jump, ladies and gentlemen. Sam Small of Great Britain now jumping."

Sam trotted up and sailed over. The crowd applauded. The other lad gave a mighty leap and jumped over. The crowd applauded again.

Then the loud-speaker began to shout about how this would be a new world's record, and all the photographers came rushing over and Sam took his little trot, and soared over with inches to spare. The noise and excitement was tremendous. Then the other lad tried, but he couldn't make it. A crowd began to gather about Sam, and the officials rushed over with tapes to make sure the bar was set right. They had a great argument, till Sam said.

"Well, lads, to make sure, just shove it up a couple more inches."

Quite amazed, they did so. And Sam sailed over.

Then Dickie Hogglethwaite ran up and threw the dressing gown round Sam and pulled him away. The officials wanted Sam to see how high he could go.

"Nothing dewing, lads," Dickie said. "Now Ah'm his manager and Ah'm his trainer too. We got two more events and Ah won't let ma man tire hissen out."

Then he got Sam in a corner of the stadium and began rubbing his legs again with training fluid, for all the world as if Sam were Jem Mace or Jack Dempsey or somebody.

"The dirty buggers," Dick muttered. "They pulled a ringer in on us. That jumping lad were one o' t' best i' t' country. But Ah were sure tha could beat him."

"Aye, Ah could ha' done moar nor that," Sam said.

Dickie fluttered about Sam like a hen with a chick, and after a while took him out for the pole vault. Of course, it was the same story. Sam made a new world's record at 15 feet 3 inches. Then came the broad jump, and Sam was tempted to jump one hundred yards, but he considered that might cause trouble and Dickie wouldn't get his bets paid off. So he just jumped thirty feet for a new record.

All in all, the two chums had a fine day and they felt righteously happy as they went home and fed all the dogs and counted their winnings. Then Dickie sent out for four cans of beer and he let Sam break training and drink one of them.

It was quite a day, indeed.

When Sam set out home that night the reaction from the excitement of the day set in. He felt lonesome and depressed and homesick. He wanted to talk over with someone his new and strange power, and who, of course, would be better than Mully?

But when he got home Mully and Lavinia were all adither. Vinnie had just signed a five-year contract with G-M-G Pictures, and of course, the excitement was tremendous. Sam couldn't get a word in edgewise, and he went to bed feeling very lonely.

THE NEXT MORNING Sam's troubles began. The newspapers were all full of it, about the man who had broken three world's records in one day. The front pages had photographs of Sam in his jersey and sweat pants, sailing over the bars with his white moustache floating in the wind behind him.

And the articles were, as they say in Hollywood, terrific. One Los Angeles paper had one paragraph of Sam and the rest of the column saying it showed what California climate could do for a man of 53. Another one said it was partly the climate and partly the California orange juice that allowed a man of 57 to break world's records.

One paper thought that it was the high amount of California sunshine that put extra glycogen into the blood and allowed all California athletes to be better than those from the rest of the world. Another said it was the exhilarating California air that made athletes on the Coast do better; while a tabloid said it was the much higher quality of California tracks that accounted for it.

The papers in the East said it was another California hoax, and that the officials in California always used special California tape measures which accounted for the records. In Florida there was a petition sent to the A.A.U. to disallow the new records because one of the men who fired the starting pistols in the sprints didn't have A.A.U. sanction.

One sporting editor said it showed the United States, with the help of Southern California, would be sure to win the next Olympics; and another said that since Sam was British it showed the United States couldn't win the next Olympics unless Southern California took even more of the load.

A San Francisco paper had an article saying that as long as Southern California could develop men like Sam we were safe from Japanese imperialism, and another paper said that since Sam wasn't American it showed clearly that Congress should do something about new fortification programs along the Pacific.

One famous columnist took nearly his whole column on Sam and said it only went to show that although there were undoubtedly some races in Africa which produced men who could jump even higher than Sam, a white man's brains were many cubic centimeters larger than a Negro's, or a gorilla's, for that matter, although a gorilla was stronger than either, and that while 40,000 Japanese planes could wipe out Los Angeles in less than an hour if they could fly as far as from Japan, it just showed what it was to be a white man.

There was no doubt about it, Sam was important news, as he and Mully soon found out before the day had really started. He was upstairs when Mully found him.

"Now what's tha been up to?" she began.

Sam burrowed down into Mully's clothes closet.

"Why, nowt," he said. "Ah were just sayin' to mysen, Ah sez: 'Ah'll just give Mully's boots a bit of a blacking and get 'em right nice and shiny the way she likes 'em.' "

"Nivver mind soft-soaping ma about ma boots. What's ta been up to?"

"Why, Ah telled thee, nowt at all," Sam said, innocently.

"Nowt! Then what's twenty newspaper reporters yammering downstairs to see thee for? And what's this?"

She jammed a newspaper under Sam's nose, and there was a picture of him doing the broad jump.

"Why, Ah were just dewing a little bit of athaletics yesterday as you might say. It ain't a varry good likeness, dosta think?"

Mully grabbed the paper from him.

"Eigh, Sam Small. They'll be cooming fro' Menston for thee ony day now. Ah doan't knaw what's happened to thy yead. A man o' thy age, callorpering and hopping around at athaletics. What in the name o' God coom ovver thee o' late?"

"Ah ain't gate a word to say," Sam muttered, stubbornly.

Mully looked at the paper, and then she looked at Sam, squatting there in the closet with her best boots in his hand.

"Sam Small," she said. "Come and sit ovver here o' t' sofa."

Sam did as he was bid.

"Now lad," she said. "There's summat behind all this. Spit it out. Now what is it?"

Sam looked at Mully, and he swallowed once or twice, and then he decided it was no use lying to Mully.

"Well, Mully," he said. "It's summat like this. Ah found out Ah could fly."

"Tha found what?" Mully asked.

"Fly," he said. "Sitha! Ah'll show thee."

So he took off and did a couple of turns round the room and then glided down on tiptoe beside Mully again.

"Now, tha sees. Ah can fly," he said, triumphantly.

"So tha can," Mully agreed. "And varry nicely tha does it too. What caps me is that tha didn't tell me about this when tha married me."

"Nay, it nobbut come ovver me lately."

"Well, a varry handy accomplishment it is, too, if tha axes me," Mully said. "Tha'll be able to wash windows that Ah cannot reach and mony things like that. Here, Sam, just hop up and wipe off that cobweb on t' ceiling there. It's been worrying me for two days now."

"Sitha," Sam said, as he went up after the cobweb. "Ah can fly like a sea gull or like a pigeon, but Ah can't yet fly like a lark."

"Well, don't be discouraged, lad. Happen that'll come wi' practice. Ah think tha does reight well for a beginner. How long's ta been at it, did ta say?"

So Sam told her the whole story, about Faith and Mountains, and the truth about the suicide arrest and how he'd met Dickie Hogglethwaite.

"Well, he were a nice sort o' chap, and a Huddersfield lad on top of

it, and when he axed me to do soom jumping, like, well, it were a
chance for him to clean up a few bets."

"Well, there's nowt wrang wi' makking a little brass," Mully agreed.
"Ah always like to have a sixpence on the Darby mysen if Ah can.
But it seems tha's stirred up summat, what wi' all these newspaper lads
downstairs, and a committee o' gentlemen to ax thee to try out for the
British Olympic party."

"Well, us can settle all that reight fast," Sam said. "All us has got to
do is just explain the truth, like—that Ah'm no athalete, but Ah just
did it by flying. Thee just run down and tell 'em while Ah gate these
boots blacked nicely for thee. Tell 'em Ah'm sorry Ah hoaxed 'em
and there's noa newspaper story for 'em, properly speaking."

Despite the fact that he had made a fortune on his self-doffing
spindle, Sam still liked to black boots—especially Mully's. It gave him
a great deal of pleasure, putting on the dauby blacking, brushing it
off, then taking a nice soft cloth and rubbing and rubbing until the
boots were burnished like glacé kid. So he lost himself in the job,
feeling sure that Mully with her apt tongue was enough to settle any
bunch of reporters.

After lunch, which was sheepshead stew with suet dumplings, with
a few side dishes of mashed turnips and pickled beets and fresh dough-
cake, with curd-lemon-cheese tarts and a pint of ale and a few toasted
biscuits and cheddar cheese, Sam took a stroll to sort of ease off his
belt a little. The minute he got on the road a young chap came up and
said his name was Jim McGillicuddy.

"Is ta a newspaper lad, happen?" Sam asked.

The young man said he would tell the truth, but he was.

Sam went on walking up the hill, beside the orange groves with the
irrigation standpipes neatly between each row of trees, and the young
chap walked beside him, explaining that he had to have a good story.
If he didn't get a good story he would be ruined. Really he was only
starting in as a reporter, so he wanted a really good story.

All the other chaps had gone back to write a funny story on what
Mully had said, but he wanted a story from Sam himself and that's
why he waited around.

"Well, there's nowt moar to it," Sam said. "Ah can fly, that's all."

"Fly?"

"Aye!"

"You mean, in an airplane?"

"Nay, just on me own hook."

The chap didn't say anything for a while and they went on walking in step.

"Well, Mr. Small," he said, slowly. "I don't want to trouble you too much, but—if you're in the mood now—would you mind just—flying?"

"Surely, lad," Sam said. "Here's a nice bit of a place here."

So he went over to where the road was near the slope of the cañon and took off. He did a turn or two over the cañon, circled over the edge of the Rogers' ranch, glided back and came neatly to earth beside the reporter.

"Holy jumped-up Geesis," the young man said. "Holy jumped-up Geesis!"

Then he went off running down the road.

"Bloody balmy Yankee," Sam said to himself.

He went on up into the hills, leaving the places where the automatic lawns lay neat, and then coming to a sort of hilly desert land where the sage-brush and tumble-weed and cactus grew. He went on a path, past this, higher up, and suddenly the land changed again as it does in California, and there Sam found it was exactly like England, with rolling turf-covered crofts and bleak skylines. It was a lonesome place, so Sam took off and had a fine hour, gliding around, catching currents that came up the cañons, and feeling the exaltation of the music on his face.

Then he went home and was just sitting down to tea when the reporter lad showed up.

"Come in," Sam said, in his usual affable way. "Sit thee down and have a little tea."

"No, thanks."

"Eigh, come on," Mully said. "Have a little summat—some short-cake, happen? Or some scones, muffins and raspberry jam, cheese tarts, a little sliced ham or pork pie—or there's a bit o' cold pigeon pie here? Or happen some polony or a bit o' cold finnan haddie here?"

But the lad only shook his head.

"Is ta feeling poorly, lad?" Mully asked.

"Aye, what's up?" Sam put in. "Tha looks like tha wished tha'd died when tha had t' measles."

"I got fired."

"Tha gate what?"

"Fired! Bounced! The gate! Discharged!"

"Oh, tha means tha gate t' sack," Sam consoled. "Why lad, Ah'm that sorry to hear it. Ah thowt Ah'd gi'n thee a reight exclusive story."

"I went back and wrote it," the lad cried. "And they fired me. They said I was drunk on the job. I told them it was the truth—the story I mean. And they were too dumb to believe it. They're just like the guys who got the Kitty Hawk story on the Wright brothers—two sticks on page umpty-nine. And this is bigger than the Wrights! Bigger than the Dionne quintuplets! It's the biggest story the world has ever known. Do you know that?"

"Tha's being varry polite," Mully said.

"I may be drunk or I may be crazy, but I definitely am not polite, ever," the young man said. "I do believe I'm nuts though. Look here, maybe I am nuts, but would you—that is—if I did see you before, will you do that again—fly?"

"If tha likes," Sam said, not wanting to put himself too much forward.

"No, really. I'd be utterly delighted."

"Righto," Sam said. And he took off in a straight-up. Immelman, went around the dining room, hovered a while over the table and then floated, inch by inch, back into his seat.

"It's that simple," Sam explained.

"Simple!" the chap exploded. "Why, you don't seem to realize that this is the biggest thing in the last fifty centuries of man's progress. Man can fly under his own power. It's big! It's colossal! It's terrific! Why, with me as manager, we'd set the world on fire. We'd make millions!"

"Millions?" Mully asked, getting interested.

"Yes. We'd give exhibitions."

"Think o' that, now," Mully breathed.

"Ah were thinking o' giving an exhibition," Sam said. "Ah were thinking t'other day, that since it were at Sister Minnie's Ah first got t'idea, happen she'd like me to fly so it could be a sort of evidence of what faith'll do, in a manner of speaking."

"Sister Minnie, hell!" the chap said. "You don't think she'd give up the center of her stage to a man that could fly. No, sir. Look, you sign with me and we'll make a tour—a world tour . . ."

"Nay, Ah doan't want to mak' no world tour. Ah just made one," Sam moaned, "and Ah doan't want another one only so far as it goas back to Yorksha."

"Sam!" Mully warned.

"Now Mully—it's ma flying and it's off to be ma judgment on what Ah do wi' it."

"Aye, and it were thy self-doffing spindle, too," Mully rebutted. "But if it had been thy judgment Owdicotts' mill'd still be using it for their own. Whose judgment were it we should gate us a lawyer and sue for their rights? It were mine, weren't it? But for that we'd still be on two pound ten a week as a mill foarman, instead of rich as we are, wouldn't we?"

Sam said nothing.

"When it comes to addling brass, thee leave it all to me," Mully said. "Now if a little bit of a thing like flying can mak' us another fortune in America, then us'd be ninnies not to tak' it. Now thee forget t' money end, and me and this young chap will settle everything."

"What about our Vinnie? We're not off to leave her."

"She's gate her own career to think on. Now, Ah fancy she'd be glad to have us goa and clear up her background. Onyhow, when us has made a few millions, us'll come back here and retire."

"Oooah, ma goodness," Sam moaned. "Ah wish Ah were back hoam, Ah do."

THE NEXT DAY the papers were all drawn up and signed.

"Now, we're set," the young man said. "It's no use fooling with the movies, because people seeing a picture would only think it a fake. We'll hire Madison Square Garden in New York. All you'll have to do is just once each day, take off and fly round in the Garden. I'll get the plane tickets and we'll fly East tomorrow."

"Fly," Mully said. "Why lewk, then. Happen tha'd better get nobbut two tickets, and Sam could fly alongside us. Us'd save one fare that way."

"That's a champion idea," Sam said. "But there's ma luggage."

However, Jim would have none of it and when he pointed out that Sam might freeze solid going over the Rockies, Mully gave in and agreed that he should ride inside the plane.

The next day they took off and after that Sam hardly knew what did happen. Things came so fast that the poor lad got fair dizzy.

The minute they landed at Newark they were raced off by motor car to the grand suite of a hotel in New York. Then the room got full of people who talked to him and talked at him and pinched him and prodded him. Then they asked him to fly.

"Hey, why should all these people see it without paying?" Mully asked.

"This is a publicity stunt," Jim explained. "It's the press. We've got to stir up interest."

So Sam did a few turns round the hotel room, but you never saw anything as suspicious as that bunch of New Yorkers. They climbed on chairs and felt for wires; they prodded Sam again to see if anything was fastened to him; they asked Mully to leave the room so she couldn't possibly hypnotize them, and finally they asked Sam to take his clothes off and fly so they could see there was no trickery, like a little motor in the seat of his breeches.

This was too much for Mully.

"Ah will not leave this room," she said stoutly, "and if ye think ma owd man's off to fly round naked as the day he was born showing everything he's gate, well ye're all bahn to hev another think cooming. Now put that in your pipes and smoak it."

They went out and more people came and Sam flew around for them. Doctors tapped his chest and tested his metabolism and took his blood pressure; psychologists asked him if a ton of feathers was lighter than a ton of lead; he was examined by a hypnotist, an alienist and a committee on psychic research.

Then the photographers started, taking pictures of Sam standing and Sam flying and Sam looping the loop and the room got so full of smoke that Sam could hardly breathe. So finally he escaped into the bedroom. There he saw a little old man sitting on the bed.

"Nah lad," Sam greeted.

"How do you do," the old man said, courteously.

"Well, that were a good show Ah put on for 'em," Sam said. "But Ah'm rare fagged out."

"It was a good show," the old man said. "But they won't believe it."

"Won't believe it?"

"No, alas! The cheap modern education of the scientific world abhors that which surpasses its factual knowledge. So your newspaper-men will write all about mass hypnotism and wires and Barnum and auto-suggestion. They'll use lots of phrases they don't understand about matters they can't comprehend. They'll find any excuse but the simple truth—that you are capable of levitation—in other words, that you can fly."

"Ah can that," Sam said.

"Of course you can," the old man said gently.

"Thank you kindly," Sam said. "Here have a pipe o' my baccy. It's varry good. And what did tha say thy name was?"

"Oh, it's just a string of vowels and consonants," the old man said, stuffing his pipe with Sam's tobacco. "You wouldn't be interested. I'm just a student, that's all, at the Research Center. I'm trying to find out how to defeat the rebellion of man's body and brain against modern life, modern cities, modern foods and modern thoughts. Why is cancer growing, mental ills? Why do cells multiply malignantly?"

He lit his pipe slowly and looked at Sam fondly.

"Now you! I am still sitting in wonder that I should have the luck to be alive in an age when you should manifest yourself again."

"Again?"

"Yes. Are you becoming rarer? Will this age develop more of you? We've had you before, you know—Daedalus, Icarus. They could fly, too."

"Then Ah'm not the first?" Sam asked.

The old man shook his head.

"Lots of you," he said. "You have been excommunicated and tortured, drowned and burned at the stake as wizards and vampires and incubi and succubi. All because the world is weak and ignorant and—human. And I, too, am human. I wish to circle your life, observe you, make a laboratory specimen of you. But I won't. I'd just like to ask one question."

"Nay lad, Ah've been axed soa mony another wean't hurt."

"Tell me, do you find it harder flying at some times than at others?"

"Nay lad," Sam said. "Well, Ah like best flying alone and out-doors. . . ."

"At night?"

"Aye, at neight. That's reight. And it does get a bit hard for me when people's around. Like this afternoon—it were like the air were varry sticky and soft and a bit harder to get through."

The old man nodded and puffed his pipe. Then he got up, and patted Sam on the shoulder.

"It has been a rare privilege to talk to you, Mr. Small," he said. "I wish I could protect you, but I can't. You see, the world will do anything but believe. Although they see, they won't believe.

"Even back when the world was much simpler they wouldn't. They tried to explain it within their knowledge. When Icarus went soaring into the blue and kept on flying away from their disbelief and never came back, they said undoubtedly his wax wings had melted because he'd flown so high he was too near the sun."

"Why, the higher up tha goas t'colder it is," Sam said, soberly. "That would set wax even harder."

"Undoubtedly. But the explanation satisfied them within their limited knowledge. And so, even today, man will get an explanation to satisfy him within our present limited knowledge. Today that knowledge is even more fiercely narrowed between the bits of misinformation we scientists have predigested for man. And you—poor lonesome Icarus, returning through the centuries—arrive at a world in which the more we prove the less people believe.

"For you have come back to a world where biologists prove virgin birth; chemists can turn water into wine; doctors with insulin raise men from the dead; surgeons perform miracles; electricians make telepathy practical; scientists prove matter lives forever, and mathematicians show that the hereafter in time and space is indisputable. And all this in a world that no longer believes in the virgin birth, miracles, telepathy and the hereafter. The more we prove, the less the rational mind believes.

"There is no more faith, simple and blessed. For the world has had too much proof and too much logic—and in getting them we have lost the faculty of having faith in the incomprehensible."

"That's funny," Sam said. "It were a sermon on Faith that started me out flying, as you might say."

"Of course," the old man said.

"Nay, Ah doan't care what they believe," Sam said. "Ah know Ah can fly, doan't Ah?"

"Yes, Mr. Small. But don't you see that their disbelief could . . . well. No, I cannot interfere. I must not do any more harm to the world. You must go on alone—but just one thing. If at any time . . . if you

find it gets harder than usual . . . just say to yourself: 'I can fly. I can!
I *can*!' and don't ever disbelieve it."

And the little old man pattered away.

SAM HADN'T MUCH TIME to think of what the little man had said, for
his days were full of other cycles of doctors and reporters and agents
and psychiatrists and photographers. Then, as suddenly as a clap of
thunder on a summer day in Cumberland, the big night possessed him
and he was in a dressing room and Mully was handing him a bunch of
spangles and a few inches of silk.

"Ah will net wear it!" Sam raved.

"What, after all t'bother Ah hed makking it! Tha'll wear it or Ah'll
know why."

"Eigh Mully, Ah'd lewk like one o' Tetley's Brewery horses at the
Sunday School feast," Sam protested. "What is it?"

"Ah embroidered it," Mully said. "Sitha, there's a Union Jack on
thy right chest, and a Stars and Stripes on 't'left, out o' courtesy, as you
might say. Now coom on, lad, put it on just to please ma."

So Sam looked at Mully and felt that sorry about her sitting up
nights doing the embroidery, that he put on the costume. When Mully
came back he was seeing how his backside looked in the mirror.

"Eigh Mully," he groaned, "Ah lewk like t'lad on t'flying trapeze,
Ah do, for a fact."

"Well, tha couldn't expect to go out there flying around in thy best
serge suit," Mully said. "And it's ovver late to change thy mind now—
change thy su-it and tha'll be sure to rue it," she quoted.

"Well, Ah changed me suit already," Sam pointed out. "And that's
bad luck reight off."

But they had no chance to argue. Jim came rushing in and dragged
Sam down to the entrance. They went through corridors and Sam felt
just like a bullock going down the chutes in that Chicago slaughter
house trip.

Jim held him by the doorway, and Sam could hear the loud-speaker
systems announcing him.

"Now you're sure you can do it," Jim asked. "Because there's the
biggest crowd the garden ever had—at a twenty-two dollar top, too.
You won't miss out?"

"Of course not," Sam said, irritably.

Then he was being pushed out, and there stood Sam Small, dressed in pink fleshings all embroidered up, and his white moustache jutting out. He stood dazed a minute, staring at the lights and blinking. He put out his arms to take off, and then, suddenly, he began to think of what would happen if he didn't fly.

There he stood, down in the middle of the enormous building, a funny little figure in pink silk and spangles, with his arms out and his jutting white moustache echoing the arms, parallel. Terror seized him and he stood still. For the thousands of people had begun to laugh. That laugh boomed and echoed and gathered until the whole place rang with it and laugh echoes bumped into new laughs and strange over-tone laughs were thus created that no one had given birth to.

Poor Sam stood wishing the earth would swallow him. He was so struck with stage-fright that he turned to run away. But Jim stood in the doorway, waving and motioning frantically.

"For God's sake—go on and fly," Jim shouted.

Sam turned, and putting his arms out again, got ready to take off. But his arms seemed heavy.

He was gripped by a horror. Perhaps it had all been a dream heretofore—and now perhaps he couldn't fly at all?

He was seized with panic, and he ran forward a few steps with his arms out, attempting to get the feel of the air. But it was like being paralyzed. He couldn't feel the air. He knew it would never hold him. Something was holding him down.

So he ran and ran with his arms out—and that's what the people saw: a funny little man running round like a chicken—a man attempting to fly.

And they laughed and roared, and the harder they laughed the faster Sam ran and hopped. He jumped and skipped until he was almost dead of exhaustion, and then he stopped, knowing he was hearing a different sound. The people were booing and roaring with anger. He looked up and saw programs and newspapers sailing through the air.

In a half-daze, he felt himself being hurried and dragged along the corridor. He had cinema-like sensations of policemen drawing their clubs and pushing people back. And then he was in the dressing room again, and Mully was beside him and Jim was looking into his eyes.

"It's all reight," Sam said, thickly. "Gi' 'em all their brass back

again. Ah'll pay for the hall and everything if it tak's ivvery penny us
has got."

Jim stood up.

"All right, Mr. Small," he said. "I don't want you to feel bad."

"That's nice, lad," Sam said. "Hurry away and tell t' folk they can
have their money back."

Then Sam sat alone with Mully, and she looked at him.

"Ah suppose tha's mad at ma," he said.

"Nay lad," she said. "Ah'm not mad, but tha did lewk a bit funny
out there, hopping around. Go on and change thy clothes, and let's
nivver say no moar about flying again."

Then she went out, and Sam changed his clothes.

"Happen Ah only dreamt Ah could fly," he said to himself. Sadly,
he got dressed. What hurt him more than anything else was the way
Mully had looked at him. She would never again have faith in him.
Faith! But that had started the whole thing!

Then it happened. Just as Sam was pulling on his breeches he remembered the little man—the little professor with the beard, saying:
"Say to yourself: 'I can fly! I can! I *can*! and don't ever disbelieve it.' "

Quick as a flash Sam slipped his braces over his shoulders, and in
one breath yelled:

"And, by Gow, Ah *can* fly. Oppen that bloody door!"

As the door opened he took off and went out over the heads of the
policemen, who ducked and fell flat to get out of the way of his soaring
body.

He shot down the corridor over the heads of the people, and then
zoomed out into the great auditorium.

"You bloody buggers," he yelled, "Ah'll show ye!"

He raced up in a tremendous climb and looped over so his belly
almost brushed the ceiling. Down below most of the people had gone
home, but he saw a small knot, faces white in the lights as they stared
up at him in disbelief.

"Ah'll show ye, ye buggers," he yelled, and he shot down at them
like a plane in a power dive. They scattered in terror and fell over
themselves, and Sam streaked away for the entrance. He screamed over
the heads of the jammed crowd and shot out into the street.

"Now, can Ah fly?" he shouted, and he looped and zoomed and dove
in the night, streaking past lighted windows, skimming over taxis and
heads of people, shooting up to the tops of the houses.

Lightly he perched on a roof, and watched the scene below. Taxis smashed into each other and people grouped round women who had fainted. Police whistles blew, sirens screeched as police cars and ambulances and fire engines raced up.

He heard people yelling at him and saw below the white mass of their faces. The fire apparatus began to raise the ladder.

"Come down off there, or you'll break your damned neck," a policeman shouted.

"Ah'll show ye," chanted Sam.

"O.K., tough guy," the policeman said. He started up the fire ladder, his gun in his hand.

Sam advanced one foot off the parapet, and then stepped out. Women screamed and collapsed. But Sam merely laughed. He flipped over, did a slow spiral round the fire ladder, and suddenly shot down at the crowd. At the last second he banked up again a few hundred feet.

Then he swooped again and raced along over the heads. He tore up through the city, he zoomed round Broadway and floated up the side of the *Times* building. He shot along the streets, leaving tangles of traffic in his wake.

Then, suddenly, his anger left him, and, feeling weary of all the people, he circled slowly, up, up into the night, until the city was a spangle of lights down below. He could hear only faintly, now, the roar of the metropolis. Beneath him was the island, a lace of light: the shimmering strands were streets, the delicate filaments of fiery beads were bridges over rivers, the crawling glow-worms were ships in the harbor, the incandescent little caterpillar that inched along far away was a train. In the majestic blackness far above the city, there was nothing to share the purity of the lonesomeness with Sam except the drone of an airplane, far to the south in the vast night sky.

The music on his face brought him sad calm and then sanity. He glided down slowly toward the city. He looked over it in wonder and confusion. And as he did so all his native caution came back.

"Eigh now, Sam Small," he said to himself, "tha has gone and done it. How the blooming hell is'ta off to find out where tha lives?"

He looked down, but not knowing New York, all the streets looked alike. He had only a vague idea that one of the tall buildings below must be his hotel. But they all looked the same. Sadly he flew up and down, but he knew he couldn't recognize his hotel even if he saw it.

"Eigh, what a dew. Ah wish Ah were home i' Yorksha," he said.

Disconsolately, he flew around until he saw a roof that looked fairly comfortable. It was a sort of projecting roof that had a little lawn and a fountain, and best of all, a porchswing.

"Eigh, gardins way up on top o' buildings," Sam said. "What an idea! However, lad, here's a soft place to kip, and 't first thing i' t' morning, tha can get down quietly and find out where tha lives."

WHEN SAM WOKE he found the sun shining brightly on his face and a policeman holding his arm.

"By gum, Ah maun o' overslept," Sam said.

"Now, how did you get up here?" the policeman asked.

"Why, Ah flew up, lad," Sam said, honestly.

At this a woman in the background, standing by the penthouse door, gave a scream:

"The bat man!" she yelled, and then fainted dead away.

"So, I've got you," the cop said, drawing his gun. "And don't you try any flying tricks on me to escape."

But the minute Sam saw the gun he decided. He was sick to death of the whole silly business, so he shot straight up in the air twenty feet, went over the edge of that building, and raced away in a power dive. It was so fast that the cop had only time to take six wild shots. Sam heard them banging behind him, and felt the bullets tearing through the air—for he had become so sensitively attuned to air vibrations that he could feel even the rip of a bullet that was not near at all.

The bullets scared Sam very badly, and made his heart flutter so fast that he had to stop and rest. He came to rest on a convenient parapet. He had perched there for only a minute, when he heard a sound behind him. He turned and saw a nice-looking young lady, naked as the day she was born, taking a sunbath on a mattress.

"Hoops, ma'am," Sam said, turning away politely. "Ah'm right sorry Ah interrupted."

The woman gave a scream and fainted away, too. Sam perched there, scratching his head and wondering whether or not he should get help, when the woman's husband came racing out with a shotgun and began blazing away.

"Drat ma bloody buttons," Sam said, "they maun think Ah'm a cockpartridge or summat, and this is t' open season."

Of course, he was thinking that as he flew, because he was going away from the sunbathing lady at top speed.

THAT MORNING was something for a man to remember. Every time Sam came down to land, the people below began yelling:

"The bat man—the bat man," and they raced up the streets keeping Sam in sight. All Sam wanted to do was to land and find his hotel, but each time he got near the earth the people crowded and clutched at him and traffic stopped and there was no chance for him to slip down unobserved.

"Ba gum, Ah'm fair sick o' this," Sam moaned.

He flew up again and finally came to rest on one of the gargoyles of the Chrysler building. Even then there was no rest, for people opened the windows and stared at him and shouted. As the morning went on they began to run sightseeing airplanes past the tower, and people inside shouted to Sam and begged him just to do a little bit of a flight for them.

Then there was a stir on a balcony below him, and a policeman shouted to him to come down.

But by this time Sam had lost his age-long respect for the majesty of the blue uniform.

"Now lad," he warned, "if tha climbs up here Ah'll just fly away to some other building and tha'll have it to do all over again. Ah'm staying where Ah am, and the only person Ah want to talk to is ma Mully. Fotch Mully here and Ah'll talk to her. Ah'm fair sick of all this, Ah am. Ah'm right sick of it, Ah might almost say. So tak thysen and thy gun away and fotch Mully here."

Sam hopped off and flew a little higher, until he was sitting right against the pole of the spire on the Chrysler Building.

And there he sat, hour after hour, until it was late afternoon. They tried to coax him down, but Sam had his Yorkshire up and was just stubborn and set that he wouldn't come down till they brought Mully.

Finally there was a shout below, and Sam saw Mully's bonnet showing up on a little bit of a balcony. She came climbing up, and Sam flew down and gave her a bit of a hand until they were both on a ledge, snug as could be. Mully stared at him and almost got tearful for a moment.

"Eigh Sam," she said. "In thy shirtsleeves all night, perched up here like a cock-sparrer. Tha maught ha' caught thy death o' cold."

"Mully," Sam pleaded, "now doan't start in plaguing ma. Help ma gate out o' this mess, and s'welp me, bob, Ah'll never lift ma two feet off the ground together again. These bloody bobbies hev been shooting at ma. Tell 'em Ah nobbut want to get down and goa on hoam to Yorksha again."

"Nay lad," Mully said. "Tha's put thy foot in it and there's owd Nick popping below."

"What's up now?"

"What ain't up," she said. "Tha hasn't awf done it, now. Tha's tangled the city up. There's been dozens killed in traffic accidents from people staring at thee. A skyscraper company has offered a hundred pounds a day if tha'll just light on their flagpole once a day."

"Nivver heed that, lass. Let's get down fro' here and get away."

"Nay, lad. Tha's started summat. Tha sees, Sam, tha's upset things. People are suing thee for damages and Ah doan't knaw what. Like one lass were in the family way at that place last night, and when tha flew out she hed a slip and now she's asking a half million dollars for thee killing her bairn that weren't born."

"Oooah, drat ma buttons," Sam moaned.

"That's not awf on it," Mully said. "One awf o' t' city wants thee shot as a bat man, and scientists say tha can't be true, and ministers say tha maun be a devil, and ivvery woman i' t' city is barring her windows. Tha's a menace, that's what tha is. They hed to call off all t' schools, for mothers is flaid tha'll fly away wi' their bairns. Police want to lock thee up because tha could rob ivvery skyscraper i' t' city at neight by flying i' windows.

"Them that doan't think tha should be shot want thee deported as an undesirable alien, and just as mony folk want thee kept here behind bars."

"What on earth for?"

"Well, tha can fly, lad. Why, one chap wi' slant eyes offered ma a hundred million dollars if Ah'd gate thee to goa to his country."

"What for?"

"Why, soa tha can teach his army how to fly, then they could strap a bomb on every sojer, and the whole army could fly on its own hook ovver any city in' t' world and bomb it to pieces and then land and capture it wi'out trouble."

"Ma gum," Sam said, "that's so! If there was an army of chaps could fly like me we could conquer t' whole world. What did'ta tell him?"

"Why, Ah told him straight that tha were a Britisher, and if any army is off to have men 'at can fly on their own hook, it's the British army. But a newspaper chap heard ma say that, and now all the papers demand that they doan't let thee leave this country till tha gives up thy secret."

"Ah have no secret," Sam moaned. "Ah can nobbut fly, that's all."

"Aye, but they doan't know that. Eh lad, tha's upset the whole world. Why, the minute they saw tha could fly, aireoplane stocks all went to bits, and then railroads and boat shares went to bits and steel followed them, because they summed it up that if people could fly they're not off to need any aireoplanes or boats or railroads or motor cars to ride in. It was so tarrible they hed to close up t' markets."

"What did they do that for?" Sam asked. "They still got to buy groceries, hevn't they?"

"Ah don't know sewerly," Mully sighed. "But t' paper said t' President ordered t' markets closed. Then he called a special meeting o' their Parliament or whativver it is to pass a bill for new money to build national defenses against flying men. In fact, to put it in a nutshell, Sam Small, tha's mucked up the whole bloody world."

"Eigh," Sam moaned, "it were that California 'at's to blame. It were a balmy climate for fair—it turned me balmy onyhow. And all Ah ivver wanted, Mully, was to be back hoam i' Yorksha, wi' a good pint o' ale, and a few lads to pass a nice evening wi'—or sitting hoam workin' on a nice rag rug. And now Ah'm in a proper mess."

He perched on the ledge, moodily.

"Well Mully," he said. "It's ma fault. Go thee down and tak a train for California and stay wi' Vinnie. Ah'll tak care o' mysen."

"Nay," Mully said, indignantly. "Ah'm noa less to blame than thee, making thee come to foreign countries where a chap gets ideas into his head that's contrary to common sense. So here Ah am, and here Ah stay, wi' thee!"

Sam thought a while, and looked out over the city. The sun still

shone where they were, but below it was getting almost shadowy and
dusk. Then he looked at Mully decisively.

"Millicent Small," he said. "Dosta luv ma, lass?"

"Nay lad, doan't talk so soft."

"Ah mean it. It's important. Dosta luv ma?"

At that Mully began to weep—much to Sam's astonishment. Finally
she looked up at him.

"Sam Small," she said finally. "Tha hesn't axed ma that for nigh on
twenty year."

"Well, Ah'm a man o' few words," Sam said. "Happen Ah've often
thowt about axing thee; but tha knows how a chap is. Soa now, Ah'm
axing thee."

Mully sniffed and looked at Sam.

"Sammywell Small," she said, "Ah've stuck by thee for twenty year,
Ah have. Ah took thee for better or worse, and happen it were worse
than Ah thowt it would be. But still and all, Ah stuck by thee through
t' strikes when we didn't have a penny and us popped ma wedding
ring to get summat to eat; and Ah nursed thee the time o' thy accident
i' t' mill; and Ah've put thee to bed when tha's been poorly. Ah've
bore thy bairn and washed thy clothes and cooked thy meals and shared
thy bed. And then tha axes ma if Ah luv thee. If Ah doan't, lad, then
for the last twenty year Ah've been living under false pretenses."

"That's all Ah want to hear," Sam said.

He got up and squared his shoulders.

"Now put thy hand in mine," he said, "and don't be flaid. Just have
Faith in me, that's all."

Mully got up and looked down at the evening streets, hymenopterous
with humans, far, far below.

"Eigh, lad, there's off to be a hell of a bloody splash if tha mak's a
mistake," she said.

But she put her hand in his.

"Awf a minute, Sam," she said. "Happen this'll work, happen not.
But if it doan't, there's one question that's been burning ma for a long
time."

"Fire away, lass."

"Well—Sam—did'ta really have owt to do wi' that widow i' Harro-
gate that summer we went there on us holidays?"

"Mully," Sam said, "true as us is facing us Maker reight now, there's
nivver been nub'dy but thee."

Mully looked at him a second, then she tied the strings of her bonnet tighter under her chin.

"That's all Ah wanted to hear thee say, lad," she said.

She put her hand in his again.

"Count three for me, lad."

"One—" said Sam.

Mully took a deep breath.

"Two—" said Sam.

Mully shut her eyes.

"Just have Faith in me," Sam told her.

"All reight," she said. "Ah do believe in thee, Sam."

"Then here we goa! Three!"

Mully stepped forward with her eyes shut. She felt the air rushing past her. It was a sweet, glorious flow of air. She opened her eyes. Then she smiled; because there was Sam right beside her, the tips of his fingers touching hers, and they were swinging around in a big circle, volplaning as smoothly as a couple of albatrosses. And like that, together, they went up and up in a great spiral.

And that's the last New York ever saw of them. The people in the buildings, staring out, and the black crowds far below on the streets, craning their necks backward, could see that twin flight of two bodies, near to each other, matching their movements with the telepathic exactitude of birds, going up and up until they were dots against the washed sadness of the evening sky—up and up until they could be seen no more.

And thus it was that Sam and Mully Small escaped New York and flew back to Yorkshire and settled down again.

And if you ever go to Yorkshire and get to a place called Polking-thorpe Bridge, near Huddersfield, you can test this story. Any evening you wish you can go down to the Spread Eagle, and there, with a pint of nice ale before him, a blazing fire behind him, and a handful of chums beside him, you can find a chap named Sam Small.

He's been all 'round the world. He has a wife named Mully. He has a daughter named Vinnie in the movies, who was married not long ago to a young American chap named Jim McGillicuddy.

But it's no use asking him if he can fly. Because if you do he'll look you straight in the eye and say:

"Nay, lad, that's not me. Tha maun be thinking o' t' other Sam

Small—the chap what dropped his musket and held up t' battle o'
Waterloo."*

* Sam here refers, no doubt, to a more famous Sam Small, who was also a
Yorkshireman. But our Sam makes a highly regrettable error in saying his name-
sake "dropped his musket." He didn't drop it. It was knocked down by the sergeant,
which started the whole ruckus. Sam maintained, not without reason, that the sergeant having knocked it down, the sergeant should pick it up. Lieutenants, cap-
tains, majors, colonels, brigadiers, all came successively to argue with Sam, but he
was true Yorkshire and wouldn't retreat from his stand, and there was all history
held up with armies waiting and Napoleon scheming and Blucher marching. Finally
none less than the old Iron Duke himself showed up and took the matter in hand.
Being a great general he had a command of language that was not only fluent but
quite the sort of stuff Sam could understand. According to the Yorkshire poem,
unexpurgated edition, Wellington roared:
"Sam Small, you —— —— ——! —— you! Do as you're —— well bid! Pick up
that —— —— —— musket!"
   And eigh, ba gum, Sam did.
   "Now," said t' Iron Duke,
   "Let t' battle commence!"
   Which it did, with results that are familiar to every schoolboy as Punch might say.

Snow in Summer

BY

Helen Hull

Snow in Summer

HAZEL ran down the stairs to the basement, caught her heel on a step, flung out her hand against the white-washed cement wall, and just didn't fall. She stared at her outstretched smarting hand, and shook it gingerly. Nothing sprained, thank Heaven! Her tongue lapped at the reddening scratches and she crossed more cautiously to snap off the racket of the washing machine. At the final subsiding rumble she gave a sigh of relief. There was always the chance that the whirling rhythm confined in that sleek, white-shining drum might someday get the better of her, explode, fill the whole basement with its froth and din. She wouldn't have told George about the animosity between her and that machine, but she knew that someday she would fail to make something fast, and it would electrocute her or drown her in suds, or flail her to bits. George had given it to her for a Christmas present, two years ago. She could see him now, explaining how it worked, a clear flush like a boy's standing out on his cheekbones. She had demurred a little. Think how much it costs! Why, that would pay the laundry for weeks and weeks!

"But this will last for years, Hazel! Years! I can keep it in order. Don't you like it?"

He would have laughed at her if she had explained how it terrified her. She took a deep breath of the quiet in the basement, and watched the motes dance in the morning sun-shaft through the low window. Her tongue took a last dart along her abraded palm, and she flexed her slim fingers. It would have been too awful if she had wrenched something! Her mind picked up the game with time it played so constantly these days. She'd be back in half an hour. Another hour to rinse and hang out the clothes, ten minutes to brush up the living room, she had

55

the salad ready. Well, say ten o'clock. If no one telephoned, she might have two hours—but she must be careful. A kind of warning, the narrow escapes she'd been having. Just because she rushed so.

She held herself to a sedate pace up the stairs, a propitiatory offering to this household *poltergeist*. After eight, the Dutch clock over the yellow breakfast table said, and Lorna hadn't touched her breakfast. From the living room came voices, George's, exasperated, "But if you'd just watch, you'd see how I do it. See, this spring—" and John, "Gee, Dad, I'm late now. I tried to put that spring back. Where's Mother, anyway?"

Hazel was there instantly, her eyes round with dismay under the crisp fringe of lashes. Had John upset that typewriter again? George was hunched over the table, elbows, square shoulders absorbed, the tuneless hum with which he always worked (like a little dynamo, thought Hazel), breaking into a satisfied, "There it is. Now don't throw it on the floor if you can help it."

"I never did," said John. "Ole second-handed thing." He peered over his father's shoulder as George rattled the shift bar triumphantly.

"Will it run?" asked Hazel. "I warned you to be gentle with it!"

"Oh, sure." John croaked a little, being casual, and reached for his schoolbag. "It's time we got a move on."

George turned, brushing at the square tips of his fingers. "Lucky John spoke of it if you want to use it. Thought you sent the bills all out." He came briskly across the room, a sturdy, compact figure, blond and well-scrubbed, his blue eyes alert and sanguine.

"Yes," said Hazel, vaguely, while she made automatic inspection of her son. He looked—well, grubby and stringy—beside his father. Growing so fast this last year or so. His face had a thin, surprised look. Hazel slid two fingers into a sagging pocket of his coat and drew out a limp, smudged rag which she dangled, her fine nose crinkling.

"Aw, gee, I thought I had a clean one." John squirmed past her and started up the stairs, three steps at a stride.

"Tell Lorna to come along this instant," Hazel called after him. "I'm getting the car now."

"I don't see what she does all this time." George opened the front door. "The postman's late, too, and this is the day my dental journal comes. He's not even in sight."

Hazel pulled a blue felt hat down over her soft hair, called, "Lorna! You must drink your milk!" and ran out to the dining room. The keys

should be there on the buffet, in the silver cup, behind the candlesticks
. . . in the corner of the top drawer. Where had she left them? Oh, not
in the car again!

"Looking for something?"

(Oh, darn! Now he would know—) Her glance darted sidewise at
him, caught the round bright expectancy in his eyes. "You've got them!
Oh, you—" she thrust out her hand. "Please!"

"And where were they?" He spun the chain in a flash of metal on
a taunting finger. "Lucky for you I happened—Ouch!" He jumped
back, as Hazel, lunging for them, stubbed against his polished toe.
"The time you'd save if you had a little system!"

"Meet you at the front door," called Hazel, hurrying out through
the kitchen. Fall chrysanthemums and marigolds marched in rows
of bright disks along the straight gravelled drive to the small garage,
and in the next yard, beyond the row of barberries, Polish Annie was
hanging out sheets. Well, Mrs. Marks could afford a washer-woman;
she had no children. Hazel swung back the doors, edged along the
fenders of the small sedan, and slid under the wheel, wriggling to
free her knees from the pull of her blue piqué frock. She fitted in
the key, made a few indeterminate movements of her hands, her face
serious in concentration. Brake, gears, clutch. "It's valuable practice,"
George insisted. "I won't get the car out any more. You know how to
drive, only you won't relax and let it be automatic." At least she
hadn't driven into the back of the garage for days! Her toe pressed
the starter button, and holding her breath she emerged in a bucking
and erratic course which landed her, after a final parabola, in front
of the house. George was probably right, but if only she could start off
head first perhaps she wouldn't mind so much. Like that nightmare
in which she went leaping backward through all the streets of the
town, unable to stop because she'd forgotten the word. She laid a
finger on the horn, but before she pressed it the front door opened and
George stepped out on the tapestry bricks of the entrance. For a moment he stood there, hands lifted to fit on his new gray hat. For a
moment Hazel looked at him, clear of the mists, the manifold subtle-
ties of her intimacy with him, her emotion toward him. He might have
been a stranger, seen for the first time in one of those intuitive flashes
when she could see almost the stranger's image of himself, the way he
hoped the world saw him. Confident, not exactly jaunty, but full of
a kind of well-being which was a matter of equilibrium, inner and outer.

He really likes his life, she thought. Teeth are terribly important, they're fascinating, a dentist is practically the mainstay of the world, he likes the town, he likes this house, having a family. He's really as happy as anyone I ever saw. As he called into the house, "Come along, you two! Mother's waiting!" Hazel shivered, and her tight fingers swung the wheel a trifle. When he found out what she was doing, he would think it very funny. Now with driving, he enjoyed teaching her, he didn't really mind that she was stupid about learning. It would be dreadful if ever she did anything to shake this content of his. Not that he was smug; he worked too hard.

The three of them, George, John, and Lorna, were rushing at the car, and Hazel, tipping forward the seat beside hers, forgot the moment of strange inspection.

"Did you get any breakfast?" She saw, in the fresh curls at the back of Lorna's fair head, the cause for her delay. That rose sweater was growing too snug over small young breasts; Lorna liked the color and refused to wear anything else.

"She's banting, Mother." John plumped in beside his sister. "I hear her jiggling the bathroom scales every time I want to get in."

"If I was as skinny as you, I wouldn't say anything," began Lorna.

"All nonsense," said George, dropping the front seat and pulling shut the door with a sharp bang. "Eat what you want and work hard and you'll be the way you're meant to be."

"My goodness!" Lorna's voice came shrilly over the clash as Hazel, sliding forward, poked the gear lever toward reverse. "Just because I don't enjoy guzzling!"

Hazel could feel the restrained patience with which George held himself until she fumbled into third gear and popped down the street. It would be almost better if he spoke out, except that when he just thought she could pretend she didn't know it. Now she was reasonably safe until she had to start up again after she dropped the children at school.

"Guzzle? Who guzzles? We, they, it est guzzledator."

Poor John and his Latin! Hazel laughed, partly a crumb of nervousness, partly amusement, and George, turning a moment from his alert vicarious driving, said, "You remember I like my girl as she is! None of your anemic slats for me!"

Of course Lorna did take after his people. Hazel drove along her thoughts drifting, melting one into the next, just at the edge of aware-

ness, hazily beyond the focus of her attention on this hazardous business of driving. Lorna was a trifle on the solid side, but she had George's
coloring, fair skin and hair. She wasn't exactly pretty, but later, when
her character had firmed out— This corner was a bad one; Hazel peered
left, right, and met George's blue glance as he peered first right then
left. She pushed down her toe and leaped across the intersection. Just
last summer, while she was in camp, Lorna had jumped out of childhood into—well, not maturity, but some of its superficial concerns.
As if something had stepped too hard on the gas. Life ought to have
a good driver, going along smoothly— She swerved, sucking in her
breath, as a brown and woolly dog trotted across the road. George
seized the wheel as she bumped over the curb, and swung the car
back into the road. A long blue car rolled past, the chauffeur grinning.
Mr. MacAndrews, on his way to the factory. Her knees had that untied
feeling!

"You missed that one, Mother," said John. "Better luck next time!"

"It's those impulsive movements," said George, "that keep women
from driving as well as men."

"Would you run down a dog?" cried Hazel.

"I never have. But if I had to choose between hitting one and
wrecking the family——"

Hazel found herself biting hard on her upper lip. She pushed it out
and ran the tip of her tongue over it. That was why she had that little
fringe of chapped skin always after she had to drive. The shadows under
the tall maples along the street were full of dogs! Why had she ever
thought it would be nice to live out at the edge of town, in the new
residence section? Three, two blocks more; she turned up a side street
to avoid the few business blocks, and came through the small park
to the high school, rocking the car as she pushed valiantly with both
feet on clutch and brake. George got out, and the children clambered
after him; John's books caught on the hinge of the seat, and as he
stooped to free the strap he winked solemnly at Hazel. She watched
a moment after George sat again beside her. Lorna had called out, a
group of girls had turned, and she went toward them, her dark skirt
tight with the quick movement of sturdy legs, the sunlight brilliant on
her hair. John dawdled behind her, banging his strapped books against
his thigh. Then Hazel peered sidewise under her lashes at her husband,
and for a fleeting instant saw, in an unfamiliar contraction of muscles
between his brows a kind of puzzled wonder. But all he said was, "John

ought to try out for one of the teams. He's spindling. Needs filling out."
Then the wonder disappeared, and he was comfortable again, knowing
what to do. "Well, time to be off."

There was again a moment of suspended attention, of withheld
comment while Hazel got under way, fairly smoothly this time. Then
George said, in the uninflected, almost talking-to-himself tone of one
who has no doubt of his listener's response, "I think I'm booked every
hour today. That means night work again. Mrs. Wills's upper, and
there'll be two sets of X-rays."

(Monday night. If I get the children off to their rooms early, I'll
have sat two more hours.) Hastily, as George's silence nudged at her,
"It seems forever since you've had a free evening."

"I really need a laboratory assistant, a mechanic." His hand darted
toward the emergency brake. "Look out! That truck——"

With a squawk of the horn Hazel dodged around the red bulk as
it swung out from the curb. "I saw it," she said. Well, she had, just
as George spoke. "You'd never find one to suit you," she added, incau-
tiously. These few blocks of morning business traffic took her mind
off her words.

"I'm not unnecessarily particular," said George, calmly. "I didn't
want another fender crumpled. And as for my work, it just has to be
right. Take an inlay. It fits or it doesn't. And bridge-work——"

"I just meant—" Hazel was a trifle breathless, slowing behind the
huge gray bus from the city, and then swinging past it as the one
traffic light of the town, on the bank corner, showed green—"that
you do everything so well yourself—" There, she drew up at the curb
without grazing the tires. Sunlight glinted on the brass sign beside the
entrance to offices above the bank. Dr. George Curtis. On the whole
she'd done pretty well this morning. "You're a kind of genius, everything you touch, now aren't you, darling?"

"Well, I shouldn't go that far." George smiled. "Pulling my leg, eh?
Just because I like things right. Anyway, I couldn't afford an assistant.
Not till the X-ray machine is paid for, and the kids are educated, and
the Building and Loan is settled. The more I make, the harder I work."

"But look at the reputation you're getting." Hazel was serious now,
pride luminous in her eyes. "Even Doctor Brown sending you cases,
asking you to consult with him— You're really educating the town."

George nodded, his mouth firm at the corners. He didn't need her
encouragement exactly; he had no doubts about himself. But he rather

liked a salvo of trumpets before he rode away into his busy day. "Yes, I think all that new equipment is justifying itself. If only John wasn't so clumsy! Lots he could do to help me, a boy his age. I wouldn't dare trust him in the door. Take that typewriter this morning. Why, any boy could have fixed that. Sometimes I suspect he's putting it on, too lazy to try."

"Oh, no! I know just how he feels! Things like—like cars and type-writers are just malicious, the way they go wrong. John isn't lazy. He just knows you can fix it, whatever it is, just as I do."

"But John's a boy! He makes me uncomfortable he's so stupid."

"You don't really think he's stupid." Hazel laid her hand over George's, her finger-tips pressed, sensitive and light, against his knuckles. "He hasn't got your hands, but you wait!"

"You'd think I'd nothing to do but sit here and chin!" George gathered himself up alertly, brushed her cheek in a kiss which was less a caress than an absent-minded symbol of affection established past inquiry, and let himself briskly out of the car. "Blow twice when you come this noon, then I won't waste time waiting for you." He wheeled; his erect head and straight sturdy back vanished in the hallway.

At least he no longer waited to inspect her departure. Hazel smiled, remembering the day he had run after her for a block to tell her to release the brake. She could drive home now in her own way, and leave the car in front of the house, safe for her noon pilgrimage.

As she drove at a snail-easy pace out the wide street, she thought, it would be like a fairy tale, so much so that it can't happen. I'm just a silly fool, having a dream. That's why I don't dare speak of it. George would try not to laugh, but he'd get that rosy, amused look. Ten thousand dollars. Think what I could do! The mortgage, the X-ray machine, college.

It had all started with the typewriter. If George hadn't brought that home! She let herself into the quiet house, and stood at the door of the living room, looking at the thing, the round white disks of the keys dancing under her intent stare. He'd picked it up cheap, second hand, and set it in order. Better business to have his bills typed. Could she learn to run it? She had learned, after a fashion, holding herself to the attempt in spite of clatter and extraordinary results until she no longer wasted George's excellent stationery. If other people do it, then you can, she told herself. She had been telling herself that about a great many things, ever since her marriage. Such as keeping the house in order. She threw aside her hat, and moved quickly about the living room, gathering sheets of the Sunday paper, plumping cushions on the divan, brushing kernels of popped corn into the ash of the fireplace, straightening lamp shades, magazines. It was queer about marriage. You expected it to be—well, a prolongation of a state of feeling. There was that about it, of course. But what you didn't expect was that you had, suddenly, to become an expert at all sorts of things you'd never dreamed of doing.

Until she had married George, she had never done anything, in the sense of tackling the great variety of material items out of which life seemed to be composed. Her mother had spoiled her, of course, but like George her mother had been so competent that she forestalled activity from less skillful competitors. And they had been so proud of her, her mother and father, for her graceful accomplishments in school. The darlings, she thought, as she hurried into the kitchen for a dust cloth. If they knew what I'm trying, they'd be sure— She felt that queer jerk deep in her consciousness, like the sensation of being dropped too quickly in a swift elevator, with which she came upon the fact of their being dead. It had happened so suddenly, and had interrupted the pattern of her life with George so little that for long busy stretches she almost forgot.

If her father had not gone to that training camp on the Lakes the dreadful winter of the flu epidemic, he would still be alive. And she might never have known George. There had been too few doctors, and her father had worked night and day trying to save the boys. When, finally, he had almost died himself with pneumonia, Hazel and her mother had gone to Chicago, had waited until they could bring him home. Hazel, seventeen, had met George, had thought him an archangel, Michael himself, his bright hair and fair skin brilliant in his uniform of petty officer making him a thing of life in a scene of appalling death. Her father had said, "We need a good modern dentist in Lounsberry. If you ever get out of this, and want to locate, think us over."

Her father had come home with a heart never the same, and so, in a way which faced life and not death, had Hazel. When, a year later, her father said that a fellow named Curtis had turned up, sort of prospecting for a dentist's office, Hazel knew she had just been waiting. And later—she could see her father's face now, as he had talked with her, waxy, wrinkles down the long cheeks, around the deep eyes like a bit of used paraffin paper—"But, good Lord, Hazel! I thought you'd want someone different—someone you'd meet at college—" she had said, "He is different. I don't want to go to college."

"And I'm responsible for getting him here!"

"You've always got me what I wanted!"

"I'd like to, as long as I can." Something had happened to his face, like a hand giving the paraffin paper another crumple.

He had died before Lorna was born, and her mother, rather like a clock there is no one to wind, had quietly run down a few years later.

Then for years Hazel had gone about her new business of housewife and mother, thinking, when she at rare intervals looked at herself, that the slim, dreaming girl who had written poetry, who had delivered the class valedictory, who—but what did it matter? She was gone, perhaps her bones were still the same, but her very flesh was different.

An hour later the clothes-horse in the backyard oscillated gently with its burden, the planes of linen and garments making in the sunlight a design of labor done. Hazel came into the living room with two square black hatboxes which she set one on each side of the straight chair. She seated herself between them, and for a moment relaxed, spine soft, suds-crinkled finger-tips pressed against cheekbones. But she couldn't be tired, not until this job was done. A month ago she had dropped into a bog of consternation: she had been mad to start such a thing, she was too ignorant, too ill-equipped, she had better throw hatboxes and all into the fire. That had been just after the children had returned from their summer at camp, and George had come back from his fishing trip. Perhaps she had worked too many hours while she was alone. At any rate, after a few days she had swung herself into the double rhythm of taking care of the family and stealing time for herself, a half hour, an hour, whenever she was alone. Second wind, her father would have called it. "People don't begin to use themselves, there's an inner reservoir they don't tap. I see it often enough in a crisis. I tell you, Hazel, some of the old boys that did so much, generals, geniuses, what-not, they'd learn how to dip in, how to work up second wind."

Hazel wasn't sure just what her father had meant, but she knew she had to finish this task if she wanted to be at ease with her self-esteem, and the very compulsion seemed to produce the necessary energy. She pushed back her shoulders, and her face lost its soft, relaxed aimlessness. The upper lip looking long and Irish under the fine nose, pulled down, its curve straightening, and the eyebrows, even, fine accents of the structure of wide brow and eye sockets, drew together. She whisked off the lids of the two hatboxes, picked out of that on the left an exercise book with a mottled cover, and from that on the right, sheets of white paper. She propped the copybook open against a pile of George's *National Geographics*, and slid the paper under the roller of the machine.

It had really started with the typewriter, she thought, again. Until George had brought it home, she had just scribbled in her copybooks; she would buy them for a nickel at the drug store which kept school supplies, and no one ever wondered what she did with them. She couldn't remember just when she had started that. After the children were both old enough to go to school, and she was efficient enough so that she no longer lost the frantic race between the length of a day and the tasks she must finish,—or was it when George began to go back to his office after dinner? At first he had had time during the day, poor boy, because not many people noticed his shiny new sign. She could remember well enough the first day he had been busy every hour. "Wasn't I right, Hazel? Even if I offended Mrs. Betts, insisting that she had to pay when she forgot her appointment, you see it made them think I was busy and couldn't be fooled with. Now you see!" What she saw, among other things, was that now she had long evening hours on her hands. She couldn't leave the children, and there wasn't much to do if she had left them, as she didn't care for bridge, and the moving picture theatre was open only on Saturday. George said, "We can get a maid pretty soon, if you want one, although with all this modern equipment—" Then, before they reached even the point of discussing a maid, along came the depression, so that people couldn't pay their bills, even when they could no longer put off a visit to George, and George worked harder than ever.

She had tried reading. But she knew most of the books in the small library, and she found nerves twitching so that her feet jumped, as they had when a little girl she had sat beside her mother through a long sermon. Reading for hours and hours would be all right when she was an old woman, but now it was too like watching someone else run and dance and live when inside her something turned and twisted and pressed to break into its own movement.

When the children were little she had told them stories, about her own childhood, about her father, about his people. Lorna never listened long, but John loved them, and gradually Hazel had woven a long serial which went on night after night, held rigorously by the boy to fidelity in every statement. "No, Mother! You said he had his possessions tied in a handkerchief on a stick, not in a bag at all!"

She had always liked her father's yarns about his people. Restless footed, he had called them, coming from Ireland and southern England to this country, settling in the east, and then the restless footed moving on, west again. Perhaps, after all, it had all started with the unused copybook she had found the first summer the children were in camp, and the sharpened pencil. Put the two together, and there was Hazel, starting to set down the story she had spun so many nights for her son. When she had filled one book, a nickel bought another. Her hand-writing was amusingly uncertain, a product of the period when the public schools swung from Spencerian script to round and horizontal letters; Hazel had made a queer combination of the two. But at the end of an evening with the copybook, slipped into a table drawer as she heard George at the door, she had a half-guilty, warm-cheeked contentment.

When she had started the first copybook she had no clear notion of what she meant to do, and telling George seemed too like confessing a private vice, trotting out a fragment of day-dream. When she had filled two books she hid them in a hatbox on her closet shelf, under a winter hat. She was finding writing like wine, and tippling on words she set down many things she had never known she felt. It was unlikely that George would have curiosity enough to read all the scribbled pages, but she ran no risk. And she didn't want him to point out with patient good humor that she was wasting hours of time. Then last spring, at the final meeting of the Ladies' Literary Society, a lecturer from the University had given her the final push into what seemed at moments a life of crime. Certainly it took as much scheming and equivocation as a clandestine love affair. She typed CHAPTER SIXTEEN at the top of the sheet, and, a little ridge of concentration between her brows, began vigorously to peck. "The country is looking for new voices," the lecturer had said: "The middle west must grow more articulate. There may be someone among you ready with the next great novel." Then as proof of the country's eagerness he had cited awards, fellowships, prize contests. "Here's a new publishing house, just being launched. Does it look for established authors already with repute? No. It offers ten thousand dollars for the best first novel from a writer who has never published a thing."

A good many of the club ladies had gathered around the lecturer to ask questions. After all, they had paid him twenty-five dollars just to come over from Ann Arbor, and he had talked only an hour. "But don't you think, Professor Elson, when so many things in the world are unpleasant, that our writers should give us what is pure and sweet?" Hazel, being part of the refreshment committee, was passing cakes. If she could get him alone for one second, could ask him one question! No hope. Miss Emma, one of the two Buckley girls, who wrote poems for the Lounsberry *Weekly Record,* was holding her cup of tea dangerously near his crisply buttoned coat and bubbling at him through her very new teeth. Hazel offered cakes to them, with a protective glance at Miss Emma. (George had been funny, about the way her transformation had slipped while she was biting on plaster for the upper plate.) But the young lecturer wasn't laughing at her; he was concerned with escape, he had an engagement, he had appreciated the audience very much indeed, very receptive, and he had edged past the barrier of silk bosoms and teacups disappearing just as the ladies' quartette started the Spring Song.

She couldn't have asked him without someone overhearing, anyway. But after two days in which she dodged and twisted only to find the same idea in the middle of her thoughts every time she opened her mind's eye, she wrote to Professor Elson. A friend of hers was writing a book, would he please send her the name of the new publishers he'd spoken about. When he didn't answer, she wrote a second time. She was sorry to trouble him, but would he please? Then she watched for the postman, and luckily reached the door first the day the envelope addressed in her own hand came back to her, with a printed announcement, and an apology scrawled in the margin: sorry, my secretary overlooked your request.

October first. Ten more days. She tapped more briskly, and the paper slid crooked as she reached the bottom of the page. She managed to finish the line, if slightly on the bias, and pulled out the sheet. Page 292. She wasn't sure how many pages a book should have. Some of Dickens seemed very long, and she'd looked at "Anthony Adverse" with dismay. Well, a man might find time to write as many pages as that; she couldn't. "Pere Goriot" was much shorter, and her father had liked that. She was a little troubled because the typewriter lacked quotation marks and authors seemed to use them. On one page she tried inserting them by hand, but the pen marks looked unprofessional. Lucky for her the machine had capital letters and periods. She adjusted the next sheet. Yes, the typewriter really was responsible. She had been struggling with the exercises George had brought home, until she was sick of the sly gray fox and the aid of the party, and she had suddenly thought it would be more fun to copy a piece out of one of her copybooks. That had done it. Almost like seeing one's self in print to have the transformation from intimate careless scribbling into the uniform impersonality of printed letters in straight rows. (Or almost straight; a few hops and glides of letters.) For the first time she had thought of her own words as standing out apart from her, making a shape for someone else to see. The idea that she might make a book had started right then, although she had waited for the circular from Professor Elson before she admitted it.

John alone had suspected anything. "What on earth do you pound that ole typewriter so much for?" he asked. "I woke up last night and you were just a-going at it!"

"Just practicing." Hazel thought: I can't tell John, because I'd be so mortified then if I didn't get the prize. I should have taken up painting. That doesn't make a noise.

She had time for another page before starting luncheon. Only part of this last copybook left. Do not insert name of author on script. Script was this thickening pile of sheets. Write title of book and name and address on separate sheet, and enclose in sealed envelope. She had already done that. "Your Hand Upon the Gate," by Hazel Browning Curtis. She had thought of naming the book "Restless Feet," but decided it sounded too much like horses. Her concentrated haste had brushed color over the narrow bridge of her nose and under her eyes when at quarter before twelve she tied the covers on the two hatboxes and carried them upstairs to the closet shelf.

Five minutes behind schedule, having turned the gas low under her lunch dishes, and set the table, she ran out to the car. She could drive fairly fast with no passengers aboard. High school was already dismissed; she kept a quick eye out for her two, among the drifting groups, girls with sunlight on their curled heads— (I'm positively the only girl in my class who hasn't had a permanent, Mother!) —boys dawdling behind the girls in noisy pairs or trios . . . scuffling, shrieking out jokes which the girls pretended not to hear. They act just as we used to, thought Hazel, in spite of all the talk. Playing up to each other before they know why— There's John! Straddling a hydrant at the corner. He propelled himself with a minimum of effort into the car. "Here we are again," he said.

"Have you seen Lorna?"

"She went on over town."

"I'm not very late, am I?" Hazel let the clutch pedal jump up, the car bucked gaily down the street.

"I haven't waited more'n an hour or two." John had a solemn drawl.

"Yes, you!" Hazel laughed. "Have a good morning?"

"Lousy."

"John!"

"Pardon muh. Stinko, then. Honest, I bet I'll flunk that Latin. No sense to it."

"Nonsense. You never flunked anything yet. Don't say that to your father!"

"He'll know soon enough. Then I'll be more popular than I am now."

Hazel stared straight ahead, her mouth firm. She'd have to talk to George; he had been riding John too much about—oh, springs out of typewriters and such! "If you were more popular," she said, lightly, "you'd—" she jammed down the brake as the traffic light jumped red at her, and a car following cracked against the bumper. She peered guiltily over her shoulder, but the grimy face of the truck driver behind seemed unperturbed. Too much to handle car and domestic nuances together! As she drove across the street she saw Lorna, standing in the triangular recessed entrance of the drug store, her face lifted in gay absorption to that of a strange young man whose red head bent toward her, shooting up from broad shoulders on which stretched a grayish sweat shirt with extraordinary inked designs. Hazel poked the nose of the car toward the curb, and peered at John. Something startling about the pose of the two figures, obliviousness, challenge. John was staring gloomily at his father's sign, as if he hadn't seen Lorna. "Who's the boy?" asked Hazel. It couldn't offend John's code to tell her that.

"What boy?" John overdid his inspection of the neighborhood. "Oh, him! He's new this year. Daniels his name is. He plays football."

Lorna had given a little start, spying the car, and after a moment of concentrated animation, quick words too low to reach Hazel, strolled out to the curb, her creamy blandness implying that she had been waiting tedious hours. So this is the next one, thought Hazel. Just a day or so ago she'd asked Lorna where Tommy Burke kept himself, and Lorna had said, "That dope! My goodness, how should I know?" This boy looked—well, older. John got out, muttering he'd like a back door to the car so he wouldn't have to move around all the time, and Hazel punched the horn button twice. Unnecessarily, because as she blew George appeared at the doorway, hat under his elbow, and beside him a young woman. Hazel was thinking: Lorna's only sixteen, but she looks older. Something about that red-head I don't like. Just the way Lorna looked at him. Lorna tossed her head as she climbed into the car, and her smile at Hazel was bright with defiance. Don't worry, darling, I won't say a word; I know better than that! Why didn't George come along, and who was the woman, anyway? Hazel leaned forward; the edge of the door cut her view. "You'll have to wait," drawled John, "till Dad finishes his lecture." A hint of laughter crinkled at the corners of Hazel's eyes, but she kept her mouth sober. It was true, George did have his serious, now-I-will-tell-you-all manner, one forefinger beating against the palm of an outstretched hand. His hat slid down as his finger grew emphatic, and he stooped for it, brushed it off without losing a word. The woman was very smart, like a red-winged blackbird in tailored suit and scarlet purse to match the long quill on her small hat. Even her hair lay in a black and shining swirl, like feathers, and she had certainly repainted her mouth if she'd been having anything done to the teeth that gleamed as she laughed. "I'll think it over." She waved her purse, and strolled away, her dark, indifferent eyes not even grazing the car or Hazel's half curious face. It is time for fall clothes, thought Hazel. But George hadn't sent a glance after that smart figure. A suit does things for you, her thoughts jumped along. But she must have at least a dead tooth! She wondered if George's habit of monologue had grown a little, perhaps because his listener so often had a mouth too full of cotton and rubber dams to answer back! But John mustn't laugh at his father. Just because George was so much in earnest —

He sat beside her, the clean whiff of antiseptic soap filling the car as he banged shut the door. "I'm glad to sit down," he said.

Hazel backed gingerly out from the curb and drove down the block of stores. At the corner where the large sign LOUNSBERRY HOUSE announced progress in neon letters, she turned, just as the woman in the black suit started across the street. The woman moved ahead with an arrogant indifference to small town traffic, and Hazel stalled the engine. "I wish people would look where they're going!" she said, as she trod on the starter.

"It is a good idea," said George.

(Only he means me, thought Hazel.)

"I wonder if she's staying at the hotel." George craned his neck.

Hazel couldn't say "Who is she"; suddenly she felt too cross to say anything. But Lorna asked. "Is she a new patient, Father?"

(Even her voice sounds excited, thought Hazel. She's trying to start something else, so I won't ask about her new boy friend.)

"She may be," George was saying. "She's making a canvass for a dental supply company, she's a representative of the concern, but we got to talking about her own teeth. She's practically agreed to come back for some X-rays. She's a very intelligent woman."

"Be kinda hard on her," said John, reflectively, "if she had to have a tooth pulled every time she got an order."

"She said," continued George, "that she seldom saw an office, except in the largest cities, so well equipped as mine."

"My goodness," said Lorna, "I shouldn't think she'd like to go all around like that!"

"I don't know." George stopped eying the street ahead for a moment to turn his head toward his daughter. "Not that I'd like you to go on the road. But she has her own car, and she seems to like it."

She does, does she, thought Hazel, with unexpected wryness. Well, I hope she doesn't sell George something terribly expensive. Like that new washbasin with footpedals, so he didn't have to touch the faucets after he'd washed his hands. Oh, *dear!* I mustn't be so edgy. Nothing's happened. Lorna's had beaux before, and George—as she rounded a corner into their own street she let her elbow rest against his arm, and her tension relaxed. She even smiled a little, remembering George, years ago. "A dentist is about as safe as a man can be. Any woman knows she hasn't got a throb of sex appeal left when she gets her mouth wide open and a drill going in it." Even a swanky saleswoman was a dead tooth to George. Typing always made her nervous, this double life was getting her down. If she weren't so near the end— When she brought the car successfully to a stop in front of the white house, she had pushed herself into her usual busy and quiet acceptance of the three of them as her family home for lunch, all separate undercurrents submerged.

On Friday afternoon, the last day of September, Hazel was hunting for a piece of paper large enough to fold around a box. It would be a joke, she thought, if after all these months of work she couldn't send off her book because she couldn't wrap it properly! She rummaged through the pile on top of the broom closet, and off it slid, grazing her nose. Odds and ends; the only thing in the pile large enough was a brown paper bag from the grocer's, rumpled but intact. Hazel smoothed it out on the table. Something fatally appropriate, a tag of domesticity. She might better save the money the postage would cost. Her fingers were listless with dejection as she lifted the tattered lid of the box— (the paper on which she had copied the book had come in the box, and she might have been more careful of it if she had known she would use it as casket). Yes, casket. That was just the way she felt about it! She'd expected elation and triumph; if she didn't hurry she wouldn't have the courage to send the thing away! There lay the sealed envelope, her name inside, "Your Hand Upon the Gate" somewhat aslant on the outside. She tied a piece of twine about the box, and slid it into the paper bag. With a little folding over along the sides, at the end, she could make it serve. Ship by express or first class mail said the directions.

She stared at the window, where fall drizzle and fog pressed flat and gray, seeming in its monotone to be without depth, drabness painted on the glass. If she went to the Lounsberry post office, Mrs. Pickett or Sam would come to the window. "What's in it, Hazel?" The Pickett back yard had touched the back yard of the Browning place when Hazel was a girl. People had complained that Mrs. Pickett was worse than a daily gossip column, but after Sam came back from the war his amputated foot carried him right through civil service and change in administration. Hazel couldn't hand under the lifted grill such a parcel as this, with the inscription: Prize Novel Contest, Horn and Westerby, Publishers. She could hear Mrs. Pickett. Like the time she had told George about the money order for the new office chair for Christmas! That would be a way for George to hear what his wife had been doing! "I'm not a bit surprised," Mrs. Pickett would say. "Hazel always had her nose in a book when she was a little girl." Brr! Her very skin felt too tight, chill-shrunken, at the inevitable calamity.

If she had time to go into the city— But she had to send the thing today or never at all, and even if she had time—already the clock pointed to half-past three—she couldn't conceal a trip to town. "But whatever did you go in for? You didn't say you were going!" Hazel decided that a life of crime presented unique difficulties. She might drive to the next village. The postmaster there didn't know her, and if she took a back road out of Lounsberry— "You have to be careful," George had said that noon. "These damp leaves falling are almost the worst hazard." She saw herself in a ditch, she heard George or Lorna or John explaining, in sombre, tragic tones, "We don't understand what she was doing, she never went to Roseville," and hastily, before her imagination could bog her into immobility, she buttoned on a raincoat and pulled a hat well down on her troubled head.

She reached Roseville without a skid, parked the car in front of a chain grocery, the one note of color in the drenched, deserted street, and the box bulging under the raincoat, to keep it dry, she darted from the car into the one story building, the sign almost lost in the dinginess of the window. The postmistress was fat and suspicious. "What's in it?" she said, as Hazel had feared. "Typewriting," said Hazel. "I—I'd like to register it." The postmistress turned it round and round. Did she smell a bomb, or hear it ticking? "You oughta seal it, then."

After a despairing ten minutes Hazel had found glue at the shoe-repair and fruit shop on the corner, had stuck down the ends of the grocery bag, and talking too much, she couldn't seem to stop, about weather, roads, the automobile plant between Roseville and Lounsberry, at last had the stamps affixed, and the thin strip with the registry number in her fingers. "The mail goes out today, of course," she said, finally.

"Gone," said the postmistress.

"Oh!" Hazel crumpled the receipt in her palm. "But this has to go today!"

"Postmarked the thirtieth," said the postmistress. She reached for the surrendered box, as if to sniff out the reason for such urgency, and Hazel, backing toward the door, murmured something.

As she drove toward Lounsberry, the windshield wiper keeping a rhythmic half circle of clearness, she tried to remember what she *had* said. She thought: of course Roseville people know George. Lots of them come over. Maybe the postmistress herself— Then she remembered the woman's mouth, with the white china display, and drove more swiftly along the rain-dark road. That postmistress didn't know George. But what did people do when they had something like—well, like a murder, say, to hide?

She came in to Lounsberry by the upper road, past the schoolhouse, down into the business block. Too late to pick up the children, too early for George. She'd stop for oranges, and if anyone asked her, that was where she had been. As she passed the bank corner she glanced up toward the windows of George's office. The neatly shirred pongee curtains she had made caught streaks of red from the traffic light, bars against the amber glow behind them. Well, she thought, I've wasted a dollar and sixty-seven cents. And how many hours! And now it's all over, but anyhow, George needn't know.

THE judges appointed by Horn and Westerby, Publishers, were having their committee meeting. As the date for release of the prize announcement was January fifteenth, and this was January thirteenth, they knew severally, and in various irking ways, that they must, today, commit themselves. They met in Mr. Horn's new office, thirty-two stories above Fifth Avenue, and Mr. Horn himself had dropped in for a few minutes. "I don't intend to offer suggestions," he said. "I just want to repeat that this isn't a Nobel Prize you're awarding. We want a book to sell. We've got the organization, we've got a staggering sales campaign—did I tell you we're planning to ship by motor truck and trailer, with loud speakers?—all we need is a book." He was a dapper little man, with an exaggeration of grimace and gesture which kept his hair rumpled and cut premature wrinkles in his thin face. He whirled now and darted from the room as if the loud speaker had summoned him.

The members of the committee looked at each other. "Nice little pep talk," murmured Carlton, a plumpish, bald book-columnist on a daily paper. He was irritated at his presence at the committee meeting anyway. He had no recollection of making Horn any promise to serve as judge, but Horn had cited place and date, a cocktail party a year ago, when the staidest firm in town showed what they could do for a novelist. Either the Scotch had made him incautious, or he hadn't believed Horn would find anyone with funds to back him. He'd told Horn he never read novels any more. Too ephemeral. He didn't tell Horn he found it easier to establish himself by expressing violent opinions on books no one else was likely to read. But Horn had promised real publicity for the judges. He was a good salesman; that was why he'd hooked Westerby as partner. "The advertising agent turned into the custodian of our literature," Carlton added.

Letitia Thomaston blinked her myopic and large brown eyes in Carlton's direction, and the lavender orchid which she had bought for herself that noon trembled on her silver fox scarf. Carlton had never spoken of *one* of her books, although for several days after each of her latest serials appeared in covers she looked at his column. She didn't read it, she just glanced at the title he had so captiously selected. When Alf Horn had spoken to her about being a judge, he had said, "Carlton's one of them. You might get chummy with him. He could do a lot for you." Not that she needed much done, but what she always said was, when thousands of people just run to get the next issue of my serial, it seems strange that no reviewer can understand my message. Carlton's face, well outside her radius of clear vision, was an amber egg. He looks just like a changeling, she said to herself; a disagreeable baby. "I need you on that committee, Letty," Horn had urged her, "to balance Carlton. You know what the public likes. He's too—" Now had Alf called him erotic or exotic? Not that there was much difference. And as Alf had promised, there weren't many manuscripts left to read by the time the office had combed out the hopeless.

"It is a great rethponthibility," said Letitia Thomaston. "Bestowing such a large thum on an unknown writer when we don't know who it is and our own names are attached to the award!" She spoke in accelerated tempo and the listener was not sure whether she really lisped or just slid over some of the consonants. "Personally I think it was a mithtake to limit the prize to new writers. Everybody who can write is in print already, and a great many of them ought not to be."

"I know what the mistake was," said Carlton, gloomily. "I should have written a novel instead of being a judge. I could use the ten grand."

"I always meant to write one," said Mrs. Rudolph Arner, the third judge. "But I never have had time."

For an instant Letitia and Carlton stared at her, united fleetingly by hostility toward an amateur. Mrs. Arner, sleek, plump, well clothed in a dark frock so simple and extreme that Letitia had felt a doubt of her own velvet, had a way of appearing on committees, a pleasant little moon illumined by her husband's reputation as essayist and editorial writer. She entertained frequently and well, and she seldom interfered much with committee decisions. She was a little troubled at present, because her second cousin's daughter had submitted a manuscript for this contest, and Mrs. Arner thought in glancing at papers, she had recognized it. She had said, firmly, "You must not give me an inkling, otherwise I can not be on the committee." Her second cousin Minna had cried. "You know what it would mean to us!" Mrs. Arner did know, among other things, that such an award would mean Rudolph could stop sending a monthly check to Minna. But she knew, too, the untemporizing scorn Rudolph would feel for any shade of nepotism, and that knowledge of Rudolph buttressed a certain crack of practicality in her own honor. The trouble right now was that she thought she knew, without intending to know, without pre-knowledge, which manuscript had come from Minna's girl. Should she lean backwards in an attempt to escape suspicion from Rudolph, and vote it down? Especially when she wasn't sure?

"But then, if we had all written books, we couldn't give each other the money, now could we?" Her secret dilemma heightened the slight accent of her husky, rich speech.

"We might as well get down to business." Carlton's implication was that the women had been talking for hours. "Shall we vote at once, or do you (grudgingly) prefer discussion?"

"What's the use of being a committee if you can't talk?" Mrs. Arner jumped her chair forward until she could reach the pile of manuscripts on the glass-topped table. "I can't remember them by name, anyway. Names seem to have nothing to do with what's in a book nowadays." If she got them to talking she could see whether that one had a chance. She couldn't help it if they chose it; even Rudolph couldn't blame her for that. Only five had survived the earlier meetings.

Carlton twirled his wrist until he could see the face of his watch. "I've got to get out of here before night," he said. "Let's vote."

"Before we vote—" Miss Thomaston's orchid was choreatic—"I must go on record. There is one book there I think we should discard. If by any chance it has two votes I should be compelled to resign from the committee. I could not allow my name to be associated with such— such—" She had wound herself into such tight sibilance she had to stop.

"You mean my choice, I suppose," Carlton's face had no expression, except for a widening of nostrils. "'Alley Cat.' The only book in the lot with any guts."

"That's just it! That's all it's got! No, Mr. Carlton, your jaded palate may relish that rank taste, but my finger has rested for years on the pulse of the reading public. I know how their heart beats!"

"Oh God!" Carlton's lips made the words without a sound, and Mrs. Arner wriggled on her chair. Something stimulating about real argument, especially when she could see each side so clearly! Carlton said, aloud, "Since you have been so frank, may I explain that your choice offends me even more? Obsolete and immoral saccharinity. Resigning wouldn't be enough! I'd have to commit suicide!"

"Then those two cancel each other," said Mrs. Arner. "I don't believe either would fit a loud speaker."

They voted on the three remaining, three times, and each time each book had one vote. Mrs. Arner did not vote for the book she thought Minna's daughter had submitted, and she couldn't decide from the printing on the slips which of the other two had chosen it. Carlton looked as if at any moment his boredom would become complete paralysis, and Letitia Thomaston wore a glaze of indignity.

"I'm tired of this," said Carlton. "Let's draw lots. They're all tepid. Horn will blow hard and get his money back. What difference does it make?"

"It makes a difference to me. I am not part of a lottery, I am a judge. My first choice is thtill 'Ordeal By Love.'" (And mine is "Alley Cat," muttered Carlton.) "But since I have no co-operation, and since it is almost five o'clock—" she blinked hostile eyelids toward Carlton, and then turned toward Mrs. Arner bending forward to pull some focus around the woman's face. "I should think *we* might agree—"

"I'm not a bit dogmatic," said Mrs. Arner, hopefully. "I don't really know which to pick, and so I voted for 'Aspic and Honey.'"

"At least it begins with an A," said Carlton. Mrs. Arner smiled at him. He didn't bother her at all; Rudolph could be much more sarcastic.

"But I'm willing to change." Mrs. Arner took a long breath. Not even Rudolph could impute partiality to her now. She didn't really know it was Ethel May's book; she only knew that Ethel May had a modern way of writing, without ordinary aids to the reader such as punctuation and capitals, and the pages of this book had the same queer nakedness. "I'll vote for the one about the hand on the gate, if you will."

"And this," said Carlton, as he agreed, "is the way democracy works." When he opened the door, Horn leaped up from a chair, with the capped and spurred air of one whose horse paws and prances to be off. "Yes," said Carlton, "it is the unanimous decision of the committee. And if you ever catch me again!"

"OH GOODNESS, don't tell me it's meat pie night again!" Lorna gave a wriggle intended for a shudder as Hazel slid the casserole onto the mat in front of George.

"We have to finish the roast." Hazel spoke indistinctly, nibbling at the tip of a finger she had just burned.

"What's wrong with meat pie?" asked George, bisecting the brown crust neatly. "Especially your mother's."

"They're so—so common." Lorna leaned her forehead against her hand, but at her mother's glance she thought better of that elbow on the table and sat upright again, while John muttered, "Just a little taste of pheasant, please."

(Nothing suits her, thought Hazel, when she comes out of her trance far enough to see us at all!) George, knife poised for a transverse cut, looked at his daughter. "You'd do well to learn how to make a pie like this," he said, tranquilly. "Your husband will appreciate it some day."

"He looks like a hearty eater, too," said John, very low. Hazel shook her head at him, and Lorna decided not to hear him.

"I can remember—" George served with a dexterous turn of the wrist— "when your mother's pies weren't like this."

"Why bring that up?" asked Hazel, her finger still smarting.

"Oh, well!" Lorna disposed of the argument. "Cooking's old fashioned. You buy things in cans and boxes. Just listen to the radio!"

A sharp buzz of the front doorbell caught George with his mouth just opening for a homily upon the home, the hearth, the kitchen.

"That's probably for me—" but although Lorna pushed back her chair and flung aside her napkin, John beat her in a dash for the hall.

Hazel saw George glance at his daughter, his blue eyes candidly alarmed, saw him seal back a protest. He's worried, too, she thought, about that Daniels boy coming so often, although he won't say a word.

Lorna expected him; she poised at the edge of her chair, every nerve waving toward the front door, to catch his voice. They all heard John's "H'ryuh, Bo," and, "How long you been working there?" and then the door shut. John strolled back, exasperatingly slow, thumb and finger pinched at the corner of a yellow envelope.

"'Satelegram," he said. Lorna slumped. A telegram was adult disaster, and did not touch her suspense.

"Let's have it!" George reached for it. "Now who on earth ——"

"It says Hazel Browning Curtis," said John, parting with it reluctantly.

Well, I don't know anyone who'd be dead, thought Hazel, and she
opened it. It roared at her, each printed word, the room rocked up
at a queer arc, and faintly she heard George, impatient, "Who is it?
What does it say?"

"It says—" her lips were stiff, "it says I got it."

John stood behind her chair and read it aloud. "Delighted to offer
you congratulations your book unanimous selection of judges for award
send photo wire biographical details immediately representative will
fly west to arrange trip to New York presentation of check publication
being rushed."

"That's a queer mistake," said George. "John, you better call up the
office at once and tell them. There may be some other message for us."

Hazel's heart, buffeted by consternation and amazement, began to
beat swiftly; the blood burned in her ears, her temples. "I don't think
it can be a mistake," she said. "It says my name."

"But what—" George stared at her. ("What have you been up to
that I don't know about," flickered in his eyes, a premonitory doubt
of stability as if the earth's crust heaved slightly.) "Here, let's see it."

Hazel waved the sheet toward him, and pressed her fingers against
her temples, trying to push back the flush of guilt, of shock. If only the
news had come when she was alone! Giving her a minute to get used
to it.

"Horn and Westerby," said George. "Never heard of them. Whose
trip to New York? What book? If you know what it's about ——"

"Yes, I know." Hazel took a long breath, to inflate the feeble squeak
in which her voice had come out. "I must have got the prize. I didn't
expect to."

"What prize?" asked George, and Lorna said, "Did you win a trip
to New York? Why, *Moth-* er!"

"I won more than that." Hazel thought: I'll say it, and see if it's
true. "I won the prize. Ten thousand dollars."

George's eyes were round and light blue, just the color of his broad-
cloth shirt, the pupils contracted to dots. John loped around the table

to lean over his father's shoulder and stare at the yellow paper. "Ten thousand bucks! Oh boy oh boy oh boy!" he chanted.

"It doesn't say ten thousand," said George, slowly.

"That's the only prize there was." Hazel gave herself a little shake. There, she wouldn't cry. She'd been afraid she might. The paroxysm in her chest was quieting. "I thought I wouldn't say anything—I didn't really expect to get it."

"I don't understand yet what you did." George's expression of doubt thickened.

"I wrote a book. A novel." Hazel's color had subsided, her eyes were bright under the fringe of lashes, her pallor, the uncertainty of her mouth had entreaty. They all looked as if she'd suddenly stood on her head in the middle of the table! "You aren't any more surprised than I am," she said, and as her eyes met those of her husband's she caught a flash of the clairvoyance which lived at times between them. You shouldn't ever be so sure you know everything about me! She smiled at him.

"You mean these people—" he laid a finger on the telegram, "whoever they are ——"

"They're publishers," said Hazel.

"Are going to give you ten thousand dollars for something you wrote out of your head?"

"Of course," said Hazel, "there's a good deal of work getting it out of your head." She had, suddenly, a new feeling, a tardy response to the stimulus of an unfamiliar drug. Her book had been selected. Unanimously. She, Hazel Browning Curtis, had written it! "Let me see that telegram!"

"I don't see when you found time."

"That's why you pecked away on that ole typewriter!" John dropped into his chair, his face screwed in dark concentration on this phenomenon in his own house. "Ten thousand bucks! Why, you're rich, Mother!"

"I haven't got a photograph, except that one with the children years ago. I couldn't wire biographical details. What would I say? I think you might congratulate me! You haven't one of you ——"

They did then, George adding stiffly, "If we'd known anything about it—have to get over the shock." Lorna thought it was like something in the movies, exactly! And wouldn't people's eyes stick out! George said he wouldn't say anything about it until they saw the check. Hazel did not notice until late that evening, when she cleared away the dishes, that he had scarcely touched his dinner. He had said, "Well, we ought to celebrate. But I promised two inlays for tomorrow. Even if I've got a rich wife, I suppose I must go on working." Hazel went to the door with him. "You know," he said, slowly, "I knew you had something on your mind. I felt it. Only I thought for a while it was another baby. You were absent-minded, that way."

"Well, aren't you at least glad that wasn't it?"

"I don't know." George held his muffler in place with his chin as he jerked into his overcoat. "I'd understand that. But ten thous— Why, my best year I didn't clear— And never saying a word—"

Hazel's hand wavered upward. She wanted to poke a finger into the buttonhole of his lapel, to explain that her silence had been a lack of confidence not in him, but in herself. "I never expected to win the prize," she began.

"I'm surprised you confided that in us!" George drew himself stubbornly away from her finger. "Mere accident, perhaps, the telegram coming as it did."

"I hadn't made any plans." Hazel shivered as the raw January wind pushed around George's stiff figure into the warmth of the hall. It was too bad of George not to be whole-heartedly pleased— "How could I when I never expected—you're just surprised because you didn't think I was smart enough to do it!" She didn't know where her sudden anger leaped from, the words curling like a wave over the blond rock of her husband's face.

"I didn't say that." He shrugged, and thrust his hands into pockets. "You needn't get mad just because I'm surprised. Only how—" his breath puffed out a great white feather in the frosty air, "however can I tell what else you're up to? But you're cooling off the whole house. Shut the door." And he strode with finality out of the range of light toward the car.

Hazel shut the door, hand braced against a desire to slam it. She ought to be high with excitement, delight, and instead George had done this to her. That was why she hadn't told him: she had known just how he would take it. She broke the thin string of accusations, seeing his face just before he had swung down the walk. Oh, poor George! The delicate, assured balance of their lives knocked suddenly out of kilter! A balance of expectancy, habit, knowledge. And she had been resentful, instead of wise. She'd heard that success was bad for people;

was she already proof of that? She heard Lorna at the telephone, in the muffled effect of lips sealed against the receiver. As she walked past her daughter, the murmur ceased, and the blue eyes rolled up at her ingenuously. John sat at the dining room table, one hand rustling in a large cracker box, the yellow telegram propped against his tumbler.

"Are you still hungry, Johnny?" Hazel glanced at the table. He'd had the rest of the gingerbread, and all the milk. But she hadn't noticed much about what he ate.

"I guess not." John munched. "Just thought I'd eat a cracker. Say, Mother, are you sure it's ten thousand dollars? It just says award."

Hazel opened a drawer of the buffet, and from under the imitation leather box for knives and forks took out a folded paper. "You can read it," she said, and John frowned as he smoothed out creases and read the announcement.

"Maybe they won't pay it," he said, darkly. "Lots of those prize things are fakes. I knew a fellow and he drew the number for a car, but they gave it to someone in the firm. He never saw it!"

"Oh, but this is different!" Hazel's fingers closed over the telegram, and she read it slowly. "Books aren't like drawing numbers for cars! Why, a professor gave me that notice. He'd know if it was a fake! And here's my name and address ——"

"John's just being smart, Mother!" Lorna was at the door, dark beret pulled toward one ear, coat over her arm. "Don't let him fozzle you."

"Just because I have brains enough to raise a question!" began John, but Hazel interrupted.

"Are you going out, Lorna? Tonight?"

"Why, I told you, Mother! We're meeting at Agnes' house to talk over the Senior play. I explained this afternoon. You must have forgotten, with all the excitement and everything." Lorna was forbearing, kind.

"Didn't you meet last Friday?" asked Hazel.

"Of course *one* meeting can't decide *everything* about a thing like that!"

"Not when you think who's there," said John in falsetto.

"You know—" Hazel hesitated. Lorna was so intrenched in righteousness, and her forbearance was so egg-shellish— After all, if George didn't want his daughter going out during the week, he might see to it himself! "That coat really isn't warm enough for tonight," she finished.

"I can't wear that other old thing!" Lorna tugged the coat over her shoulders, buttoned it with an air of drama. "Honestly, I'd rather freeze to death! *Mother!*" her face changed from its slightly reserved hostility into glowing supplication. "Oh, Mother! I just thought—with all that money— Oh, could I have a fur coat? Could I?"

Hazel looked down at the yellow paper, and again, slowly, there expanded within her a bright bubble. Somehow, among them, they had almost obliterated the extraordinary fact that she, Hazel Browning Curtis, had won the prize!

"We'll see," she said, deliberately. "After I know more about this."

Lorna's hands, pulling the belt through the buckle, stopped, and her eyes stopped too, round, and almost thoughtful. "Would you rather I didn't go tonight? I—if there's anything——"

"Any little thing like a fur coat?" queried John, reaching for another cracker.

"Don't be late," said Hazel. Her hands, automatically, began to pile together dishes from the table. The silver clattered.

"Of course I said I'd be there," Lorna waited.

"Of course." Hazel pushed open the door into the kitchen, and blinked her lashes. It would be ironic if after all her care in handling Lorna, her tender noninterference, her attempts to erect invisible safeguards just to keep the child from blundering too early into what she thought was love, bribery should now prove effective. Lorna would stay home, if Hazel wished, with a fur coat in the offing! Money was a weapon Hazel had never had a chance to try. It might be stronger than words or wisdom. A reminiscent flush of embarrassment showed in Hazel's face as she poked her head through the shoulder loops of an apron. That night last week when she had tried to talk with Lorna! She'd been strictly contemporary, using bold and simple words about what a strong instinct sex was, and how it might blot out all the other interests that were important for her development, and that would be all right if she belonged to a primitive tribe, but she had to think about earning her living, getting a proper education— Hazel had been proud of her little speech, and at the end Lorna had looked at her pityingly and said, "Of course, Mother, we belong to entirely different generations!"

She hadn't even been surprised that her mother had written a book! I suppose—Hazel turned the faucet and held a finger in the stream of water, testing the temperature—I was as self-absorbed as she is, at her age. Maybe I hid it better. I don't know. Lorna's like George, you know just where they are. George had been surprised. She clattered the dishpan into the sink. That water wasn't hot. Never was, unless the furnace was roaring. Why—she stood motionless, and the water purled over the edges of the pan. She could install a new heating plant, if she wanted to. That oil burner, automatic, that the agent had been so persistent about last summer. She could do anything she liked! Almost. Of course, at this very moment, whether she liked or not, she had to do dishes in lukewarm water. Was that a way to celebrate?

There should be someone to tell, someone who would say, "Marvelous! Wonderful!" Her mind clicked off a line of people, neighbors along the street, women in the church, in the literary society, girls grown older who had been her best friends when she was a girl. Queer, the way marriage altered your intimacies, absorbed whatever it was that ran out searching for friends. Turned you into a small principality with guards along the border. Well, it would come out in the paper, and then they'd all know. As George said, better wait until she had the check.

In the quiet kitchen, above the soft note of the water, the ticking of the porcelain clock grew louder. A queer, hard tone, the beat of metal under porcelain, like a premonitory whir which might someday shiver the china into fragments. Hazel listened, her upper lip caught between her teeth, her eyes bright and rebellious. She didn't like that clock. It had run her life for her too long, measuring her inefficiency against its methodical progress. Time you had those dishes done, it said right now! Hazel looked at the stacked plates. She didn't like them, either. George's mother had sent the set, not as a wedding present, just as an extra. "We don't need them, now the family is so small," she had written. "It will save you buying any."

Heavy, old-fashioned ware, with a design in yellowish-green which crawled and twined around the borders. George had been delighted. "Makes me feel at home," he had said. One of the hired girls who helped out a few weeks after the birth of Lorna or John had broken one plate. That was all. Hazel stared at them, the design began to swim around the plate, the clock had the vibratory tone of breaking china. Suddenly Hazel seized the pile, thumbs on top, fingers spread, held it well away from her body, and with a little push to help out gravity, dropped it.

John poked the door open and looked in, his face solemn. Hazel with her toe spun off the top plate, sole survivor among the shards.

"Migosh," said John, "another revolution in China!"

"I can buy some more," said Hazel.

The telephone burst into a prolonged and unnatural clangor.

"Gleeps!" said John. "They gone crazy, too?" He vanished, the ringing ceased, and in a moment John was at the door again, his thin face twitching, as if his air of nonchalance had grown too tight for his skin. "New York calling for Hazel B. Curtis," he paged her in his deepest tone, holding the door ajar.

New York calling, or Mars would like to speak to you. Hazel slid past John, sat down at the telephone stand, and after an instant blew a somewhat winded "Hello," toward the mouthpiece.

"Is that you, Mrs. Curtis? Someone in New York *says* he wants to talk to you." That was Flora Robb, Jessie's oldest girl. Hazel had heard she was night operator. "At least they have your address."

"Yes," said Hazel firmly. Flora needn't sound so incredulous! Well, George's caution about saying nothing would do no good now, with Flora on the line.

"Here's your party."

The brisk, staccato voice was, as Hazel said later, just as clear as if he'd been right in the room. Yes, she was Hazel Curtis, yes, she'd written the book, yes, she'd had the telegram, yes, she was delighted. Something both stimulating and breathtaking in the rapid pelting of words. A little information for a news story to be released at once. Had she ever written before? What did she do? Oh, fine! Two children, husband was what? A remote voice interloped, words about three minutes, and the staccato bristled. How did you happen to write a book? (John had crept near, head bent as if he listened to New York.) Hazel floated above the earth, herself the golden bubble, even the intent and repressed astonishment in John's face a remote thing, caution quite gone. How had she happened to write—those lonely evenings, with George at the office— Any message, how you feel at winning the prize? What will you do with it? And now, Mrs. Curtis, we want you to drop in for a few days. We're rushing the book through the press, need you for publicity hints. No, we've decided it's much better for you to come to New York, meet all of us, sign contracts, of course you can manage, matter of paramount importance. Wire me, I'll meet you. What's that?

Can't afford— Nonsense, you're rich. I'll mail you a check for expenses.
Work up radio and movie ends when you come. Congratulations.

The hall door opened as the voice ceased, and Hazel swung dizzily
around on the stool, finger-tips tingling. George, both hands embracing
a pyramid of green paper, kicked the door shut behind him. The kick
jarred his hat forward, and he peered from under the brim with raffish
suspicion. "I thought you weren't going to tell anyone yet."

"I wasn't." Hazel giggled. George did look comical! "He was telling
me." (This must be like being drunk, she thought. It's a grand feeling!) "But he's going to put it in all the papers!"

"Was that the very guy that's handing you ten thousand bucks?"
drawled John.

"How'd he get here so soon?" George pushed his chin over the
crackling paper.

"New York calling, Dad. I bet Florabelle got an earful that time."

"I hope what I said was all right. Goodness, I can't remember what
I did say! But how could I go to New York?" Whirling away from
them, across a continent— "I could hire someone to come in— Oh, it's
too—too ——"

"Utter," said John. "Just too utter! That's the word."

George set down his parcel on the console-table, propping it against
the wall. "I'll have to put up the car," he said.

"Lemme, Dad." John angled past him a whoop floating back as he
slapped the door shut. George took off his coat, folded his muffler
into a pocket, and opened the door of the hall closet, his movements
deliberate and prolonged.

"I wish you could come to New York with me," said Hazel. "I'm
not used to going places by myself."

"It sounds as if you would be," said George into the closet.

"Would you rather I just stayed here?"

"Of course not." George turned, and smiled, just a quirk of the
corners of his mouth. "I mean of course I would." He shoved the green
bundle along the table. "I bought you that. They didn't have much
to choose from. Maybe you won't want it—if you're going away."

Hazel pulled off the metal clips, folded away the noisy paper, the red
azalea danced.

"Of course I want it!"

"He had some roses, but I thought this would last longer." George
cleared his throat. "You—you didn't think I wasn't pleased, did you?

I mean I just never thought of your writing a book, and then to have it turn out that it was my wife——"

He's trying so hard, thought Hazel, looking up from the red blossoms. She could see only the shadows cast by his quick and secret thoughts, in a shifting of tautness about his mouth, about his grave blue eyes. Not the thoughts. Never the thoughts themselves. Suddenly she stepped close to him, her hands slid between his arms and rigid body, clasped tight against his hard back. "Darling!" she said. His arms strained around her, urgent, and they kissed, the wryness of shock or fear or strangeness gone as their blood remembered all their knowledge of each other.

"You know—" Hazel sniffed, liking the faint clean odor, the cool firmness of his cheek— "I'd rather give it back than have it make any difference. It couldn't, now could it?"

"I hope not, old lady." George's embrace relaxed. "Not if you keep your head. You couldn't give back ten thousand. That's a lot of money."

Hazel withdrew slowly. Too bad, the way saying things changed your feeling— "Goodness!" she spoke briskly. "I haven't even finished the dishes! You put the plant on the living room table. I'll be through in a little while."

She slipped through the door into the kitchen, and stooped to gather up the fragments of china. She didn't, suddenly, want George to see that mess. As the pieces clinked softly into the waste basket, she thought, and the back of her neck prickled, almost with fear, that perhaps it was a bad omen, this first gesture of hers. You'll always have to pick up the pieces, if you smash things, she told herself. But what a silly way to feel. As if good fortune was too much for her!

Hazel left for New York late in March, after three changes of the date. The first time John had the flu. He had pretended that he felt perfectly well, but at the very moment when Hazel kissed him good-bye, she caught the unmistakable faint whiff of fever about him. Stripping off her gloves, she took his temperature, ignoring the awful faces he made. (Never worry about your children, her father had told her. Find out right away.) When she read the thermometer she asked George please to send a wire that she couldn't come. John hadn't been very sick, but only, she was sure, because she popped him into bed that minute. The second time the housekeeper left just as Hazel meant to go. George had something to do with it, although Hazel couldn't ask him what. "All I ask is a women competent enough to take charge of things," he said. "I can't give up all my business, unimportant as it may seem to you, to look out for the children." The news stories had done that to George. Mr. Horn had played up the, "Wife seeks solace for lonely hours in writing. Beside the cradles of her sleeping children she composes great book. Domesticity palls upon this remarkable woman." The first time George read that he had been too outraged to listen to Hazel. By the tenth time Hazel had ceased any attempt to explain the difference between what she had meant and what the stories said. It was too bad they'd called George a struggling young dentist. Hazel couldn't honestly blame him for being angry, but she blamed him for not believing her when she protested that she hadn't told reporters such things. George did drive her into the city for her train this third time when she made an actual getaway; a formal George who made comments on the state of affairs in Michigan as indicated by objects of the landscape. He left her at the stairs which led up to her track, and his kiss had the effect of chastisement. "When you come back," he said, "I hope I'll recognize you."

Hazel brushed away tears which burned her lids, and suddenly parting, blade-sharp, cut through the layers of awkward hostility, of self-reproducing misunderstandings, and she was in his arms. "Don't let anything happen to you while I'm gone! Oh, George, darling! I don't want to go."

"You're the one things will happen to. We'll be all right." But he kissed her again, and this time he loved her and reassured her.

"Nothing that will make any difference between us, will it? Say it won't. I couldn't bear it!" Never had she loved him more, the firm clip of his arms, the little wave of his chin as he tossed off too much emotion, the everything that was George.

"When you get this all over and settle down again—" A porter jostled them, climbing past with luggage, but the moment was gone, anyway.

"I don't want to settle down." Hazel folded her hands under her collar, pushing the soft beaver against her chin, and stared at George, her eyes startled. "I didn't mean that. I mean—but you know!" Challenge rang like a silver disk struck softly, clear under the hubbub of the station noises. We can't go back as we were, exactly, she was saying. But we do still love each other.

"You mustn't miss your train." George retreated into practical matters. "Send me a wire in the morning."

She couldn't sleep. There was, she thought, something appalling about a train trip. Surrendering yourself, giving up your freedom. You kept an illusion that you were free to make choices: you could eat dinner or go to bed early, but all the time you were being propelled through space, your destination fixed. Wasn't it a good deal like life, except that on the train you had at least chosen your destination? Who bought the ticket for life? Weren't you propelled along as inevitably, with as much illusion of freedom, through time instead of across miles of country? When she had started to write a book she hadn't said please give me a ticket away from George, and yet look! She wouldn't have thought George would take it as he had. But she couldn't be sorry she had done it! As the train rolled eastward George was diminished by more than space, and the next day, vague and brilliant, seemed to come to meet her minute by minute, just as she rolled toward it mile after mile.

After the first flurry of news stories, people in Lounsberry had acted almost as if nothing had happened. Except George. The Ladies Literary Society had thought it would be nice to have Hazel tell them about the book, but they had their meetings all arranged, and of course they hadn't read the book yet. Was it laid in the town, and had she put them in it? Insurance agents, numerous and persistent as English sparrows, had rung the telephone and doorbell, automobile salesmen, young men representing investment companies. It seemed silly to hide in one's own house, but Hazel tried that, instructing the new housekeeper to say that she was out. The woman complained that she couldn't do a lick of work for arguing at the door, and George came home one evening, stiff and cold with indignation. Two of his patients had cancelled appointments, one for herself, one for her little girl whose teeth George was straightening. Mrs. Wills and Mrs. Parsons. "They're insulted because you wouldn't see them when they called. Must you ruin my business, too?" Hazel had written notes to them, trying to soothe them, and Mrs. Parsons did bring back her child, as the brace had to be adjusted. Mrs. Wills said that some people couldn't stand good luck.

After that Hazel answered the bells herself, when she wasn't trying to decide which letters should have answers. Advertising letters, begging letters—(the world was suddenly crammed with worthy institutions for seamen, blind men, orphans, Lithuanian cripples, indigent actresses, and worn out horses, all of which institutions would totter unless she remitted . . .) letters from women in Oklahoma, Alaska, Texas, and the Bronx who had written novels they wished to send her, letters from men in prison, in a lumber camp, on farms, in the haberdashery business who had plots for novels they would share with her, one dreadful note on brown paper threatening the children unless she mailed a thousand dollars to X B, General Delivery. George had taken that up with the police, and they had watched for a while to see if anyone claimed the envelope thus addressed. But as the officer said, "A real gangster wouldn't bother with chicken feed like that. Just some nut."

Weeks ago the crest of the flood had dropped, almost as suddenly as it had risen, and the postman no longer made his joke about needing an extra mailbag just for Hazel. She wondered whether someone in some other town had unwittingly made himself such a target. Even Mr. Horn ceased to wire or telephone so often. He was rushing the book through, proofreading it in the office to save time; he consulted her about various matters of which she knew nothing, and Hazel caught the wind stirred by his rush even over the telephone.

She tried to fit the solid Pullman pillow between shoulder and cheek, tried to wriggle into comfort under the tight blanket. Here in the dark cubicle, with unexplained shafts of brilliant light striking at intervals under the drawn shade, she could admit that she had liked it. Not everything, of course. Like being transposed into a different key. Hazel, with variations. I wouldn't tell George that, she said. But I like it. And New York should be more exciting still, because that would concern the book itself, not just the prize. People would read her book. She hoped the dresses she had bought would be all right. As the clerk had said, black lace was always good. George couldn't have stood it if she'd bought that red dress with no back at all, although she had looked at herself for a long time before she let it slide down to the waiting hands of the saleswoman. She hoped her speech would be all right, too. She hoped she wouldn't be frightened. She hoped John and his father would get along while she was gone. Better, perhaps, than these past weeks while she was there, with George so edgy, and John so quick to catch moods.

And Lorna—Hazel frowned, a concentrated and baffled tenderness expanding through her body at the thought of her daughter. She must have quarreled with the Daniels boy. Queer, Hazel had worried about their intimacy, and yet when she saw the boy downtown with that red-headed Gwendolyn Baratsky, who had more reputation of the wrong kind than any other girl in town, she was furious. John ceased to tease Lorna, an ominous sign. Hazel tried unobtrusively to assure Lorna of support or sympathy or whatever she most needed. (At her age a heart, even broken, should heal quickly, like your bones.) But Lorna went about with a surface hard and prickly, resisting intrusion. She shut herself into her own room, and said she supposed they wanted her to do some studying, didn't they? She carried her secret, whatever it was, in a sort of fourth dimension, where no one could touch it. When Hazel said, "Don't you want to go to the movies?" or "Why don't you and Tommy go to the Club dance tomorrow?" Lorna had looked at her, and for an instant her fair, round, unchanged face had seemed a mask over lean torment. "When I want to go places, you and Father say I'm going too much, and when I want to stay home you won't let me alone." I just have to stand by, thought Hazel, waiting for contact. I'll get something for her in New York, a new dress.

The next morning she was the first passenger to appear as a finished and civilized product, being driven by anxiety lest the train arrive at Grand Central and she find herself ejected, like one of those dreams in which you walk down a street with your clothes over your arm! The porter found her a seat forward, beyond all the bulging green curtains, and she looked out at the great river running down in the sunlight as fast as the train, at patches of dingy snow, at gulls on old sunken piers, her fingers tense over her new brown purse.

"Take a taxi to the hotel," Horn had written. "I'll engage rooms for you there, and drop in early." It was strange to get off the train and know that not one of the people at the gate waited for her. Always George or the children waited for her, with that grand moment of recognition exploding like a Roman candle between them. Unless, indeed, George and the children were with her on the train. But the red-cap rushed her to a cab, and the cab rushed her in spurts to the hotel. New York wasn't unlike the other cities she knew, except perhaps that the chasms of the narrow streets were deeper, cut sharper angles, and the blue sky was buttressed incredibly far above by towers extraordinary and varied. Her name, the name of Alfred Horn meant nothing to the hotel clerk, and Hazel searched in her bag for the letter. Surely he had said this hotel! "Will you please register, Madam?" Why, he had known, all the time! The bell boy whisked her to the elevator, the swift ascent reminded Hazel she had had no breakfast, their feet were silent on the deep nap past polished doors, and then the bell boy lingered, having indicated ice water, radio, phone. "Yes, it's a nice room," said Hazel, and then the persistence of his shrewd, pimpled face reminded her, and she opened her purse again. How much should you give him—she'd given the porter more than George said, because he seemed to expect it . . . oh, dear! . . . She found a quarter, and then a dime, and sighed as he withdrew with no excess of gratitude. Outside the windows lay New York, superimposed silhouettes, with shadow-accents, city haze dimming the sky color. Hazel gazed at the mulberry and blue of rug and hangings, the reddish cast of modern maple, she wondered how they made the pleats of the valance, and decided to unpack her dresses.

As she unlocked the case, the door trembled under a tattoo. Hazel opened it, and was swept back into the room by the influx of several men, Mr. Horn himself, a photographer, a reporter. Mr. Horn all but embraced her, holding both her hands. "Hazel Browning Curtis, at last! Well, well, this is wonderful! Just a minute for some pictures." The next hour was a blur of holding her head this way and that while silver bulbs exploded in silent dazzles, of answering questions, no she didn't know how she liked New York yet, no, she hadn't started another book, (keep George out of it, she warned herself; don't mention George!) Mr. Horn seems very young, she thought. He'll wear himself out, he's too intense. Then the photographer disappeared, the reporter folded up his sheets, and Mr. Horn said, "Now we'll go over to the office. I've made a luncheon engagement for you, good chance, Mrs. Canterbury's literary luncheons. One of her speakers fell down, and she'll tuck you in. She has a crowd of females, soaks 'em plenty, tells them about books, dames lap it up, don't have to read, see? They don't buy books, but Canterbury gets good notices."

"But I couldn't think up a speech——"

"You don't have to say anything. Get up and give 'em a look. Come along."

"But do I look all right?" cried Hazel, desperate to brace herself against the rush. Mr. Horn was worse than the train, the way he propelled her inevitably ahead.

"Why, yes." Mr. Horn looked at her, the crease deep between his bright, dark eyes. "Little brown wren from the middle west. Yes, you're fine. We'll play up that aspect. Homebody."

Wren, in her new coat that even Lorna had said did things for her! But Mr. Horn wouldn't hear her if she told him what she thought of his wren. And when he stopped at the florist shop in the lobby, and bought a spray of gardenias tied with silver ribbon for her, she decided to say nothing about his bird lore.

The offices of Horn and Westerby seemed a trifle bare. Perhaps she had expected something more like a library, instead of this series of cubby-holes in and out of which moved men and young women, each with an air of being in a great hurry to reach some other spot before it was forever too late. Hazel sat beside Mr. Horn's flat desk, trying politely not to read any of the fascinating letters which littered the top, and meeting in such rapid succession that she never sorted them out the sales manager, the advertising man, the business manager, the publicity head, and what else. The telephone rang often, and Mr. Horn, hooking the mechanism between chin and shoulder, talked into it and over it at the same time. Finally he said, "Well, that's about the line-up. Reviews ought to begin Sunday. If we get a good break— Is there anything else you'd like to ask?"

"Could I see it? The book, I mean?"

"Good God, haven't you seen it?" Horn pressed the buzzer. "*Didn't* we ship you some?" A thin dark girl in horn-rimmed glasses looked in; her glance at Hazel said plainly, what is a mere author doing here? "Bingham, get me a copy of 'The Hand,' willya?"

"If I can find one. We sent out all we had around."

"Well, find one. And order a bunch sent up here. Mrs. Curtis ought to sign a few."

Then for a few minutes he was intensely silent, looking over papers, and Hazel wondered whether only a homebody would ask to see her book. The Bingham girl came back, and Hazel had it in her own hands, her own book, "Your Hand Upon the Gate" in zig-zags above white palings on a red ground, a gold band sealing it, announcing the ten thousand dollar prize award. She was afraid she might cry, her throat hurt, but Mr. Horn said, "Take it along. Canterbury may not have a copy. Hold it up when you get up to talk. Pretty neat job, we think here at the office."

So Hazel held it through the luncheon, although she found it hard to keep her knees stiff enough to support bag and book. Mrs. Canterbury had swept up to her in peach lace, a gold cap on assisted-gold hair, her animation as applied as her lipstick. So sweet of Mrs. Curtis to consent to come, she hadn't read the book, but she would say all she could, and Mrs. Curtis could speak just a few words to the ladies. A remarkable group, highly intelligent. Then she swept away to project herself around a plumpish man with white hair and a pink face, evidently her favorite guest. Hazel was seated well down the long table, between two women from the suburbs who talked across her, and across the table to the women opposite. If they knew I had a book, thought Hazel, they might talk to me. But as she swallowed tomato bisque, thick and not too hot, the dismal emptiness, partly physical, began to ease away.

The woman across stared at her, the wired bow on her turban quivering. "Aren't you one of the speakers?" she asked "I didn't catch the name."

"Curtis," said Hazel.

Never heard of it, signalled the woman's well-pruned eyebrows. "We hoped to hear Stark Young today," she said. "Mrs. Canterbury is very good usually about taking up only the books you have to know about. My life is too full for reading, but I think when someone gives you a good digest it is really better than if you read the book yourself, because she can pick out just the salient points, don't you agree with me?"

Fortunately she did not wait for Hazel's answer, but turned her wired bow toward the woman on her left, and the two confided in undertones, while Hazel jabbed at her chicken à la king. For the first time in her life she felt the apologetic uneasiness of a performer. Because she had written a book she ceased to be one of the ladies lunching, and became a questionable part of the entertainment for which they paid. Getting up to speak would be exposing herself to all their arrows. But Mr. Horn said it would be good for the book. Her left hand spread over the smooth surface of the book, pressed it hard against her flesh. She had to stay.

The ladies adjourned to a reception room where gold chairs stood in rows before a low platform. Mrs. Canterbury strolled back and forth on the platform, fitting the gestures of her jewelled hands less to her words than to her intended emotional effects, while she offered her digests of the books on her program. She was gay, very feminine, she made little jokes, she referred at times to the quality of her audience, she pattered briskly through the story, and at crucial points of deaths or lovers' meetings she quoted lines with elocutionary histrionics. She really works hard for her money, thought Hazel. Wouldn't the Lounsberry Literary Society love her! Hazel wound her ankles tightly together and clasped book and purse. What would she say when she had to stand on that platform? She tried to remember lines from the speech she had written for the dinner. They wouldn't do; she couldn't thank these women for giving her the prize!

Mrs. Canterbury swayed at the platform edge, hands extended gracefully.

"And now, Ladies, we have a little special treat. We hoped for Stark Young, but fate intervened, fate in the form of a teeny little flu germ. So we have a new writer. I can't tell you about her book, as I haven't read it, as I didn't know until this morning we would have the pleasure of hearing her. But since it has won a prize of ten thousand dollars I am sure we will all want to read it if only to see why it should be given so much money. I present Hazel Browning Curtis, who will tell us the story of—what is the title?" And to Hazel, in an undertone, as the latter rose, she said, "The ladies are getting a little restless. Don't talk too long."

Hazel didn't. As she collapsed in the taxi on the way to her own hotel, her face burning, her heart still racing, she was sure only that she hadn't talked too long. She scrambled through her mind, trying to hear echoes of what she had said. A spurt of anger had lifted her clear of the symptoms of stage fright, and she rather thought she had said that perhaps someone there would read the book out of curiosity, as Mrs. Canterbury had suggested, and as she'd written the story she wouldn't bother to tell it over, there was the book, and she'd held it out, flaunting its gold band, and she didn't know how to make a speech, this was her first, and so she'd stop. Had she said thank you or not? Her mouth quirked at the corners. "My goodness, she got my dander up, as George would say. Now, see here!" She sat forward in the cab, her pulses calming. "Can't go 'round losing your temper. But acting as if she were doing me a favor, when I thought I was the one——"

She decided that if she moved fast she could bathe and dress before Mr. Horn called for her. Quarter to five, he had said. A cocktail party. She supposed she couldn't wear the black lace. She'd have to come back again to dress for dinner. She wished she had bought that red one, just to dispose of the wren idea. She was in the tub, having scrubbed it thoroughly with her wash-cloth (how did she know who had last used it!) when the 'phone rang. She popped out, seized a bath towel, and left a trail of damp prints across the mulberry rug. Mr. Horn calling. Was she ready?

"I thought you said quarter to five!"

"I got wind of another tea. For an English author, but we'll drop in. Bound to meet some people there."

"I'm taking a bath," said Hazel.

"Bring it right along! How soon can you make it?"

"Five minutes."

She did, too. Being a mother was good training in speed at one's toilet. The gardenias had brown smudges on the outer petals, but Hazel repinned them to her coat. She powdered her nose, and wondered whether she might buy a lipstick, just to use in New York. George always liked her own color better, but of course he had such close-ups of mouths.

At midnight Hazel closed the door of her hotel room, brushed back her hair with a slow, heavy hand, and sank down on the bed. Someone had turned down the blankets. Nice. If ever she could stir again! She did not feel tired, so much as extinguished. Blotted out, scattered, lost. As if, presenting herself again and again to all these strange men and women, hostile or indifferent or bland or self-absorbed, none of them coming out to look for her, some of them cagey, suspicious (don't think you'll get me to write you a good review by smiling at me!) she came at last to non-existence, annihilation. The teas were easier than the dinner, although just as annihilating, for when Horn convoyed someone up to meet her—most of the names she didn't understand—the someone murmured, "Ah, Horn's prize!" or "How do you like New York?" and then hailed an acquaintance or strolled off toward the bar. One darkish man seemed friendly, and asked whether she was at work on a second book. Just as they had begun a real talk, Horn dragged her away. "Has he got you signed up yet?" Mr. Horn's cocktails had accelerated his ordinary tempo. "Biggest pirate in town, steals authors under their publisher's nose." At the second party, which a literary agent, a friend of Horn's, was giving for him and his author, Hazel thought she met again some of the guests from the first. But she wasn't sure. Her face had stiffened, her mouth felt dry from too many smiles, but she found corners of tables and windowsills where she could set down the cocktails presented to her whenever anyone observed her without one.

At the dinner, however, she had to sit at the speakers' table, and try to talk. On one side sat Mr. Carlton, a member of the committee which had chosen her book, and Hazel, although partially extinguished, had thought, he at least must have read it. But when she said she was glad to meet him because he had liked her book well enough to select it, he stared at her gloomily, the light strong on his bald forehead, and said, "Don't thank me. Now I suppose you'll write another. Or per-haps—" a spark through his gloom, "you're one of these one-book authors."

"I don't know," said Hazel. "I haven't thought of another one yet." Then, slyly—she couldn't help it, he looked so cross—"Would you mind if I did?" (After all, someone had to write books if a critic kept his job!)

"Mind? Oh, no. Not at all." (Nothing in his life!) "You know, I've been considering a project. I think authors should be licensed before they can practice. Like doctors, or lawyers." The tip of his thin nose twitched, and he stroked his chin thoughtfully. That idea would do for a column. "Board of examiners, penalties for illegal practice— why hasn't it been done long before?" He turned to the woman at his left, and Hazel heard him repeating his proposition with sardonic elaboration. Mr. Horn explained later, in a rapid two-minute survey of the evening before he handed Hazel into her taxi; "That's just Carlton's line, being rude to authors. Likes to bully 'em. What he said about your book wasn't bad. Some quotable phrases. Couldn't very well pan it when he helped pick it. Never heard him enthusiastic about anything except a treatise on the family life of the three-toed sloth. On the whole the evening was a great success. You made a nice little speech."

"I didn't know it was going to be broadcast. I was frightened." That awful disk, set up between her and all the staring eyes! If she'd known, she could have told John to tune in.

"One of my last minute breaks. One of the things I do best, getting breaks that way. Get a good rest. I'll give you a ring in the morning."

Hazel pushed back her coat and let it lie in a mound around her. She hadn't thought of needing a real evening wrap. In Lounsberry everyone just wore a winter coat because it was so cold at night, but here even the new beaver collar looked—well all right! wren-like— among velvets and ermine, even if the ermine was rabbit. Not that it made any difference. "If I'd been a Hottentot princess in beads maybe someone would have seen me. I'm not sure." But in her handbag was the envelope, heavy cream, with her name, and inside it an engraved slip. Not the real check. "I'll give you that tomorrow," Horn had said. "Have to figure out the deductions I've advanced." And on the table beside the bed lay the book.

Hazel reached for it, the black lace falling away from her arm. Her dress had been all right, she thought, although not striking— She turned the volume slowly, and slid the gold band carefully off. Then she opened it. She looked at the first page, and the printed words spoke to her in her own voice. Reading them was like life flowing back into her, it was like writing them again, and yet different, almost creation in reverse. She turned the page and read the next, wondering how she had happened to say just that, and yet feeling the words drop softly, rightly, as if she held within her the archetype from which they had been made, and each word fitted into its own place.

A long time later Hazel closed the book. She didn't know, really whether it was good or not, not being able to tell how much was there in words to reach other people, and how much was in her own feeling. But she had written it, and for the first time she had read her own book. It's not like having a child, she thought, with sudden scorn for that old comparison. A child is separate from you right away, and a book— She laid the volume on the table. It's more like ectoplasm, it seems to be separate, there it is, and here I am, but it's really me, all the copies everywhere. She wondered, in alarm, what she had been up to, scattering herself in pieces all over the earth! But she did like that last scene, where the restless footed one of the third generation came home at last, and the woman he loved welcomed him, her hand upon the gate. She'd always liked the poem.

Her foot had gone to sleep, and she hobbled across to the dresser, unclasping the string of pearls (George's present last Christmas: he'd said he wished he could give her real ones, but these were pretty good). She poked them, still warm, into a double circle, and stamped on her prickling foot. She must get to bed, or she'd look dreadful tomorrow. She did now, with smudges under her eyes and a mazed whiteness on her face. Presently, her purse safe under her pillow and the table lamp drawn so close she couldn't miss it in the dark, she lay small and flat in the strange room, and looked out at the amber haze which filled the sky, a haze which was not steady but fluctuated to the rhythm of flashing signs and beacons.

Mr. Horn telephoned the next morning. He was rushed, number of things just came up, but he'd made an appointment for her with Grawn, an agent, to talk over movie possibilities. Just run over and have a chat. "Don't commit yourself to anything. See what he says. I'll take care of any actual offers. Then drop in here at the office. A few advance reviews have come in. Um, fair. Fair."

Hazel waited for a long time in an outer office, with engrossed and oblivious people rushing past her until she suffocated under the dull cloak of invisibility. She peered at herself in a small mirror. She'd bought a lipstick that morning and tried it; now she wasn't sure it helped. At last a bored young woman escorted her down corridors and into Mr. Grawn's office. He sat with a dingy window at his back, a little man with a large head gray-crested, and a slow, deep voice.

"Ah, yes, Mrs. Browning. Horn suggested I see you. Just what have you in mind?"

"Nothing," said Hazel, trying to arrange herself easily on the hard chair. "Mr. Horn told me to come."

"Ah, yes, let's see, your book is going well, is it?" His small, white hands moved slowly among papers, found a memorandum. "'Your Hand Upon the Gate.' I don't believe that title would sell. Ah, yes. Prize book, Horn says he's launching big publicity campaign. Frankly, Mrs.—" he glanced at the memorandum— "Browning Curtis, it would be well to wait. If the book is a smash hit, we can work up good bids for it. Otherwise, I may say the motion picture business is incalculable. No one can prophesy. Why, I could tell you—" And then for what seemed hours to Hazel, blinking her eyes against the light, seeing Mr. Grawn's stiff gray crest prismatic, he did tell her, stories of books he had sold, of books he had not sold, of fabulous prices, of extraordinary rivalries, until he ended, accusingly, "If it had been serialized, that would help. You could, of course, run out to Hollywood? If the book is a hit, I often place authors. Say five hundred a week, to begin with? It's valuable experience for a time. You mustn't stay too long, though, or you lose your public. Nice of you to drop in."

Hazel, dropping down in the elevator, wasn't sure whether she would find herself in Hollywood when she walked out upon the street. It was still New York, and she asked a traffic policeman how to reach the offices of Horn and Westerby, if she walked. If she went under her own power, she might step out of the Alice-in-Wonderland daze. Five hundred a week. How could she go to Hollywood? Anyway, who had asked her to go? Three blocks over, five up. But walking in New York was not like walking in Lounsberry. Her usual firm, smooth stride, which could shake nonsense out of her mind, turning into dodgings and delays. It's not really walking, she thought, it's wriggling through.

Again she waited, although not so long, in the triangular little reception room at Horn and Westerby's, watching the telephone girl shift plugs and say "Who's calling? Just a moment, please, Who's calling? Just—" Mr. Horn burst into the room, seized her hand, ushered her swiftly along the corridor. Had she seen Grawn? Of course, it was just a wedge. An opening attack. Oh, Grawn never read anything! You bet he'd grab it if it showed signs of going over big. Now she must look at the lay-out for the ads. He whisked smooth sample sheets past her, rattling off names, the *Times*, the *Tribune*, some of the trade journals, these little ones for daily papers. Hazel's color deepened. All those about her book! "Of course, Mrs. Curtis, a publisher can do only so much. He can launch a book, and we're doing a big job on the launching. After that, it's up to the book. Word of mouth is what does it. If people like it—get to talking about it— If you have any suggestions, any original publicity— I'm sorry to say some of the reviews aren't as whole-hearted as they might be. Trouble with a prize novel, reviewers like to say why in the name of God was this book chosen! Don't mind them. I suppose you'd like to look them over? This one's the best. Good selling review. Tells the story, see, catches interest, calls it good wholesome book of familiar type. Carlton comes out and says he preferred 'Alley Cat.' That was runner-up, going to put it out next week. Here, look 'em over." He pushed toward her a pile of clippings and blue-penciled sheets. "Remember, a panning's better than no attention. May start talk. Yes, Bingham?"

The secretary's spectacles glinted at Hazel. "You here again?" they suggested. Aloud she said, "Mr. Smith says he has an appointment with you."

"So he has." Horn jumped up. "I'll leave you here, Mrs. Curtis. Amuse yourself."

When, an hour or so later, he came back, Hazel was sitting straight and still beside the desk, on which she had ranged the papers, her eyes dark with bewilderment under the thick lashes, petals of vivid color on her cheekbones. Mr. Horn's tentative glance investigated her mood.

"Mr. Horn," she asked, "did you by any chance read my book?"

"Why, yes, certainly. Of course." He flung himself into his chair, lighted a cigarette. "You smoke? No."

"What did you think of it?"

"Damned good book, of course. Now don't let some of those cracks disturb you. I never knew an author yet who could take criticism. Have to take it. Part of the game."

"Are you sure these are all about my book?" Hazel pointed at the clippings. "I thought maybe they mixed up the titles."

Horn jackknifed into a sudden laugh. "Say, that's rich!" he shouted. "That's a good one on reviews!"

"I wasn't sure. They blame me for so many different things I thought there might be a mixup." She shivered, as if she had been driven confused and stumbling down a long gauntlet where men cracked whips of phrases as she fled. No book ignoring the social and economic problems of the present deserves consideration. Style is spontaneous and fresh, but plot is hackneyed. Style is labored with affectations of modernity, although the plot has originality. Another family cycle; surely the time has come when we might be spared this banal repetition. Refreshing to find an authentic picture of the American scene, although the characters unfortunately are mere wooden types. The characters have a three-dimensional vitality; it is a pity that the action is nothing but moralizing, a projection of Miss Curtis' ideas of good and evil. The book has promise; the prize will give it undue attention, and no doubt destroy the author's future growth. Carlton's column had been the worst, perhaps because she had met him, and could hear him saying the words as she read. "There was another entry, virile, salty, full-bodied, with the tenacious hold on life hinted in the title, 'Alley Cat.' Not a pretty little book to win a prize. But Horn and Westerby, having presented the circulating library readers with a chocolate marshmallow, may put themselves on the publishing mat with a real book. Watch for it."

"Anyway—" Hazel thrust out her chin, her upper lip drew down long and Irish, her color deepened—"I did get the prize! Even if it made them mad. That's the way they sound, just mad!"

"Sure," said Horn, "they're all frustrated novelists. Don't let 'em worry you. Now, what have you got on for this afternoon?"

You couldn't say nothing to a question like that. Hazel shook her head.

"I have to run out of town. Terribly sorry."

(Golf, thought Hazel. Or fishing. She knew that masculine air of inevitable, foredoomed preoccupation.)

"I thought you might like to shop, look around a little. The office is closed Saturday, of course. But Monday is a full day. In the morning I want you to see a pair of the cleverest radio agents in town. Fleeman and Flower. Chance to do a program for them. One of their biggest clients is looking for something new. In the afternoon you're to autograph books at one of the department stores. I've got the girls here all lined up to drop in at intervals, get a book, get it autographed, suggest there's a big demand, see? We can use 'em later. Why don't you look around for a place to settle here in town? You might as well stick around."

"But I've got a family," said Hazel.

"Bring 'em along. Good thing for a writer to be here on the ground. Get to know the right people."

"My husband wouldn't leave his business." Hazel braced her heels on the floor. If she didn't watch out, Horn's dynamo would have whirled her forever away from Lounsberry and the three there. She would be a star sucked out of her proper constellation by his velocity, and go spinning alone in the dry unreality of his orbit.

"He's a dentist, isn't he? Hm. Might be openings here. I wouldn't know. Out of my line. You aren't planning to leave him, then? Not that divorce or separation is much use as publicity. Too common. But more than one woman when she pulls off a big thing of her own finds it makes a difference."

Hazel set her teeth into her lower lip. It wouldn't do to tell her publisher that he was impertinent. Anyway, his inquiry had a terrible impersonality, quite as if she were a horse he had entered for a race, and he looked at her teeth, ran a hand over her hocks.

"Let's see." He flung out his wrist, read his watch. "Why don't you run down to Atlantic for the week-end? I can telephone for a reservation. Now, why isn't that an idea?"

"No." Hazel got to her feet quickly, before he shipped her off. "You needn't have me on your mind. I'd much rather stay here. Only I'd like some of my money."

Mr. Horn's face changed; he became almost husbandly. "Certainly. Now, you've had five hundred. I suppose if I give you the rest, you'll spend it before you leave town!" He waggled a finger at her.

"I'd like a thousand now," said Hazel with dignity. She hadn't meant to ask for so much, but he drove her to it.

After further persiflage Mr. Horn arranged to deposit it for her, and wrote out a card of identification. "Not a bad little publicity stunt, prize author goes shopping. See if I can't get one of the sob sisters to do a story. I'll be seeing you Monday, then. Have a good time, and don't buy Brooklyn Bridge!"

Hazel went back to her hotel, and as she ate luncheon she wrote on a slip of paper the names George, Lorna, and John, with dotted lines after each. A dress for Lorna. A watch for John, a good wrist watch, something like Mr. Horn's. For George—he'd like something for the office. She found the telephone directories in a long corridor of booths, and studied the Red Book until she had several addresses. The desk clerk, being urged, indicated which one was not too far from the hotel, and presently Hazel had convinced a supercilious young woman in an outer office that she was in earnest about buying a piece of dental equipment, and followed a tall, thin salesman into the show rooms. She wanted something quite expensive. No, she wasn't a dentist, her husband was. No, not in town, in Lounsberry. That was in Michigan. (Still there, solid and familiar, in spite of these strange days!) He had a good office chair. And an X-ray. In the next room she stopped, entranced, as if George stood beside her, and all his delight in perfect mechanism flowed into her. "These are the newest units, chromium and a new treatment of steel." Marvelous shining robots, with hinged and crooked elbows, dazzling metal threads through intricate wheels. The salesman swung the arms, turned a button and the drills sang and water gurgled. "You can spend as much as you like, depending upon the accessories." She was one with George again as she signed the check and arranged for the shipping. Just as quickly as possible. Freight was too slow. Express. She wished it might go by air-mail!

Lorna's dress was easy, and John's watch, and when at the end of the day Hazel returned to the hotel she was thoroughly happy. She could even stand being called a chocolate marshmallow! She bought an evening paper, and rode up to her room. For a time she sat at the window, watching the geometric silhouette of the city flatten against the sky, the sharp forms merging into dimness, light-pierced. Then she spread the paper open on her knees. At the third page she stopped, the sheet crackling in her fingers. "Prize-winning Housewife Visits City." It stared up at her, shadowless, blanched by the flashlight, startled, a picture with her name beneath it. Hazel read through the article, a half column. Then she re-read it, her face white as anger closed a tight hand over her heart, her breathing. At least, she thought, George would never see it. Nobody at home would see it. "Modest, pleasant little middle-aged housewife comes to city to claim prize. From hamlet nestling in hills of distant Michigan—" I suppose they think we have Indians and buffaloes—"Slight air of distracted anxiety, as she thinks of babies she has left for this momentous trip." Hazel folded the paper, picture inside, and thrust it into the wastebasket. "Somewhat dazed by the city, by the whole adventure, she finds herself figure in fairy tale." I never said that! "She thought it would be nice to write a book, and here she is! We can see housewives all over the land hearing of her good luck, neglecting pots and pans to dash off best sellers."

"I'm not middle-aged! I'm not modest. I—I certainly don't feel pleasant!" Hazel confronted her reflection in the mirror, and color ran up her soft throat into her face. She wondered who wrote the article. One of those smart, hard young things at the dinner last night. "It's dreadful, having to know how I seem to strangers, who don't know me, don't care—" She looked about the room, her anger changing subtly into desperation. Suppose she had to stay here always, with such articles, or such book reviews all she had! She would cease to exist, that was all. She wouldn't be herself any longer, because no one would know what she was. She moved swiftly to the telephone on a stand; she couldn't even stop to sit down.

"I want an out-of-town number," she said, her voice urgent. "In Michigan. Lounsberry. Two eight six three. No, I'll speak to anyone there."

"What's your room number?" and then, "I will con-nect you with long distance."

Listening, Hazel heard the quick calling of exchanges across the country, Buffalo, Cleveland, Detroit, each transporting her nearer home, strides on seven-league boots across the land.

"Here's your number!" and then John's voice, his blessed telephone voice, affecting boredom, the quality thinned a trifle. Tears in her eyes, in her throat. "It's Mother, John!"

"Why, hello!" His drawl quickened. "How are you? Say, you sounded swell on the radio. Dad saw in the paper about the broadcast, and we all sat up."

"You did! Are you all right, John?"

"Sure. How's ole New York?"

"Oh, it's fine. Is Father there?"

"No. He went in town to a meeting."

(He hadn't said anything about a meeting—)

"And Lorna went off as soon as she ate her dinner."

"Where did she go?"

"I dunno. Ketch me asking that gal anything."

"Poor Johnny, all alone!"

"Well, I got my hat on, all set for the movies. Some of the fellows are going."

"Don't be too late, will you, dear. It's not long since you were sick." Hazel closed her eyes, her fingers tight over the instrument, straining for each inflection of his voice. She could see him, thin shoulders hunched as he bent toward the telephone there in the hall.

"Say, when you coming home?"

"Very soon. Next week."

"Not till then?"

"I have to do some things Monday. I have to see some radio men, John! Maybe they'll give me a job. And perhaps I'll be in the movies." She laughed, and the excitement she had not felt suddenly prickled through her veins as she offered it to John. "But I'll tell you all about it soon. Good-night, Johnny. Tell Father and Lorna I'm sorry they weren't home."

She held the receiver hard against her ear until the click which followed his "So long" broke the thread between them. She felt better. Like having her foot go to sleep, the way these two days had made her feel, and John's voice sent blood racing so that her own self woke up. She wouldn't let them get her down again.

Monday evening Mr. Horn escorted Hazel to the Wolverine, although he protested her departure. "To be sure, there weren't many customers at the bookstore, but you can't rush things. If you'd stay a few weeks——"

Many, thought Hazel. Two, besides the girls from the office who had pretended to be customers, and she'd sat on that chair for three hours. "If you really need me, I could come back. But I don't want to stay now." She had been stern with herself on Saturday and Sunday, buying a little guide book and booting herself over town to see what a visitor to New York should see, but she wasn't going to put in any more days paying solitary visits to fishes at the Aquarium or marbles at the Museum. She was going home.

Mr. Horn advised the porter about the placing of her bags. On the seat beside her he piled a large box of candy, all red cellophane and bows, a smaller glossy florist's box, and several magazines. Then he lolled against the arm of the seat, knee up, ears pricked for the "All Aboard," which would release him. "I hope you've had a good time," he said. "'Sbeen a pleasure to meet you. You try a few scripts for Fleeman and Flower, and I'll see if I can get a contract out of them. Of course they felt, too, that you ought to stay here, be on hand for conferences."

"I couldn't do what they want," said Hazel, and for a moment Mr. Fleeman's face swam out from the green plush of the opposite seat, coming too close to hers as it had in the morning interview, black velvet hair, deeply lined white skin, sharp beak. "Something like Amos and Andy, only not colored, with a touch of Eddie Cantor, a few old songs thrown in (people like hymns), a real heart interest, and perhaps room for a touch of amateur hour."

"They don't know what they want," said Horn, briskly, "except they know what's pulled the best the last year or so. All those radio guys are crazy, but if you give 'em something good they'll pay real money for it. You try."

Hazel had her face set toward home. Although the train had not yet moved, she had already surrendered herself to the journey, and Horn's words danced like the final faint notes of a fantasia terminating with the wind instruments.

"Don't worry about your book," he was saying. "We're backing it with all we've got. Well, happy landing!" He pumped her hand, and was gone.

Hazel arranged her coat and hat neatly on the opposite seat. She untied the metallic cord and peered into the florist's box. More gardenias. She'd give them to Lorna, if they lasted until morning. She opened one of the magazines, turning the thick, smooth pages of advertisements until she reached an illustration. Posed against a pillar, a stairway winding below her to nothing at all, urns and palms behind her, incredibly tall and slender and arching backward, one arm above her head, so that the satin sheath of gown caught highlights on every curve she owned, stood a girl, her eyelids inscrutable not with the weight of ages of sin, like Mona Lisa, but with well applied eyeshadow.

Hazel stared at the photograph. Now that, she thought, is the way you're supposed to look. What it really is is just a picture a man took of a girl in a dress that wasn't even her own, a girl from some small town who had that kind of figure. Like that girl Lorna knew who got a job modeling. The train was moving now, and Hazel leaned back, hands folded on the magazine, her face close to the window. If she could put her finger on it, she'd know something about New York that was like that photograph. The New York she'd seen, at least. For here, outside the window as the train climbed above street level and pried its way between dingy, close-pressing apartment buildings, was another city, washing flying on a fire-escape, a woman leaning with elbows on a dirty cushion, and then as the train gathered speed, too quick a winding past of interiors for Hazel to see anything but lights which marked rooms where people lived. She sighed. The whole fantasia of the past days, with its abrupt rhythm, its dissonances, was growing very faint. Later she might decide what it all meant. But if she'd known what happened when you wrote a book—no, not when you wrote it; when you had it published, when you took a prize! She could see dark water now, and great advertising signs flooded with light, and dimly on the window the shape of her own face. She thrust out her chin, and worried a little at her lip. She'd do it again.

HORN walked jauntily through the station. It was late, but Millbeau, the salesman for the eastern territory, had agreed to wait for him. Like to run over the order sheets with him, tell him about the campaign for "Alley Cat." "The Hand" wasn't going to do much here in the East. Carlton had crabbed it, but he'd have to howl for the "Cat," he'd committed himself. Out in the sticks the "Hand" might move better. Women like Hazel ought to go for it, prize band on it and all. But he'd cut the advertising, at least till reorders started. Jeese, was he glad to be rid of that woman! He paused a moment at the curb, snapping his fingers, eyeing a girl that passed, her tight dark dress catching the good line from thigh to knee. Not that she wasn't a good sort, nice eyes, if she knew how to use 'em. But personally he didn't fall for that flower of the field type. Didn't get on with 'em. Something appalling about that kind of naïveté. Probably never see her again. Didn't think she had another book in her. If he didn't get his money (Westerby's!) back on her, he would on "Alley Cat." First book sweet

and pure, second strictly modern and soiled, good beginning for the
firm. Then he had at least another half dozen manuscripts he could
spread over the summer and fall, if nothing better came in. Just as
he'd thought, the prize had been good bait, giving them a quick choice
for their list, even if Westerby'd been skeptical about the sales value
of a prize. "Make it a million, someone'd hear you. Ten grand? Bah!"
And Horn had snapped, "What you think this is, a relief project?"
That had tickled Westerby. He knew how to handle him! Then Horn
darted across the street, swinging his arms in excess motion, jostling
the crowd as he hurried, his nostrils wide, his face shifting in quick
grimaces, all the superficial aspects of the city, the brilliance of the shop
windows, the concentrated drive of the crowds, the rhythm of traffic
the stimuli which nourished him.

HAZEL had not wired that she was coming home. The children would
be in school, and George would not like to leave his office. She took
the bus out from the city, watching with content the familiar, flat country wheel past, fields winter-brown, farm dooryards muddy, the only
hint of spring some quality in the sunlight, as if the angle at which it
struck meant a stirring in the earth. The bus stop in Lounsberry was
just across from George's office. She wanted to see him so much that she
felt in every muscle the climbing of his stairs, the pushing open of
the door. And then she'd find someone waiting in his office, thumbing
over a magazine, and George, white-coated, bending over a patient in
the chair. Their meeting must be more than that! No interference. No
static! But how to get home? She could telephone the Murphy boy. If
he were home, he'd come for her. As she turned toward the grocery
store, Bill Pakaloupus, the owner's son, came out, arms full of bags
and baskets, the morning orders.

"Morning, Mis' Curtis." He bobbed his head. "Just going out to your
place. You going away?" He saw her luggage.

"No, I've been," said Hazel. She glanced at the Pakaloupus car, a
battered sedan converted into a truck on week-days by removing the
rear seat. "Could you give me a lift, Bill? I don't want to bother Dr.
Curtis."

"Sure. Climb right in."

Hazel did, her eyes bright with amusement. Famous author comes
home.

"I seen a woman at your house Sattiday," said Bill, as he clattered around the corner. "I thought mebbe you was sick."

"No. I've been to New York."

"Yeuh? Was you down on Washington Street? The old man lived there when he first come across. Guess you're glad to be back, ain'tcha?"

Hazel hung on to the rattly door-frame as they swooped up the street.

"Can't waste time." Bill grinned, his teeth white in his swarthy face. Then when he swung into the driveway at the Curtis house and stopped, with all the groceries bouncing, he refused Hazel's money. "Ain't you one of our good customers? 'Sa real treat to have company." He carried her suitcase to the front door, and disappeared around the house with a basket.

The front door was locked, and Hazel waited. Bill backed out of the yard, waving to her, and presently the housekeeper opened the door. "Why, Mrs. Curtis!" Her high, firm bosom pumped reproachful breath through her words. "I didn't know you were coming home today!" She was larger than Hazel, with an effect of polish on the planes of her wide, hard face.

"No, I didn't send word," said Hazel, managing to enter her own house. "Everything all right?"

"The Doctor said he wouldn't be home for lunch, and the children said they'd get something at the drug store because it was too far to walk and so I never planned a thing for this noon because all I ever take is a cup of tea."

"I'll call up my husband," said Hazel. "I guess you can find something."

She waited until Lizzie's broad and still reproachful rear had vanished into the kitchen. Then she called George. Yes, this was Hazel. No, she wasn't calling from New York, she was home! And George said, "For heck's sake, why didn't you let us know?"

"I knew you'd be busy this morning." Hazel swallowed a thistle before she went on. "You've got the car, haven't you? Can't you pick up John and Lorna, and come home for lunch?"

"Of course I want to see you! But I didn't know you'd be here. I made arrangements—if I can get hold of the party, I'll let you know. But it's pretty awkward." And then, almost caustically, "Have you had a grand time?"

"Oh, yes. Wonderful. Don't bother about lunch." Hazel held the instrument at a distance, hating it. "I'll see you tonight."

"It's not that lunch is a bother, Hazel. Please be reasonable. How could I know when you were coming? You told John you didn't know—" After a moment's pause he went on, and now his voice had lost its self-vindicating tone, had grown crisply professional. A patient must have come into the office. "The party I have the appointment with isn't in town yet, but if I can get hold of them, I'll explain. But it's a piece of business. Quite important."

"Well," said Hazel, "if I have to have a tooth pulled, would you have time to see me?"

"What's that? Is that tooth I filled bothering you again?"

She laughed. "No. *That's* not bothering me. See you later."

Ridiculous to feel such disappointment. She knew how George disliked suddenness or change. He planned his day, and he wanted it to go by schedule. He planned his life—and what a jolt she'd given him! Her mouth was soft and contemplative, and the pencil in her fingers drew a row of little birds with cocky tails and stiff legs, a row that marched across the cover of the telephone directory. Suppose he never accepted the jolt. She bent her head a trifle, evoking the quality of his voice. Clear, fresh, each syllable, each word distinct; it's a blond voice, thought Hazel. No shadows. But strong, like sunlight. She had heard it all these years, and never thought before how precisely George it was. Things have got to be all right, she told herself, ignoring the way a shred of apprehension clung to her mood, for all she brushed away her disappointment.

She considered telephoning to the school. But John and Lorna would not have time for the long walk home, and perhaps they, like George, had made dates for their sandwiches at the drug store counter. She'd been gone only—she counted off the days on her fingers—five days, and when she came back, she found the pattern so changed it didn't include her at all! What would happen if she went to Hollywood? But women did do things like that, lots of them. She heard Lizzie stomping about overhead, her feet expressing annoyance that Hazel had taken advantage of her, arriving unheralded before the roomwork was done. Better wait till she's through, thought Hazel. The living room was in stiff order, the small rugs each in the wrong place. Hazel moved about quietly, changing the rugs, pulling chairs out from the wall, until the room was hers again. She glanced over the mail piled on a corner of the table, advertisements, circulars, letters from three clipping bureaus enclosing several of the reviews she had already endured. Then she carried her bag to her own room and unpacked, alert for signs of what George had been doing these five days. He must have worn his new gray suit today. The blue one needed pressing; she'd call the tailor. Then she saw, on the lower shelf of the night stand between the twin beds, her book! Her heart gave a thud, and she couldn't move. An end of the gold prize band showed; George had marked his place with it. Where had he got it? And what, dear God, what did he think about it? Imagine him lying there, turning page after page in his slow, deliberate way, George, who never read anything except the paper and his dental journals! He might have said something, when she telephoned.

Her hands trembled as she hung away the black lace dress, the new silk dressing gown. She took off the brown silk, and buttoned herself into a clean linen frock. She peered into the bathroom cabinet. Those cold tablets had been moved. Now which of them— Still seeking news, she went into John's room. The brown rep curtains hung in straight folds, the brown and yellow cover was spread smooth on the bed, a few books stood between the bronze lion bookends she had given him Christmas. His neckties were a stringy jumble in the top drawer. She sat down on the bed, crossing her ankles, and her heel struck something hard. Her hand, groping, touched smooth leather, and she was on her feet, drawing out a suitcase. John's, bought for camp last summer. She sank to the floor beside it, her knees weak, and pushed at the catch. John's suitcase, packed! Pajamas, shirts, sweater, little balls of socks, the case with brushes, the cup he'd won in the Junior tennis match. She closed the lid, snapped the lock, and pushed the case out of sight beneath the bed. Then she got to her feet, brushing out wrinkles in the blue linen. Whatever he'd planned, he must come home first. But where, this time of year— Had George said, done something? Once, when John was just a little fellow, he'd run away. But all boys do that—Hazel could see him, riding home with the milkman, dirty and tired, but proud because the man let him hold the reins. Was he in school, after all? If he'd packed the suitcase, he meant to take it. She wanted to run through the streets to the school, to be sure he was there, safe. But he'd never forgive her. She would have to wait. Perhaps it was some school trip, some legitimate plan she had not heard about. Oh, John!

She went quickly to the door of Lorna's room, her eyes dark, her lip caught between her teeth. Rose and blue, ruffled and feminine orderliness, surely she would find no clue to disaster, no vague threat here. She looked at the small painted desk, her hand lifting, fingers curved, importunate. The drawers there might have notes from that boy. That was different, prying. Fair enough to look for clues, when she had such hunger. But no prying. She opened the closet door, and the dresses swayed on their hangers, neat blue pasteboard containers for shoes, for stockings, sat in decorous rows, and a whiff of sachet blew out. Hazel closed the door and went away. Her daughter's room kept secrets as well as did her daughter. But she's like George, thought Hazel. She has his passion for fitness, for orderliness. If she has it about her own life ——

Lizzie served tea, toast, and an egg, with an air of that being more than one might expect, especially as she'd been trying to finish the ironing. She'd ordered the things for dinner before she knew Mis' Curtis was coming, and she hoped it would suit. Hazel wandered into the living room. She supposed she'd better keep the woman for a while, at least. "Although I might feel less an interloper in my own house if I had the dinner to get."

She tried to take a nap, but when she lay down the clatter of the Pullman trucks over the ties began again in her head. The minister's wife telephoned. Would Mrs. Curtis meet with the Ladies' Aid on Friday, and give a little talk about her trip to New York? They would charge ten cents admission for the tea and sandwiches. "I knew you were back," she added, "because I saw you with the grocer boy." (You would! thought Hazel.) Yes, she could come Friday, unless something came up to prevent.

"You aren't going to Hollywood right away, are you? I said I'd never believe Mrs. Curtis would leave her family to mingle with the kind of people we hear of out there, even if we do try to be charitable, where there's so much smoke ——"

"Who said I was going?"

"It was in the paper, how you were considering an offer."

Mr. Horn must have put it in! And George must have seen it! "I'm not going immediately," said Hazel. "Nothing's settled. I won't go before Friday, anyway." She could see the face of the woman, spare, dun, with a look of bitter exhaustion in the sagging folds about mouth and chin, like that of a swimmer spent from the effort to keep above the surface of gentility. Not since the depression had the church made up the full amount of the Reverend Mr. Morrison's small salary. She must almost hate Hazel for her sudden fortune! "I'll see you then," Hazel finished, "I'm sure I can make it."

That would account for George's tone on the telephone. He saw her alighting for a moment, en route to California. "We'll play it up," Horn had said. "That's the way to create a demand, make those fellows think someone else is hot on your track." She went uneasily upstairs, thinking that if she had alighted she had found a threat of quicksands where the earth had always been firm and stable. She'd change her dress. Not one of the new ones. The blue silk with the lace collar that George always liked. She dressed slowly, watching the hands of the small clock crawl. The children couldn't possibly come before four, and they might be later.

It was five when John came. Hazel sat in the living room, the evening paper unread on her lap, her cold hands folded over it. She heard a car stop, heard John's, "So long. Thanks for the lift." She went quickly into the hall, the secret and ignored dread of the long afternoon peeling away like a dry husk. He pushed open the door and looked at her, silent, but she saw a great gulp move in his thin throat. "Hello," he said, "when'd you blow in?"

"Oh, this morning." She had to kiss him, had to run her fingers, feather-light, over his stiff young head, although she held tight to the passion of tenderness which cried in every nerve-end for release. "How are you, Johnny? Come tell me what you've been doing. Did you miss me?" She slipped a hand under his arm, pulled him into the living room, down on the divan beside her.

John let his strapped bundle of books plunk to the floor, and dangled his hands between his knees. "I noticed you weren't around," he drawled. "You don't seem much different."

"You haven't changed much yourself." Hazel laughed. She thought, that line his head makes, rising from his neck, that sweet boy line— But his color isn't good, too white.

"Say, did they really give you the money?"

"Yes, they really did. I brought you something. It's there on the table, the small box."

John looked at her, his mouth moving around words, and then, without speaking, he crossed to the table, his coat hitched up in funny wrinkles. He came back with the box, and opened it slowly. The flat gold rectangle lay in his palm, and he twitched at the leather strap. "Gee, it's a pippin! It's a good one, too. But you know—" his face twitched, "Dad'll probably say I oughtn't to have it."

"What nonsense, John! Father isn't like that." Hazel pushed back his cuff, and buckled the watch about his thin wrist. "There!"

"You don't know." John held out his hand, shook down the sleeve to see how much of watch remained on view. "You don't know—" and suddenly his face had despair, complete because without perspective, his parted lips dry, his forehead creased. "He's fed up with me. He said so." He gulped. "He'll tell you about it, don't worry. First I meant to clear out, get the hell away. Only then you called up, and I didn't like to run out on you. An' I was talking with a fellow down by the freight yard, and he says times ain't what they used to be and you can't bum your way any more because if you haven't got a job then you have to go on relief or in a camp, and I couldn't because they'd look up my family. So I thought I'd wait and talk it over with you."

Hazel sat very still. He seemed balanced so precariously on a thin taut wire of confidence that a clumsy move from her would knock him headlong beyond her reach, into what pit of foolhardiness or danger? "Would you mind," she asked, "telling me what happened? I'm glad you waited. I should have felt let down if I'd come home—" She couldn't go on. That suitcase!

"The car got smashed." John hunched forward, knees pressing his hands together. "I was just driving along, and this fellow comes around the corner too fast and skids into me. It was sleety, see? Honest, I didn't do a thing wrong, but the fenders were crumpled and the running board stove up, and Dad said I oughtn't to be out loose."

"He'd be upset, John, but he didn't mean——"

"You didn't hear him!" John's fingers dug into his hair. "I can't help it if a mug skids into me! I can't help it if I haven't got a license yet. I just took the car to go down town, I wasn't going on any joy ride the way he said."

"You weren't hurt," said Hazel, softly.

"I wish I had been."

"Oh, hush! The car can be repaired, and your father was just worried——"

"He stays mad—" a glint of humor touched John's mouth, "because he has to walk and that reminds him all the time."

"Anyone may have an accident." Hazel spoke briskly. "Now you unpack your suitcase and hang around with us a little longer. I sort of like having you here."

John straightened his shoulders, and rolled his eyes at her, round and surprised. "You knew—" he began, when outside another car stopped. "See here," he said, "when you go to Hollywood ——"

"Sh!" said Hazel. "They're coming." And close to his ear she added, "You stick around, and if ever I should go, I'll take you along."

Then George and Lorna were in the hall, Lorna with little shrieks of welcome, George with a restrained and somewhat questioning heartiness.

Lorna loved her dress, white chiffon, soft and swirling. She held it up and posed before the hall mirror, and Hazel thought, she looks happier, less subdued, something has happened to her, too. "And this is for you." Hazel handed George the catalogue of dental supplies, open at the smooth cut of the marvelous dentists' unit, all black and shining chromium. "Only I couldn't bring it. It's coming soon, by express." George looked.

"You mean you ordered it for me?"

"Yes, sir." Hazel stood close to him, her finger on the page. "That very one! Don't you like it?"

"Yes, yes. It's just what I've needed."

"If it isn't exactly the one you want, we could send a wire—" Hazel pushed herself against that skim of reservation over his acceptance. "What isn't right, George? I wanted it to be perfect."

"It's quite all right. This is one of the best supply houses. I am afraid you were pretty extravagant."

Hazel shook her head. She knew that almost uttered *but,* that withholding of the kind of delight he should have. Better let it alone, rang a small warning. She couldn't, she had to dash on, no matter what! "You might as well tell me," she said. "It's really not a trifle, and we might still change it ——"

"Trifle! Of course not. There's nothing to tell. I was just wishing you might have consulted me ——"

(Dear Heavens, was his pride hurt again?) "But George, darling, you don't consult about presents!"

"You see, I practically gave an order for just such a unit this very noon. That shows I really want it!" He was defensive, prodded into explanation. "I meant to buy it on time, of course. But it would have been nice if you could have placed the order here. I've taken a good deal of her time."

"At luncheon?" asked Hazel, and down the street like a picture on a banner unfurling in a gust of angry wind marched the figure of that saleswoman, that red-winged blackbird person, arrogant and smart. You had luncheon with her, you wouldn't come home, said Hazel's sealed, dark look. And why not, after all you've been up to, answered George's steady, unrepentant gaze. This, thought Hazel, can't go on now, with the children listening. It must wait. Her stiff smile at George was a rain ticket. That was one thing about having children. You had to postpone settling difficulties, and sometimes after such postponement you couldn't find them again. Either they had evaporated, or you had mislaid them and they waited to trip you in some dark corner of your life.

"Dinner should be ready," she said. "I'm famished. Last night, on the train, I was too tired to eat, and Lizzie wouldn't give me much lunch. She, like the rest of you, hadn't expected me. Wash your faces, my lambs, and let's sit down."

With the soup, Hazel began an account of her trip to New York. As she talked, she listened, thinking, Mr. Horn should hear me! He'd give me a job as publicity liar right away. She had moved in a glitter, in a dazzle, rushing from triumph to triumph, meeting famous men and women, being toasted in cocktails, dined and wined and fêted, sought after by radio (they said my voice was excellent!), by motion pictures, pursued by rival publishers (Well, Mr. Horn said she was!), Lorna leaned forward, elbows on table, chin propped on crossed hands, her blue eyes wide, her lips parted. John listened more soberly, frowning, glancing at his father. And George ate methodically, with an air of one who has often heard such recitals, but as Hazel mounted with animation from one glory to another, his color changed, until instead of his usual clear flush on cheekbones, his face was pale except for a curious dull red along the line of jaw. She couldn't stop. She was saying, see, you never guessed how wonderful I am, you don't believe it now, this is the kind of life I could have, and you are indifferent, cruel, you take saleswomen in black suits and red feathers to lunch!

"Do they just have parties all the time? Honestly, Mother, I don't see how you can bear it to come back to Lounsberry!" Lorna sighed.

"They implored me to stay." Hazel was reckless. She'd decked that little brown wren of Mr. Horn's out with bird of paradise feathers until she almost believed the bird had worn them! "They said you had to be on the ground to catch the early worms. (Confound that bird.) I mean to meet the right people, work up radio programs, everything."

"You had to come home sometime," said John, "unless you stayed forever. Don't they know you've got folks? Parties all the time would be sickening, if you ask me."

"Oh, I'd love it!" said Lorna, and George did not look up from his plate.

After dinner Lorna wished to try on the new frock. Hazel watched George settle himself with the evening paper. "You don't have to go back to the office?" she asked, brightly, from the doorway.

"How can I, with no car? Or didn't John tell you about his latest piece of brilliance?"

John bolted up the stairs as if his father's words yapped at his heels.

"Oh, yes. Well, I'm glad something keeps you home. I mean you drive yourself just too hard."

George shifted his paper. "That was why you wrote your book, wasn't it? Those lonely evenings while the struggling dentist struggled."

Hazel drew a quick breath, and mounted the stairs, her feet clipping each step sharply. If he was going back to the very beginning, if those first silly interviews still rankled— For the first time, with a galvanic shock as if the thought had physical existence, Hazel said to herself, "Perhaps we are finished. I've destroyed his contentment, his notion of our marriage, of me, his sufficiency. He feels belittled." She paused at the top of the stairs, one hand clinging to the rail, and everything about her, the light, the walls, the sounds of the house receded. She was alone in a dark void, her blood had curdled in that keen pain under her heart, and no stimuli could touch her. She mustn't faint, that would be absurd. Somewhere she found her will, she stirred her curdled blood, she drew light and sound and the shape of walls and floor back into her consciousness.

"See, Mother, how do you fasten this?" Lorna was calling her, and Hazel went quickly into her room. She would finish with this, she would say good-night to Lorna and to John, and then, and then! Eagerness beat up in her, as if the very chemistry of her body had changed. She wanted to confront George, to have this out. She was through with side-wise fencing, with gentle subterfuge, with postponements.

She fastened the girdle, catching the sweet warmth of her daughter's round, soft body. Lorna pirouetted, the toes of her gold strapped dancing sandals shining. "It's adorable, Mother! Put on your new black dress and let's pretend it's a party. We could show Father."

"Not tonight." Hazel adjusted the puffed caps at the shoulders. "It is sweet, and it fits very well."

"It's only a paper moon, it's on-ly a painted sky—" sang Lorna, taking dance steps. "Did all the people have on lovely dresses at the parties? Didn't they think you looked simply swell in yours?"

Hazel sat down on the bed. Her exhibition mood had vanished, and she said, drily, "No one spoke of it." She sat there, her brow crinkling, while Lorna swept down stairs to show her father. Just what had happened to Lorna? Suddenly she had it, tangible as if it lay between her clasped fingers. Why, Lorna was actually thinking about her, Hazel! Little, first attempts— She had moved a step out of the childish prison of her self. Hazel watched the girl draw the soft clinging folds carefully over her head, watched her move about the room, thinking how sweet she is, that milk and honey white and gold, just that bra' and panties— "However do you keep warm enough?" she said.

"Oh, I couldn't breath if I had to wear more clothes!" Lorna hung away the dress, tied the cord of a blue bathrobe firmly around her waist, and sat down beside Hazel. "You know—" she studied her pink toes, and then rushed on. "The girls think it's wonderful, to have a mother that can do what you do. They ask me everything about you. And Miss Chalmers, in English class, said we should be very proud, and maybe I might inherit some of your ability. I don't think I'll get married for years and years." She sighed. "I'm not really very smart, yet, but maybe—if I worked—I could do something, and go to New York and get my picture taken and everything." She hugged her round knees and brooded.

It hasn't been a total loss, then, thought Hazel. She relaxed, quiescent, receptive, waiting. At long, long intervals, and always after the girl had come out at the end of some experience, some stiff ascent in her development, she had a moment when she wished to talk. Just a few phrases, a seal the child placed on something she was done with.

"It isn't always being in love, is it, when you go all soft and squidgy inside being kissed, even if you think it is? Anyway, some boys just work too fast. Only when he got another girl right off, just because I wouldn't— But it's all right now. I see my future much more clearly."

"That's good, darling," said Hazel, quietly. She must keep her horror out of her voice. That dreadful boy!

"Good-night!" cried Lorna. "Look how late it is, and me with scads of homework." Confessional was over, she would have no more of it. She jumped to her feet, tugging at the cord about her waist. "I'll just say it was so exciting having you come home that I forgot about work!"

Hazel gave her a quick hug. "Good girl," she said, and Lorna pretended to be absorbed in the book she had opened. John's door was ajar, and Hazel laid one hand against her throat, as she saw what the boy was doing. The trophy cup sat on the dresser, and John was stowing away in a drawer the contents of his suitcase. She stepped past silently, and went down the stairs.

George stood at a window of the living room, hands hooked together behind his back. He did not hear her, and Hazel looked at him, gray suit snug over truculent square shoulders, smooth light head well up, heels together. Her glance hurried about the familiar room, and all the furniture, the rugs, the lamps, chosen over so many years, lived with, looked back at her bleakly, meaning gone from them. George hadn't even turned on the radio! She walked in, selecting a strip of bare wood beyond the rug, and George said, not moving, "I thought you must have gone to bed."

"No," said Hazel. "I haven't."

"I thought you probably were pretty tired after all you've been doing."

"No, I'm not."

He turned then, reluctantly, as if he heard in her voice the restrained violence of her intention to get at him, as if he preferred more silence, more dodging, more sly undercuts.

"I just want to say this. I don't mean to stand in your way at all. You can go on to Hollywood or New York or wherever you want to. As Lorna said, Lounsberry isn't much to come back to. I can't compete with your offers. Lorna can go to college next fall. And John—a good stiff school somewhere would be good for him. He needs some sense pounded into him. We'll close the house. I'd rather live at the hotel. And later——"

Hazel sat down. "Yes," she prompted. "Later?"

"Later we could arrange for a divorce. A nice, quiet one, that wouldn't upset the children. You could stop off at Reno, say, on your way to Hollywood."

"You've got everything planned without even asking me——"

"Ask you? What was there to ask you? When you've shown in every move you've made what you really want! When all our life meant was that you were so bored you had to say so publicly! From the minute that telegram came about the prize you were different. You haven't known I existed. You haven't thought or cared about anything except what was happening to you, what was being said about you." George spoke with a quiet, unmodulated fluency which meant that all these words, worn round and smooth from constant turning in his mind, rolled out with no effort. He could not know they were amazing, because to him they were rote-familiar. "I've always known you didn't really care about my work, you never listened when I tried to explain it, it was only the way I made a living for us, and now that you can make so much more money you don't have to pretend. I waited till you'd been to New York. I don't know quite what I hoped for. But now I see it's no use. All these grand things—I won't stand in your way. You wouldn't say this to me, because you'd think, mistakenly, 'Poor George! I mustn't hurt him.' But I believe in extracting dead teeth. I can't stand things as they are. It's upsetting my work." His blue eyes had a sudden wintry gleam. "Do you know what I did yesterday? I mixed up two sets of X-rays, and I pulled out the wrong tooth. That is, it was the right tooth in the wrong mouth. The plate showed a shadow, but it wasn't Mrs. MacAndrew's shadow." He broke off with an impatient gesture, his hand implying, *but you don't care about that!*

Hazel sat back in her chair, her hands limp, her heart beating so heavily she felt it in her wrists. Dear Lord, it was like reading another terrible interview, or review of her book, this trying to see what George saw of her! The self she thought she was had shrunk into a dried pea, rattling in shells provided by other people! She didn't care about dentistry. George had told her that before. But who else could, the way George did? Was it true, that she was selfish, indifferent, absorbed? That grand picture she'd built up, of herself in New York! She'd come rushing home, and now George was pitching her out, making her over into a hard, demanding creature— Perhaps——

"George Curtis," she said, fiercely, "are you getting rid of me for another woman? Are you—that woman you took to lunch? That saleswoman? Are you in love with her?"

"No," said George. "Not yet. We have things in common."

"Oh!" cried Hazel. She flung out her arms, her eyes brilliant under the heavy lashes. "George, you idiot! I won't be extracted. I'm not a dead tooth! You—" was it laughter that sprang from the tight coil of feeling?—"you've mixed your X-ray pictures all up. Oh, don't you know I've thought about you every second? I've been so wretched because you didn't like it—I've been terrified! I had to make you think I had a grand time, didn't I? I didn't even feel real until I got home—and then you wouldn't come— Oh, I won't let you be so stupid that you don't know what I want first!"

"You mean you'd give up your Hollywoods and everything?"

"I didn't mean that. We could leave that till it came up. But I mean if we tried, I'd get used to being somebody, not a big somebody, and you'd get used to it, and it wouldn't make any more difference than— than your filling a tooth!"

"You don't think I mind that all this happened to you?"

Hazel looked up at his strained face, the light gleaming on his forehead, on his neatly brushed fair hair.

"I had a feeling you were a different woman, not the girl I married. But I——"

Hazel slid to her feet, clasped her hands behind his head, and kissed him. "There!" she murmured, against his lips. "Same girl."

Later they sat together on the divan, hands linked, Hazel's head on his shoulder. She thought: he did mind, terribly, just what we neither of us ever will know. But I've got him back. Dear Lord, help me look interested in dentistry or machinery or anything else he wants to talk about! I do love him so much.

George said, clearing his throat, "I bought a copy of your book. Two-fifty. They had quite a pile of them in Hudson's."

Hazel held her breath. She wanted to sit away from him, to watch his face, but she kept her head down against the solid shoulder.

"It's a good story. I don't see how you thought it all up. It wasn't exactly like your father's folks, although I recognized some of it. I was glad you ended it that way."

Hazel relaxed again. "I tell you," she said, dreamily, "when I write the next one, you can read it as I go along. You could make suggestions."

Season of Celebration

BY

Albert Maltz

Season of Celebration

At Nine in the Evening

AT NINE in the evening Baldy White, night man of the Hotel Raleigh, opened the door to Room B and poked his head in. He stood there chuckling. "Hey, Benson," he said, "here's some one wants to know if the beds is clean."

Except for a sick youngster, who was asleep in a cot further down the aisle, the man called Benson was the only one in the big room. He was lounging on the back end of his cot with his scraggly shanks hanging down loosely over the iron rim. Benson was a lank, ugly man of fifty, a farm hand and migratory worker. Thirty-five years of high-balling over the forty-eight states, from one job to another, from railroad jungle to Jesus flop house, had lined and grooved his weary face into a steady, bitter scowl. Now he sat grimly, hunched over, with an old newspaper spread on his knees to hold his game of solitaire. He ignored the night man.

"Tell him, Bill, tell him," Baldy repeated laughing.

Benson sighed. He screwed up his face into a grimace that was weary, sour and impatient at the same time, jerked his thumb, and sluiced a stream of saliva on the floor. Then he looked down at the cards again.

The night man laughed and smoothed the top of his bald dome with a thick, white hand. His mouth opened wide and the gold capped teeth gleamed yellow in the sharp light. He liked Benson. Benson was an old customer—a glum mutt with a cranky disposition, but no teeth left. Nice feller, Benson.

"Take a look," Baldy said. He closed one eye and inclined his head slightly toward the door.

A young man of about twenty-seven came into the room. He was shivering with the cold. His face was hollow and curiously serious with the brows knitted and the deep, brown eyes, which were liquid and soft like the eyes of a woman, set in a peculiar stare. He wore only overalls and a scrappy sweater which had lost its buttons a long time ago. It hung down loosely from his angular shoulders and he had it fastened at the throat with a safety pin. Under his arm he carried a brown, paper parcel—the suitcase and wardrobe trunk of a stiff on the bum.

Baldy watched him with an expressive grin on his face: A number one boy—he knew the type!

The young man examined the long bare room with great care: the triple row of iron cots, the narrow lockers, the hanging electric bulbs encased in wire mesh; he took a long time for it. Then he rubbed one hand over the stubble of soft reddish hair on his face while a finger of the other hand played nervously with the string on his parcel.

"Ah cain't sleep if there's bugs," he announced finally.

Baldy laughed. He knew the type! He knew them all! He was sixteen years in the business and he had seen the endless, murky river of men with an old shirt on their backs and two bits in their pockets. Number one was the working stiffs out on their uppers: the scared, bitter stiffs floating from town to town with their teeth locked together and holes in their shoes from scraping the streets at six bells every A.M., trying to find them a job, trying to keep their poor schnozzles out of water. Yes, Jesus Christ, when Baldy looked at them, he thanked his Aunt Lizzie he had this job. And the second was the bums, the boozers, the guys who had given up: two feet down already; tomorrow in a doorway or frozen by a curbstone or keeling over in the street; the morgue boys waiting to be laid out; finished but still crawling, scratching, coughing, panhandling, hanging on they don't know why; buy 'em an' sell 'em for a nickel. And number three was the fish in between: the men on the skids with their guts dryin' up, stiffs with their juice runnin' out; you don't look for work so hard any more; you've given up tryin' for a job nowadays; you're startin' to get drunk on smoke when you get it: Oh the boot in the backside but they don't know it yet, slidin' down hill but they can't see the ground go past. Oh yes, Baldy had seen 'em all! Sixteen years of faces he had forgotten. New ones comin' up every day like somebody had planted them. Here was a number one boy: a stiff with his nose for a job—but a boy with the trimmings; one of the specials—looking for a bed without bugs—banjo eyes like he just came out of the incubator, didn't know how babies were made—there were them kinds too!

"Texas," Baldy said clapping the young man on the back, "Texas—you find a bug an' I'll eat it. Louse, bedbug or any kind of roach." He laughed again. "We kill 'em all with kerosene. There's none in here you don't bring with you."

"Ah'm from Arkansas," the boy said seriously. "Mah name is Luke Hall."

"That's fine, Mr. Hall. I knew somebody from Arkansas. Fine feller! Bill," he said, "tell Mr. Hall how you always come here on your business trips to New York."

Mr. Bill Benson looked over at the gentleman from Arkansas, screwed up his face wearily and looked down at the cards again. Baldy wasn't as funny as he thought. Benson wished he'd get through and go wiggle his tail.

The night man chuckled. He had a round, full, good-natured face the color of fresh dough. The laughter made his fat cheeks shake. "Finest hotel on the gay, white Bowery," he said. He waited for the boy to make up his mind.

Hall was silent.

"Unless you want a flop to yourself," Baldy suggested suddenly. The boss gave him a commission on the private rooms and Baldy pushed them whenever he could. "You get side walls an' chicken wire on top so nobody can't reach in. It's strictly private."

"What's the charge on that?"

"Fifteen cents more."

Hall shook his head. "Ah ain't got a job. Ah'll tell you, Mista," he added confidentially, "that's why Ah've come t' New York. Ah'm hopin' t' get me a good job heah."

"You ain't got a job, eh?" Baldy wriggled his thick lips humorously. This son of a bitch was a daisy! "Most men come here got fine paying jobs. They just like it here." He held out a hand that was like a cut of prime fatback: "That'll be twenty cents!"

Hall fumbled in his overalls pocket. He drew out a small woman's purse. "Anyway," he said, "anyway it's New Year's Eve an' Ah'll be right glad to have company. Ah'm right fond of company."

"That's right fine," Baldy replied with a grin. He mimicked the boy's speech: "Mr. Benson's right fine company. Regular entertainer.

An' it's a cold night . . . this room'll fill up pretty soon. You'll have plenty of right fine company."

The stranger from Arkansas fished out two dimes. "That's good," he said. "Ehhh—" he felt hesitant about asking—"you don't have anything special on heah tonight, do you? Ah mean—like for your patrons?"

Baldy scratched his dome with exaggerated thoughtfulness. "Well no . . . a' course," he said, "we have our regular New Year's Eve dinner—you know . . . soup, fish, duck, chicken, plenty of nuts . . . just the regular five courses—an' entertainment a' course: some of the Park Avenue dames comes down for the dancin'."

Benson, four cots down the aisle, raised his ugly, grinning head from the cards. "Don't miss it, buddy," he croaked in his hoarse voice, "it's a picnic."

Luke Hall looked doubtful. "It ain't free, is it?"

"Well no," Baldy protested. "But it ain't so much either—four-fifty a plate!"

"Four dollars an' fifty cents?" Hall smiled wistfully. "Ah reckon that's a little too steep for me, Mista White."

Baldy shook his head sadly. "It's too bad, Mr. Hall." He held out a key which was fastened by wire to a piece of wood. "This is for your locker. There's a right smart toilet and washroom through the door on the other side."

Benson burst out into a snort of laughter. Baldy turned around with an appreciative grin on his face. Then he smoothed his bald dome and looked solemn again. "One more thing, kid," he advised kindly, with amusement, "don't leave your duds around loose—not if you want 'em again."

"Ah won't," Hall replied. "Ah know *that*. But thank you, Mista." He walked down the line of cots searching for his number.

The boy who was asleep suddenly groaned aloud and flung his arm away from his face. Hall stopped, startled. Baldy lumbered over. "O'Shaughnessy!" he called.

There was no reply. The boy twisted in his sleep. He was muttering to himself.

"Is he sick?" Hall asked.

"He's all right," Baldy replied. "He's had ptomaine for a coupla days."

"He looks turrible," Hall said.

"He don't look good," the night man agreed. He called again: "O'Shaughnessy!"

The sick boy subsided. He slept quietly with one arm flung out and his head twisted to the side in a strained position. The bright lights overhead colored the pallor of his flesh giving it an unpleasant, wax-like appearance. His face was emaciated: the cheeks sunken in, the jawbones protruding, there were deep pockets under the eyes. He was breathing hard but now the low muttering had stopped.

"Hey, Bill," Baldy requested, "call me if he wakes up, will you?"

"What's the matter?" Benson croaked, "you hafta blow his nose for him?"

"You call me, Bill!" Baldy said. "I'm worried! He owes me for a whole week."

"Aw, c'mon," Benson persisted, "you blow his nose for him. He ain't had it blowed all day."

"Say—" Baldy turned to Luke Hall. "Wanna buy an overcoat?"

"It's cold, ain't it?" Hall agreed. He rubbed his chin. "Ah didn't know it got so cold up heah in December."

"It'll get colder, son," Baldy warned. His tone became business like. "I know where you can get a good coat for a buck an' a quarter."

Baldy's rule was a coat or a hat for an unpaid bill. What the boss didn't know didn't hurt him and there was a good turnover in it. Hell, Baldy only got twenty-five a week an' he had three kids an' an old lady to support.

Hall shook his head. "That's too much for me, Mista."

Baldy frowned. A bargainer, hey? That was fine. A bargainer an' cold sober. The drunks were better; they forked right over. "There's one for four bits I can pick up," he suggested confidentially.

Hall shook his head.

"You're gonna need one!"

"Ah ain't got a job yet," Hall explained.

"Okay!" Baldy gave up in disgust. The Arkansas rummy must think overcoats grow on trees. "Okay then!" Baldy turned quickly and left the room.

Hall sat down on his cot. He was wondering if it had been a mistake to let the overcoat go. That was a good offer Mr. White had made him. Still—he didn't have much money. It was more important to keep eating. He could buy one later, when he got him a job. Yes!

But how if he didn't get a job? The thought frightened the boy.

But that couldn't be! It couldn't be! In a big city like New York there'd bound to be *somethin'* a man could do—if he was willing to take anything at all. Wouldn't there?

He felt reassured again. That was sensible! And prayer! Prayer would help too.

Luke shifted on the cot and began taking off his shoes. He wore no socks and his feet were white with cold. He rubbed them slowly. He thought of the fine dinner that was going to be served at midnight. He wished he had the price of that fine dinner.

O'Shaughnessy twisted in his sleep. He was muttering to himself.

Luke watched him pityingly. It was terrible to be sick when you were away from home. It made you so lonely. Luke knew how lonely it made you feel.

He picked absently at the dirt that was caked between his toes. He hoped that the sick boy was a believer. It'd help him in his sickness if he believed. And it was good to be in a warm room. He could bathe himself here. When the disciples came back from a long journey, the first thing they did was to bathe themselves.

O'Shaughnessy subsided. The bright light was cruel on his white face.

The street noises of the Bowery drifted in. They sounded melancholy. They carried the dreary feel of a dark, winter night.

As BLESSY swung around the corner of Delancey Street onto the Bowery, walking quickly with his hard, hurried stride and his big head crooked down against the flurries of wet snow, he ran smack into a young girl. He was in a hurry to get up to the Raleigh and see how O'Shaughnessy was doing and he hadn't been looking where he was going. The impact of his heavy, driving body almost knocked the girl down.

Blessy grabbed her, and the girl regained her balance. She leaned her head back against the plate glass window of the cigar store and burst out into an abrupt, foolish giggle. "Poosh poosh!" she said. She was very drunk.

"Did I hu-u-u-u—hurt you?"

Blessy flushed painfully. There he was—stammering again. Whenever he became excited, like a goddam ninny. How the hell did he get like that in the first place, he asked himself savagely. Since he was a kid.

"It's awright," the girl said. "It's a pleasure." She looked up at him and smiled drunkenly. It was a warm, free, abandoned, drunken, New Year's Eve smile that meant nothing.

Blessy looked dumbly at the girl's red, smiling mouth. Then he saw her body. Her drab, cloth coat had become unbuttoned and she wore a gay, party dress underneath. She was not a pretty girl. Her face was dark and thin and there were tired circles under her eyes. She looked Italian, like a factory kid, he thought. But her mouth was a warm red smear and Blessy could see the flesh of her throat, naked and sensuously white against her dark face, and the slight curve of her breasts where the dress swung low, and the round, hard little nipples pressed tight and warm against the blue silk—and her youth, her warmth and her youth!

A keen desperate desire for the girl swept over him. It had been so long since he had left home and no one, not anyone, since then! A molten, quivering flame licked through the veins of his body. It tongued warm and bitter at his flesh, stripping away the lonely wall of security, leaving him weak and trembling and desperately hungry. A painful bubble of noise rose up in his throat. He felt choked. He stared at her—but he couldn't find words to speak.

The girl stopped giggling. For a moment she eyed the youth closely. Her head was swaying a little. He stood directly in front of her, a heavy, muscular, peasant-faced youth of twenty-four in an old lumber jacket and blue corduroys, without a hat on, standing there without speaking while the wet snow fell soft on his face and hair, standing there staring with hot, blue eyes that stabbed into her.

Blessy's face was fiery red from the wind and the out of doors and his features were extraordinary: big, thick, hard with high, prominent cheekbones; a wide, hard, heavy jaw and a big, wide mouth with thick, firm lips. He looked as though he had been cut rough out of a quarry. And like a crown on his flaming face there was a wild, magnificent shock of yellow hair shot through by flecks of gold. He stood there, planted in front of her, gripping the earth like an inarticulate, powerful animal and the girl could see the full tide of his desire, the humble, passionate, naked yearning written like script on his face.

If she had not been drunk, she might not have spoken to him. Her thin, dark face suddenly seemed full and soft and she leaned forward a little. "Well, so long," she said. She put her hand on his arm.

Then she stepped to one side and walked with stiff and drunken dignity to the curbstone. On the other side of the Bowery there was an automobile crowded with young people. The girl crossed over. She got in. The car moved off.

Blessy walked again, more slowly now. His head had sunk down into the collar of his lumber jacket.

It turned colder. The snow became a dry, fine powder. It'd stick to the pavement now and if it kept up all night, there'd be a couple more days' work. That was good. Blessy thought about it slowly. Snow was good. You made much more that way than selling the white sheets. If Jimmie hadn't gotten sick now, they could've cleaned up.

Blessy walked slowly—past the eating joints and the gin mills, past the pawnshops and the two pairs of pants joints, the Salvation Army flop and dark doorways where bums were sleeping, kept warm for a little while by smoke, but tomorrow morning they'd be picking up every third one with the sweat froze stiff on him.

In the instant that the automobile had moved off Blessy had forgotten about the girl. Not really forgotten—she was just gone, that's all, the way a fire leaves you when it dies down to ash. You walk along the street and you can't hardly recall what it was like. It had happened to him before. He wondered why.

A bum see-sawed blindly across his path yelling "Hooray for the bums from Idaho," yelling it at the top of his tin-horn voice. Blessy stepped to one side. He stopped to look at a neon light winking first yellow and then green with the snow falling soft in front of it: "Beer, Beer!" It looked nice.

Perhaps, he thought, when a guy didn't have a job or a home or anything like that, he had enough to do just to keep alive. A man most always needed his belly full to start wanting a girl. Feelin' kind of tired all the time was about all the feelin' a man could have. Yes, you were always that way, always sort of half tired. Yet once in a while it hit you like a streak of lightning and then it felt like somebody had poured gasoline all over you and struck a big match. That woman in the subway was like that.

The snow scuffed under his feet. He felt washed out. He wasn't used to heavy work any more. All day long shoveling in the cold. Better to have his supper first. No—no, he thought, Jimmie might be awake now. See him first. Poor Jimmie!

A current of emotion welled up in Blessy at the thought of his friend. Yes, God Almighty, there weren't many things he had left in life. You hung on hand to mouth, a dog keepin' house in an alley. Outside people walking, you all alone in the dark countin' the cramps in your belly. If Jimmie hadn't been there to pal along with him, he'd agone crazy.

He thought of the future. Well, that was somethin'. Jimmie was trained, a mechanic. Two an' a half years in the State school. That prepared a man. One of these days they'd be needing trained men again. Jimmie'd get on, teach *him* something—maybe some day they'd have a machine shop together—I'm tired, he thought.

He passed a bonfire in the gutter. Half a dozen stiffs were hugging the flames. Something in the color of it made him stop. Then he saw what it was: blue from a tar barrel. At home, when the rain came down, the coal dump burst into a hundred little fires. You'd see them just like that, flickering blue-red all over the side, way high up sometimes like ghost fires, with the odor of coal gas blowing down over the camp. Well, it was never so good in that lousy coal camp—but it was better than this—aw, what the hell, he thought. No soap in mining any more. So many machines coming in, five out of ten men were out, even the old-timers. It was better to be in a city. You could dig yourself a hole in a city.

Blessy crossed the street. A limousine touring car streaked past him like a black locomotive. A fat man in a college boy overcoat leaned out of the front seat and hollered "Happy New Year, bud." The limousine shot hell bent uptown and a burst of warm, careless, woman's laughter rippled back to him.

They were waiting for midnight. Blessy had seen that headline in a newspaper: "America Waits For Midnight." A happy country was waiting for midnight.

A surge of bitterness rose up inside him. What was he waiting for? Something, but not midnight. Sure, a job, a woman, a home. Christ, everybody was waiting for that. And tired waiting! Your bones were beginning to crack with waiting! O'Shaughnessy was sick from waiting. Free, white and waiting!

He entered the doorway of the Hotel Raleigh. A man was sitting halfway up the flight of stairs that led to the office. Blessy knew him, Jed Killifer, a bargeman from Boston. Jed was the one put him and Jimmie wise to the white sheet racket. You wait till two when the morning papers hit the stands. You buy 'em for three cents and then beat it over to Fourth Avenue where the night club traffic is scooting home to Brooklyn. You can always get rid of some at a nickel a piece and that's the price of your flop.

"Hello, Jed," Blessy said. "How you doin'?"

Jed was blind drunk. He didn't recognize Blessy. He stood up and grabbed him by his lumber jacket. "I'm from ol' Bean town," he said belligerently, "an' a guy from ol' Bean town's as good as a guy from New York. Ain't that right?"

"Sure," Blessy told him. He removed his hand.

"They had fifty million dollars for the bankers," Jed announced fiercely, "an' not a goddam cent for me." He grabbed Blessy by the jacket again. "Ain't that right?" he demanded.

"Right," Blessy said. He sat Jed down and brushed past him. "You better turn in, Jed, you're loaded."

Jed burst out laughing and smacked his hands together. "Oh boy, oh boy," he whooped, guffawing, "oh boy, what she did to me for a dollar!"

"How much was the dose?" Blessy asked. He walked up the stairs laughing.

"Happy New Year," Jed called after him. "Everybody's gotta have a happy—oh boy, oh boy!" He clapped his hands together again.

Blessy opened the door to the landing where the office was. There was no one in the cage. He crossed the floor and started up the corrugated iron stairway that led to the rooms. Baldy White, the night man, met him at the turn.

"Hello," Baldy said quickly. "I wanna see you."

"I'll be right down," Blessy told him.

"The kid's asleep," Baldy said. "No use in goin' up."

"Oh! Say, that's funny," Blessy speculated aloud in his slow, heavy manner. "He must be sure played out. He's been sleepin' all day."

"All day?" Baldy pursed his thick lips sarcastically. "Let me remind you somethin', boy: he's been sleepin' here *free* all week."

Blessy gestured impatiently. "I told you I'd pay you, Baldy."

"Awright, pay me!" Baldy snapped out his thick, white hand.

"I ain't got it now. . . . What's the matter with you anyway?" Blessy asked suddenly. "You know I been working on the snow for three days an' you know the city don't pay off right away. I told you, when I get it, I'll pay you. Jesus, we're good customers."

Baldy hooked both thumbs under his belt. For a moment he was silent. His plump, doughy face was flushed and he was breathing hard and angrily.

"You make me tired," he broke out finally, "you stiffs make me god-damned tired. Who's doin' the favors around here anyway? Does O'Shaughnessy owe me or do I owe him? For Godssakes," he burst out, "*I* don't own this joint. I been puttin' twenty cents in the till every goddam night your pal's been layin' around here. Why the hell should I do that for you?"

"I'm gonna pay you, ain't I?" Blessy insisted stubbornly.

"How do I know?"

"I'm tellin' you!"

Baldy snorted. "*You're* tellin' me! A lot of other guys has told me but *I* had to pay for it because I'm nothin' but a good-natured slob. Listen—" he shoved his face close to Blessy's—"so far O'Shaughnessy's overcoat makes it even. I can take *that* in trade. But that's all! I ain't carryin' him a day more! Tomorrow mornin' he goes out!"

Baldy lumbered into his office: "Don't forget it!"

Blessy stood rooted. The night man's threat was too unexpected and it had come too quickly for him to comprehend it. Then his brain blazed and he walked over to the cage with slow, heavy deliberateness. "You gonna thruh-thruh-throw him out even if he's still sick?" he asked.

"Listen," Baldy said, "I ain't no Rockefeller Foundation. There's a *lotta* sick people in this world. I can't carry him!"

"I won't leh-leh-leh-let you!" Blessy said. His body hunched down a little and his thick neck became red and swollen. "I won't leh-let you!"

"Oh!" Baldy surveyed him calmly. "You gonna make trouble, I'll get a cop that's all. If you want a month in the can, okay with me."

"Listen—" Blessy said thickly—"you be careful! You throw him out, you be careful!" The youth's face had suddenly become murderous. He shoved a big-knuckled fist under the night man's nose. "You listen," he said thickly in a voice that trembled with emotion, "you throw him out I'm go-go-gonna *get* you. I'll—I'll—" he searched for words—"I'll wait ten years but I'll do-do it!"

Baldy slid out of his swivel chair and backed to the other end of the wire cage.

He was scared stiff. This bull-headed bastard looked crazy mean. No, it was too risky. Blessy was only a foot away. He couldn't make it. Baldy cast a quick glance over at his billy hanging by the cash register.

"You be ca-careful," the yellow-haired youth repeated in a thick, choked whisper. He was still standing hunched over with his big, sledge-hammer fist poised in the air.

Baldy's doughy cheeks quivered as though he were about to cry. "For Godssakes," he said in a burst of pleading, "what can *I* do?"

"I'll pay you," Blessy said. "But you got to luh-luh-leave him alone."

The night man's head wagged exasperatedly. He started to speak, then stopped.

They stared at each other. Finally the youth straightened up. "Don't worry, I'll p-p-pay you," he said. . . . He walked out of the cage. "I'm goin' back to Dooky's—get some grub. . . . You tell Jimmie if he wakes up, will you?"

Baldy sighed resignedly. Now, God help him, he was doin' favors again. . . . "All right, I'll tell him," he said wearily.

The big youth nodded in his slow, heavy manner. He went out.

Baldy sat down. He wiped his forehead with his sleeve. This was a hell of a note. He wiped his forehead again. On the one hand—stuck with an unpaid bill. Fine! He could hear his old lady hollering already. But on the other hand this big lug—hell, he was built like a bull and crazy enough to do anything. "Jesus!" Baldy exclaimed aloud. He wiped his forehead for the third time. But maybe the boy *would* pay. Baldy considered the prospect. He *said* he would. He wasn't trying to weasel out on the charge. It might be better to wait. Yes, he decided, he would wait. He could always grab the overcoat.

"Some job, hey?" he asked himself suddenly. He leaned back in his swivel chair and swore softly with slow, keen relish. For twenty-five a week—him and J. P. Morgan.

Blessy stepped out on the street and pulled his lumber jacket around him. It was brutally cold and he felt the deep, long-time weariness heavy inside of him. It had been a mistake to come home without eating.

The holiday traffic roared past him as he trudged downtown. It gave him a lonely feeling. He wished Jimmie were well again.

Nine Twenty P.M.

LUKE HALL came out of the washroom. He approached Bill Benson hesitatingly. Benson was still grimly playing his solitaire with his face

screwed up into its steady scowl. Now and then he reached into his
pocket for a bottle of liquor. It was a smoky, white fluid, a bottle of
murderous home-brew that he had picked up for two bits. It coursed
down his insides like streaked lightning and after each drink he
coughed and spit on the floor.

"You want t' play some cards with me, friend?" Luke asked in his
soft drawling speech. He was holding a piece of toilet paper to a cut
on his chin where his ancient razor had left its signature. Now that the
stubble of beard was gone his face seemed even more pallid and emaciated than it had before, but there was a curious softness to it, in the
curve of his lips and the liquid expression of his eyes, that made him
look wistful and young. Luke waited for the answer to his question.

Benson didn't reply. He kept his face down at the cards.

"Didn't you hear me, friend?"

Benson snapped his head up. He opened his mouth as though to
speak, took a swift breath, clamped his wolfish-looking jaws together
with an angry click and then looked down at the cards again.

Luke walked back to his cot. His lips were curved in a pout and his
face showed his distress. He hadn't expected to find people as non-
sociable as this. He'd expected they'd feel different on New Year's Eve.
They always did at home. They had fun at home.

The sick boy stirred in his sleep. He uttered a long, drawn out sigh
and raised his legs under the blanket. Luke watched him. He hoped
this ptomaine wasn't catching. A fellow who got bad sick and didn't
have a home was in a bad fix. The sick boy sighed again. His knees
relaxed.

Luke stretched out on his side and pillowed his head in his arms.
He felt lonely all of a sudden. Unhappy too. He wished he could do
something to make himself feel better. Back home on New Year's Eve
they used to sing songs. That was nice to do. Perhaps if he did that
now it'd make him feel better. Yes, he decided, that was a *good*
thought; he would sing a song and pretend he was home again.

He began quietly in a fresh, clear voice. It was a hymn:

> "All people that on earth do dwell,
>   Sing to the Lord with cheerful voice;
>   Him serve with fear, His praise foretell,
>   Come ye before Him, and rejoice."

He rolled over on his back and began the second verse. He sang it tenderly lingering over the notes.

Benson interrupted his solitaire. He glared over at the hymn singing grease ball with savage contempt.

New Year's Eve or no New Year's Eve, this was more than Benson could take. He gulped down a drink, spit a blob of juice onto the floor in bitter indignation, took another drink.

"The Lord, ye know, is God indeed,
    Without our aid He did us make ——"

An old man limped into the room. He stopped when he heard the singing. He was a small, round, plump little package of about sixty with rosy cheeks and a thick, white Van Dyke beard stained by dirt and tobacco drippings.

"—We are His flock, He doth us feed,
    And for His Sheep, He doth us take!"

The old man smiled, the gentle, benign, foolish smile of senility. He commenced to sway his head from side to side in time with the music. With his tattered suitcase which had to be tied by cord to keep both sections together, with his tattered, cast-off clothes that were a mixture of rags and fancy patterns—the coat was brown, the trousers tweed, the shirt and tie green, the shoes had once been white—he looked like an unemployed, street-corner Santa Claus who had, a long time ago, dreamed of becoming a band conductor. He stood beating the air with his locker key, a plump, little pigeon of a man with an ancient derby balanced precariously on the back of his head.

"Abide with me! Fast falls the eventide ——"

Bill Benson swung his body around. He was finished! For over four years now he'd been forced to trade an hour of Jesus singing for a mess of goddam fly-stew. He was goddamed if he'd take it for nothing.

"Awright, Jesus," he burst out in his croaking, whiskey voice, "awright, awright, that's enough! You can go to sleep now. It's time t' go to sleep!"

Luke flushed. "Why cain't I celebrate a little?" he asked. "It's New Year's Eve, ain't it? The lights ain't out yit, are they?"

Benson shot a stream of saliva between his shut teeth. "Yours is gonna be, yours is gonna be," he warned. "You wanna celebrate—get in bed'n have a good time with yourself—but shut your hole."

The old man limped forward. "Don't you mind him, boy," he broke in. "You sing fine. Go right ahead."

Benson glared at him. His face was drawn with rage.

The old man sat down on Luke's cot. "My name's Knox." He thrust out a plump, little hand. "Knox with an 'x' not 'knocks on the door.'" He laughed gayly in his free, joyous, senile manner. His beard wriggled and his round, little belly rumbled with laughter. "Go ahead, sing something else."

"Where the hell do you think you are," Benson demanded violently, "in a *ho*tel or a goddam Jesus society?"

"Do you know this hymn?" the old man replied pertly; "it's a fine hymn." He began it:

> "The birds without barn or storehouse are fed;
> From them let us learn to trust for our bread ——"

He smiled warmly at Luke. His face was amiable and rosy. Luke smiled back timidly.

> "—His saints what is fitting shall ne'er ——"

Benson flung back his head. His voice exploded in the room, howling out an old, raucous, wobbly tune picked up somewhere in his fighting days:

> "At the cross, at the cross,
> Where I lost my shirt and drawers,
> And the but—tons they all
> Rolled away, rolled away ——"

Luke and the old man stopped singing. They stared at the man in amazement. Benson glared back at them. For a brief moment there was silence. Then the old man bristled like an angry little cock. He snapped his head up. "Come on," he urged Luke, "come on":

> "No strength of our own, nor goodness ——"

Benson leaned back, took a deep breath and howled again. He drowned the old man out:

"Scissor Bill, he is a little dippy,
Scissor Bill, he has a funny face.
Scissor Bill should drown in Mississippi,
He's the missing link ——"

Baldy White came racing through the door. He was breathing hard from the run up two flights of stairs but he looked ready for trouble. His ugly, little billy hung by a leather thong from his wrist.

Benson stopped singing. Baldy approached him crabwise. He scrutinized him carefully with the growing but unwelcome realization that poor Bill was slipping at last. "By God, Bill," he said in a low, concerned voice, "you ain't lost hold like this in the last five years. What in hell you *got* in that bottle?"

Benson sprang to his feet. "I gotta do somethin'," he cried wildly. "There's a coupla Jennie Linds you put in here—can't keep quiet." He pointed with majestic contempt. "Those blue-nosed punks 're singin' hymns."

"Oh! . . ." Baldy stifled his desire to laugh. He knew this crotchet of Bill's. He swung around at the other two. "Now listen," he said severely, "no noise! Get it? No noise!"

"*Noise?*" Knox replied, "*noise?*" He tugged excitedly at his beard. His round, little face was swollen with insult. He tried fruitlessly to speak. Then he tugged at his frayed, wing collar. And for the old man to tug at his wing collar was a sign of complete and final rage: because first Mr. Knox had been a street car conductor in Brooklyn; and then the street car system had become a bus system and he had been laid off; and then (after refusing many offers) he had become a book salesman; and finally he had adopted a wing collar as a sign of respectability and the more his fortunes declined the more he relied on the morale which a wing collar gave him. The one thing he could never do was tug at it—it was too old to withstand tugging.

"Noise?" Knox repeated for the third time when his rage permitted him to talk. "*He's* the one who made all the noise. We was bein' *quiet, peaceful,* and *gentlemanly.*"

"Monkey nuts!" Benson shot a stream of saliva at the old man's feet. "You been eatin' so much beans you can't keep the wind from comin' out."

"You're a dingle dangle," Knox shouted with his voice rising shrilly, "you're a low-down dingle dangle."

Baldy burst out laughing. "Now what in hell's a dingle dangle?"

"Ain't we allowed t' do a little celebratin' on the New Year's?" Luke asked sitting up. "We just bein' sociable."

"Well, you can't sing hymns," Baldy told him. "Bill here's got a grudge against hymns. Makes his pecker rise." Baldy's cheeks quivered with silent laughter. He smoothed his bald dome and shook his head weakly.

"We just bein' sociable," Luke repeated in a hurt tone. Luke hadn't expected things to be like this in New York. It wasn't nearly as friendly as at home.

O'Shaughnessy suddenly groaned and threshed his hand on the bed. He muttered something agitatedly. Baldy walked over to him. "How do you feel, kid?" he asked.

The boy's eyelids fluttered. He fell into his troubled sleep again. His lips were curved away from his teeth in a kind of snarl and his forehead was wet with perspiration.

"You see"—Baldy said—"you woke him up. No more singing now or I'll throw you out."

Baldy left the room chuckling to himself.

Benson sat down and gathered up his cards. His ugly, grinning face expressed the keen satisfaction he felt over his victory. There was one thing Benson knew: his rights. When *he* paid out good money, there was no Jesus singing allowed in the vicinity.

Luke Hall lay back on his cot. He felt lonely again. He wondered how many of the men in the hotel were going to be present at that fine dinner at midnight. He was feeling a little hungry. When he got a job he was going to have a good dinner every night. With meat in it. And potatoes and beans. And a sweet cake. Yes!

The old man found his locker and stored away his top clothes. Then he opened his suitcase and began fussing over the contents. He had to be ready in case some business came his way. A good salesman was always ready and Knox was a good salesman.

The room was quiet.

Nine Forty-Five P.M.

THE PATRONS of the Hotel Raleigh were beginning to usher in for their night's rest. From this hour until one in the morning men would be straggling up the corrugated iron stairway to Baldy White's cage, to be shunted from there into one big room or another. On a cold night like this everyone with the price would be heading for an inside bunk. It was a good night for business.

Two men entered Room B together. One was Charlie, a well-known figure on the Rialto. It was he who had shouted at Blessy an hour before. He came in still yelling "Hooray for the bums from Idaho," yelling it at the top of his tinny voice. Charlie was about forty-five. He was what Baldy called a "number two" boy. His unwashed hands and neck and face were so black with coatings of accumulated grime that he looked as though he had been crawling through a coal bin. Through the dirt on one side of his face could be seen the mottled flesh of a scarred and blistered cheek, at one time burned by fire. It gleamed dully making his face hideous. This cheek was the sign of Charlie's life. The fire, which had scarred his flesh, had seared his mind away in the same, blinding moment. It had happened in a freight crack-up when Charlie, in another world, had been a railroad engineer. He lived now, an idiot, a drooling, scratching unwashed member of that great fraternity of men who are not born to this final glory but are somehow nurtured to it, the forlorn, nameless herd who must once have sprung from women's loins as naked, unscarred babies but who now would be recognizable neither to mother, father, brother nor God.

And so Charlie, shouting at the top of his voice "Hooray for the bums from Idaho," sat down upon the cot to which Baldy, the night man, had directed him and issued the command of "Whoh, whoh!" as he might to a horse.

Baldy, chuckling with genial amusement, turned to Luke Hall and said: "What do you say, Arkansas? It's filling up like I told you, ain't it? Here's Charlie. He's right smart company."

And so, having successfully short-changed Charlie of four cents, Baldy hurried down stairs again; at the same time he made a mental note to get some candy for his kids since there was nothing they liked better than penny candy and since they didn't have candy very often.

As Baldy left the room, Charlie, with some strange urge troubling his maggoty brain, stood up abruptly and stepped away from his cot. He lost his balance. He tumbled backward, clawed at the bed and slumped down to the floor. He lay for a moment and then rolled over on his back. Sprawled out, with his body twisted and with one hand pressed convulsively to his throat, he lay quiet. His ruined mouth sagged open, exposing the broken stubs of teeth and the festered, yellow gums. He slept, the sleep of the innocent and the good.

Only now did the man who had come up the stairs with Charlie decide to enter the room. He was a tall, swarthy man of forty with the solid, muscular body of a laborer. The skin on his pockmarked, clean-shaven face and on the thick trunk of his neck was tight and firm. He walked slowly, with dignity, carrying his cap in his hand, his heavy shoes scraping the board floor, and as he passed the crooked figure of Charlie he muttered a low "drunk bum" to himself and his mouth twisted in contempt. It was the contempt of a sober, industrious man for one who was not sober and industrious, it was the contempt of a workingman for a bum.

Methodically this man, Michael Zets, an unemployed laborer, set about preparing for the night. His overcoat came off and was hung in the locker; then the torn, brown sweater; then the shiny, blue trousers. He stood finally in his woolen underwear and bare feet and began pulling small parcels from his overcoat pockets.

First he fished out a corn cob pipe. He smelled it, tapped it on the bed rail, filled it and began to smoke. Then he opened a paper bag containing a rusty towel and a sliver of soap. Next came a crumpled newspaper. Carefully he smoothed it out and put it to one side. Finally he took out half a loaf of rye bread and an onion. Sitting down, he set the pipe on the floor, spread the newspaper on his knees and began to eat and read. He rubbed the onion on the bread before each bite.

Old Knox, who had been watching the newcomer with increasing interest, suddenly dug into his suitcase. He sorted rapidly through the contents and fished out a pair of horn-rimmed spectacles. Holding them behind his back, he limped across the room.

"Pan, razuma Popolska?" he asked with a friendly wave of his hand and thereby not only carried out Rule No. 3 of the book on salesmanship he had read in the Public Library in Cincinnati (a rule which advised all drummers to establish intimate relations with their prospects), but at the same time he exhausted his entire knowledge of the Polish language.

Rule No. 3 worked. The man turned. One cheek bulged with a hunk of half-chewed bread. His sombre, heavy-featured face was flooded with warmth. He started to speak, stopped, chewed hastily and gulped down his mouthful. Then he broke into excited Polish.

Knox smiled benignly at him. "No spik Polish," he said. He offered the spectacles. "These are for your eyes. *Eyes*"—he pointed—"help you read."

Zets looked at him bewilderedly.

"My name's Knox," the old man said briskly. He held out his hand. "Happy New Year! What's your name?"

Mechanically the big man shook hands with him. "You no Polish feller?" he asked.

"I have many good friends among the Polish race," Knox assured him still holding his hand and smiling at him warmly, "what did you say your name was?"

"Zets," the man replied. "Mike."

"A good Polish name," Knox told him, "good Polish name."

The man took his hand away. "Zets is Rooshan," he said sullenly. His sombre face was a little flushed.

"All the same to me," Knox assured him. "I'm not prejudiced. Here's a pair of glasses for you," he continued. He displayed them rapidly from all angles. "A man of your age has to be careful of his eyes. Try them!" he shoved them toward the Russian's nose.

Zets drew his head back. "No want glass's," he said.

"Only a quarter, friend. Save your eyes!"

The big Russian champed his teeth down hard on a piece of bread.

Knox shrugged expressively: "All right, friend, but I've studied the eyes for forty years. Great specialists consult with me. How about you, son?" He darted over to Luke Hall and broke into a jargon he had carefully memorized: "Your pupils are distorted showing eye strain and nervousness. Try 'em on. A quarter of a dollar."

Hall put them on. His gaunt face was illumined with excitement. The old man darted to his suitcase and hurried back with a handful of magazines.

"Here you are, son; take a look at these. The beneficial effect is immediate." He held one open.

Luke studied the print for a few moments. "Ah cain't see nothin' at all," he announced.

The old man laughed gayly. "The wrong pair, that's all, the wrong pair." He snatched the glasses off. "Now let me see—" He seized the boy by the overalls and peered closely into his eyes. Luke flushed in embarrassment and tried to back off.

"Ah yes—fifty-four-forty—slight relativity and pupils a little to the oblique side."

He hopped back to his cot. The limp in his short leg scarcely seemed
to interfere with his agility. He fussed through the suitcase like a
plump little tom-tit on the search for worms.

"Here you are, boy!"

Luke ignored the glasses. His eye had caught sight of the magazines.
"What's that?" he inquired curiously. He was fond of reading matter.

"*That?* Ahhhhhhhh!" The old man screwed up his face, shut both
eyes tight and stroked his beard. "That, m'boy, is a pamphlet—" —he
drew a deep breath—"a pamphlet explaining the great mystery of life—
love between the sexes! This one proves conclusively that love is caused
by vapors. I have others—intended for men only—little, spicy stories
full of humor and situation, illustrated by pictures of many different
kinds. Then—" —he added with emphasis—"then I have some religious
pamphlets!"

Three cots down the aisle Bill Benson raised his eyes from his game
of solitaire. His liquor bottle was half empty now and the mellowing
effect of the pint of rot gut in his belly showed on his face: the frown
was still there and the weary, acid mold had not altered but there was
a slight, grudging smile on his lips and a shimmer of interest in his
eye. He surveyed Knox with amusement.

The old man winked over at him in bawdy, senile suggestion. "Pictures of every kind," he repeated. "Ten cents."

"What's vapors?" Luke Hall asked.

"Vapors, my boy?" Knox put his hand paternally on Hall's shoulder.
"Vapors is what passes between man and woman."

Benson spit a mouthful of liquor over the floor. "Sounds like crabs
to me," he said snorting with laughter.

"Nothing of the sort, nothing of the sort," the old man sputtered.
He thrashed his arms like a flustered hen. "A vapor's like air. It's a
spark! Philosophical term is effluence! You look at a young girl, a
young girl looks at you, and a spark passes between."

Benson exploded with laughter. "What passes between?" he demanded. "What passes between?"

"A spark," the old man shouted. "A spark! It's a vapor!"

"If that's a spark I'm a Presbyterian minister," Benson laughed. He
leaned back weakly on his cot.

Knox howled and shook his fist. "I speak twelve languages and you're
a fool! You're an ignoramus! You don't even know who I am! Some
day you'll consider it a privilege to have known me." He pulled a little

notebook from his pocket and thumbed the pages rapidly. "I'm writing a book! A book of life! Containing the meaning of all religions, a little humor, philosophy, poetry. It'll be published in every language in the world, a million copies in each language and a hundred thousand free copies will be given away to my friends. You won't get one!!!" He turned to Luke Hall. "You'll get one! What's your address?"

Luke emerged from a day dream. "Have you got any writings on the Essenes?" he asked.

Knox clapped him on the shoulder. "My boy, I wrote fifteen books for fifteen years while I was a street car conductor in Brooklyn. They haven't been published yet but I'll give you copies."

"Ah'm grateful t' you," Luke said. "Ah like t' read. You know Ah've been studyin' about the Essenes. Have you got any pieces on them?"

Knox cocked his head reflectively and stuck a stubby finger in his nose. "Essenes . . . Essenes . . . one of the lost tribes of Judaea ——"

"Oh no," Luke corrected, "they was in the time of John the Baptist. They ——"

"Of course," said Knox interrupting, "John the Baptist—twenty-four B.C. ——"

"Oh no," Luke began ——

"I've been a student of the Bible for twenty years," Knox continued ——

"They believed that there should be no fornication between man and woman unless it was to begat children," Luke said softly, dreamily. "They said you had to conserve your strength so you could wear the armour of the Lord and do the good work."

"Very interesting," the old man exclaimed. "I know all about it!" He clapped Luke on the shoulder again. "My boy, I'm interested in you." He darted to his suitcase. "Here's a little book soon to be published in which I take down notes of interesting people as I go along. You'll get one."

"Ah'd like that," Luke replied shyly. "If Ah had books Ah'd read most all the time."

"I've visited every famous library in the world," Knox announced. "Known well in all of them."

"You know," Luke said dreamily, "since Ah've been converted Ah don't have t' go to whores so often. Ah used to go for them turrible, but Ah got converted to the Pentecostal a while back an' now Ah don't go to whores more'n two or three months at a time. Ah'm tryin' to' conserve mah strength."

"You'll have to visit me," Knox stated emphatically. "We'll study religion together. I've lived eighteen years in Cuba. You'll spend the winter with me. I have hundreds of famous people from all over the world come and visit me every year. I'm working my way down there now."

"Ah'd like t' see Cuba," Luke said smiling warmly at him.

"I'll be expecting you," the old man replied. "Ask for me anywhere."

"But Ah'm thinkin' of changin' from the Pentecostal to the Presbyterian," Luke confided. "The Pentecostals are too much for speakin' in the tongue. Ah don't think that's necessary. Ah don't see that in the Scriptures."

"Here's the Gospel by Paul," the old man said with a sudden return of business zeal. "Eight cents—marked down."

"Ah'll take the one on vapors," the boy replied. He fished down into his overalls for his purse. "Have you got any hymns?"

Benson heaved himself up and seesawed down the aisle. He was not quite steady on his feet. He buttonholed Knox with heavy joviality. "Hey, gran'pa, gimme a look at 'em."

"Which one do you want?"

Benson grabbed a magazine out of the old man's hand. "Not the hymns, hophead, I ain't a virgin." He flipped the pages and paused at the photograph of a girl who was lounging naked and seductive on a couch draped with a bearskin. His mouth split into a loose grin.

"Ten cents," Knox said.

Benson ignored him.

"Ten cents!" Knox repeated.

Benson grunted over the pictures making little, sensual smacks with his mouth and lips.

"Ten cents," the old man said, plucking at his sleeve.

"Some bettle!" Benson commented. "Ain't that somep'n, gran'pa? Some ham on it," he observed admiringly.

The old man hopped frantically from one foot to another. "Ten cents, please! Ten cents!"

Benson leaned down with a genial grin and blew into Knox's face. "Poppa, I'm not that kind of a girl an' besides I don't do it for ten cents."

The old man grabbed the magazine. "You can't look at it then. You can't —"

"Now listen," Benson said, "I ain't seen a goodlooking dame like this in a year. Let me look at it, will yuh? I ain't got ten cents."

"No sir," Knox said, "if you can't pay, you can't look."

"Jesus!" Benson shouted in sudden, flaming rage. "Jesus!" He tore the magazine from Knox's hand and flung it violently to the floor. "Jesus!" He strode away in a drunken fury.

Knox picked up the magazine and ran after him. "You can have it," he cried, "you can buy it. What do you want to pay?"

"Beat it," Benson ordered. He began shuffling his cards.

"Razor blades?" Knox offered pulling a package from his pocket. "Five for fifteen!"

Benson uncorked his bottle of liquor and tilted it to his mouth.

The old man watched him drink and his little, blue eyes commenced to shine greedily. He sidled over to him. "Slip me a drink of the lush, hey, boy?" he requested.

Benson jerked his head and sluiced a mouthful of liquor into the old man's face.

"Tit for tit," Benson said. "Have another!"

Halfway down the aisle, Zets, the hulking, sombre-faced Russian, sat up abruptly.

Knox wiped his face and limped away muttering. He looked like a hurt child wounded to the point of tears.

Benson regarded him with sour satisfaction. "Have another, pop," he called. "It's good for that bush on your face. Keeps it growin'."

Slowly Zets got up from his cot. He set his pipe carefully on the floor. Then he walked over to Benson. His heavy-featured, pockmarked face was dark. The angry blood was pumping in it, swelling thickly in the veins on his forehead. "What for you spit in ol' man face?" Zets asked. His deep, slow voice had a leaden feel to it.

Benson looked up in amazement. "For Chrissakes," he said.

The big laborer repeated the question coldly, slowly. "What for you spit at ol' man?"

"Well for Chrissakes!" Benson burst out angrily, "mind your own goddam business."

Zets spit in his face.

Benson jumped to his feet swinging his liquor bottle. Zets flung him back furiously and Benson toppled backward onto the bed. The

Russian stood over him with one huge fist, like a block of stone, poised in the air ready to smash down.

Benson lay inert.

Zets lowered his hand slowly. "You dirty sonambitch," he said and then, in a tone of disgust and incredulity, "spit at ol' man!"

He walked back to his cot and picked up his pipe again. He was finished. He had done what was right.

Old man Knox limped over to him. He shifted from leg to leg and finally pulled the pair of spectacles out of his pocket. "Go ahead," he offered, "take 'em."

Zets looked at him blankly.

"Free," the old man said. "Go ahead!"

"Never min'," Zets replied. He reached under the pillow for his towel and soap and turned down the aisle.

Knox ran back to his suitcase, snatched up a magazine and hopped after him. "Here," he offered, "something to read."

The Russian shook his head. "Never min'," he said. "You ol' man," he added seriously, "nobody spit at ol' men!" And nodding his head slightly by way of ending the matter he continued on his way to the washroom.

Knox looked after him. "Happy New Year," he called. He walked back to his place and stood thinking. His head was cocked at an angle and his red lips were pursed thoughtfully. Abruptly he plunged himself down on his cot, took out his notebook, searched energetically until he found a pencil and then began to write. He wrote busily. Occasionally he stopped to scratch his beard or frown heavily in an attitude of profound reflection. He was adding to his storehouse of "Interesting Events and Characters," a compendium of life and philosophy soon to be published in all the countries in the world, a million copies in each country.

The room was quiet. Luke Hall sat absorbed in the pamphlet on vapors. A nervous finger picked absently at the dried cut on his chin and one bare foot slowly massaged the other. Benson lay motionless, snoring. Both hands were fastened around his liquor bottle in an unconscious, vise-like grip. And off to one side O'Shaughnessy slept fitfully. His slow, thick breathing was like a sigh in the room.

From outside there came the caterwaul of taxis and the occasional pound and rumble of the elevated trains heavy with holiday traffic.

And now and then from off the East River there was the deep bay of a fog horn like a hound dog far away on a scent.

Ten P.M.

IT SEEMED to O'Shaughnessy that if he could only throw back the blankets, he'd feel much better. Hot. He was hot. On a summer's day it was crazy to make him lie there with so many blankets on top of him so hot.

When I get a job, momma, it'll be different.

It was obvious that the blankets were tied there with safety pins or a strong rope that went to both sides of the bed.

"Momma, Momma, Momma," the sick boy cried. But she didn't ever hear him. Never! I guess she's down at the stand. But on New Year's Eve it was foolish to have the stand open.

Oh God, it's so hot, momma. If I can only push them all the way down to my feet, I'll feel better: I'll be able to sleep then.

And he was so thirsty.

If he could get the blankets down off his feet, then he could get up. But if things ever picked up, then he'd have a chance. A tool and die maker—they need them. Poor momma, you've been workin' like a truck horse. Let it go tonight. Let's go to a movie and a burlesque Burlesque tonight.

There was a spider as big as a cat sitting on his stomach. It had its claws in his flesh. Each claw was poisoned, and sent a pain through him. Right there!

And he was so thirsty from the hot blankets.

THE FIRST thing Blessy saw when he came into the room was the little knot of curious men gathered at the foot of O'Shaughnessy's cot. It gave him a shock that was apprehension and anger mingled together and he ran forward shouting: "What's the matter? What the hell's goin' on here?"

Zets shook his head soberly and wiped his face with a yellow scrap of towel. "This feller pretty damn sick maybe. He yell!"

"He's got ptomaine," Luke Hall announced, and then, in a murmur to himself, "it's catchin', ah reckon."

"Jimmie," Blessy said, "Jimmie."

O'Shaughnessy didn't reply but he stopped tossing. The whispered name seemed to calm him even in sleep. He lay quiet.

"You buddy wit' dis feller?" Zets inquired.

Blessy nodded. "When did he start yellin'?"

Luke Hall said, "Just now, Mista."

Zets bent down and wiped O'Shaughnessy's wet forehead with his scrap of towel. He showed the towel to Blessy. "Boy bad sick maybe. You give him bicarb? Bicarb good for belly."

"He don't need that," Blessy replied. He rubbed his forehead reflectively. A troubled frown creased his big, bony face. What the devil was wrong? Jimmie had been swell just that morning. He'd even gone out and shoveled snow for a few hours till he got tired. An' he was sure all cleaned out by now.

Old man Knox suddenly hopped at the big Russian like an agitated flea. He seized the towel. "Let me smell," he demanded. He pushed his little stump of a nose deep into the material. Astounded Zets pulled it away from him.

"That's ptomaine all right," Knox chirped. "I can tell. Comes from poisoned food."

"You crazy," Zets said.

"Don't be ignorant," Knox rebuked him loftily. "All diseases have their smell. You just have to be trained."

"You crazy!" the Russian repeated. "Keep still," he added harshly. "No wake boy up!" He turned to Blessy. Blessy grinned at him. "You want tow'l?"

"I got one," Blessy said.

Zets nodded. He went back to his cot. Methodically he folded the towel and set it in its proper place in the locker. He stretched out on his back and lit his corn cob pipe. He smoked and stared soberly at the ceiling.

Blessy began to undress. He needed a shower after the day's work and there wasn't much time before they turned the heat off. By God if there was anything colder than a flop house toilet in winter, Blessy had never seen it.

The youth tossed his lumber jacket on the bed and unbuttoned his shirt. Then he stopped and stared absorbedly at the boy in the bed. It was bad. There was something the matter. Jimmie had been sleeping all day and that was a good sign. But still—still, he just didn't look good. Worse than this morning.

O'Shaughnessy lay quiet. One knee was slightly raised under the faded, army blanket. There was no curve or roundness to his neck any more and the cords of his throat strained tight against the lined, waxy skin. His face was still wrapped in its ghastly pallor and the sunken cheeks and the sharp lines that bit into the taut flesh made him look pained even in sleep.

Now, in an instant of sudden clarity, the truth slashed through Blessy's mind like a blow from behind. O'Shaughnessy looked terrible— like a corpse. He might be really sick now. He might be bad off.

The youth groaned. What should he do? A doctor. He didn't have any cash on him. But maybe Dooky— Or take him to a hospital.

A hospital? Jesus Christ, he wasn't as sick as all that. You don't take guys to a hospital for just a bellyache.

The youth rumpled his hair with blunt, nervous fingers. He sat down on his cot and put his head in his hands. He had to get straight on it. Jimmie looked bad now but God—there were reasons. Even the drugstore man said he'd be knocked out for a while. No grub—all that castor oil—it'd make anybody weak.

The thing was to wait. When Jimmie waked up, then you could see. If he wasn't no better, sure, get him a doctor. There'd be two bucks comin' from somewhere even if he had to roll somebody.

Blessy stowed his lumber jacket in the locker. He felt better now. The thing was to wait and see.

A hand plucked diffidently at the youth's arm. He turned around. Old man Knox was standing behind him with a bottle of pills balanced in the palm of his hand.

"Young man," Knox said hastily, "I have a vast medical knowledge. I have something here—" he displayed it— "get rid of that ptomaine by morning."

Blessy grinned and shook his head.

"Nature's remedy," Knox advised. "Don't cost much."

"No!" Blessy reached for the chunk of kitchen soap in his locker.

"Why don't you give it a try?" the old man persisted plaintively. It'd be awful if he couldn't sell *anything* in a place like this. He could get a turkey dinner with stuffing for twenty-five cents tomorrow if he could make one more sale. "If it don't work, you don't have to pay me," he offered.

"No, listen, pop," Blessy explained patiently, "he's had about a quart of castor oil since Monday night. He don't need any more of that."

"But this is Wednesday," the old man argued.

Blessy burst out laughing. "What do you think he is, a gah-gah-goddam elephant?"

O'Shaughnessy groaned aloud and awakened. He threw back the covers on his bed and raised up on his elbow. Then he sank back on the pillow again. He looked around with glazed eyes.

Blessy ran over to him. "Hello, kid," he whispered. His tone was full of warmth and affection and the love he bore this comrade of his was written unashamedly on his hard, coarse-grained face.

For a moment O'Shaughnessy didn't reply. He was awake but his mind was still clouded by the sick nightmare he had been having. Then he recognized Blessy. He smiled. It was a tired, drowsy smile. The skin wrinkled back from his mouth and his teeth jutted out like the teeth of a cadaver making his young face look piteous and ugly.

"How do you feel?"

O'Shaughnessy drew a deep, tired breath. "I feel better, I think." His eyes dropped shut again. He muttered to himself.

"What did you say?"

"Water," O'Shaughnessy mumbled.

"Do you want some water?"

The sick boy opened his eyes. "No, I don't want any water."

Blessy was puzzled. "You *said* 'water'," he told him.

"Before. I wanted water before," the boy replied. His voice took on a weak, complaining tone: "I wanted water this afternoon but there was no one to give it to me."

"Gee, I was out shoveling, kid," Blessy apologized. "But I brought you a sandwich to eat. Do you feel like eating it?"

"I'm still kinda sick to my stomach," O'Shaughnessy answered. "Can't you eat it? We don't wanna ——"

"Stop worrying about money," Blessy ordered. "It's snowin' again. We're gonna have a coupla more days' work."

"I guess I shouldna shoveled this morning." O'Shaughnessy reflected drowsily. "But I felt better. I thought I was all cleaned out."

"Sure you are," Blessy said heartily. "But you're pooped that's all. That's why you need sleep."

"Sleep is nature's remedy," Knox interposed from the foot of the bed. "Sleep and vitamins." He looked over at Blessy to see if the comment had registered. He was still trying hard for his turkey dinner.

O'Shaughnessy moved one hand laboriously under the blanket. He was feeling for his belly. When he touched it, his face twisted in an expression of disappointment and despair. "Gee," he said, "my stomach's still puffed up the way it was. It hasn't gone down at all."

Blessy touched the blanket over the boy's middle. He wanted to say something to comfort the kid but he couldn't think what.

"That always goes with the ptomaine," Knox advised. "Dropsy's the same way. And elephantiasis. Elephantiasis too!" He looked over at Blessy significantly. "I have a whole medical library. Keep it in Cuba."

O'Shaughnessy tossed his head. "Aw," he said confidently, "I'm gonna feel all right in the morning. You wait an' see. That castor oil cleaned me out. I'm all right."

"Sure you are," Blessy agreed fervently. "Listen, kid," he promised, "tomorrow night you're gonna be over at Dooky's peelin' spuds ——"

"That's the trouble," O'Shaughnessy interrupted. "We peel spuds for him an' he don't feed us right. Gives us garbage." He squirmed restlessly, fretting. "He oughta feed us better, oughtn't he? He don't hafta pay us in cash."

"Now don't worry about that, kid."

"Did you go?" O'Shaughnessy asked suddenly.

"Where?"

"To the burlesque?"

Blessy laughed. "Forget it, kid. I wouldn't go without you. We're gonna go together . . . celebrate New Year's."

"When's New Year's?" the boy asked drowsily. "Ain't New Year's tonight?"

"No!" Blessy laughed. "New Year's is when—" he stopped talking. O'Shaughnessy had fallen asleep.

Old man Knox frowned. "I'm afraid," he began ——

"Sh!!" Blessy jerked his thumb for the old man to beat it.

Knox sniffed. He walked off with an offended air. "That man won't take my advice," Knox whispered loudly to Luke Hall. He looked pityingly at Blessy. "He's a fool!"

"Are you a doctor?" Luke inquired.

"Never practised," Knox replied briskly, "but I consult very often."

Blessy got up and tiptoed over to them. "Hey, for Chrissakes, shut up, will you?" he whispered. "I want him to sleep." He went back to the cot alongside of O'Shaughnessy. He took off his shoes and lay down on his stomach with his head pressed into the pillow.

Luke Hall rolled up one leg of his overalls. "Do you know what this bump is?" he asked Knox in a whisper.

Knox peered at it. He scratched his beard thoughtfully. "I never make a diagnosis without an x-ray," he replied, "but that type of symptom often indicates a serious tumor necessitating operation."

Luke laughed uncertainly. "Why shucks, Ah've had this all mah life," he protested. "Ah don't think it's more'n a birthmark."

Knox probed one nostril with a stubby forefinger and regarded Luke with disdain. "M'boy," he said, "there's many a dead man thought that." He turned away, ending the matter.

Luke stared after him. His brow was furrowed and his soft, brown eyes were suddenly anxious. It'd be turrible if he had to have an operation. Where would he go? And he wouldn't be able to work for a long time. What would his folks do? Luke sat down on his cot and stared gloomily at the bump on his leg.

A newcomer entered the room. He was a small, comic-looking man of about thirty-five. He wore dungarees and a sailor's pea-jacket. His head was massive, bulging and partially bald and he had a thin, sharp-featured, over-serious face. One eye was swollen and the injury gave his serious face a blinking, cock-eyed expression. He crossed the room quickly and went into the washroom. In another moment he returned with a wet handkerchief pressed to his eye. He found his cot and lay down on it. His name was Reynolds. He was a ship's cook out of a job.

Out on the street an automobile sputtered and then backfired loudly. Blessy started up out of his doze. He glanced over at O'Shaughnessy. The boy had not been awakened. Blessy lay down again.

Bill Benson, who had been lying inert from the moment the big Russian had flung him down in their quarrel, now pulled himself to his feet. He yawned, rubbed his eyes, took a drink. He had forgotten all about the incident. He looked around the room and then seesawed down the aisle into the toilet.

Blessy pushed his head deep into the pillow. He knew he ought to be taking his shower but he was too tired. He'd rest a little while first. He caught the strong oniony odor that came from his perspiration. In the mine it was different, you smelled like coal gas, you and your pit clothes and the house. But that was a good smell. An image of the girl on the street corner came back to him. It was almost gone now, her face was almost gone, but he could see the faint outline of her body, the white flesh and the little, warm nipples pressed hard against the dress. Blessy stirred. He felt a twinge of weary, lonely desire. God, what a different New Year's for a guy who had a job and a girl. God, you could go crazy year after year, year after year. It had to stop sometime. A man couldn't . . . all the time.

He fell asleep.

Ten Thirty P.M.

As BENSON came back from the toilet, a boy with a pack on his back came in through the open door. They met in the aisle.

The boy was no bigger than a lad of sixteen but his face could have belonged to a man of sixty. It was old, dead-white and cold.

Sharp lines like little scars ringed his thin, cruel mouth. Under his blue eyes there were grayish, baggy pockets. His shoulders were hunched and his head was shaven clean except for a stiff brush of straw hair at the front. He carried his head erect and on his lips there was a thin smile, self-assured, sneering.

He came in slowly, coughing, looking at the numbers on the cots, eyeing the men in the room. His eyes were knowing, distrustful; the slight smile was steady on his lips.

His name was Hunchy. On the box-car highway some called him "Coughy." He didn't care. He knew what he had to know. He knew how to take care of himself. He was seventeen years old by a week and three days and he knew how to get along. He had been learning since he was twelve. He didn't want any help. He wanted to be left alone.

As Hunchy came up the aisle, Benson hailed him with drunken joviality. "Hello, punk," he said, "where'd you blow in from?"

Hunchy stopped walking. "Don't you call me 'punk.' I ain't anybody's punk." His voice was slow and coldly venomous.

Benson laughed. "Okay, Hunchy, I ain't after you. I ain't no goddam wolf. Whenja blow in?" he asked. "You look like hell. You look like you been in the coop for six months."

The boy's thin lips twisted into a sneer. "Listen," he said slowly—"don't be such a friggin' pal. Go suck somebody else."

Benson stared at the boy with rising anger. "Well for Chrissakes," he burst out, "you're a snotty little pup, ain't you? I oughta fan your tail for you." He took a step forward.

Hunchy stood where he was. Leisurely he removed his right hand from his pocket. A knife blade snapped open. Benson leaped back.

The boy held the knife low down in front of him. The short, thick blade gleamed in the sharp light.

"Keep away from me," he said slowly.

"Well for Chrissakes," Benson exclaimed. "Why," he said surveying the boy, "you're what I'd call definitely *anti-social*." He stepped between two cots. *"You certainly are!"*

Hunchy held the knife loosely in his hand. He sauntered down the aisle looking for the number on his locker key. He found the place and sat down with the open knife blade resting snug at his side.

Benson shook his head, swigged a mouthful of liquor and teetered back to his bunk. He shuffled his cards and resumed his game of solitaire.

Old man Knox limped down the aisle. He planted himself a few feet away from Hunchy and coughed politely. Hunchy ignored him. He was busy peeling off his clothes. Every so often he coughed. At those times he would remain still, holding himself tight, while the cough racked up through his chest. Then he would spit and pause wearily for a moment before continuing to undress.

Hunchy's clothes were odds and ends, patched, worn. His overcoat had evidently belonged to a full-grown man and had been sliced off to bring it to size. The ends hung down now frayed and uneven. Beneath the overcoat he wore a thin sweater, then a layer of newspaper wrapped around his body and tied in place by twine, then another sweater. He stood finally in a dirty, white summer shirt from which his scraggy elbows protruded, and carefully folded up the newspaper. He would use it again the next day.

Old man Knox coughed politely for the second time. "Happy New Year!" he offered. He smiled warmly. "My name is Knox—Knox with an 'x' not 'knocks on the door.'" He chuckled with his round little belly rumbling with laughter.

Hunchy ignored him. He fished a paper bag out of his pack. There was half a cocoanut pie inside. He wielded his knife deftly cutting an enormous chunk.

The old man's eyes glittered. He watched the boy wolf the first mouthful. "Got some for me, kid?" he whispered. He glanced around cunningly to make sure no one else in the room had seen the pie.

Hunchy looked up coldly and crammed another slice into his mouth.

"Where'd you get it, eh?" Knox asked. "Lifted it, eh?—off a baker's truck! You're young," he said enviously. "Got t' be young t' do that."

Hunchy sighed. "Listen," he said, "you ain't gonna get any, so stop hangin' around."

"I'll trade you, sonny," the old man whispered. "Just gimme a little taste." He looked around hastily. "Some magazines! Got pictures in 'em! Young girls with nothin' on! Give you two!"

Hunchy paid no attention to him.

"Want some razor blades?" Knox asked. He pulled a little box out of his vest pocket. "You need this all right: 'Nature's laxative!' Always handy to keep around here. Here!"

The old man dropped the bottle on the cot and made a grab for the pie. With the speed of a young adder Hunchy struck out hard, rapping him on the knuckles with the flat blade of his knife. The old man retreated with a cry of pain and surprise.

"You make me tired," Hunchy said wearily. He flipped the bottle of pills to the floor.

The old man picked it up. "I wanted to trade, didn't I?" he complained.

Hunchy got up coughing. "For Chrissakes go away," he said angrily. "How can I eat with your stink around me?"

Zets turned around to see what was occurring. Luke Hall raised his head from his magazine.

"I don't stink, I don't stink," the old man cried. "You oughtn't to say that."

"Sure you stink," the boy snapped. "I'm smelling you, ain't I?" He took a step forward. "Get away from here!"

Knox retreated. "I don't stink, I don't stink," he wailed. He shook his fist. "You lousy bum, you dirty little—" Knox stopped! From O'Shaughnessy, the sick boy, there had come a sudden heart-rending, nightmare cry. It was shrill, frightened, incoherent, a cry of sick agony that paralyzed the room.

In an instant the quarrel was forgotten. Hunchy stood still, glued in his tracks, and for a moment his face was convulsed; for a moment it was the face of a wild thing caught in a snare. Old man Knox pawed at his throat and turned, trembling and sweaty, to look at O'Shaughnessy.

And all over the room men jumped up in a start of fear.

Eleven P.M.

WHEN MEN lose their sense of security, fear waits inside of them. To each man in the room O'Shaughnessy's cry of agony was the touchstone of his own fear; in that moment, fear coursed the room like a living thing, thrusting deep into each man there, turning the flesh clammy, gripping the heart and the nerve. And for a moment no one could be sure who had screamed—himself or another. Each man waited to find out, crouching, waiting to be told: "It was you: your time has come!"

Then it was gone. Now they stood clumped together watching the boy in the bed. They were safe now. For a time they were safe. It was someone else.

And O'Shaughnessy didn't know either. When he finally heard Blessy speak to him, when he saw his friend's anguished face and saw the men clumped together at the foot of his cot, he became aware that the scream had been his own, that it was not only in a dream. And then he knew that he was sitting up in bed and that Blessy's big hand was on his shoulder.

O'Shaughnessy groaned and fell back on his cot: his stomach was on fire.

The nightmare was gone. O'Shaughnessy could scarcely remember it but it had left its sick feel with him. He had wanted something—and he had lost it. He had wanted something with such terrible, concentrated need—and someone had wrenched it from his hands. And at the moment of loss a hot, sharp needle had been thrust deep into his flesh and somewhere far off a voice had screamed.

And now, as he lay still on the narrow cot with that burning fire in his belly, he thought of his life, the loss and the waste of his life, and slowly his head turned on the pillow and the weak, salt tears trickled out of the corners of his eyes. The pain and the struggle, the long, bitter years of pain and struggle—useless! His mother had tended the paper stand, she had been up at six and never had been back till one; she had given pennies for candles and never once accepted the wafer with false heart—useless! All their hopes, the years of effort—to no good! None! And now he was lying in a flop house and the pains had started again and he must be bad sick now and his mother wouldn't

be there to help him because he was far away and she was dead. And
he lay weeping.

"IT'S ALL RIGHT, Hal," O'Shaughnessy said. A few minutes had passed
and he had become quiet. "I had a pain, that's all."

Blessy drew a deep breath of relief. "You got no business with
pains," he told the boy in an awkward attempt at humor. "You're all
through with pains."

O'Shaughnessy didn't reply.

Sam Reynolds, the little ship's cook with the swollen eye, inquired
softly what the matter was. Luke Hall answered him. Old man Knox
scratched his belly and explained the matter loudly: "It's the toxins.
They pass through the corpuscles and stop the circulation."

"Ptomaine?" Reynolds echoed softly. His Adam's apple jiggled
sharply as he spoke giving him a comic quality. "Ptomaine?" he said
again. He looked into the face of each man there. His glance was hot
with challenge. He seemed to be questioning, probing their thoughts.
"Well," he said finally, "it's fine, ain't it? Fine!" He paused. When he
spoke again his voice was soft but fiercely, tremulously passionate. "I'm
a ship's cook," he said. "*I* know what gives men ptomaine. I've dished
out swill myself." The little man choked with repressed fury. He
rubbed his mouth with a red, calloused hand that seemed strangely
big for his thin wrist and arm. His deadly serious face, his bald, hen's-
egg head were comic to look at. "Ain't God's food clean?" he burst out.
"Ain't it?" He fixed his gaze on Zets. The big Russian looked back at
him soberly. "No, I guess it ain't," Reynolds answered himself bitterly.
"I guess it damn well ain't. Not for us!"

O'Shaughnessy groaned and pressed his hand to his swollen belly.

"What's the matter?" Blessy leaned down over him.

"I got another pain," O'Shaughnessy said with a sigh.

"Like Monday?"

"No," the boy said, "it's worse now."

"For Godssakes!" Blessy wiped the boy's brow with a towel. "I don't
understand it, kid. You're sure all cleaned out."

"It's all right," O'Shaughnessy said. Then suddenly he groaned
again. The blood drained out of his face and he ground his teeth
together. The sweat was pouring out on his forehead.

"Jimmie, Jimmie," Blessy cried. He grasped the boy's hand feverishly. He wanted to help him. His mind was racing wildly trying to think of something to do. It was terrible. It was terrible to watch him. Jimmie was just a kid. It shouldn't happen to a kid like that.

The attack passed. O'Shaughnessy closed his eyes and rested back on the pillow. His breath was like a deep sigh in the room.

Reynolds cupped a hand over his injured eye and peered at O'Shaughnessy. "This boy had a doctor?" he asked. "Looks to me like he needs one."

"*I* can treat him," Knox said. "I've got some pills here. Special!"

"Shut up!" Zets ordered harshly.

"I don't want a doctor," O'Shaughnessy told them. "It's a waste of money."

"Jesus, kid," Blessy begged, "forget about the money, will you? We'll get it."

"We can take up a collection," Reynolds suggested. "We can go through all the rooms."

Hunchy, who had been standing off by himself, spoke out abruptly. "You'd better get an ambulance!" His voice was cold, matter-of-fact.

"What for?" Blessy demanded. The suggestion frightened him. "It's just some cramps. He don't ——"

"Get an ambulance," Hunchy repeated.

O'Shaughnessy opened his eyes. "No," he said. His voice trembled. "I don't want no hospital."

"Get out of here," Blessy said to Hunchy. "Shut your face. Beat it."

"Okay!" Hunchy sneered and walked away. He got into bed, coughing. He turned his back to the others.

"Hal," O'Shaughnessy pleaded, "I don't wanna go to a hospital. I'm afraid of them."

"Don't worry, kid," Blessy assured him. "You'll stay right here. I'll crack that little bastard in two," he muttered to himself.

O'Shaughnessy raised his head. "You know what they do?" he said. "They give you the Black Bottle. When you're a charity patient and can't pay, the nurses give you the Black Bottle. They gave it to Mary Croggins when I was a kid."

"That's *right*," Luke Hall offered. "Ah heard that too."

"Lay down, kid," Blessy pleaded, "you don't wanna get excited."

"There's more ways'n one a *poor* man gets screwed," Reynolds said softly. "A poor man gets screwed every day in every way. There's only one thing protects him—" he paused and looked from one to the other, blinking his swollen eye, "organ-eye-zation." He spoke the word with difficulty but with a strange flavor, with a sense of love, like a lonely man speaking of a woman. "Organ-eye-zation"—he repeated it—and he raised his head in a gesture of pride and dignity. He looked from one man to another, searching for their response.

The others were silent.

O'Shaughnessy stiffened. His pains were commencing again. He murmured something and then suddenly pushed himself up in bed. A frantic, bitter cry burst from his lips. "Ain't we tried to get along?" he cried. "Ain't we been tryin' to get work?" He clutched at Blessy's arm. "Peelin' spuds—hustlin' the white sheets. Goddamit, we tried, we tried, didn't we?" He was choked with sobs.

Blessy pushed him back. "For Godssakes, Jimmie," he said, "you gotta lay down. You gotta keep quiet."

The boy fell back. The sense of loss that had been present in the dream swept over him again. What was their life anyway? No place to sleep—no job—couldn't have a girl. They ought to have a right to *something*, he cried to himself. Didn't they have a right to *anything*?

O'Shaughnessy's anguished body writhed under the blanket. "Hal, Hal," he cried, "it hurts me, it's hurting again."

Blessy jumped to his feet. "I'm gonna geh-geh-get you a doctor." He stammered with excitement. His big, hard face looked tortured with pity.

"No," O'Shaughnessy said. "No doctor." He was suddenly delirious. "Toilet. Gotta go toilet." He sat up in bed and tried to lift his feet from under the blanket. His eyeballs were glazed and his glance was the glance of a blind man.

"Wait a minute," Blessy cried. "*Jesus Christ!*" He lifted O'Shaughnessy from the cot.

O'Shaughnessy stepped down. His heavy, woolen underwear was unbuttoned leaving his belly exposed. It looked enormous against his thin body. "Toilet," he mumbled.

"Let's carry him for Godssakes," Reynolds said agitatedly. "He can't walk!"

"Can you wah-wah-walk?" Blessy asked O'Shaughnessy. "Wah-wah ——"

O'Shaughnessy started to answer. There was a loud, gagging noise in his throat. His legs buckled under him. He pitched forward.

Blessy grunted and caught him. O'Shaughnessy was bent double. His body hung grotesquely over Blessy's arm like a misshapen sack of meal.

"Jimmie," Blessy cried in a sudden, stricken tone. "Jimmie!"

O'Shaughnessy didn't answer.

Reynolds ran over and lifted the boy's legs off the floor. "Take 'm t' bed," he ordered.

Blessy didn't move. He stood panting, looking down at the body in his arms. His face was stupid, stricken.

"C'mon, feller," Reynolds said. "What's the matter with you? *For Godssakes!*"

An inarticulate, little cry burst from Blessy's lips. He came to himself. They carried O'Shaughnessy to the cot. "I'll call an ambulance," Reynolds said. He ran out of the room with one hand cupped over his swollen eye.

O'Shaughnessy's head lolled to one side. His eyes were half open. His breathing was slow, tortured. With each breath his chest heaved and his mouth sucked hard for air. When he exhaled, there was a hard, cruel rasp in his throat like phlegm rattling. Then he was silent for a long time. Finally he would breathe again, his chest heaving, his open mouth sucking for air, his lips drawn back from his teeth in a snarl.

Zets bent over, slipped his hand under the covers and felt for the boy's heart. Blessy stared at him with the same stricken look on his face. The big Russian took his hand away and stood up.

"You feel sah-sah-somethin', don't you?" Blessy whispered.

"Maybe get hot wat'r bottle!"

"He's not *d-dead*!" Blessy burst out in frantic, unreasoning anger. "He's *breathin'*! Can't you feel him breathin'?"

"No, no boy; he no dead," the big laborer said reassuringly. "Just hot wat'r bottle *good.*"

Old man Knox tugged at his wing collar. "Not for this, not for this," he put in excitedly. "An ice bag!"

Reynolds ran back into the room with a red-knuckled hand still cupped over his eye. "The ambulance is comin'," he said. "How is he?"

The men looked at O'Shaughnessy. He was deathly still, not breathing. His young face was a muddy gray, the skin drawn tight over the bones with a thousand, fine wrinkles to it.

"Is he daid?" Luke asked.

"What's the matter with you?" Blessy cried turning on him. "What do you mean, dead? He's br-br-breathin', ain't he? Ain't his eyes open?"

"He ain't breathin'," Luke said.

"He's breathin', he's breathin'," Blessy shouted. "Shut your goddam face."

Baldy came running in. "The ambulance'll be here right away. How is he?"

No one answered.

O'Shaughnessy's chest heaved and he sucked for air. The ugly rattle sounded in his throat.

"Jesus!" Baldy exclaimed, "he looks like an old man." He rubbed one hand over his bald dome. "I'll be goddamned!"

The men were silent.

Hunchy got out of bed and walked slowly down the aisle.

"Have you got an ice bag?" Knox asked. "That would fix him up."

"You crazy!" Zets said. "Hot wat'r bottle."

"I ain't got nothin' here at all," Baldy replied.

Hunchy spit between his teeth. "I told you," he said. "An ambulance won't do no good now." He spit again and went back to his cot.

"I'll wait in the office," Baldy said. He walked down the aisle. He spied Charlie, the bum, lying asleep on the floor and jiggled him with his foot. Charlie snored with quiet unconcern.

"Hey, Arkansas," Baldy called to Luke Hall, "commere—help me a minute."

They lifted Charlie onto his cot.

"There's always a cop comes in with the ambulance," Baldy explained. "Nobody ain't supposed to sleep on the floor."

"Do—do lots of people die in this heah hotel?" Luke inquired timidly. It was a bad omen to be near death this way. Luke wouldn't have come here if he had known all this was going to happen.

"They do an' they don't," Baldy replied angrily. "What do you expect?" He turned on his heel and stalked brusquely from the room. Luke remained where he was in an attitude of gloomy foreboding.

"Kid take long time for breathe, hey?" Zets said to Blessy.

Blessy nodded nervously. "Ain't it time for the ambulance?"

"They said ten minutes," Reynolds told him. "Don't worry," he added, "they come quick." He blinked sympathetically at Blessy with his good eye. He started to speak, then stopped and muttered to himself. He wanted to say something to take the big fellow's mind off his friend but he couldn't think what. Jesus God— "organ-eye-zation," Reynolds muttered to himself. His Adam's apple twitched in his stringy neck. Then "he'll be all right," he said aloud. He raised his hand as though to pat Blessy but dropped it to his side.

O'Shaughnessy's mouth opened. He sucked for air with a dry, harsh rattle sounding long and thick in his throat. He lay still again with the bright light cruel on his muddy face.

"Goddamit, why d-d-didn't I get a doctor earlier?" Blessy burst out bitterly. "Such a gah-goddam fool. But he was all right this morning," he said turning to the others in pleading and explanation. "He was shoveling snow this morning."

"I think he's dead," Knox stated abruptly.

"Shut up!" Blessy said.

"That was a death rattle," Knox persisted.

"You're crazy," Blessy shouted furiously. "He's been breathin' like that right along. His eyes are open, aren't they?"

They waited! They were half a dozen men in a flop house waiting to see if James O'Shaughnessy, a blond lad from Pittsburgh, who was a good Catholic and a good tool and die maker, would breathe again. And within each man there was a secret fear that waited in company with him. Within each man there was the fear that came in the still pause of the night when he lay on his cot alone and wondered when *his* turn would come, and how, how!—pushing it off, next week, next year, the man alongside, not me, please, not me, not that way, not my number yet! And to each man the young, blond boy with the muddy face was himself.

And then Benson said it; into the silence at the foot of the bed his tongue, thick with drink, blurted out the word "me." "Me," he said, "that's me!" He swayed drunkenly, Bill Benson, a seamed, ugly man of fifty, and his voice rose in a strange mournful cry of bitterness and defeat: "I'm the best goddam harvester mechanic in the whole United States," he cried. "I've got a pair of hands can handle machinery like a goddam, newborn baby. But they turned me into a bum," he cried. "An' I let 'em. *I* let 'em!" He stood swaying. His mouth hung open in helpless anguish.

No one spoke to him. Reynolds cupped his hand over his swollen eye and muttered to himself.

"Pray for me, Jesus," Benson suddenly cried. He lurched forward and struck Luke Hall on the shoulder with his clenched fist. "Pray for the Lord inside Benson! Look at me, Jesus. The Lord's inside me, inside you, inside each and every back house in the world."

He stumbled blindly, drunkenly from the room.

There was a moment of silence.

Then Luke spoke up fervently. "That man's lost," he said. "You look to Jesus, Jesus helps you. Ah don't know what Ah'd do without Jesus. When a man's hungry or lyin' out in the rain, he's got t' do *somethin'*." Luke's voice trembled. "Ah'd hold up somebody, or rob a bank, if Jesus wasn't there to stop me. It's Jesus keeps me safe."

"It's Jesus keeps you weak," Reynolds burst out fiercely, "keeps you down, keeps you from fightin' back—talkin' pie in the sky while you got wind in your belly. My God, when ——"

Blessy swung around angrily. "Shut up, you guys. Can't you keep quiet a minute?" He turned back to O'Shaughnessy and resumed his fixed stare at the still form.

"There's too much keepin' quiet," Reynolds muttered in a low voice. "That's the trouble." His Adam's apple twitched in his throat.

There was silence. They waited.

Eleven Twenty P.M.

BALDY WHITE came in calling "This way, here!" A bulky, middle-aged cop followed him in. He had his nightstick clamped snug and ready under his arm. "Somebody get knifed?" he asked.

"No," Blessy cried. He ran past the cop to a young interne standing in the doorway. "Over here, doctor. There's a sick kid here. He's very s-s-s-sick."

The interne followed him in, walking quickly. He was a young man, small, with warm, dark, Jewish features.

Blessy ran to the cot. "Look out now," he said, "leh-leh-let him through. He's a doctor."

"C'mon," the cop bawled, crowding the men, "out of the way."

The interne bent over swiftly and felt for O'Shaughnessy's pulse. He paused; his eyes were intent on the boy's face. Then he dropped the hand and reached into his bag. He cast a quick, sharp, inquiring glance at Blessy.

"He's not d-d-dead, is he?" Blessy whispered.

The interne was silent. He pulled down the covers and put the stethoscope to the boy's chest.

"I'll bet he *is* dead," Knox remarked loudly.

"Shut up!" the cop bawled.

Blessy watched. His shoulders were hunched and his big, bony face was agonized.

The interne removed the stethoscope from his ears and pulled the covers down, exposing the swollen belly. His mouth twitched a little.

"Is he dead?" Blessy asked.

The interne nodded. He stood up with a slight sigh.

"Can't you do nothin'?"

"No!"

"I read in the papers—there's an injection in the heart—" Blessy pleaded feverishly.

The interne shook his head. "Not for this. He'd die all over again. It's been hopeless for the last twenty-four hours. Before that it would've been easy."

"*T-t-twenty-four hours?* But he was b-b-better *last night!*" Blessy cried. "He was better all day! *Jesus Christ* he was all right till just now."

"I know," the interne said. "That's the way it acts—but he's dead now," he added gently.

Blessy turned away. Tears welled into his eyes and streaked down his big, hard face.

The interne pulled the covers up over O'Shaughnessy, hiding the body from view. He began writing his report.

The cop took out his notebook and thumbed the pages. "Death on arrival, hey, Doc?" he asked.

The interne nodded.

"Wasn't I right?" Knox inquired loudly. "I have forty-five years of medical experience."

The interne looked up with a startled glance.

"Great specialists consult me," Knox told him.

"Shut up, you," the cop bawled.

The interne nodded at the old man and returned to his report.

"You'll leave him here for the morgue wagon, huh, Doc?" Baldy said.

"Yes."

"I sure hope it don't take as long as usual," Baldy said mournfully. "This is a big night for me. I can fill up every room. But not with him here. It'll all go down the street."

The interne shrugged.

Baldy went out with a heart full of bitterness. It was a hell of a break to get. It always had to come on a night like this.

The interne touched Blessy's arm. "What was his name?"

"James O'Shaughnessy," Blessy said. His voice was hoarse.

"Irish, huh?" the cop observed. "How old?"

"Twenty-one, I guess," Blessy replied. His head was turned away.

"Where's his home?"

"He didn't have any."

"Parents both dead?" the cop asked.

"His mother is," Blessy replied. "The ol' man's on the bum somewhere."

"Occupation?"

"Tool an' die maker," Blessy said. "But he didn't have a job."

Sam Reynolds edged over to the interne and tapped his report. "He had a job," he remarked. He blinked his swollen eye. "Tryin' t' keep alive. That's a big trade nowadays."

The cop chuckled. "Guess that's true enough. Make it unemployed, Doc."

The interne stopped writing. "It's too bad," he said gently to Blessy. "If the boy had had medical attention soon enough, he wouldn't have died."

"That's fine," Blessy answered.

"Where was he born?" the cop inquired.

"Oh, what the Jesus difference does it make?" Blessy said irritatedly.

The cop shrugged and jotted down a memorandum. "Cause of death?" he asked the interne.

"He didn't have a job," Reynolds said.

"The devil with that," the cop replied. "What did he die from?" he asked the interne again.

"He died from not having a job," Reynolds burst out savagely. "He died 'cause he couldn't eat right an' he couldn't live right an' 'cause he didn't have sense enough to fight. An' that's the truth!"

"Oh, so you're one of *those?*" The cop observed contemptuously. "Now you just keep your mouth shut till we fill out these records, or I'll shut it for you good."

Reynolds spit on the floor. "I'll talk till I'm blue in the face," he announced flatly, "an' you or nobody else won't stop me. There's one fink hit me already tonight so you can try the other eye."

The cop stepped forward. The young interne put his hand out. "Ruptured appendix," he said pointedly.

The cop stopped. "Appendix, eh?" He made the memorandum. "I figured it was ulcers, Doc. Lots of 'em go by ulcers."

"That was no cause," Reynolds muttered savagely. "That was a result."

The interne looked up. He smiled. "The medical professors wouldn't know what you were talking about," he said.

"Then they're goddam dumb," the little man replied.

"I wouldn't say you were wrong," the interne answered. He patted Blessy on the arm and walked down the aisle. "Good night, Lehane," he called back to the cop. He went out.

Under the flesh of Blessy's cheek a nerve quivered, beating a tattoo against the skin. His eyes were dry now, the tears on his face were dry, his look was stony. He sat on his cot and stared at the floor without moving.

The cop put his notebook away and opened the dead boy's locker. He examined the contents.

Zets walked over to Blessy. His pockmarked, peasant face was sombre with pity. "No feel bad, boy," he said. He sighed. "Goddam life no good." He shook his head. "For poor men no good."

"Say, buddy," the cop called to Blessy, "if you're this kid's pal, you can take this stuff."

"I don't want it," Blessy said.

Knox scurried over to the locker. "I'll take 'em," he cried. He reached inside.

The cop shoved him back. "Wait a minute. What's the matter with you?"

"It'll just go to waste," Knox cried petulantly. "What do you want to waste it for?"

"Take your time," the cop barked. "You old stinkpot," he added humorously, "you're a goddam gravedigger."

Luke Hall approached Blessy hesitatingly. He wasn't quite sure how to begin. "Mista," he said finally, "Ah'm a God fearin' man all right—" he paused—"but Ah ain't got no overcoat an' if your buddy had an overcoat an' if you ain't gonna dispose of it—Ah sure could use it awful well."

Blessy kept his eyes fixed on the floor. "Go ahead. Take what you want."

"Thank you, friend," Luke replied softly.

"Awright, you goddam ghouls, fight over it," the cop told them. He stepped aside and chuckled out loud.

Knox leaped to the locker and began feverishly sorting over the contents.

"Ah can have the overcoat," Luke cried rushing over, "the overcoat's for me."

"Jesus," the cop laughed, "it's like the war. A guy'd kick off an' then they'd strip him. . . . Well," he announced, stretching himself and yawning, "I ain't got anything to do now till the morgue wagon comes an' that's liable t' take an hour or two. If you boys'll keep an eye on him, I can go out an' get a beer." He sauntered down the aisle. "Don't let him run away," he added jovially. He went out.

Hunchy got out of bed. "Cops stink!" he observed loudly in his cold, metallic voice. "If everybody in the world turned to Jesus Christ over night—cops'd still stink."

Hunchy walked down the aisle until he came to O'Shaughnessy's cot. He looked down at the rigid form hidden beneath the blanket. He commenced to laugh softly. "Well," he said, "he's dead! He's dead an' they'll take him down to the morgue an' make out a little slip for him. Then they'll pump the blood out of him an' when he's all pickled proper, they'll hang him up on a hook that'll hold him nice an' steady right through the ear."

Blessy sprang to his feet. His face was sick with pain and rage.

"An' it'll be the happiest day of his life," Hunchy finished bitterly. "Hallelujah!"

"You shut your face," Blessy cried, choked.

"Hallelujah!" Hunchy repeated. He went back to his cot and crawled under the covers. Then he buried his old man's face deep into the pillow.

BLESSY SAT crouched over. Hunchy's remark festered in his brain, stabbing his mind like a delicate, poisoned needle. He thought of O'Shaughnessy—his friend—the kid he had stuck to for over a year now. Dead! Hanging on the wall by a hook through his ear. Dead! "Oh God, Oh God Jesus," Blessy cried to himself in mute agony, "Oh my God Jesus."

Blessy had been a miner. Death was no stranger to the routine of an eight hour mine shift. He had seen men crushed by a fall of rock; he had seen death on a picket line; he had in his eye the image of his stoop-shouldered uncle caught between a slate car and a wall—crushed bloody like a soft bug between pincers.

It was not just death. No, Blessy knew that. What was it then? It seemed important to know and the youth's mind groped painfully for the answer.

He was not a thinking man, this Blessy, this huge, rock-faced miner's boy, brought up in a coal camp, learning what life was in a shack by a smoking coal dump, going into the mine at fourteen. He had never formulated his views on life, or wanted to particularly. He had never done more than grow up, and work, and now, more lately, try to keep alive.

But this was different. It required thought. It was not just the death, the dying. . . .

Yes! It was clear now. The waste! It was the waste! Yes, Jesus God, the useless, crazy waste! Good coal on a slate dump. Jimmie O'Shaughnessy junked for nothing. Good for so much and now he'd hang by a hook through his ear—for what?

"God," Blessy cried aloud and he didn't know he had spoken.

Zets walked over to him. "No cry, boy," he said. "No good cry."

Blessy heard the soft, deep tone. No, he thought, he wasn't going to cry. What for? What the Jesus for? You cry an' they get you down. He wasn't gonna lay down. You lay down an' they step on you. They turn you into a bum.

A bum! God Almighty was that what he was gonna become? A bum like Benson? A blind, scratching, panhandling stew bum? No! Jesus Christ, no! Not him. Not in a million years. He'd turn the whole goddam world upside down! He'd tear it to pieces first!

The youth jumped to his feet. The long, bitter years were flaming blindly within him. He felt choked. In one moment he had become on fire with a thousand days and nights . . . the cold and the loneliness, the horror, the unspeakable indignity. And there flamed up in him a blind, unreasoning, overwhelming need to strike out, *now, now, at this moment, now!*

He screamed! It was like the cry of a hurt beast. He seized a cot and flung it over. He grabbed a shoe out of Knox's arms and smashed an electric bulb. He flung the shoe violently at the wall. *"Not me,"* he yelled, *"they don't make no bum outa me. Not me! Not me!"*

He raged through the room smashing everything he could get his hands on, tearing at the bedclothes, flinging down the lockers. His big, bony face was flaming, his mouth was open, his hair was like a wild crown on his head.

The others stood speechless, backing off before him, frightened by this stricken, inchoate fury.

Baldy, the night man, ran shouting into the room. "What the hell's goin' on here?" he demanded. He grabbed Blessy by both arms. "Stop it, you son of a bitch! You gone crazy?" He shook him violently.

Blessy became still. The change was abrupt. He stood limp, his body spent. His hands were trembling and his face was haggard from rage and pain.

"For Godssakes, boy," Baldy said, stepping away from him, "you gone loony? What's the matter with you? What you tryin' to do?"

Blessy didn't answer. He stood hunched over, breathing heavily.

Reynolds walked over to him and put a hand on his arm. "I know what you want to do," the little man said softly, "but you don't know how to do it. Not the walls! You don't wanna fight the walls!"

"I'm a son of a bitch," Baldy observed, "I'm runnin' a nut house." He rubbed his hand over his bald dome. "You gotta pay me for everything you spoiled, Blessy, you hear?"

Blessy went to his cot. He picked up his cap and lumber jacket. Baldy caught hold of him. "Where you goin'?"

"It's all right," Blessy told him. "I ain't runnin' out. I ain't r-r-runnin' out on anything!"

"I'll see you tomorrow," Reynolds said.

Blessy shrugged his shoulders and went out.

"He'll learn," Reynolds said softly. "He's got good stuff in him, that boy. He'll learn."

"You too, eh?" Baldy observed. "You're crazy too?"

"Go ahead an' laugh," Reynolds told him. "You get hit hard enough, you'll find out too."

"Me an' Morgan," Baldy said. He yawned. . . . "Listen, you stiffs, I'm gonna turn out the lights. . . . Happy New Year an' for Godssakes nobody else kick off tonight."

"Do we have t'sleep with him in here?" Luke asked pointing to the body.

"Well, I can't keep him in the office with me, can I?"

"Ah sure don't like him in heah," Luke said.

"Too bad about you," Baldy told him. "Go to sleep. They'll pick him up in an hour anyway. Hey!"—Baldy noticed the mackinaw on Luke's arm. "Where'd you get that coat?"

"It was given to me."

"O'Shaughnessy's, isn't it?" Baldy demanded.

"Ah reckon so. What about it?"

Baldy grabbed it. "He owes me for a week's rent. This stays with me."

"You can't take it away from me," Luke protested fiercely. "*He* gave it to me. That man."

"Let go of it— For Chrissakes I'll run you in for stealing."

Luke's hands dropped to his sides. "That ain't fair," he said.

Baldy grinned. "Happy New Year, Texas." He went out.

Zets suddenly spit on the floor. "Whole goddam world no good," he said.

Reynolds laughed softly. He cupped a red-knuckled hand over his swollen eye and blinked happily at the big Russian. "That's the first lesson," he said. "That's where I began too. The second's to know why. Do you know why?"

Zets looked at him soberly.

Reynolds laughed and pointed to his swollen eye. "Look at this," he said. "A subway guard socked me for sellin' a newspaper, a *working-man's* newspaper. You know why?"

Zets regarded him blankly.

"C'mon," Reynolds said. He took Zets by the arm.

"Where you go?" the big laborer asked.

"C'mon in the toilet," Reynolds said. "I wanna talk to you." He led him by the arm. "There's more'n one thing you can do in a toilet," he added happily. He cupped a hand over his eye and laughed.

They went inside.

The lights switched out.

Luke Hall approached old man Knox. "Do you mind if ah sleep by you?" he inquired timidly. "It's New Year's Eve an' ah'd sure like some company."

"Certainly, certainly," the old man replied politely. His voice dropped to a whisper. "I'm sure glad that man didn't see these shoes." He had the dead boy's shoes clasped tightly, one under each arm.

"Ah'm goin' t' sure miss that overcoat," Luke said mournfully.

"You know something?" the old man exclaimed with a sense of discovery in his voice. "I've had a hard life! Yes sir! It's New Year's Eve an' I can say it: I've had the life of a dog!" He smoothed his beard. "Now I always wanted to be a doctor," he reflected, "but somehow I couldn't ever get the schooling. First I was on a farm with my folks but they couldn't send me. Then I was a street car conductor in Brooklyn but that didn't seem to pay either. Nothing ever seemed to pay." He paused. "I guess it's just too late now," he finished sadly.

"Ah wish Ah could get rich," Luke joined in, "but Ah nevah get anythin' that pays enough either."

"Yes," Knox observed, "come to think of it, you might say God has been hard on *all* of us in here. Now personally I feel I had the makings of a successful man in me, but somehow I never could get ahead. The harder I worked—the less I got. Still—I'm trying. Maybe I'll succeed yet."

"Ah'd like to tie up with a big business in Wall Street," Luke said. "Ah understand *that's* the way t'do it."

The old man rubbed his eyes with both knuckles, like a sleepy child. "I'm all tuckered out," he complained. He crawled into bed. He put the dead boy's shoes under his pillow. "I don't even trust the locker with these," he said—"not good shoes like these." His head touched the pillow. He fell asleep.

Luke moved his things to the cot beside Knox. He took off his overalls and lay down. It felt good to have the blanket tucked up around his chin.

The room was quiet and dark. The street noises from the Bowery drifted in.

Luke turned to the old man. "Do you want to sing a hymn with me?" he asked. "Ah feel lonely. Ah wanted to celebrate New Year's."

Knox didn't reply.

"Are you asleep, friend?"

The old man snored.

Ah'd like to have sung some hymns at least, Luke thought sorrowfully. It's New Year's Eve. We always used t' do that.

He sniffed a little and turned over. That good dinner would just be starting upstairs now. And he was hungry. He wondered how it was at home. Maybe his folks were hungry too.

He was quiet for a few minutes. Then, softly, he began to sing to himself. He sang in a whisper:

> "Count your blessings,
> Name them one by one ——"

He paused; then went on—

> "Name them over
> See what God hath done;
> Count your many blessings,
> Name them one by one—
> Count your many blessings,
> See what God hath done!"

"That's a good hymn," he remarked to himself.

But what if he didn't find a job?

A sob rose up in his chest. He pushed his face into the pillow and wept quietly.

"Oh Jesus God," he prayed, "Ah need a job bad. You got to give me one before Ah die like that poor man heah tonight. You'll help me, Jesus, won't you? Please God?"

Twelve Midnight

THE ROOM was still.

The men slept.

Benson staggered into the room. He found his cot and lay down on his back, staring up at the ceiling. Hunchy turned over and coughed. Old man Knox slept soundly. He was snoring. And Luke lay curled up like a child with his face still wet with tears.

In the toilet a little man with a swollen eye and a comical Adam's apple walked up and down with a pockmarked Russian laborer. The little man was talking and the big man was listening, attentively, with his swarthy face serious in concentration.

And the city lay waiting for midnight.

Outside the sound of horns and bells and shouts broke out in a sudden, mad, abandoned tumult. The church cells pealed and the taxis honked and men called to one another and embraced.

It was midnight.

It was the eve of the New Year.

It was the season of celebration!

Turnip's Blood

BY

Rachel Maddux

Turnip's Blood

Turnips do have blood, you know,
Thin and mauve and lighter than air.
And almost always so confined
One never sees it there.

Only when it spurts
As when a knife cuts through,
Or when the quantity becomes so great,
The turnip hurts

And lets it free, does one learn
That it was all the time
Made of multi-colored bubbles
That arise, expand and shine.

ALL HIS IRRITATION at having been called out of bed at three o'clock in the morning was gone now. It had been a nice piece of work, he thought, as he walked out of the hospital toward his car. He decided to drive the long way home and see the dawn because he wasn't sleepy and the weather was excellent, and he hadn't seen a dawn for years.

The long way around led through Miner's Village, a town of one street lined with two rows of identical stone houses. Lawrence had always liked Miner's Village and this morning he tried to think why. He felt quite sure that no one, not even the people who did live there, wanted to live there. Yet why was it so pleasing to him? The monotony of it must be the reason, he decided. Yes, surely the monotony . . . that was it. A lovely word in itself. He realized that he had gone

through this reasoning before about liking Erik Satie's *Gnossienne.*
Well, he thought, that was the difference between life and art—in art
you liked monotony and in life you didn't.

If he knew more about art and less about life he might be able to
write a treatise on that distinction which would forever shut up those
stupid arguments about Is Art Nature? or Should Art Reflect Life?
And then, Miner's Village miles behind, he thought if he had known
more about art and less about life he might not have had the idea at
all. He said, "Damn!" and knew he might as well be back at the
hospital or asleep in bed for all the good he was getting out of being
outdoors with the dawn coming up in a minute.

He stopped his car by the park when he got into town and got out
to walk. It was a strange sensation to know that no one would be worried or conscious or even aware that he was wasting an hour. He felt
a slight bit of guilt wash over him almost as though he had said he
was glad that Edna was dead. It wasn't that Edna had not been a good
wife; it was just that. . . .

He had missed the first moments of the dawn and that made him
angry. He set his shoulders and determined to enjoy himself. And of
course just when he had made up his mind to think of nothing but
spring and dawning and being alive, there would be a whore sitting
there on a park bench.

"My God!" he thought. "They're everywhere." The next moment he
was terribly ashamed of himself because he saw that he'd been wrong
and it was only a child—a very thin child sitting very still.

"Probably lost," he muttered to himself. David Lawrence had found,
identified and returned to their mothers more lost children than any
other one man in America. Lost children and beggars and women
without tickets in railroad stations—he could spot them a mile off,
and they knew it.

He sat down on the bench by the girl and realized that she was
almost as tall as he and that she had an unlighted cigarette in her
hand. So he had been right the first time! He had smiled reassuringly
at her as he sat down and now he felt like a fool. What a ridiculous
situation! Should he just get up and walk off? He was becoming more
irritated every minute. She seemed to be unaware of his presence and
went on just sitting there and staring in front of her looking fragile
and contented and not like a whore.

"I beg your pardon," David said as he stood up. "I thought you were a child." Still she looked straight ahead.

"Yes, I know," she said.

"That's absurd," he growled. "How could you know what I was thinking?"

"But I am a child." And this time she did look at him.

"Well, why don't you go home then?"

"It isn't time yet."

"I suppose any time before six o'clock in the morning is too early to go home?"

"Exactly."

He could have walked away then, but he kept thinking she'd say something else. The air hung heavy with her silence and his anger and he wished she'd speak so that he could make a sarcastic retort. He wanted to make her angry. The seconds thudded by and he felt weaker and weaker and finally sat back down again.

"What are you doing with that cigarette?" he asked.

"Holding it."

"Why don't you light it?"

"I don't have a match."

"Why don't you go get one? There's a store a half block away."

"It isn't worth it."

"If you have a match you smoke and if you don't have a match you don't smoke, is that it?"

"Is it so difficult to understand then?"

"And I suppose if you don't have any food you don't eat, and if you have food you eat?"

"Of course," she said. "It would be stupid not to eat if you had the food."

"Oh, God!" David said to himself. "It was such a lovely morning and I'm so mad. I'm so mad I could kill her."

"Look here. Don't you have a family?"

"Yes, but they aren't here."

"So they kicked you out?" he asked hopefully.

"No, I just left."

"Were they mean to you?" How could they have helped being mean, he asked himself.

"No, they were very good to me."

"Well, why did you leave then?"

"I was restless. They talked too much."

The city was thoroughly awake now and trucks and trolley cars filled their lungs with air and screeched for sheer joy. David Lawrence had a smile that he reserved for special occasions. He used it in the operating room when a clumsy nurse trod on his toe or when a piece of catgut broke. The internes at St. Mary's knelt by their little white beds every night and prayed to Our Lady: "Please teach Doctor Lawrence to swear instead." He smiled so now and called over the noise of the traffic: "And you find it quiet and peaceful here?"

"Yes," she shouted, "I find it quiet here."

"Oh," he said, "you find it quiet here."

"And why is it," he asked, "that you can't go home until six o'clock?"

"It's because of Alice."

"Oh, I see. . . . It's because of Alice. And *what* is Alice?"

"Alice is the girl who lives at night where I live in the daytime."

"And what does Alice do in the daytime?"

"She works."

"And you . . . you work at night—and sleep in the daytime?"

"Yes, that's right."

"If you don't mind my asking, are you working now?"

"No. I get off at four-thirty."

"Oh," he said, "you 'get off' at four-thirty."

Quickly she said: "Charlemagne immediately dispatched his herald, accepting the challenge, and said 'Bring me some soup.' There, repeat that!"

David Lawrence's spine snapped upright. "Charlemagne immediately dispatched his herald," he said, "accepting the challenge, and said 'Bring me a . . . bring me a . . .'"

"Bowl of soup," she said.

"Ah, yes . . . a bowl of soup."

"That's wrong."

"What's your name?"

"Eve."

Eve on a park bench, Lawrence mused, in a green sweater and skirt at ten minutes of six in the morning, still holding in her hand her four-thirty cigarette. He scratched a match and held it for her. She lighted her cigarette and looked up to thank him. Her eyes were green, too—very green, very narrow and very slanting. Her hair hung not very tidily down to her shoulders. It was vaguely curly and very thick.

"Your skin is very white, Eve," Lawrence said.

"Because it's never in the sun."

"What is this work you do until four-thirty in the morning?"

"I scrub floors in an office building." He looked at once, of course, at her hands.

"That's a lie," he said.

"I wear gloves."

"So you saw me look at your hands?"

"No."

"Then—how?"

"It is the way one expects a surgeon to solve a problem."

"Then you know who I am?"

"I scrub the floors in your building. You're quite a legend there. The stenographer is in love with you."

"Which one?"

"The one with glasses."

"I think they both wear glasses," he said, suddenly aware that he had never recognized either of his stenographers as personalities.

"This one has gray eyes."

"I don't know what color their eyes are," he said, as though Eve were ridiculous to have thought he would have known.

"She has freckles—just a few."

"That's no good, either."

"She wears a pink dress, often."

"Pink dress," he said, "pink dress. No, I don't remember it."

"Her right shoulder is low and her left hip is high. She . . ."

"Oh, you mean Miss Simmons!"

"Yes," said Eve, "I suppose I do."

"Well, well. Miss Simmons. And what makes you think Miss Simmons is in love with me? I'm sure I never noticed it."

"She comes back nights to work and she has a newspaper picture of you on her desk which she puts in the middle drawer when she leaves."

"And *you* scrub floors!"

"Yes."

"Why? Is that all you can find to do?"

"I like it."

"You *like* it?"

"Yes, I like it."

"What's so charming about it?"

"Night work."

"So you don't like to work in the daytime?"

"Sun hurts my eyes and, besides, it's noisy."

So she's not a lost child, he thought, nor a whore; neither a salamander nor a shop girl.

Eve stood and yawned and stretched. "I have to go home now," she said, "it's after six."

"How can you tell?"

"By the noise."

"I have my car. May I drive you home?"

"No, I have to walk."

"Why?"

"It's on account of Rameses. He's afraid of cars."

"Well, may I walk, then, with you and—Rameses?"

"If you want." A sound came from Eve's throat—a hybrid sound half coyote and half bubbling brook. She turned her head toward David apologetically and said, "I can't whistle, you know."

"So I see," he said.

Infinitely nonchalant and dripping with sleep, Rameses padded slowly through the bushes, one ear alert, the other caressing his cheek.

"I see what you mean," David said. "It's hard to tell whether he's looking forward and going sideways or going forward in profile."

Rameses licked Eve's shoe. He put his elbows on the ground and let his shoulders melt into them. He sighed heavily and then stood up.

The three of them started off through the park, Rameses walking first in front, then behind, then between the man and the girl. David stumbled a great many times.

"The dog gets underfoot just a little, don't you think?"

"He isn't used to walking with two people."

They walked four or five blocks from the park and then down an alley. They came to a fire escape and Eve said, "Are you hungry?"

"Starved."

"What time do you have to go to work?"

"Nine o'clock."

"You'd better eat then. Come on." They climbed two or three miles into the sky and Rameses and Lawrence had a hard time of it because Rameses was far from agile and Lawrence was dizzy. When they got to the top Eve pushed open the door and said, "Don't bump your head."

The floor was bare and clean. There was an odor of damp wood and laundry soap not unpleasantly mingled. The walls and ceiling looked like a freshman art student's idea of cubism. In fact, they looked like anybody's idea of cubism. Against one wall there was an unpainted wooden table with two straight chairs; along the adjoining wall, a wooden bed with neither head nor foot, slightly too wide for a coffin. The third wall had shelves holding books on one side, dishes on the other, and a door leading into the bathroom. The other wall was cut into by a window and the door they had just entered. The room looked restrained rather than poverty stricken; severe rather than bare.

"Sit down," Eve said, and disappeared into the bathroom. Lawrence heard her splashing about and presently she reappeared very shiny and barefooted in a clean but shapeless gray garment which came to her ankles.

She raised the window and reached outside into a box fastened to the ledge, bringing back cheese and milk, two fresh pears, unsalted butter and a loaf of pumpernickel. She set these down in a chair while she spread a coarse but very clean cloth over the table. Then she stacked everything in the middle of the table, and set on opposite sides of it two squat red glasses, two blue plates and two blue cups. She put a knife by each plate and a bread knife by the loaf of bread. She disappeared into the bathroom again and came back with a pot of coffee.

She went once more to the window box and brought out a package of meat which she put on a newspaper for Rameses.

"All right," she said to Lawrence. The whole process had not taken more than fifteen minutes, and yet in that fifteen minutes Lawrence had learned more about the power and the courage of color than he had dreamed of in his fifty years.

When Lawrence had been thirty he looked and acted forty and now that he was fifty he still looked forty. It seemed to him that he had always been forty and not feeling fifty, he did not allow himself to say those things that people of fifty can say quite naturally without being thought too sentimentally sincere. So he did not tell Eve that the red glass seemed to be the source of light for the room, but he said instead, "I never knew a table could look so pleasant," hoping she might think he referred to the food and to his appetite.

"It's because the walls are white and the room is bare and my dress is gray. Then, too," she added, "pottery is so much warmer than china."

"Young girls," he thought, "can say things like that and it sounds all right." They ate and did not talk much except for a slight discussion on coffee and its noble qualities.

"Do you call this breakfast?" David asked. "I've always been curious about people who turn day and night around."

"I eat only once a day," Eve said, "like Rameses, so it doesn't matter what I call it." When they had finished Eve lit a cigarette and pushed her chair back against the wall. She asked David if he liked to smoke a pipe.

"I smoke a pipe at home," he said, "but I never carry it with me." She went to the bookcase and brought him a pipe and a can of tobacco.

"You can smoke this one if you want," she said.

David chuckled. "Alice's?" he asked.

"No, it's mine. I always run out of cigarettes at the end of the month."

She sat down and tilted her chair against the wall again and finished her cigarette. Then she got up and put the remainder of the food back in the window box, took the dishes to the bathroom, set them in the tub and turned on the water. While it was running she took the cloth from the table, put her chair in place, transferred Rameses' newspaper from the floor to the waste basket and returned to the bathroom. She turned off the water in the tub and as she dried each dish she set it on the shelf, except for the coffee pot which she left on top of the stove in the bathroom.

She spread two blankets down on the floor and opened the window. She put a blanket on the table by Lawrence. "It gets cold sometimes," she said. She went into the bathroom and washed her teeth. Coming back into the room, she set the alarm clock for eight.

"I have to go to bed now," she said. "Don't let Rameses out when you go." She sat down on one edge of the blanket and covered her feet securely. Then she lay down and, catching the upper corners of the two blankets in her teeth, her arms at her sides, she rolled over and over until she had exhausted the blankets. Rameses, from his corner, oozed over to her side and lay down. Slowly he lifted one ox-like paw in the air, reached and touched her like a priest giving his blessing. He closed his eyes, sighed, and slowly his leg relaxed and slipped to the floor.

David laughed at the sight until Eve's head popped turtle-like out of the bundle of blankets.

"Why don't you sleep on the bed?" he asked.

"It's Alice's," she said and withdrew her head.

Lawrence sat and smoked Eve's pipe and listened to the breathing. Eve had gone to sleep at once and her breathing was even and rapid and quiet. Rameses snored erratically and now and then a leg twitched and the toenails scratched back and forth on the bare floor.

"Dreaming of rabbits, no doubt," Lawrence said to himself as he knocked out the pipe and laid it back on the shelf on his way out.

II

LAWRENCE was a man of considerable mental discipline. As he said, "he had to be," and so he neither neglected his work nor lost his sleep over Eve. But he was cursed (or blessed) with an accurate and vivid memory. The same thing that made him able to remember every patient's name and idiosyncrasies made him see Eve in her long gray robe when he smoked his after-dinner pipe at home.

The next day a patient, a young girl, came into his office wearing a green sweater. He found himself being less brusque, less professional in his manner with her. The day after, he asked Mrs. Darling, his cook, to get him some pears for dinner and as he ate them he pronounced Eve "plain stupid," but he got up at five-thirty the next morning all the same and drove to the alley and parked by the fire escape to wait for Eve. He would have liked to go to the park again, but he didn't feel up to another tango with Rameses.

Presently Eve turned the corner about a hundred feet from him and came into sight. Rameses trailed behind. She pushed her hat onto the back of her head and began hop-scotch jumping, landing with one foot on each block of sidewalk. Each time a foot came down she paused for a moment stork-wise and said, "He will come," or "He won't come." She ended face to face with Lawrence just as she said, "He won't come." She was out of breath and looked surprised to see him.

"So much for superstition," she said, and started up the steps, her hat still on the back of her head. David stood bewildered on the sidewalk.

"Aren't you going to invite me to come up?" he asked. She stopped climbing and, leaning over the hand rail, looked down at him.

"Oh," she said, "didn't you come to see me?"

"Of course I came to see you."

"Why are you standing there, then?" she called.

As he started the long climb the doctor muttered to himself, "For this I get out of bed at five-thirty in the morning."

As he bent his head to go through the door he saw the flowers on the table. He went over and stood in front of them for a moment before he took off his topcoat.

"How many years it's been," he said, "since I have seen larkspur!"

"I hoped you'd come before they died," she said. He knew then that they had been bought for him and he was pleased and felt shy. He turned to look at her, but she had already gone into the bathroom and closed the door. Presently he heard her splashing and singing in a cheerfully loud, but not very good, voice.

Everything was the same as it had been before except that there were apples instead of pears, and after Rameses had been fed and the dishes washed, Eve didn't go to bed but sat on with her chair tilted back against the wall.

He had thought of a lot of questions he wanted to ask her, but it didn't seem to be quite the right time.

Suddenly Eve jumped up and, taking him by the wrist, pulled him into the bathroom.

"Shh!" she said.

"What's the matter," he whispered.

"The collector for the gas company is coming up the stairs," she whispered back.

"I don't hear anything," David said, forgetting to whisper.

Eve frowned at him for answer and after a few seconds David, too, could hear the steps. While he stood there he realized that the bathroom was the one place that could not be seen from the window.

"Must have done this before," he thought. He wanted very much to laugh.

Eve said "s-s-s" through her teeth, and Rameses went to the door. In answer to the series of knocks that followed, Rameses sent back terrible sounds. They were frightening enough, but not exactly what one expects of a dog. David visualized his looking back over his shoulder and saying sweetly: "I can't bark, you know."

The collector left and Rameses gave one look around for approval and went back to his corner.

"Is it safe to go out now?" David whispered, enjoying the secrecy of a shared danger.

"It's all right now," Eve said.

"Can I go after him and pay him, Eve?" David asked.

"Don't bother," she said. "It's only a week till I get paid, and besides the coffee's gone too, so it just came out even."

"You mean they turn the gas off?"

"Sure."

"How'd you know who that was, by the way?"

"Recognized the footsteps. He has metal plates on his shoes. Didn't you notice?"

"You should have been a detective," he said.

"Or an Indian." She smiled and walked over to Rameses to reward him for his bravery with a pat on the head which he acknowledged with a yawn.

"Shouldn't you go to bed?" Lawrence asked.

She didn't answer for a few seconds and then she said, "You'll come back again?"

"Yes," he said. Then he remembered the flowers and added, "If I may."

"Then I'll go to bed."

He felt that he should have gone then but he couldn't resist watching the blanket rolling ritual, so he sat down and had another pipe. He looked at the flowers and smiled and then he looked around the room more conscious of detail than on the previous visit. There were a dozen or so worn books on the shelf and he put on his glasses and went over to look at them.

Conrad Aiken's *Jig of Forslin* was there and *Easy Recipes for Newlyweds* and a sagging, shabby dictionary. *Sanine* and Huneker's *Painted Veils* stood erect with difficulty to support Anderson's *Winesburg, Ohio* and *Care and Feeding of the Dog*, which were aslant. *Daphnis and Chloe,* thin and shy, stood between a history of alchemy and *Gargantua and Pantagruel.* Carlyle and a Norse mythology approved each other over their beards of ravelings, while *The Circus of Doctor Lao* stood aloof, blatant and conspicuous in its newness.

"They could be Alice's," Lawrence told himself as he tiptoed out.

He got in his car and drove down to the gas company. He wondered if she'd be angry at his paying her gas bill. He knew he was a person that many people feared and he had always rather enjoyed helping his temper out a bit and so he was amused at finding himself a good fairy.

"I'll have to get a wand," he thought. He stopped the car and strode into the office, unconsciously adjusting himself to the civilization of "business."

"I'd like to pay a bill," he said to the man-at-the-desk.

The man-at-the-desk said, "Do you have the bill with you?"

"No, I don't," David said.

"What is the name?"

"Eve," said David. He blushed and looked around him in panic. He didn't know her last name. Why hadn't he thought of that? Nor did he know the street number or the apartment number. It was impossible to say to the man: "You go down Chestnut Street, see, and then you turn left down an alley."

"I beg your pardon," he said. "I have forgotten the name." He almost ran out of the building and pushed the revolving door so hard that he had to go around twice before he could get out.

He climbed into the car and swore as he saw the man-at-the-desk running toward him.

"You left your billfold, sir," he said.

Lawrence took Eve for a ride the next morning after Rameses had been fed and left in the room. They stopped to eat at a restaurant and Lawrence started to order his usual breakfast, but thought in time to order cheese and bread and fruit and coffee. He was surprised and rather pleased to find himself capable of such subtle and flattering tact, but Eve spoiled it all by asking him what he usually ate for breakfast.

David was not after all so different from those very people who were in awe of him that he could resist the telling of something that had embarrassed him, and so he told Eve about the episode at the office of the gas company wondering, as he told it, whether she would be angry at him for having tried to pay her bill or properly chagrined at not having told him her name.

If it has been said that the doctor had a smile, then it should certainly be said that Eve had a laugh. It came straight from the belly without suppression or apology. It was robust; it was sustained; it was loud. The tears streamed from her eyes and after she had found her handkerchief and blown her nose, she said, "Did the man ask if you were Adam?"

Lawrence was at first shocked that she showed no sympathy for his

embarrassment, but he soon came to see the picture in Eve's mind of
Adam, dressed in his fig leaf, holding his billfold (for which he had
no pocket) and saying to a twentieth century man-at-the-desk: "I have
come to pay Eve's gas bill." It was the first time Lawrence had laughed
with Eve and he found it pleasant.

When they had finished breakfast, David asked: "Eve, what do you
want to do?"

"Oh, I'll have to go home," she said.

"I don't mean that," he said. "I mean, what do you want to be?
Aren't you ambitious? Do you want to go to school, or what *do* you
want to do?"

"I went to school."

"How long?"

"Through college."

"You mean you got a degree?"

"Oh, no, I didn't get a degree."

"How long did you go to college?"

"Four years."

"What was the matter—did you fail?"

"Oh, no."

"Well, why didn't you get a degree then?"

"Well, you see, you have to be present at Commencement."

"Of course, weren't you?"

"I couldn't bear the thought of it," she said.

"But didn't you think you'd need it when you went to get a job?"

She laughed at this as she had laughed at the picture of Adam and
Eve and said: "Oh, can't you just see Mrs. Glutcher and Mrs. Peabody
and me all standing in a row holding our mops in one hand and our
sheepskins in the other?"

He realized as he became irritated with her that he must have been
thinking more about her than he would have liked to admit. He saw
that he had made of her a child with an impossible dream and of
himself a benefactor.

"Then you're not ambitious," he stated rather than asked.

"No," she laughed, "I don't care what I do when I'm grown up."

He knew that he had said a thousand times that ambition ruined
women, that he would love, just once, to find a woman who wasn't
ambitious, and now that he had found her he was provoked. He had
occasion almost weekly to comment unfavorably upon what he called

the modern generation, yet when Eve refused to fit his idea of that very generation he was angry with her for it.

"Did you learn anything in college?" he asked.

"Oh, yes," she said. "I learned to hate football and vocations and efficiency and routine."

"Didn't you learn to love anything?"

"You don't *learn* to love things," she said in dismay at having to explain such a simple fact to him, "they happen to you."

He was no longer irritated at her, only amused now and relieved that he had solved the mystery. "The purely emotional type," he tagged her mentally and smiled to think of the various complex solutions that had crossed his mind vaguely since he had known her.

He took her home, his mind quite at rest, and as he left her, knowing he would not come back, he was aware of being disappointed that she no longer interested him.

It occurred to him on his way to the office that he still did not know her name. Then he realized that if he ever wanted it he could ask the building manager.

III

THE DOCTOR, certainly, was not a "purely emotional type." His mind was of that reasoning texture which makes of a geometrical theorem a pleasure, of the elimination of irrelevant details a habit, and the deduction of a logical conclusion a necessity. So it was inevitable that the little details about Eve, inconsistent with his classification of her, came to insert themselves into his consciousness until they got on his nerves.

"What I ought to do," he said, "is to have a look at her academic record just to satisfy myself." So, supposing she had gone to the state university, he wrote for a copy of her transcript (with the building manager's help) saying that he wished to give her employment. He realized that he was not being very much of an adult about the thing and that he might just as well have asked her himself.

He got a polite letter in answer reminding him that he had forgotten to enclose the customary fee. He swore and reached in his pocket to find that as usual he had no money with him. He wrote a check and mailed it, wondering after he had sealed the envelope if he had remembered to sign it.

By the time the transcript came he had ceased to think about it and for that reason the record amazed him all the more. She seemed to have excelled in all possible fields with the exceptions of domestic science, pedagogy and sociology which she had not studied. She had, Lawrence saw by a more careful scrutiny of the record, failed consistently in physical education, hygiene and economics. She had once failed in metallurgy, but had repeated the course with a high mark.

Had he asked for a letter of recommendation he might have learned a great many other interesting things about Eve, but he never felt it necessary to take another's estimate of a character when he had a chance to form his own.

"Can the universities really be so bad," he asked himself, "or is it that I was so wrong?"

But finding Eve not academically stupid did not change his attitude. "If she's not stupid," he growled to himself, "she's arrogant . . . and that's worse." But he had to admit that he had always cherished his own arrogance.

"Well, at any rate," he decided, trying to settle the matter, "I wasn't in love with her and that saved me from being ridiculous." The fact that he had stayed sane and impersonal and unimpressed seemed to please him and then:

"Or did it?" he asked himself. He thought of blackmail, he thought of finding an hysterical charwoman in his office. He saw the facts divorced from their situations: a man fifty, relatively well to do, a girl nineteen or twenty scrubbing floors, unable to pay her own gas bill.

"It's all too possible," he said, "I'd better put a stop to this before it happens." He put on his hat and strode out of his office and realized that Eve would be asleep at this time of day. He decided to wait until the next morning, but by that time he had come to see that Eve could not be put into facts, that no expression of years would describe her naïveté, nor would facts express her charm.

He was angry at himself for being so suspicious, so unimaginative and he was glad that he had not gone to her in anger about something which he felt she would not have been able to comprehend.

He might never have gone to see her at all but for a book he read one night in which there was a minor character, a child of fourteen of whom it was written:

"She had always an air about her of a recent scrubbing and a robust appetite which made her hands singularly incongruous. They were so delicate, and the bony structure was so little concealed, that they looked brittle."

He never finished the book nor learned what became of the child with the "brittle hands," for a procession of Eve's hands as he had seen them in a hundred different dynamic attitudes passed before his eyes and obscured the print. He laid the book aside and counted up the hours before six o'clock in the morning when he should touch Eve's hands for the first time.

As he fell asleep that night he did not wonder if her hands would be brittle or soft or firm or cold or warm. He thought only that they were somehow pathetic.

He got there at six o'clock and, when she didn't come, he thought she might have come home early or his watch might be slow, so he went up alone. There was no answer to his knock and it occurred to him that she might have gone away. He wished frantically that he had not waited so long to come back. He tried the door and found it unlocked. He had not really expected it to open and he ducked his head and stepped in feeling very guilty. The books on the shelves were still there and he found her gray robe hanging in the bathroom.

He grew impatient waiting for her and so aware of the silence that he wished for some kind of activity. It occurred to him that he might have the meal ready when she came, but he could not find the first thing he wanted. He marvelled at the ease with which Eve had made the little meal appear and at his own inability to make the first definite move. He stood in the middle of the room looking vaguely about him as though to find a tablecloth and silverware hanging from the ceiling.

So Eve found him when she came. She stood speechless just inside the door and automatically kicked it shut behind her. Then, as though she had followed the thoughts that had brought him back to her, she came toward him with her arms outstretched and put her hands in his. She grasped his hands so tightly that she hurt him and then as quickly she let him go and stepped back.

He wished to confess, to apologize. She could have made it easy for him. She could have asked him where he had been; why he had not come. Because she didn't he could not make the effort and so he said: "I wanted to have breakfast ready when you came, but I couldn't find anything. Where do you hide everything?"

She laughed at him and said: "I bury it." Then she went into the

bathroom and took up her usual morning routine as though he had
been there only yesterday.

When they had finished the meal he asked, "No larkspur today?"

"It turned red," she said, "and I had to throw it away for insub-
ordination." She was thinking as she said it of all the larkspur that
had bloomed and died in that room since he had last been there, of
how, having had such luck the first time, she had become superstitious
about it and had thought at each new vaseful that he would come
before it died.

"You look tired," she said.

"I am," he answered. "I almost lost a woman yesterday. That takes
it out of you, all right. Yes, it takes it out of you."

"Do you care each time," she asked, "as though it were the first
time?"

"Yes," he said, "I guess you do. You tell less people about it; that's
all."

"I'd heard you couldn't—that you didn't dare."

"You heard wrong," he said, and then, as though the subject were
uncomfortable for him, he put his elbows on the table and leaned
forward.

"Eve," he said, "I've been wanting to get you a present, or do
something for you, but I don't know what you want. You don't want
to go to school; you're not ambitious; you seem so satisfied, and I'm
so bad at buying presents. Eve, don't you want *anything?*"

He wished he hadn't said it at all. He thought he should have left
her just as she was. He had always felt that people did harm who gave
children half dollars when they still believed coppers worked magic.
He wished he had drunk his coffee and left things as they were. He
felt clumsy and heavy and he lifted his eyes to hers and saw there the
light of conquest, the rapture of Aladdin.

"Do you mean I can have anything—that you'd do *anything?*"

"Well, I'm not Midas, you know. I have my limits." He laughed
doubtfully.

Eve, too, had put her elbows on the table and leaned very close
to him.

"I'm so excited," she said. "I'll tell you what it is I want more than
anything. I want Rameses to sit up at the table on a chair and eat
with me . . . with nice manners. I've tried and tried and I can't teach
him."

David felt as Charon would have felt had a passenger offered him a handsome price to row him to hell. Had she asked for jewels he would have been disappointed, had she asked for a merry-go-round or a ferris wheel he would have been amused. But to be asked to turn animal trainer to an aged and sad-eyed hound of doubtful if startling ancestry, that was surprising. It took him some little while to relax and arrive this far in his conclusions but suddenly he saw the really surprising angle of the whole thing, beside which the request was a mere extending of the palm.

"What makes you think," he asked, "that *I* can teach him if you can't?"

"But of course you can," she said. She did not say it to bolster up his courage as mothers say to their children: "Of course you can go to school by yourself." She stated it simply like "hot is not cold; cold is not hot."

Something like this unquestioning faith he had seen a few times in his patients taking their first unhampered steps. Some of them could not keep their eyes on his face as he told them. They could not resist looking at the floor, but a few walked toward him without once looking down. Even these were not like Eve because they tried so hard. Eve did not try to have faith in him, he saw. She could not even help it; it came so easily.

"You must think . . ." he began.

"Oh, never mind," she said. "If you don't want to. I only thought— you said . . ."

"Of course I'll try," he said quickly. "I just don't know if I can, that's all, and then I was so surprised at the request."

"Why?" she asked.

He balked at the futility of trying to explain to her, and turning to Rameses said: "Well, when shall we begin?" Rameses, unsuspecting what trials lay ahead of him, slept peacefully in the corner.

Eve went over and woke him. She pushed him toward David gently and said: "Do you be a good pupil, now!"

"I'll not watch," she said to David. "I want to be surprised."

While Eve slept, David tried in turn his bedside manner, his club manner, his manner for the children of friends, all equally without avail. He took off his coat. He lifted Rameses onto the chair saying "sit up, sit up," and patted him on the head. Then he lifted him onto the floor and said "sit up, sit up." Rameses' feet grew roots into the floor.

David put on his coat and washed his hands and left in disgust. He stamped down the fire escape, muttering to himself: "I'll be god damned if I'll be an animal trainer. I'll tell her. I'll tell her that dog of hers is too stupid to learn anything. I'm surprised he can even eat off the floor. It's a wonder she doesn't have to feed him with a spoon! Maybe she should get some seals, too. She could keep them in the bathtub and I could throw them fish. Fish!" He stopped one floor from the ground and ignored his dizziness in the excitement of his discovery.

"Of course," he thought. "You have to feed them to teach them tricks. Any fool would have known that."

He was back the next morning with a sirloin steak cut into neat cubes. Rameses, of course, didn't know the difference between sirloin and boiling beef, but David didn't know that Rameses didn't know it.

By the time that the sirloin was consumed, Rameses had progressed so far as to be able to clamber up one leg at a time from the floor to the chair. He did it with no grace whatever after the manner of a fat, rheumatic and aged Negress boarding a bus. But grace was of small concern to Lawrence; he could find that elsewhere. He was seeking accomplishment, pure and simple.

Lawrence learned, as he was urging Rameses to progress from the four-legged to the two-legged method of sitting upon chairs, that dogs as well as people have that benign and complacent acceptance of over-indulgence which makes them take after-dinner naps without pangs of conscience. For all he had once scorned the chair, Rameses now went to sleep on it, although it was incapable of supporting both his body *and* his head. He seemed to smile as he slopped over the edges of the chair as though to say: "It's silly of me, I know, but I just can't help it."

After that, Lawrence got half the amount of steak and cut it into twice the amount of cubes.

Rameses had learned to climb from the floor to the chair at command in two days. In a week he ventured so far as to sit upon three legs, lifting the fourth in the air, but sit upon two legs he would not. They were set back by the fact that Lawrence, by calling Rameses all kinds of flattering names in a gentle voice and holding the meat cube tantalizingly close, had persuaded Rameses to take both front legs off the chair for a second, whereupon Rameses fell onto the floor upsetting the chair. It was two days before he would even approach the chair again.

Lawrence petted Rameses. He fed him, cajoled him, talked to him, and finally he swore at him in German, French and Spanish.

By the time they again reached the three-legged stage, Lawrence had come to remarking to himself that by this time he could have bought Eve the crown jewels of Czechoslovakia, built her a mansion with his own hands, or raised a St. Bernard from a pup and taught him to eat with chopsticks.

Every morning for two weeks Eve asked with bright expectancy: "Can he do it yet?" to which Lawrence, from long experience, answered: "He's coming along," or "Pretty soon, now." It was difficult when she asked each morning, but when she ceased to ask and nobly, if obviously, avoided the question, David's heart sank.

He pleaded the necessity of a trip to a medical meeting in a distant town and stayed away for three days. He had planned to stay home and read in books whose pages held no word of dogs, but he found it much easier to work, or to give up to thinking more about Rameses.

"I don't know which keeps me at it the more," he said to himself, "whether I hate to let Eve down, or whether I'm too proud to admit failure."

The next evening at eight he went to Eve's apartment and asked if he might borrow Rameses for the evening and bring him back the next morning. He was a little hurt at her slight show of reluctance, but he made no comment and with one hand on Rameses' collar and the other on the steering wheel he drove to his office. Remembering Eve had said Rameses was afraid of cars, he spoke reassuringly to him all the way down to the office. Rameses shrank and trembled, but Lawrence was flattered (and at first disgusted and later amused at finding himself so) by the fact that Rameses in his fear huddled near him.

Lawrence unlocked the door of his office and found Miss Simmons hard at work. He wished that Rameses had been a mouse which he could have hidden in his pocket, a bird in his hat, a cockroach in his hand.

"I just came back to do a little work," David said. "Brought the dog along for company."

"Can I help?" pleaded Miss Simmons ardently.

"Oh, no, Miss Simmons, thank you. But it's nothing you could do. Besides, you shouldn't be working such late hours. Is the work too heavy? Should I get someone to help you? You mustn't let us impose on your good nature here, you know. Better take it easy."

"Oh, Doctor Lawrence," Miss Simmons blushed, "you don't give me *half* enough to do. I always like to come back at night and do the little extra things."

"That's very kind of you, Miss Simmons, but you must go now. You've worked enough for one day. *Somebody* has to watch out for your health. If you won't I'll have to."

The chance to be protected was too much for Miss Simmons. She put on her coat and left. She giggled all the way home and said, "Let *me* do that, Miss Simmons. . . . You shouldn't work so hard. . . ."

In the safety of her own room she allowed herself to weep. "Oh, my Darling," she said to the wall, "you're so kind."

David locked the door upon Miss Simmons's back and sighed with relief.

"Rameses," he said, "you'll make a fool of me yet." Rameses was lifted onto a table and told that he was a good dog. He was patted on the head and strapped into place. He was exposed to the emanations of the X-ray. He was then released, measured and taken in the horrible car to Lawrence's house. Here he was fed and shut in the basement for, while Lawrence had always liked dogs, he didn't believe in being sentimental about them. As Lawrence prepared to climb into bed he heard Rameses howling in defiance at his solitude.

"He'll get used to it," Lawrence said, as he pulled up the bed clothes. "A little discipline won't hurt him."

He soon learned that he could either go to sleep or else he could "discipline" Rameses, but not both, so he got out of bed and swore as he tried to get his arm into the wrong-side-out sleeve of his bathrobe. When he opened the basement door Rameses lunged at him and, unmindful of the fact that he had almost knocked Lawrence over, he wagged his tail in gratitude and made that series of sounds which passed with him for barks.

He followed Lawrence upstairs and into his room and there he made a careful olfactory search for Eve and familiarity. Finding neither, he walked the floor.

"If only you could put your hands behind your back," Lawrence said, "then it would be perfect."

They exhausted themselves finally and when Lawrence awoke it was to find Rameses by his side, his cheek upon the pillow.

David returned Rameses to Eve and at her exuberant welcome of the dog he wondered whether it were a simple greeting or relief from anxiety.

"What have you two been doing?" Eve asked.

"That's a secret," Lawrence said.

He went to his office and studied the X-ray picture of Rameses' spine. As a roller-coaster for thrill-craving couples of meningococci, or as a slow motion picture of the falling of the Tower of Pisa it would have been excellent, but placed upright it would hardly have supported a new-born fly.

Laughing to himself and shaking his head from side to side, the doctor designed a brace for Rameses. It was an intricate affair with laces and buckles and chamois-covered pads. He sent the specifications to the man who made his braces and along in the afternoon he got a puzzled and apologetic telephone call from that meticulous person.

The brace-maker had made mistakes in his time and upon his head had fallen the doctor's red and purple wrath. So he asked if he had read the directions correctly, if there had possibly been some mistake?

Lawrence repeated the dimensions from memory, assured the man curtly that all was well and closed the conversation.

Now this maker of braces believed with all his heart that if the doctor were to tell him something should be seventeen thousandths of an inch and he were to make it eighteen thousandths, Lawrence would undoubtedly detect the difference. He fussed about his work so much at home that his wife often wished he would take another job, but the brace-maker always said to her: "He worries the life out of me, all right, but I like him, all the same. You see?" His wife did not see and the brace-maker finally gave up trying to explain it to her.

He looked at Rameses' brace when it was finished and said, "Maybe a snake stubbed his toe; maybe a hunk of baloney has gone limp. I give it up."

He sent the brace to Lawrence still fearing he had made some mistake, but he heard nothing further from it.

The next morning Eve said, "What's in the package?"

"It's a secret," Lawrence said. "You're not to see it yet. It might not work."

It did work, though, and in a few days Rameses, wearing his pale pink brace, was able to sit up on his haunches and eat off a plate on the table. The time had come to show Eve and Lawrence made her sit at the table with her eyes closed until he had got the dog trussed up.

"All right," he said. "You can open your eyes."

"Oh!" Eve said. "Does it hurt him?"

Somehow, Lawrence had expected gratitude. "Oh, no," he said. "As a matter of fact, it probably feels good. At any rate, the feat is impossible without it."

Eve held her breath and waited.

"Sit up!" David said to Rameses, and Rameses jumped upon the chair, sat up and ate, his corset strings dangling behind him.

Eve jumped up and hugged Rameses. She clapped her hands. She squealed. She danced about the room and finally she sat on Lawrence's lap and put her arms around his neck.

"I'm so happy!" she screamed. "You're wonderful."

Lawrence said: "You specified 'nice manners,' but you'll have to do that yourself. I gave up at this point. Besides, that's a mother's job anyhow."

Suddenly pensive, Eve said: "I just thought of something; now we'll have to get another chair."

"Oh, no," David said, "just put mine on a newspaper on the floor."

"I wouldn't think of it," she said quite seriously.

IV ·

THEY PLANNED to go on a tour of second-hand furniture stores the next day to find a third chair like the other two, but when Lawrence parked his car in the alley Eve came flying down the fire escape at a pace that made him shiver.

"We're not going shopping," she called. "Come on up. I've had news."

David waited until he had safely climbed the steps before he spoke.

"You're home early, aren't you?" he asked.

"I've quit."

"Quit?"

"Just last night. I've a new job. Did you ever want anything for years and years and then have it come true? I'm so excited. But wait, I'll show you the letter."

She was hopping up and down in her incoherent excitement and she picked up the letter from the table and waved it in front of him so that he could not have read it even if he had had his glasses on.

"Child, child!" he said, "stop jumping. Calm down now and tell me what it's all about." He put on his glasses.

"It's a circus," she said. "Isn't it wonderful?"

"You're a circus, certainly." He took the letter from her. It really was a circus. He read the letter through and then he said, "You're not serious?"

"Of course I'm serious."

"You mean you're going to join this circus? You're actually going to travel about in a dirty little old train with a bunch of freaks, eating rotten food and ruining your health?"

"It isn't like that at all, I'm sure. Of course I'm going. I've wanted to all my life and I've been trying to get this job for three years. Isn't it wonderful? Aren't you excited?"

"No, I'm not," he said, taking off his glasses. "It's perfectly absurd. My dear, you've got a lot of crazy ideas in your head and I'm going to get them out. Now, see here . . ."

"Oh, you don't understand," Eve said, all her excitement apparently gone, "and I thought you would."

"I understand this. You're a child who needs a good spanking. You've got a lot of pretty ideas in your head. You're not a delayed adolescent; you haven't even reached adolescence yet. Why . . . Besides, what could you do in a circus? Have you even thought of that, now?"

"I'm going to a ride a white horse, so there!"

"I suppose you told them you wouldn't come unless you could ride a white horse?"

"I said a white horse or an elephant."

"An elephant would have been safer at that. Have you ever been on a horse?"

"Once; that's how I knew I'd like it."

"Oh, I see," he said, "once."

Before they had eaten, he simply spluttered his anger at her, but after the meal he had calmed down somewhat and tried to reason with her, to explain to her the sordidness of the life she was going to. He might as well have tried to convince her that the Lorelei wore a wig or that the odor of Christmas trees was dime-store perfume. He saw that it was quite hopeless and that he was only making her impatient and unhappy, so he accepted the fact and wished her luck.

"When do you leave?" he asked.

"Tonight."

"So soon? I suppose you will be so great and famous that you'll scorn the society of a mere doctor when you come back?"

"I'll write to you every day and tell you all about it," she said. "Besides, it's only for a few months, you know. I only want to see what it's like and get to know the people."

"Don't tell me you're going to write a book about it?"

"A book?" she asked. "What for?"

"You just plain don't have any excuse at all for going, do you?" he asked.

"I don't need any."

He stood at the door wishing either to try again to dissuade her or to tell her how much he would miss her, but he had not quite forgotten his anger and could not bring himself to say anything.

"Well, good-bye," he said.

She put her arms around him and kissed him. Not having expected any such show of affection, he was very awkwardly holding his hat in front of him and Eve held him so tightly that he could neither get his arms free to put them around her, nor could he save his hat from being crushed.

"If I miss you too much," she said, "I shall come back right off."

Miss Simmons came into Lawrence's private office three days later holding an opened letter in her hand. She blushed and stammered as she held it out to him.

"I'm so sorry, Doctor, but the letter was not marked 'personal' and I just supposed it to be office business. I'm awfully sorry I opened it. I do hope you'll forgive me. . . ."

Almost every day one of these letters came and, until Miss Simmons had learned the handwriting, Lawrence was continually being embarrassed. Eve, in her naiveté, never thought to mark any of the letters "personal" and, since she travelled perpetually and never mentioned in advance where she was going, he could not write and tell her to address her letters any differently.

Elkhart, Kans.
May 15th

Dear David:

Rameses and I live in a big car which is just like a house inside while the circus goes from town to town. The man on the flying trapeze's wife and the Fat Lady live here, too. They did not much like having Rameses at first, but when I had him show them the trick you taught him, they were won over. The Fat Lady laughed and laughed and asked me to ask you if you would make her a corset. She is not allowed to wear a corset when the show is on but she says she wears it while she's resting because it's more comfortable, except the stays in this one punch. She offered to show me where the stays punched, but I declined. The Fat Lady is very jolly. She told me all about her husbands. The first one was a sailor and the other two didn't seem to be much of anything. She did not mention where they are now, but I gathered that she considers herself well rid of them.

I would have written to you last night, but I was hypnotized by watching the man on the trapeze's wife do her exercises. She insisted that I feel her calf muscles of which she is very proud, and she offered to show me some exercises to get me over the horse-stiffness. I tried a few, but finally decided the horse was the lesser evil.

You were right about the food, but the coffee is good.

Love,
Eve.

P.S. The horse's name is Solomon and he really *is* white.

Hugoton, Kans.
May 16

David:

So far I've just sat on Solomon, but today I began standing on him, first on two feet and then on one. It feels just like it looks, only they won't let me laugh while I do it—only smile.

I wish you were the Tall Man or something, so you could be here, too.

The Bearded Lady came to call on me after the show, and what do you think? She's really George Bernard Shaw in disguise! She gave me the position (financial, social, marital, unmarital) of the members, a concise little paragraph for each, and offered to advise me on my choice of friends. She smoked up all my cigarettes so that I had to borrow off the Tall Man who is fast becoming my best friend. You know

without my telling you, of course, that he likes Rameses very
much, and vice versa.

'Till Sublette,

Eve.

P.S. Who does your charring now?

"As though I'd know," David said to himself. He laughed over the
letter and, as was his habit, he mechanically tore it up and threw the
pieces in the waste basket. Immediately, he wished he hadn't. The later
ones he saved, carrying them home with him at night to the desk in
his library.

Sublette

May 17

Dear David:

Whomever this town was Sublette to got a raw deal. The
dust is knee deep. Even Solomon looks gray.

On account of Rameses, I thought it wise to make friends
with the cook who is a big Negro named Sam. Today the Tall
Man told me Sam said he wanted to see me and when I went
over, what do you think he had bought for me? An orange
and a head of lettuce. I didn't dare eat it in front of anybody
he said, because they'd get sore if they caught him playing
favorites, so I stood back of the kitchen and chewed it down
like a rabbit. Sam said he used to cook in a big hotel in
Tulsa and he could tell a lady when he saw one and knew
what they liked to eat. I didn't say a word.

It seems a long time since I saw you.

Eve.

Garden City

May 18th

Mon Ami:

Today I got to ride on an elephant. There are two and I
had such a time deciding which one to choose. It is lots of
fun, like a slow motion of rocking in a rocking chair, but not
nearly as much fun as riding on Solomon. I'm glad I do not
ride the elephant in the show.

The man who rides the elephant in the parades and shows
is the only person around called "mister." He is Mr. Carmichael, and he is most impressive looking, like King George.

He joined the circus (that is, Mr. Carmichael—not King George) when he was drunk and signed a two year contract, but he takes it most philosophically.

I asked him what he used to do, but he said that it had been so long ago that he couldn't remember.

He promised to take me to visit the snake charmer who is quite exclusive and hard-to-know.

Eve.

P.S. Rameses sends you his love.

Dodge City
May 19

Dear David:

Mr. Carmichael and I found the snake charmer smoking a cigar and reading an old movie magazine. She likes Mr. Carmichael because they're both Irish, that is, she's half Irish and half Indian and that is a combination you shouldn't miss. Even without the paint, she's a scream.

Mr. Carmichael told me she didn't have time to be nice to most people because she had to paint those pictures on her every day. He was only kidding me because she's really tattooed.

She asked me where I came from and when I told her she said: "Have they got any real artists up there that can do tattooing?"

I told her I wasn't acquainted with any and she said to Carmichael: "I been thinking I'd like to have some more work done by a really high class guy. I'm getting tired of what I got and I got lots more space, but every place I go they only got the same old patterns."

Rameses is getting so fat you wouldn't know him.

Love,
Eve.

Kinsley, Kans.
May 20

Mon Cher:

Do you know this country? It is perfectly flat as far as one looks and all day I have hardly seen a tree. Yet the whole thing beats and beats as though all the people who had walked across this land in coarse and clumsy shoes had left

the rhythm of their tread. The sunsets escape being melo-
dramatic by getting over with quickly, like a farm woman in
labor who is used to having babies. It is the first time I ever
really felt "America."

Solomon has at last recognized Rameses and the three of us
are now good friends. I shall hate to leave Solomon.

I still get hungry at six o'clock in the morning out of habit.
Do you?

Yours,
Eve.

Larned
May 21

Dear David:

We had a poker game last night and I won all the clown's
money. I offered to give it back to him, but he would not take
it. His name is Arthur and he is much funnier with his own
nose and eyebrows.

He has got the political situation all analyzed and he explained it to me. At the time it seemed quite clear, but right
now I cannot seem to remember much about it except that
if the politicians would do as he says he would no longer be a
clown in a circus that only boasts two elephants. Instead, he
would be back in vaudeville juggling at eighty a week. As I
say, he explained all this very carefully to me, and after he
had aired his opinions of circuses like ours (already I'm pos-
sessive, you see) I felt that he and you would have a great
deal in common.

Arthur tried to initiate me into the fine art of juggling, but
whether it's apples or dumbbells they all come down on my
head. I do not have the slightest talent, but contrary to my
expectations, this did not make Arthur angry or impatient
with me. I had proved beyond a doubt that, just as he had
said, juggling is a very difficult art and scarcely appreciated by
the uninitiated.

Arthur says there is a revolution coming, so you must get
ready for it. You may even wish to leave the country, because
if I understand Arthur correctly, one will find, after the revolution, millions of highly paid jugglers and jugglers only on
every theatre stage in America.

The man on the flying trapeze and his wife have patched up their quarrel (for the good of the act, they say) and he has quit travelling with the cotton candy man and the ticket taker to come back to us. When the Fat Lady heard the news she said to me: "Now it won't be dull around here any longer, dearie. We'll have some roarin' good fights."

If it gets too bad I shall go live with the lion in his cage, for he is so old that his teeth are all soft and he is so fond of his keeper that it is only with the greatest difficulty they make him roar any more at all. It is for this that I call him Robert Ingersoll. Even that does not make him mad.

Love,
Eve.

Great Bend, Kans.
May 22

David:

We got paid today. It hardly seems right to get paid for having so much fun. When the Fat Lady found out how much I made (or rather, how little) she had a fit of rage and said my youth was being taken advantage of. But really I can hardly do any tricks yet and I ride sitting most of the time, so I think the Fat Lady is being quite unreasonable.

Everybody here has got kodak pictures of somebody in their dressing rooms. I wish I had one of you.

Love,
Eve.

Lyons,
May 23

Dear David:

I have been trying for several days now to learn to ride standing with one foot on each of two horses. You've no idea how difficult it is, and the only other white horse in the show is not so nice as Solomon. I am supposed to have it perfect for the McPherson show, but I don't know if I shall be able to or not.

Arthur wants to use Rameses in his act, but I am not sure if I could bear to have him laughed at or not, and yet it is hard to refuse Arthur anything. It means so much to him whether one hundred or two hundred people applaud.

If I do not lose all my money at poker, I shall buy a victrola when I come back.

Love,
Eve.

For several days David did not hear from Eve and so he read her old letters over. They so amused him that he wished there were someone he could show them to. He had few intimate friends and even with these he feared being thought ridiculous, so he laughed alone. When the next letter came he opened it before he had even examined the rest of his mail. The lines slanted across the page, characteristic of letters written in bed, and David was stiffly apprehensive before he had read the first word.

MERCY HOSPITAL

McPherson, Kansas.

Dear David:

Would you pay for having Rameses sent to you and take care of him? No one in the show could take him because they had to go on. I got stepped on by a horse, I think, and I'm in the hospital here and they won't let Rameses come in. He has stood at the door for three days now.

Please wire, because he must be awfully hungry and I can't get them to let him in.

I don't know now when I shall see you again, but at least the circus days are over.

Eve.

"The crazy little fool!" David said. "She *would* get herself hurt. And she hasn't even sense enough to write what is the matter with her, but fills the whole letter with anguish about a dog. What does she think a hospital is?"

He was so angry that he did not come to be concerned for several minutes. A long distance telephone call got him in touch with her physician and thus it was that he learned of the terrible and tragic accident that Eve had described as having been "stepped on by a horse."

He told Miss Simmons to postpone all his appointments and he prepared to leave on the next train.

Waiting in the railroad station with characteristic impatience, he suddenly remembered Eve's one request. She had neither asked him to call the hospital nor to come to her and both of these he was doing; but she had asked him to take care of Rameses, and he had done nothing about that. He called Miss Simmons and asked her to locate a veterinarian in McPherson and to wire him sufficient money to care for Rameses who could be found at the Mercy Hospital door.

Then he boarded his train. He had brought nothing with him to read and he raged with impatience at every stop. He tried to sleep and found it impossible. The rhythm of the train kept reminding him of one of Eve's songs.

> *Have you never heard of Gertie the Goon?*
> *She's half a ghoul and half a loon.*
> *She isn't dead yet, but she will be soon.*

He counted up the time he would be away from his office and tentatively arranged his schedule on his return.

> *Oh, she lives all alone in a great big house*
> *Built from the skin of a great big mouse.*
> *She sits in her parlour and she bays at the moon:*
> *"God! don't you know that I'm Gertie the Goon?"*

Damn that song! Surely Miss Simmons would telegraph if anything went wrong with that boy in 214. How many days had he been in?

> *She had whiskey for breakfast and brandy at noon,*
> *She chewed upon licorice and ate with a spoon.*
> *Her skin was yellow and her eyes were blank*
> *And once a year she bathed in an old tin tank.*

He tried to think of another tune to drive this one from his mind. The woman in the seat in front of him was chattering in a shrill voice. David rose and went into the smoking car.

> *She got high on the weed and low on rum*
> *She fastened her kimono with chewing gum.*
> *And she did up her hair with safety pins.*
> *Oh, Gertie the Goon knew all of the sins.*

Where did she learn such songs? Children these days! He remembered some of his own student days. After all, he too had once sung songs. Well, yes of course. . . . But, then. . . . He chuckled at some vaguely remembered episode and, feeling his laughter incongruous, remembered Eve's accident. How would she take it? He must be careful not to say "I told you so."

Once in McPherson, he went straight to the hospital and sought out Eve's physician. He found it somehow awkward to explain his presence there in an unprofessional capacity and muttered something about having been a friend of her family's.

"I'm very glad you have come," the doctor said to David, "because she has consistently refused to tell us how to locate her family. I don't think yet that the full force of her condition has made its impression, although I have explained to her quite plainly that she can never walk again. She shows absolutely no despair, and at the same time her attitude does not seem to be one of forced courage. Really, a most curious case—and yet, a most amiable patient."

"May I see her, now?" David asked.

Eve was much paler than usual, and there were gray splotches under her eyes but otherwise there seemed no change in her. She did not seem either very surprised or very glad to see him and for greeting asked: "Did you take care of Rameses?"

"Of course I did," David said, "but it's you I came to see. How are you?"

"I'm tired," she said. Never to walk again, without money and undoubtedly in pain, she chose of all things to say that she "was tired."

"Well, I must say," David said, "you seem to take the whole thing lightly." She seemed to be so little in need of sympathy that he was at a loss for words. In all his years of practice he had never seen a patient so unconcerned as Eve, except those who wished to die.

"You do not know," Eve said, "how comforting it is to know that no one will ever again expect ambition of me."

Was this, David asked himself, that enlightenment that America needed to understand her youth? Were these children who believed that knowledge was for pleasure and endeavor an empty thing—were these the progeny of pioneers? Was youth, then, not mad, not radical, but only tired? Or was Eve an exception, a sprite in a real world? No, he thought to himself, there is no great generalization to be learned here; there is only a child to be taken care of.

"I shall have to live on the ground floor when I come back, won't I?" Eve asked. "And not go up to the attic."

"Dear Eve," David said, "you shall have to go back to your family."

"Oh, no," Eve said, "they'd make me work cross-word puzzles, trying to keep me busy, and they'd be everlastingly sorry."

"But you can't live alone," David said.

"Then I shall come and live with you," said Eve.

"Unfortunately, you're hardly of an adopting age."

"Then you shall have to marry me," she said.

It was two months of gradual transition before David, too, came to this conclusion and in the end the two conclusions were identical and David's voicing of it did not sound as much weightier than hers as it should have in view of the fact that it took his sixty times as long as hers to be born.

In the manner in which they decided to marry they were like two people shopping for hats. David must go to all the stores and see all the hats in order that, after he had bought the first (which he had really liked), he need never in the future have occasion to doubt the wisdom of his purchase. Eve was as one who buys a hat to cover a head. This, of course, is only an analogy, for were they really shopping for hats, the doctor would have gone to the store where he had always bought his hats and where the clerks knew so well what he wanted that they would give him the right one the first time. And what Eve would actually do in a hat shop is unpredictable.

The doctor "looked for his hats," so to speak, from all angles. From thinking the situation impossible, he came to thinking that Eve was not old enough to choose a husband. She should marry a young man. Then he remembered that Eve, paralyzed, would hardly be in a position to choose.

He did not, of course, think of the matter constantly. Sometimes for days at a time the whole idea seemed so unreal and his work so real, that he scarcely gave it a thought. Then he would find himself saying things like: "I could fix over the library for her. There is a fireplace in there and it's downstairs. I could take my stuff upstairs."

He half heard some music on the radio one evening that brought Vienna back to him. There it was, crystallized before his eyes, full blown and in its glory. Eve had never seen Vienna. What fun it would be to tell Eve about Vienna—Vienna of twenty-five years ago, before anyone guessed that She was dying. He thought of Eve's sitting across the table from him (the table was so large; perhaps it would be nicer to sit around one corner) and of his telling her about Vienna and of walking in Switzerland, and of how he could tell her just enough and from such an angle as to give her a good appetite.

There were so many things that he had seen and read and learned. He could not help but realize how pleasant it would be to have a curious and eager child in the house to tell them to.

But the thing that finally decided him was a startling realization of what he would be able to do for Eve. It was remembering her remark about the cross-word puzzles that set him to thinking of this aspect, for he saw without conceit that of all the people Eve should probably ever meet he was best suited to the job of taking care of her. He would neither watch her with apprehension nor obviously ignore her limitations. He would know that there were times when she need not be "occupied" at all, and when time did hang heavy on her hands, how ingenious and varied the diversions he already knew and how many more he would think of under the impetus of necessity.

He gave himself at least twenty more years. In twenty years she would be forty something. What would become of her if she stayed with her family? If they were still alive at that time she would have had behind her twenty barren years of attention, solicitude and cross-word puzzles. And if he took care of her for twenty years? She would at least have money enough for servants and she would have a house to be interested in in a way that it is impossible to be interested in another's house. And, if he at all deserved his success or his reputation, she would not have an invalid's mind.

"When you look at it that way," he said to himself, "it seems cruel and stupid *not* to marry her."

It did not really matter that it had taken him two months to come to the decision, for Eve could not have left the hospital before that time anyhow and under no circumstances whatever could David have brought himself to feel that a hospital was a suitable place to be married in.

He made the trip to McPherson to get her when she was released from the hospital.

"I thought," he said, "that we could be married here and then go straight to my house because the drive will tire you, I expect."

"All right."

When he had got her lifted into his car and had assured himself that she was as comfortable as possible, he suddenly remembered something and asked: "But where are your things?"

"I sent them to your house yesterday," she said.

He rather expected her to follow this remark with another or with a smile which would accentuate her cleverness at having known that he would, after all, marry her, but she looked ahead at the long flat highway, apparently having forgotten her remark.

Once she turned her head to look directly at him and her smile was such a one as to make him feel warm and glad and she said: "How good it is to see people in real clothes again!"

V

DAVID FELT that he had been right about the library, for the room pleased Eve. She had been there a week, in fact, before she showed even any curiosity to see the rest of the house. David was not sure that Eve could see the rest of the house comfortably, for she had firmly refused to have a wheel chair brought into the house, saying that they, like pianos, never seemed to belong in a room. David himself carried her in to dinner each evening and, since he saw her only in the evenings and she never complained of any inconveniences during the day, he thought that in this first week she probably was still weary enough to rest most of the time and that Mrs. Darling was so far succeeding in making her comfortable.

So when Eve said she wanted to be shown the rest of the house by him and he suggested that perhaps it would be better to wait until they had time to figure out the best way (meaning until Eve had reconciled herself to some kind of conveyance) he was surprised to hear her say, "Oh, Anthony will carry me."

Anthony was a huge white-haired Negro who had come to work for David so long ago that the circumstances had been forgotten. At any rate, he had come before Mrs. Darling, who had once been the cook and was now housekeeper. For what specific duties David had hired him originally neither of them could remember. He had been retained because of his philosophy, which was neither very clear nor very constant, but always colorful.

Anthony, whom David had always thought old and lazy, Anthony knew just how to do it. Eve, like a dancer in midair, dwarfed to feather size by contrast with Anthony's bulk, looked at David over Anthony's shoulder as he followed them up the stairs.

"You see," her eyes, looking mischievously at him, said, "a wheel

chair is a clumsy and an ugly thing and for me it is unnecessary."
David was much amused, as he always was at the sight of male servi-
tude to a female whim. He was always amused at any human trait
supposed to be characteristically "masculine" or "feminine."

Eve asked a great many questions in all the rooms and then she
said she was tired and wanted to be taken downstairs.

They had slipped into a routine which they found pleasant. They
met first for the day at the evening meal. They lingered long over
coffee and cigarettes, and if David did not have to go out, he would
take Eve on his lap and they would talk about what they had done all
day while they had been apart. Then he would settle down to do the
writing or reading or thinking he had marked out for himself that day.

Eve usually sat across the room from him while he worked and,
when she got tired with reading or sitting, he carried her in to bed and
helped her to undress. While she yawned loudly he read her a bed-time
story from a book for children. While he read she held his free hand
in both hers. At first he had been alarmed at the amazing number of
bed-time stories he should have to hunt out, but he soon found that
one would last for weeks, for Eve went to sleep so quickly when she
was tired, and she was so seldom able to remember the next night
where she had left off listening, that as a result David read the first
pages over many times.

Although he read them to her to put her to sleep, he was sometimes
so defeated by the slow progress they made that he was tempted to
awaken her and plead with her to hold her eyes open until they could
get past some particular paragraph which was beginning to bore him.

One night, though, he finished one complete fairy tale and Eve was
still awake. He was so astonished that he asked her if she were ill or
restless.

"No," she said, "curious."

"Not about the story, surely?"

"Take off your clothes," she said.

The Mermaid and the Fisherman fell to the floor and David was
suddenly thankful that he had kept up his golf and his swimming.

"You look like a horse trader, the way you're staring," he laughed
at her as he undressed.

"Oh, I'm so glad," she said.

"Glad?"

"I was so afraid you might be woolly," she said. "It's so nice to know you're all smooth." She smiled and fell asleep.

He stood for several minutes estimating the possible chances of meeting Mrs. Darling if he should walk upstairs without dressing. He hated to dress, only to undress again as soon as he had reached his own room. He decided to chance it and, holding his clothes over one arm, he leapt silently up the stairs and into his own room.

"I'll bet," he mused, "that Eve would have liked to have had that in the marriage lines: 'I, Eve, take thee, David, if thou art smooth and not woolly.'"

David never failed to be surprised and amused at Eve's conversations when they talked together in the evenings. He always gave her a brief outline of what he had done during the day and usually he asked her how she had spent her day. Almost always she had some long tale of purely imaginary and highly amusing activity to relate to him, and, strangely enough, there was no tone of irony or bitterness in the telling.

Eve usually had flowers in the house and one evening David noticed a huge bowl filled with chicory flowers. They were held together by a piece of florist's paper lace.

They both had been looking at the chicory when David asked. "Well, what did you do all day?"

"I've turned alchemist," she said.

"So?"

"Uh-huh."

"Are you a member of the union?"

"In excellent standing."

"Are you making gold?"

"No, my activities are purely experimental. Today, for instance, I threw Stravinsky and Huysman and Caldwell into a cauldron. Then I stirred and stirred, all the time humming the Star Spangled Banner to make it boil faster. And what do you think I got?"

"A burn?" David hazarded.

"No, a pink elephant. A small pink elephant. Next, I put in W. H. Hudson and the elephant's ears were edged with lace. When I added Van Vechten and a little agua regia the elephant's front legs disappeared and after Cummings had finally dissolved the hind legs, the poor thing rocked back and forth on its belly most pitifully."

"You didn't leave it like that?" David asked.

"Dear, no. I said to it: 'Poor thing, how will you move?' Without any other change of expression, the legless elephant simply lifted one eyebrow and said, 'There is no longer any place I wish to go.' "

"How strange," David said, "that pink should be the mark of sophistication among elephants."

"I thought," Eve continued, "that the way things were going, the kindest thing I could do would be to make it disappear altogether, and so I reached for my copy of Jean Cocteau to that end, but by some mistake I threw in Carlyle which was next to Cocteau on the book shelf (God knows why!) and the whole thing turned into a bunch of chicory flowers wrapped in paper lace!"

"You don't say," David said.

"And there they are for evidence," Eve said, "right in front of you." And so they were.

VI

As HE MOUNTED the stairs this evening, he wondered what adventure she would have made up for today. It occurred to him that she might not have any at all. He was frightfully late for dinner. Eve had never seemed to be aware of whether or not he came home early or late, but he knew from long years of experience what a state Mrs. Darling would be in, and he did not expect Eve to remain uninfluenced by Mrs. Darling. Though she had bullied and nagged at him for years, David had never thought of asking her to leave. Mrs. Darling was plump and Irish and she "spoke out frank," as she said, but David did not believe that any other cook would be different. He had never really taken her managing and grumbling very seriously. Certainly, he never sent patients away from his office because of what Mrs. Darling might say about his being late to dinner. But, on the other hand, he did not sit down after the last patient was gone and smoke his pipe either. He came home.

Edna had agreed with Mrs. Darling that a late dinner is a spoiled one, and Edna had often repeated Mrs. Darling's scoldings in Mrs. Darling's words, but with her own pronunciation. It had often irritated him, but since he considered his tardiness unavoidable, he could ignore the comments.

Eve was still in her own room reading and so David did not find her in the dining room. He thought she might have been angry and not waited for him.

"Has Mrs. Lawrence already eaten?" David asked of Mrs. Darling.

"She has *not*," said Mrs. Darling, "though what there'll be for her to eat *now*, I don't know."

"I expect she's in her room, then," David said, eager to escape.

"Probably fainted away with hunger, you'll find her," said Mrs. Darling.

But Eve was reading a book, sitting in a chair before the fireplace, Rameses at her feet, and she put up her face to be kissed as though a dinner might be eaten without discussion at any hour.

"I'm sorry I'm so late for dinner," David said, "but . . ."

"Oh, is it time for dinner?" Eve asked.

"Mrs. Darling is in a state," David said.

"So that's what she was muttering about!"

They giggled quietly like two children who have hidden their nurse's shoes. David was as happy as he had been the day they hid in the bathroom from the bill collector. Mrs. Darling stomped into the library and found them giggling.

"You'll not find your dinner so funny," she said.

"Oh, is it ready?" Eve asked.

"Is it ready?" shouted Mrs. Darling. "Is it *ready*! It's been ready since six o'clock."

David carried Eve into the dining room and when Mrs. Darling had left them, she winked at him. David was thinking that it was all too good to last and was about to say "Two against the cook" when Mrs. Darling reappeared.

She set a steak before David and, looking slightly over his head, said: "You'll find it cold."

"That's all right, Mrs. Darling," he said.

"There's some as don't mind *what* they eat," she said. She did not leave the room although there was no further need of her staying. It was obvious that she expected, almost anticipated, further argument. David found himself enjoying the situation. With Edna he would have felt belligerent, but Eve's presence had changed the situation to one of amusement. He was startled to see unmistakable anger on her face. He felt somehow disappointed, as though he had expected too much of her.

Eve was not eating. She held her napkin clenched in her hand and her eyes were narrowed.

"Mrs. Darling!" she said, "are you a Catholic?"

In all the years that Mrs. Darling had stood near a table, no one had ever asked her such an irrelevant question, nor had anyone dared to speak to her in such a voice.

"The Lord be praised, I am, Ma'am," she said, turning to Eve.

"Would you *dare*, Mrs. Darling, would you *dare* to tell the priest you thought the Virgin Mary was an Irish slut?"

Inside Mrs. Darling was created suddenly a vacuum—a vacuum that audibly sucked air into her mouth.

"The saints forgive me should I dare," she gasped. Eve seemed to be growing taller.

"In this house, Mrs. Darling, my husband is God, and nagging at him is blasphemy. This is *his* house and if he doesn't get home until midnight, it's all right, do you understand? It's quite all right. He's supposed to have his meals when he wants them, and it's your business and mine to see that they're hot. If he didn't work so hard that he *had* to come home late, neither of us would even be here."

Nothing had ever so surprised David. He could not remember that anyone had ever defended him. He felt pleasantly important and suddenly he knew that he loved Eve terribly. The sight of Mrs. Darling, however, changed his noble reverie into sheer amusement. Mrs. Darling, perhaps for the first time in her life, was chastened. There is nothing that so throws cold water on Irish indignation as finding spirit where it is unexpected. Mrs. Darling was silent. She was silent all over. Her bristles visibly wilted. David had a fleeting wish to be a fly and to dart into her open mouth. Very quietly she said: "Yes, Mrs. Lawrence," and padded softly out of the room.

Eve turned to him, her face a picture of tender consideration. "Are you ill?" she asked him.

"No," he said. "Why?"

"Fights always made my father sick," she said.

"On the contrary, I'm convulsed," he said. Mrs. Darling safely out of hearing, David felt free to laugh. He laughed at Right Defended and at the memory of Mrs. Darling's open mouth and he laughed because he felt good.

"What are you laughing at?" Eve asked. She could have understood his being angry—even his being sick—but not his being amused.

He could hardly stop laughing long enough to ask, "What would you have done if she had been a Methodist?"

"Why, I . . ." Eve hesitated. "I should have thrown a plate at her."

Lawrence never again was scolded by Mrs. Darling for being late to meals, but he was never able to convince Eve that the incident had been funny.

Apparently without compunction Eve had left him to join a circus. She had greeted him at the hospital without surprise and she had sat through the marriage ceremony as though it had been a parent-teachers meeting. So it was natural that as the days wore on David thought that he might have interpreted her defense of him to Mrs. Darling as a manifestation of love only because it had so shocked him.

Except for Mrs. Darling's attitude, their days were unchanged. The diversions that David had planned were never necessary. He marvelled that Eve seemed never cross or restless. Almost every evening's conversation showed him new colors and textures in her mind. He found himself suddenly smiling at odd moments during the day at the memory of something she had said. He was as surprised at her knowledge of the stage directions for operas as he was to hear her singing:

> *She was a harlot and I was a thief,*
> *And we loved each other beyond belief.**

But his knowledge of her emotions rested unsteadily on her delight in Rameses' trick, her fight with Mrs. Darling and her otherwise constant equanimity. His work during the day and his evenings with Eve served to make both so enjoyable that he found himself accepting life pleasantly and easily without question, except that now and then he was puzzled about either the absence or the obscurity of her emotional depth. Had it not been for the scene with Mrs. Darling, he would not have been puzzled. Had she really married him, then, because of his remark that she was too old to adopt? But then, what of the larkspur? Had it not been bought for him? What of the hat-crushing caress? Were woolliness or smoothness essentials of pseudo-adoptions, of friendships? "Why question?" he asked himself. "She seems contented; I am quite happy. What does it matter?"

One evening after dinner he found his cigarette case empty. They searched the downstairs fruitlessly, and Eve said, "I left my cigarettes upstairs in the attic. Would you get them for me?"

* *My Uncle Oswald*, by Roy L. McCardell.

On his way upstairs David remembered that weeks ago Eve had asked him if she might redecorate a storeroom upstairs. He had said that of course she might, thinking that it would give her something to do, and, since she had not mentioned it, he had forgotten it until now. He was curious to see her ideas of decoration and he wondered if he had given her enough money.

He turned on the light and found himself back in the old attic where they had first been together.

This room was larger than the old one, but not unlike it in shape. There were the same table set for two people with the same bright colored dishes, the same two chairs, the books and the pipe on the shelves. Even Alice's bed was there. He sat down in one of the chairs and tilted it against the wall and allowed himself the luxury of memory that is not sad because it is not over. He got up and walked about the room and delighted in checking over every detail. Everything was there except the fire escape.

And then he saw that something was different. There was a niche that had been made in the wall and resting in this was a study of hands which had been carved from wood. If he did not find the study beautiful, he found it fascinating. The hands were not passive, but the fingers had been caught in movement and he was aware of knowing kinetically what the movement was going to be. And then of course he knew. They were his hands. The wood was of a mellow brownness; the surface dull from oil. The veins and hinted wrinkles were accurate testimony of his own labor. The sudden and surprising tapering of the fingers—the moonless nails—all his. Even his ring was there; the ring he wore on his little finger. It, too, was a little large. It, too, seemed to slip to one side.

He left the light burning and ran down the stairs. To Eve, whom he had left in the dining room, he said: "Those hands . . . they're mine."

"Yes," she said, "they're yours."

"Who made them?"

"I did."

"But how?"

"From sketches," she said, "hundreds of sketches in the evenings while you were working."

"The whole room . . . it's . . ."

"You forgot the cigarettes," she said.

"So I did."

He carried her into the living room and went back after the cigarettes which were on Alice's bed. That night he did no work, for he had to hear every detail of the room and of how she had carved the hands and of how often and patiently Anthony had carried her up and down stairs, and of the difficulty of buying Alice's bed. They talked very late, and Eve went to sleep on his lap. He carried her into her room aware that he held something infinitely precious and amazing.

All the next day he kept thinking that surely she loved him. Finding the room, and, most of all, his own hands there like some kind of idol in a temple, made him not afraid to voice what he had feared to read into the larkspur or the subduing of the Irish.

So, when Anthony called his office and said he thought he'd better come home, he said he'd come at once, without even asking what was wrong with Eve.

He found Anthony, Mrs. Darling and Eve all in the attic.

"What's wrong?" he asked. Anthony stood silent, the picture of helplessness, his head bowed in the presence of something too much for him. But Mrs. Darling was not silent. Mrs. Darling was frankly exasperated.

"She's been going on like that for hours," she said, "just cries and cries. She says she's not sick, but she won't stop cryin'."

David sent them both away. He found himself more irritated than relieved that the fall or illness he had imagined was really hysterics. He said all the things that he would have said had Eve been a patient. He was firm, brusque, kind, calm, patient and firm again. All this filled a pillow slip and both his handkerchiefs with tears. He resolved to wait and "let her cry it out." She seemed capable of going on forever. Finally, he did what the most stupid of his patients would have done under the circumstances. He took Eve on his lap and put her red and swollen face against his shoulder. He kissed her and patted her head and while she blew her nose an endless number of times he told her over and over that he loved her.

When she was quiet and almost dry he asked, "What was it, Eve dear?"

"I don't know for sure," she said, sniffing, "but I think. . . ."

"Yes, dear, you think . . . ?"

"I think I'm growing up," she said.

The Song the Summer Evening Sings

BY

I. J. Kapstein

The Song the Summer Evening Sings

The evening, don't you remember the summer evening when the sky faded to yellow and the wind gently whirled the dust and leaves in the gutters and a piano tinkled sadly far away and the bells of St. Joseph's rang out vespers, the kids playing in the streets and the men sitting in their shirt-sleeves on the front stoops with the smoke of their pipes drifting on the still air, don't you remember the dreamy summer evening of long ago?

A long, long time ago. The Boston *American* said NEW FIGHTING IN THE BALKANS, and Sylvie said, "Pa, where's the Balkans?" and he said, "In Europe," and Ma said, "In Europe far away," and Sylvie asked, "Were you ever there?" and Ma said, "A long time ago. When I was a little girl like you long ago."

It was suppertime, but the summer sun was still hanging above the maples and pouring light into the kitchen. There was green and white linoleum on the floor, the walls were painted yellow, the kitchen table and the chairs were streaky with the varnish you had put on in too much of a hurry last time. Ma had been baking, and it was hot. Over the table hung Pa's big calendar, and Sylvie, just learning how to read in the first grade at Laurel Street Grammar, spelled out the words:

THE PEOPLE'S MARKET
124 Water Street
H. ROBBINS, PROP.
Fresh Meats, Fruit and Vegetables

Underneath the printing was a picture of a big brown bottle of ale with a blue ribbon tied on it and under that was more printing:

DRINK GALLOGLY'S ALE
The Public Demands A Pure Ale That Will Not Cause Biliousness

"Pa, what is Prop.?" and she said slowly after him, "Pro-pri-et-or." "Proprietor, that's me, Sylvie. It means I'm the boss," and he laughed and his teeth showed white under his graying moustache.

Then Ma came in with the tablecloth with the red and white squares, saying, "Take that old paper off the table," and Pa pushed his chair back and leaned against the wall and read out slowly to you how Harry Hooper got three safe bingles off Groom of the Senators. "The boys over at the livery stable say there's a good chance of the Red Sox getting the pennant this year," you told him. And he asked, "Who said so?" and you said, "Joe Flynn," and he laughed and said, "Joe knows a lot about horses, but he just guesses when it comes to baseball. Why, the Red Sox always start off like sixty and then before you know it, they're down in the cellar."

Then he said, "It's gol-durned hot with that stove going, Martha. Do you have to bake fresh bread even in the good old summertime?" and Sylvie began to sing, "In the good old summertime, in the good old summertime," and Pa's deep voice joined in, and Ma's thin sweet singing came out of the pantry, the voices floating gently in the air warm with the smell of fresh bread, and all the sweetness of the summer welled up in your heart.

Then Ma called Sylvie, and Sylvie went out into the pantry with her and came back with the knives and forks and spoons and the salt- and pepper-shakers and a big plate of fresh bread. Pa pulled his chair up to the table and reached out with his fork and took a piece. He bit into it and called out, "We'd be rolling in money if I could sell bread like this down at the store, Martha," and Ma came in with a couple of bottles of beer and set them down, and Sylvie brought in the sliced tomatoes and pickles. Pa grabbed a pickle and said, "I'm the guy that put the pick in pickles, I'm the guy."

He looked at Sylvie and said, "Why've you got that bandage around your neck?" and Ma, coming in with the big platter of cold meat and potato salad, said, "Don't bother the child. She's got a little summer

cold, that's all, and I've put a little mentholatum on the bandage."
"Should we get the doctor?" Pa asked her, and Ma said, "No, for
Heaven's sake. You fuss over that girl like an old hen." She sat down
and served and you all began to eat.

Pa sucked the foam of the beer off his moustache, and you said,
"Can I have some, Pa?" and Sylvie said, "Me, too. Can I have some,
Pa?" And Ma said, "No," but Pa said, "Oh, a little won't do them any
harm." With relish you swallowed the cold brown tangy drink, but
Sylvie said, "I don't like it, it's bitter," and Pa said, "Look at the
temperance girl." "She's like me," Ma said, "I wouldn't touch the
nasty stuff," and Pa said, "H'm, I see we got local option in this house,"
and they both laughed.

BUT the taste of the beer had made you remember last Saturday afternoon. After Pa had made the orders up, you put them in the wagon
and unhitched old Pinky and said, "Giddap," and went down the
dusty street, holding the reins between the fingers of one hand the way
Joe Flynn had shown you. The kids came running up, hollering,
"Give's a ride, Charlie, c'mon, give's a ride," and you said importantly,
"I can't, I'm delivering orders," and clicked your tongue to Pinky and
touched him with the whip.

When you went into Riley's Saloon with the onions and pickles and
radishes and the sliced ham and the loaves of bread for the Saturday
night rush, it was cool and dark and smelled of sour beer and fresh
sawdust. Mr. Riley was leaning over the bar, talking to a couple of
men, and as you went up to him, you saw your face, flushed from the
summer sun, in the mirror behind the dark bottles and the rows of
glasses. Quickly, furtively, out of the corner of your eye, you looked at
the naked woman in the big gilt frame, and Mr. Riley said, "I'm
damned, here's Harry Robbins' boy with the order already," and the
men turned around and looked at you while you said, "I guess you'll
find it all right, Mr. Riley." You began to check the order off, and
Mr. Riley turned back to the men and said something in a low voice
about Harry's being up against it, and then one of the men said something about how he should have stayed in the little place and should
not have moved to pay a big rent to the Jew, and you went out slowly,
scuffing your feet through the thick yellow sawdust, and vaguely
troubled about Pa.

You turned off up Franklin Street, with Pinky, his ears poking up through the straw hat, just ambling along. You stopped at the Gallands' house to leave the order and when you came out, your heart jumped because Margie Golden was standing near Pinky and holding out on the end of a stick an apple core for him. Her hair was brown and cut in bangs, a Dutch cut, like Sylvie's, and when she turned toward you, you saw the little gold spots in her dark eyes.

She waved to you. "Hello, Charlie."

"Hello, Margie," you said, "what you doing?"

"Giving your poor old horse something to eat."

"Don't worry about him," you said, "he gets enough to eat. He's eating us out of house and home, my father says."

"He's a pretty old horse, I guess," she said.

"Not so old. Look." You turned Pinky's upper lip back so that she could see his big stony-looking teeth.

"Don't," she said. "It scares me."

"He wouldn't hurt a flea," you said.

She moved away a little. "Well, Charlie, I have to go in the house now."

No, not yet, you thought, not yet. "Look, Margie," you said, "want to take a ride?"

"Well, I don't know," she said. "My mother'll be looking for me."

"Aw, come on," you said. "Just a little ways."

She hesitated.

"I'll let you drive."

"Will you? Really?"

"Come on, get on."

Then she climbed up and you got up after her and her shoulder was touching yours. You clicked your tongue and touched Pinky with the whip and he started off. Her shoulder was touching yours and there was a sweet smell from her hair.

"You going to let me drive now?" she asked.

"Yup," you said, and put the reins in her hand. "I guess you better use both hands, though, till you get used to it."

"This ain't the first time I ever drove a horse," she said loudly. "Pa lets me drive the buggy sometimes. But it's kind of different driving a wagon."

"Sure," you said, "a wagon's heavier."

"Look," she said, "here comes a Stanley Steamer."

The automobile came puffing down the street, the white steam rising around it. "That's not an auto," you said, "that's my mother's old kettle running away."

She laughed. "You're awful fresh," she said.

Excited, glowing, you leaned out as the auto went by. "Get back in the kitchen," you hollered, "get back in the kitchen."

"You could get arrested," she said. "Look, Charlie, will you show me how to drive one hand?"

"Sure," you said, "but, well ——"

She took both reins in one hand, she leaned against you. "Show me, Charlie."

You took her hand in yours, your heart was beating hard. Her fingers curled in your hand, you hardly knew what you were doing, but you got the reins arranged in her fingers while Pinky ambled along. At the corner of Laurel Street she hollered, "Whoa," and jerked the reins. Pinky stopped. "I have to go home now," she said.

"Aw, no," you said, "come on, Margie."

"Nope, I have to go," she said.

"All right," you said. She stood up. Your heart was beating fast. "Wait, Margie."

"What?" she said.

"Look," you said, "will you—will you be my girl?" The wind was blowing on your flushed face, and the papers whirled in the gutter. You watched them whirling around, you couldn't look at her.

"Aren't you funny," she said.

"Honest, I mean it," you said. Your voice was thick.

"I can't," she said, at last.

"You're not mad on me for anything, are you?" you asked her.

"Nope." She shook her head, her hair swirled about, and you smelled the violet in it.

"Then, why can't you?"

She didn't say anything for a minute while you could feel the thud of your heart. Then she said, "My father's mad on your father, that's why."

"Mad on my father? Why?" Your heart recoiled in sudden hatred for fat Mr. Golden, the old fool. "What for?" you asked. "What's he mad on my father for?"

"Because."

"Because why?"

"Just because."

You were getting mad. No one could get mad on your father. You'd show them. "Why's your fat old father mad on my father?"

She turned toward you. Her voice was shrill. "Don't you call my father names." Her eyes flashed.

"Well, Margie," you said weakly, "I take it back."

"I guess you better," she said, "if you don't want to get your father in trouble."

"Gee, Margie, tell me, will you?" you pleaded. "What's the matter anyway?"

"All right," she said. "Yes, I will. Why don't your father pay my father the rent for the store?"

"He does," you said. "He does."

"No, he doesn't, only once in a while. And my father is mad on him because he fixed up the whole store for your father and painted it and put a new floor in and fixed it all up like new, and your father doesn't pay him the rent."

You were stunned. This was the first time, this, when a doubt of your father struck you with a shock, this was the first time that life laid its overbearing weight upon you—a little girl's shrill voice like a whip across your shoulders and the quick ebbing of the blood from your face in the anguish of your hurt. But you said, "No, you're making it up, it's a lie."

"It's not a lie." She turned her bright flashing eyes on you again, but now you did not care. "It's not a lie," she said, "because last night my Uncle George was over to supper and him and my father and mother were talking about your father, and my father was kind of mad, but my Uncle George said your father was a good man and worked hard and to give him a chance to get settled. And my father said he wasn't no slave-driver, but he was kind of pinched himself right now and a little from your father would go a long ways with him. And then they talked some more about him afterward in the front room after I went to bed, but I didn't hear what they said. So there. I guess you don't have to call me a liar." She jumped to the street.

"Margie," you called after her, "Margie!" You didn't care any more about her shoulder touching yours or the smell of her hair, you wanted her to ease your hurt, to lift the weight of the world from your struggling heart, but she ran straight up the sidewalk without looking back. You touched Pinky with the whip. "Giddap," you said, and slowly you went up the street all clouded and wavering through the tears hanging heavy in your eyes.

PINKY AMBLED ALONG, and you stopped every once in a while and delivered orders, but you hardly knew what you were doing because you were thinking of money. But nothing came into your mind but pictures—the ice-cream man taking your nickel and giving you a cone of strawberry, Ma's fingers opening her little black purse that she kept behind the clock on the kitchen mantel and holding out a dime to the hunchback who came with pins and needles and spools of thread and shoelaces in his old basket, Sylvie's hand putting in her State House bank the silver dollar that Uncle Gustave had given her for her birthday, a nickel into the hand of the girl for the moving pictures at the Bijou, a cent in the hand of old Mrs. Blaine for a stick of licorice, a nickel to be rung up by the conductor on the trolley for a ride to Meriden Park, a quarter and a dime into Sing Lee's yellow hand for Pa's collars, Pa, at the Bon Ton Shoe Store, saying, "You sure they feel all right, Charlie?" while his hand and Mr. Ingolstadt's were joined for a moment by two one-dollar bills, your hand putting a dime into the hand of the girl at Woolworth's for the plaid hair ribbon for Sylvie on her birthday, Pa, on Saturday nights, sorting out on the counter the nickels and dimes and quarters and half dollars and pennies, you helping him, and taking out of his pocket a thin roll of bills with an elastic around it and flattening out the bills and counting them slowly with his big thumb and forefinger turning each one back in his hand—pictures of hands joined in taking and giving money.

You would go out West. Someday you would come back, you would knock on the door as if you were a stranger, they would open it and cry with amazement, "It's Charlie!" but you wouldn't say anything, you would walk to the kitchen table, carrying your two valises, and you would open one and take out handful after handful of bills and pile them on the table; there would be so many they would cover the whole table and would be falling off onto the floor, and then you would just open the other valise on the floor and dump out the silver dollars ringing and rolling around everywhere, and you would say, "There you are, it's all for you, and there's plenty more where that came from."

Then someone was hollering, "Look out where you're going with that old plug," and you saw the kids were having a game of one o' cats in the street and you said, "You better go over on the lots to play, I just saw old Rooney the cop on his bike on Cherry Street. He'll put you in the cooler if he catches you," and you looked back just then, and Rooney was coming around the corner, and all the kids hollered, "Cheese it!" and ran. Then Mr. Rooney was riding along beside you, holding onto the wagon with one hand and saying, "Hello, Charlie, how's your father?" and you said, "Dandy, Mr. Rooney." "Ma, all right, too?" he asked, and you hoped the kids were watching you talk to old Rooney while Pinky clumped along and Rooney on his wheel hung onto the wagon. "Those kids'll get hurt some day, playing in the street like that," he said. "Well, give my regards to your father," and he turned his wheel off down Adams Street.

The way Rooney asked about your father made you feel better, but you didn't want to go back to the store yet. You turned back at the upper end of Water Street to go by the Bijou: COMPLETE CHANGE OF PROGRAM TWICE A WEEK, the big sign said, and you jumped out to look at the pictures in the lobby and see what they were going to have.

BIJOU   Mon., Tues., Wed.
TENDERFOOT BOB'S
REGENERATION
by the Selig Company
A Powerful Story Of Degeneration And Regeneration
Through The Personality Of A Mother

THE SEVENTH SON
by the Selig Company
A Thrilling Civil War Drama Of A Widow Who Gives Six
Brave Sons To Her Country Only To Have Her Seventh Son
A Coward. President Lincoln In A Leading Role

HER UNCLE JOHN   HOODOOED
A Very Funny Comedy   Another Funny
Chase   Farce

NEW ILLUSTRATED SONGS

"Looks like a good show you got here next week," you said to the man who was sweeping the sidewalk.

"Yup, you better come see it, sonny," he said. He beat his broom on the curbstone and went inside.

"Giddap, Pinky," you said.

The nearer you came to the store, the worse you felt. You didn't know how you were going to look at your father. Slowly you tied Pinky to the hitching-post and rubbed his nose and then when there was nothing else to do, you went in. Your father was sawing through a steak bone for Mrs. Cannon and old Mrs. Levy was poking around in the vegetables and Benny Martin was standing around waiting. "Hi, Charlie," he said, "gimme a pint of molasses and a box of Shredded Wheat and a peck of potatoes, and hurry up because my mother is waiting for 'em." "All right, gimme a chance, will ya," you said and went up to Mrs. Levy, and she had already picked out what she wanted, two pounds of tomatoes and a head of cabbage, and you put them in a bag for her, and then at last you went up to your father and you had to look at him, and you said, "Eighteen cents out of a dollar," and he gave you the change and smiled at you, and you could hardly look at him, wanting to throw your arms around him. Then you waited on Benny, and he and Mrs. Cannon went out together. And then you and your father were alone.

"Well, Charlie, what's new?" he asked.

"Nothing much," you said. "Only Mrs. Galland didn't pay me for the order. She said she'd pay you next time she came in."

"Hell," Pa said, "there's a woman for you. She promised me when she left the order to pay you when you delivered it." Impatiently, he whisked the bone dust off the chopping block. "Sure, she'll spend all kinds of money on a fancy picture-hat covered with flowers or ten dollars on a corset, but she won't pay for the food she eats. How's a man to get on if he can't collect his bills? And she's a suffragette, too. Sure, it's women like her that want the vote, not the sensible ones like your mother. Gosh, Charlie, it makes my blood boil. Well, what else? Riley have anything to say?"

"No," you said. Now it was coming. Now. "I met Margie Golden and gave her a ride," you said slowly, and then your voice broke and got high and shrill. "She said—she said—" Your heart seemed to explode in your chest and then the tears spurted out of your eyes and you ran to him while he stood bewildered and threw your arms around him and bawled like a baby.

"Charlie," he said, "son, what's the matter? What happened? All right now," he said, "nothing's worth that much crying about. Come on, a big feller like you, too." He was patting your shoulder. "Come on, son, tell your old man about it."

After a while you told him what Margie had said.

His hand fell away from your shoulder, and he sucked his lower lip in. "Yes, I see," he said slowly. "No wonder." You watched him through your tears. "It's all right, Charlie," he said at last. "It's nothing for you to get upset about. Margie's one of those little pitchers that have big ears, that's all." Still you watched him. "Listen, Charlie," he said, "you get enough to eat, don't you? Never hungry, are you? Always get a pair of new shoes when you need them, don't you?" He laughed and turned around. "Look, there aren't any patches on my pants, are there?" You laughed shakily. "Listen, son," he said, "I'll do the worrying for this family. And when Harry Robbins is licked, you'll be the first one to know it—I'll tell you first, and then you can take charge of the Robbins family." He laughed again. "Feel better now?" he asked. You nodded. "Don't worry about Golden," he said, "I'll take care of him all right. I'm the guy that put the gold in Golden, I'm the guy," he said.

"Gee, Pa, that's a good one," you laughed. He was funny all right, you thought. There was no one like your father. He could lick the world. And you had a sudden vision of your father punching Jack Johnson right on the jaw, knocking him out, knocking out that bright Black Tiger with one punch. . . .

ALL THAT had happened last Saturday afternoon. Now you took the last bite of meat on your plate and said, "What we going to have for dessert?" and Ma said, "I never knew a boy to be so crazy for sweets. Wait and see," she said. She got up and took the supper plates out and came back with a big plate. "That's classy," you said, "double layer chocolate cake." And Sylvie said, "I want a big piece, Charlie always gets a bigger piece than me." Pa said, "For Heaven's sake, Martha, what sense is there in your standing over a hot stove all day in the middle of the summer, baking? I could've stopped at Moran's and brought you home a cake." But he was smiling just the same, and Ma said, "It's no bother at all—so long as I was baking anyway, it took me five minutes longer to mix up a cake."

Your mother was tall and big-boned, with a deep bosom, and her hair was twined around her head in two big dark brown braids. Sylvie loved to brush her hair out for her. Coming home in the afternoon, you would holler, "Ma!" and she would say, "Yes, come in, Charlie," and you would go into the bedroom, and Ma would be sitting in front of the bureau and Sylvie would be slowly brushing her hair. Ma would say, "That's enough now, Sylvie," and Sylvie would say, "Just a little longer, Ma. Just a little." She had some gray hair, but not much, and she wouldn't pull it out because she said it would make two gray hairs grow where there was only one before. She would take the hair-combings and burn them in the kitchen stove, and after she had cut your or Sylvie's nails, she would burn the nail-parings, too. When you asked her why, she said, "I don't know, but Gramma always did it. All the women in the Old Country did it, I don't know why." Her eyes were dark, and over them her forehead was low and wide.

After Sylvie was born, you went in the next day to see Ma, and you were frightened. Her hair was spread out loose on the pillow and when you kissed her, her skin was dry and hot, and she looked like Gramma before Gramma died—her face drawn in and pale. "Now, son," Pa said, "you can stay only a minute." "Are you sick, Ma?" you said. "Are you?" "Look," Ma said, "don't you want to see your baby sister that the doctor brought last night?" and she turned back the quilt on the other side of her, and you saw the little red face and the tiny fuzzy head. "Are you sick, Ma?" you said. "Are you sick?" After all you were only seven then, and your heart was still clenched with the anguish of your mother's cries in the night, that had made you sob with terror. "Ma," you screamed, "Ma!" and your father came in and lighted the gas and sat down on the bed and patted your shoulder. His face was gray, and he said, "Now, Charlie, you go to sleep." But you kept on crying, and after a little while he turned out the light and went out, and pretty soon you heard again your mother's cries echoing and re-echoing through the house. A long time ago, when you were seven.

A long, long time ago, the years running together into one, one dreamy summer evening long ago.

You were just taking the last bite of your cake when someone knocked at the door. "Come in," Sylvie screamed before anyone else could say anything.

The door opened, and Mr. Gruner the insurance man with his little black bag came in smiling, showing his gold teeth and nodding. "Good appetite," he said.

"Thank you, Mr. Gruner," Ma said.

"Hello, Gruner," Pa said. He did not look up and kept right on eating.

"Everybody in good health, I hope?" Mr. Gruner said. He kept on smiling and nodding. "You mustn't worry the Company, you know."

"Everyone's fine," Ma said. "What can we do for you, Mr. Gruner?"

"Well, now," he said, "I don't want to disturb you at supper, maybe I better come back a little later."

Ma got up quickly with a disturbed look at Pa. "Why? Is anything wrong?" she asked.

Mr. Gruner hesitated, looking at Pa. Then he said, "Uh, well, there's a little matter of three, four dollars due on the children's policies you know."

Ma looked at him and then at Pa. Her face got red and then very pale.

Mr. Gruner stopped smiling. He said, "I been carrying them myself the last eight, nine weeks. Out of my own pocket. Mr. Robbins promised me ——"

Ma turned to Pa. "You told me you were paying on the policies, Harry. You remember you told me."

Pa threw his napkin down on the table. "For God's sake, Gruner," he said, "why don't you let a man have his supper in peace? You insurance men are a lot of damn bloodsuckers." His voice was loud and empty.

"Harry!" Ma said.

Mr. Gruner picked up his little bag. "I did the best I could, Mrs. Robbins," he said. "No one could do more. Out of my own pocket, too. I guess the policies will have to lapse."

"Don't worry, Gruner, you'll get your money," Pa said.

"Only a quarter a week," Ma said. "How could you let them go so long, Harry?"

"I couldn't be bothered with chicken feed," Pa said loudly, "that's why."

"Of course not, Mr. Carnegie," Ma said.

"Will you quit nagging me?" Pa hollered. He went out of the kitchen and banged the door. Sylvie began to cry.

Mr. Gruner looked as if he were going to cry, too. "Gee, Mrs. Robbins," he said, "I'll come back some other time."

"No, no," Ma said, "wait—I'll get you the money." She went out, too, and closed the door behind her.

"Don't cry, Sylvie," you said, "don't cry." You got up and patted her back. You felt stiff with Mr. Gruner watching you out of his little blue eyes.

"Tell Pa to come back," Sylvie said.

You could hear their voices mumbling in the bedroom. Pretty soon Pa came out. He smiled at Mr. Gruner and held out some bills and the little insurance books. "Sorry I got excited, Gruner," he said. "Here's your money."

Mr. Gruner began to smile and nod. "That's all right, Mr. Robbins," he said, "I know what it is to be a little short sometimes."

"Oh, that isn't it," Pa said. "Business worries, you know how it is, a man forgets himself sometimes."

"Sure, sure," Mr. Gruner said. He began to write in the little books.

Ma came out. "You better call here at the house every week," she told him.

"That's fine," Mr. Gruner said. He picked up his hat and his little bag. "Well, thank you," he said. "Good night, people. Good night, children."

"Good night," everyone said. He went out.

Ma sat down again. "Sit down, finish your supper," she said to Pa. He sat down and picked up his fork. "A fine meal," she said.

"Oh, give a man some peace," Pa said, "it's all over, ain't it?"

"Yes, till the next time," Ma said.

Sylvie said, "Don't fight."

"There, you see?" Pa said.

All this time you hadn't moved. You felt sick and ashamed. Ma said, "Have some more cake, Charlie."

"I don't feel like it," you said.

"Here now, you," Pa said, "don't be lippy to your mother."

You began to eat without knowing what you were eating.

Pa said suddenly, "You'll see, Martha, some day there'll be plenty of money. Worse men than me have made good. Just believe me, old girl." He got up and kissed Ma's cheek. "Give the old man a smile," he said.

"Lookit, Charlie, lookit, Pa is kissing Ma," Sylvie said. She bounced up and down on her chair. "Lookit, Charlie."

Ma looked up and gave you a long deep look out of her dark eyes. For a second everything was clear, you sensed the secret pain of being, looking into her deep eyes. Then she turned and smiled at Pa, "What a big baby you are," she said, "worse than Sylvie."

Pa laughed and went back to his chair. A cool breeze blew the curtains back and the sun lay bright upon the tablecloth.

THEN SUPPER was all over, and Pa was unbuttoning the top button of his pants and going into the parlor with the Boston *American* and the *News*. He came back again in a minute. "Listen to this, Charlie," he said, "here's a good one." He shook the paper in his hand.

"What is it?" Ma asked.

"Listen," he said:

> "Hey diddle, diddle, the cat and the fiddle,
> The cow jumped over the moon,
> The Beef Trust laughed to see the rise,
> And the citizen dined on a prune."

He laughed. "These newspaper fellers are pretty smart," he said, "pretty smart. I don't see how they think these things up."

"It is smart," Ma said.

"And true, too," said Pa.

"I can't bother now to talk politics," Ma said.

Pa laughed again. "Well, I know one girl who'll never be a suffragette, thank God," he said. He went back into the parlor.

Ma began to clear the table with Sylvie helping her, and you went to the window and looked out. The sun was touching the top of the maples. You saw Rooney going by on his bike with his helmet on the handlebars and his face all red in the sun. Two or three autos chugged down the street. You could tell what kind they were by their looks. The kids used to stand on the corner and guess what kind was coming down the street, and you could tell the most. A gray Cadillac went by, then came a Kissel Kar, and after that, a Metz. Then Mr. Connors from the bank went by, driving his buggy with the black horse that won trotting-races at the State Fair. In the front yard across the street, a couple of kids were playing peggy, their voices rising strong and shrill. You wished you lived in a house of your own and not in a three-family house. Farther down the street you could see Mr. Martin sitting on the front stoop smoking his pipe, and Mrs. Martin standing down by the gate talking over the pickets to a lady you didn't know. Then, for a moment, as in a picture, as in a dream—everybody, everything was still in a long moment of quiet, the street poised and hung like a picture in the warm still air—everything, the autos, the policeman, the black horse, the kids, the women, the trees stood still for a second—and then a long low cry sighed through the summer evening, and the street breathed and moved again. You awoke from your dream, *but are you not still dreaming of the summer evening long ago?*

You saw your best friend, Frankie Myers, thin and dark, coming up the street. *And Frankie? Where is Frankie now? In what French field still feeding the wheat with his torn body and shattered bones?* He walked along quickly, clacking the end of his baseball bat against the pickets, imitating a drum. He stopped in front of the house and looked up. "Hey, Charlie," he yelled, "Charliee-ee!"

You pushed the screen back and stuck your head out. "What you want, Frankie?"

"Come on over to the lots," he hollered. "We got a challenge from the Adams Street kids. Bring your catcher's mitt and the mask."

"You got a ball?" you asked him.

"Yes," he said, "Benny Martin's bringing his."

"Wait a minute," you yelled. You went into the pantry where Ma was scrubbing the cake pan. "Ma," you said, "can I go out?"

"I don't know, Charlie," she said, "seems to me you go out every single night."

Pa called in from the parlor, "Oh, let the boy go, Martha. The sun won't be down for two hours yet, and he worked hard enough at the store today."

"That's just it," said Ma. "He's overdoing it."

"Aw, Ma, we're just gonna play six innings," you pleaded.

Sylvie said, "Let me come, too, Charlie. Ma, can I go with Charlie?"

"No," said Ma, "you stay right here. And don't start sniffling at me either. All right, Charlie," she said, "go ahead, but you be sure and be back before nightfall."

"Yup," you said, and ran out to your room to get your mitt and mask out of the closet and went running down the stairs, hearing

Sylvie's voice through her sobs, "You let Charlie do everything, you don't let me do nothing."

"Gee, it's still hot," you said to Frankie. "Who's going to play?"

"Well, this is the line-up I made up," Frankie said. "You, catch; me, pitch; Benny at first, Joe Ruben at second, Oscar Mueller at third, Pete Menzies, or Maxie Patton at short—the one that don't play short will have to pay in the outfield—and then we'll have to pick up a couple of little kids for the daisies. They're all over at the lots now, I guess. I stopped at Francis Connors's house, but he went to the country yesterday with his mother. You think that's a good line-up?" he asked.

"Sounds pretty classy to me," you said. "We ought to skunk those Adams Street kids."

You and Frankie went down Cherry Street to the end, turned down Water Street and down to the end of Washington Street, over the railroad bridge, and up the embankment where the grass grew rank and thick, and came to the lots. Away over at the other end where the diamond was laid out, you could see the kids running around and a ball soaring into the air. "Gosh, I hope we beat them," you said.

As you came nearer, Frankie grabbed your arm. "Look who they got!" he said.

"Who?" you asked.

"Big Mullarkey," he said. "He's not going to play for them, he's sixteen, anyway. What's he want to come hanging around here for? No one on our side's more than thirteen."

"And there's Little Mullarkey," you said.

"Well," said Frankie, "we don't care about Little, he can play if he wants to, but if Big plays, we'll call the game off."

There was an argument about Big Mullarkey's playing in the game. Pete Menzies got excited and kept calling Mullarkey a big horse. "Why don't you play with the fellers your own age?" he kept saying. And then Big swung at him, and Pete ducked and picked up a bat and hollered, "You lay a hand on me and I'll brain you."

The Adams Street kids stood around looking foolish because they didn't want Big to play any more than you did. Maxie Patton said, "Why don't you fight someone your own size?"

Big pushed his brother Little forward and said, "Little'll fight any one of you."

And Little said, "Go on, leave me alone, Big. Fight your own battles. Get out of here anyway, and let us play."

Then Big said all right, he wouldn't play, but he'd umpire and there was another argument. While that was going on, one of the drivers from the Gallogly Brewery had come over. "Come on," he said at last, seeing there wasn't going to be a fight. "Come on, quit your beefing around, let's get this ball game started." He said to Big, "Go away back and sit down."

Big's face got red and he said, "What you butting in for?" and the driver said, "Listen, don't get funny with me, if you don't want a punch in the nose." Big looked at him a second as if he would like to murder him, and then he went back across the lots. The driver said, "Batter up! No, wait a minute." He turned and yelled to where the beer drays were pulled up. "Hey, Louie!"

"What you want?" the man yelled back.

"Come on over," the driver hollered, "the Hinky Dinks are playing the Starfish Giants." He turned around. "All right," he said, "play ball."

"He thinks he's smart, don't he?" Benny Golden said to you. "Listen, Charlie," he said, "you going to let me play out in the daisies?" His hair was the color of Margie's.

"All right," you said.

It was a close game. All you got was one hit, but Frankie knocked a home run and Joe Ruben got two doubles, and even little Benny Golden got a hit. When the game was nearly over, you saw Margie and two other girls coming across the lots. Your heart jumped when you saw her, but you didn't try to show off. When she got closer, she hollered, "Benny!"

"Aw, what you want?" Benny said.

"Benny, you come right home," she said. "Ma's been looking all over for you."

"I can't go now," Benny said.

"You hafta," she told him.

"Aw, Margie," you said, "let him finish the game."

"Ma'll be awful mad, Benny. Besides we got frankfurters for supper," she told him.

"Gee whiz," Benny said, "a fella can't have any fun at all around here. I don't care if Ma is mad, I hafta finish the game."

"All right for you," she told him, "you'll get it when you get home."

"I don't care," Benny said.

In the last inning you got hit on the forehead just above your mask by a foul tip, and Margie came running over and said, "Gee, Charlie, does it hurt?"

"No, just a little," you said.

"I'm sorry we had a fight," she said.

"Me, too," you said.

Your team won, 10 to 8, and then the whole bunch started back for home. It was getting cooler, the sun was nearly down behind the horizon, and coming up Washington Street with Margie walking between you and her cousin Joe Ruben, her shoulder touching yours once in a while, with the leaves of the maples whispering overhead and the light shadows running over the sidewalk, and the evening breeze cooling your hot face, you felt pretty good. Then Little Mullarkey began to whistle In the Good Old Summertime, and Margie began to hum it, and one by one all the kids joined in, walking up the street singing In the Good Old Summertime, breaking the hush of the summer evening drifting down over the town:

> Strolling through a shady lane
> With that baby mine,
> I hold her hand, and she holds mine
> And that's a very good sign
> That she's my tootsy-wootsy
> In the good old summertime.

And some smart Aleck hollered, "Hire a hall, hire a hall," but everyone kept on singing and sang it twice over.

Then, one by one the crowd broke up, and Margie and Benny turned off up Maple Street. "Goodbye, Charlie," she said.

"You going to let me play again with you, Charlie?" Benny asked.

"Sure," you said, "any old time you want to." Hating to see her go, "So long, Margie," you said. Then only you and Frankie were left, going up the street together. "You been to the libarry lately, Frankie?" you asked him. "I haven't got anything to read."

"No," Frankie said, "but I got my card with me. You want to stop and get something?"

"Well," you said, "it's kind of late, but I'll catch it for staying out so long, anyway."

"Look," said Frankie, "the way to do is to get a book for your mother, too. See? Then you can tell her you stopped to get the book for her, that's why you're late."

"That's a speedy idea," you said. "Come on."

Going up Croker Street toward the library, you suddenly heard the long roll of drums, and you and Frankie began to run toward the corner. When you got there, you saw it was the Von Steuben Cadets on their way to drill in the Armory. "Look," you said, "there's my cousin Arthur Schulz." You pointed down the rank of rifles. "Hi, Art," you hollered, but his face was set forward and he did not even turn his head.

"When I'm eighteen, I'm going to join," said Frankie.

The Cadets went by, stepping smartly, their blue uniforms trim, the flag waving over their heads, and the drums beating in their blood. "I'm going to join, too," you said, "that's if my father lets me." Then the Cadets were gone by, marching down the long street, marching a long time, marching into the Argonne and Belleau Wood and the ridge near Vimy, and Frankie marching, too, the blood marching in his veins to spill itself into a roadside ditch at Soissons.

"We better hurry up," Frankie said. "The libarry'll be closing."

In the library it was cool and quiet. "You boys ought to know better than to come in here with such dirty hands," old Miss Lord said. "I've a good mind not to let you take any books out."

"Aw, gee, Miss Lord," Frankie said, "we just came from a ball game. We'll wash our hands before we read them. Honest."

"You promise me?" she said, looking at you from under her glasses. You nodded. "Very well," she said.

And the books were waiting for you, row on row, red and black, green and gold. You knew what you wanted. You went to the shelves where the sign said *Boys and Girls*. Your finger traced along the books. *Dick Fowler, Tackle*—you had read that one twice. *Lefty Plays the Game*—you had read that, too. And *Danny Phipps, Freshman* you had had out last month.

"Did you find anything?" Frankie said.

"No, there's no new ones," you said. "I read all the others."

"Is this any good?" He took *Danny Phipps, Freshman* down.

"It's a peach," you told him. "I read it twice. It's about this feller

who goes away to school and he has red hair and is a sorehead,
and he goes out for the baseball team, and he's doing good until
he fights with an umpire and the coach puts him off the team.
Then ——"

Someone took you by the shoulder. It was Miss Lord. "Young
man," she said, "do you see that sign?" She pointed up above the
shelves at QUIET PLEASE.

"Gee, Miss Lord," you said, "there's no one else in here but us."

"It doesn't make any difference," she said, "you have to obey
the rules." Then she smiled. "What's the matter, Charlie, have you
read them all?"

"Yes'm," you said.

"Have you read this one?" she asked. She took a book from the
A's and put it in your hand. *Little Men* by Louisa Alcott," she
said.

"Yes'm," you said, "I read it a long time ago."

"Did you like it?" she asked.

"Well, not very much," you told her, "it's kind of old-fashioned.
But it was good in some places," you said hurriedly.

"I knew Louisa Alcott once," she said. "A long, long time ago,"
she said in a faraway voice. "You come with me, Charlie."

You went to her desk with her, and she reached underneath it
and gave you a brand new book. *Winning His Y,* you read.

"It just came in today," Miss Lord said.

"Gee, you going to let me take it now?" you asked her. She nodded.
"That's peachy of you, Miss Lord," you said.

"Now, mind," she told you, "if you bring that book back with
a single dirty fingerprint on it, it'll be a long time before I let you
take another one."

"Yes'm," you said.

Then Frankie came over with his book, and Miss Lord wrote
the numbers on the card, and you said good night to Miss Lord,
and were just going out when Frankie grabbed your arm and said,
"Charlie, we forgot the books for our mothers."

"Gosh, yes," you said. You turned back to Miss Lord. "Look, Miss
Lord," you said, "we want to take some books home for our mothers.
You want to pick out one for mine and one for Frankie's?"

"Now that's thoughtful of you boys," she said. "I'll be glad to."
She went to the shelves. "Now let's see," she said half to herself,

"what would they like?" She came back with two books. "Here," she said, "here are two new ones." She came back with the books. "Here," she said, *Mr. Opp* for your mother, Frank, and *The White Sister* for yours, Charlie."

"Thank you very much, Miss Lord," you said, and you and Frankie went out into the deepening dusk of the gentle summer evening.

On the way home, you talked about the ball game and how sore Big Mullarkey was. "Did you see how pale he got when that feller chased him away?" Frankie asked.

"I felt kind of sorry for Big then," you said. "For a minute I thought Big was going to take a punch at him. He boxes over at the Washington A. C. sometimes, Little told me."

"Aw, no," Frankie said, "those brewery-wagon drivers get good muscles pushing those barrels. He'd of killed Big."

"Big would have to take boxing lessons from Jack Johnson to beat that guy," you said.

"Mullarkey the White Hope," Frankie said, and you both laughed. Then you stopped for a minute in front of Frankie's house to say good night. "I'm going to run the rest of the way," you said, "my mother's going to be good and sore at me."

"Well, don't forget, you got a book for her," he said.

"You bet I won't," you told him. "So long, Frankie."

"So long," he said, going away from you, his voice already faint, his voice floating back faintly over the years. And Mullarkey, Mullarkey the White Hope, over the years? A broken-down prize-fighter battered in third-rate athletic clubs in preliminary fights, always preliminary—a chopping-block, his ears flattened, his nose broken, Mullarkey sits in the State Asylum mumbling his fingers, sitting in a corner for hours, tense and waiting for the gong, flinging off imaginary punches, Mullarkey crying brokenly, his head bowed in his hands. *Big! Mullarkey! Don't you remember me? It's Charlie Robbins, don't you remember? Big, don't you remember, don't you . . . a long time ago?"*

Frankie's voice floating away from you, and then you were going up the dark stairway and into the kitchen just as Ma was lighting the mantle. "I got a good mind to take a strap to you, Charlie Robbins," she said.

"Aw, gee, Ma," you said. "What for?"

"What for?—look at the time."

You looked at the clock—a quarter to nine. "It isn't so late, Ma," you said. "I guess I'm big enough now to stay out a little later."

"Listen to him," she said, "hardly out of his diapers!"

"Aw, Ma," you said, "don't be sore at me."

"Well, you see that you get home in good time hereafter, you understand?"

"Yes'm," you said. "Where's Pa?"

"He fell asleep over the paper—and don't you disturb him either. He'll have something to say to you about getting in all hours of the night."

"Gee, Ma," you said, "it isn't even dark yet." You went to the window. But it was nearly dark. The watering wagon was going by, and you watched the fan-shaped drench of water pouring over the dusty street.

"Where've you been anyway?" she asked.

"We had a ball game," you told her, and then you remembered about the book. "I stopped at the library with Frankie Myers— we got you a book," you said. You held it out to her and she took it. *"The White Sister,"* she read, "by F. Marion Crawford. Now when am I going to find time to read it?" she asked. "Next time you come right home from your ball games—never mind being so good to me. *The White Sister*—what's it about?"

"Gee, Ma, how should I know?" you said. "Miss Lord picked it out." Frankie was wise all right, all right, you thought. "Is Sylvie sleeping?"

And then Sylvie was calling out to you from her bedroom, "Charlie —Charlie—ee," in the baby voice that she put on sometimes.

"There now you woke her up," Ma said.

"I didn't wake her up," you said, "how could I?"

"Well, if you were home when you should be, she'd have been asleep long ago. She waited and waited for you to get home and tell her a story."

You felt a pang of guilt. "I forgot, Ma."

"Charlie—Charlie—ee," Sylvie called.

"Well, you'd better go in there, or she'll be up all night. Tell her a story if she wants one," Ma said.

You went into Sylvie's little room. She was standing up in her bed, waiting for you. "Charlie, you're mean to me," she said.

"No, I'm not, Sylvie."

"Yes, you are, too," she said. "You ran away from me, and you didn't tell me a story."

You went up to her and she put her arms around your neck. Her small warm body was in your arms and a sharp delight went over you. "Do you love me, Sylvie?"

"I love you best of all, Charlie."

You hugged her close to you for a moment, and then you said, "Now get under the cover, and I'll tell you a story."

"Two stories," she said.

"Nope, Ma'll be mad at you if you don't fall asleep."

"All right, Charlie," she said, "one story, but a long one."

"Yup," you said. You lay down beside her, carefully dangling your feet over the edge of the bed.

She pushed over till her head was in the hollow of your arm. "Now tell me the story."

"Well," you said, "once upon a time ——"

"Charlie," she said, "it's my birthday pretty soon."

"That's right," you said. "Who said anything about your birthday?"

"Pa did," she said, "I heard him talking to Ma after you went out. You going to give me something for my birthday, Charlie?"

"You bet I am," you said, "something peachy."

"Tell me what," she said.

"Listen," you said, "it's a secret. Now do you want me to go out, or shall I tell you a story? Ma'll get mad in a minute if you don't fall asleep."

"All right, tell me a story," she said.

"Well," you said, "once up a time—once upon a time there was a little girl named Sylvie who lived over the mountains far away."

"She had the same name like me," said Sylvie, stirring comfortably in the hollow of your arm.

"Yes, and one day she went for a walk in the woods." You sat up suddenly. "Ma," you called out, "the front doorbell's ringing." You heard her coming out of her bedroom.

"Yes, yes," she said, "I heard it. I wonder who it would be at this hour." You heard her go into the parlor.

"Who's coming, Charlie," Sylvie asked, "who's coming?"

"Sh," you said, "how should I know?"

You heard your mother in the parlor. "Harry," she was saying, "wake up. Someone's at the front door."

"Uh, what's that?—oh," Pa said. The Morris chair creaked as he got up. "Kind of late for a visitor," he said.

The doorbell rang again—a long peal. "Hurry up, Harry," Ma said. "Don't keep him waiting whoever it is."

"Come on, Charlie, tell me the story. So what happened?" Sylvie said.

"Wait a minute," you told her, "wait a minute."

You heard Pa's footsteps going heavily down the front stairs, then the sound of the door opening, and the mingling of your father's voice with another's. Then they were in the parlor, and your father was saying, "Martha, it's Mr. Golden." Your heart contracted with terror.

"Just a minute," Ma said, "I'll be right out."

"No, no, don't bother about me, I beg of you, Mrs. Robbins," Mr. Golden said. "Harry and me'll come out in the kitchen." They came out into the kitchen as Ma turned the mantle up.

"It's just as well," she said, "the mantle in the parlor is broken anyway. No matter how much I remind Harry, he forgets to bring a new one from the store."

"Say, Mrs. Golden is after me every second, every second, for what I forget to bring her," Mr. Golden said. You heard the scrape of chairs around the kitchen table.

"Charlie," Sylvie said, "Charlie, tell me the story."

"Yes, yes," you whispered, "wait a second, can't you?"

Ma said, "A glass of tea, Mr. Golden?"

"Your wife's a smart woman, Harry," Mr. Golden said. "That's very nice of you, Mrs. Robbins. And could you put in just a small slice lemon?"

"Certainly, Mr. Golden, I know how your people like their tea," Ma said. You heard her in the pantry, moving around, getting things ready.

"The story, Charlie," Sylvie said, pulling at your sleeve.

"So," you said, "she was walking in the woods and she walked a long ways, and pretty soon ——"

"Well, Harry, how's things with you?" Mr. Golden asked.

"I'm just getting by," Pa said, "just getting by."

"And pretty soon she was far far away from her house. . . ."

"That, I'm sorry to hear," said Mr. Golden, "real sorry. I thought maybe with the new store and a better location. . . ."

"Charlie!" Sylvie said.

"And she looked around and saw that she was lost and didn't know how to get home. . . . "

"Well," Pa said, "the mills are shut down, people are not buying, or else they're buying and owing. If I could collect what's owing to me, I'd be all right, believe me."

"So what did she do then?" Sylvie asked. She was getting sleepy, you could tell by her voice.

Mr. Golden laughed a little. "Say you took the words right out of my mouth, Harry. If I could only collect what's coming to me, I'd be all right, too, believe me. Harry, in business it's all the same. It takes a little money to make a little business go, and it takes a lot of money to make a big business go. We're in the same boat."

"So what then, Charlie? So what then did she do?"

"So she looked around and she looked around and all of a sudden she saw a black tiger coming along. . . ."

"If things was all right with me, Harry, I wouldn't care. Believe me, I wouldn't care. I could let six, seven months' rent go, I could wait till things picked up for you," Mr. Golden said. "Do you think I would have fixed up the whole store like new for you if I didn't think you could make a go of it there? Say, Harry, I'm a business man, I know what I'm doing. But right now I'm pinched myself. I got to pay interest on mortgages, I got office people to pay. People are out of work, they're not paying their rent."

"Charlie," Sylvie said. "Come on, tell me the story."

"So when she saw the black tiger, she got scared and began to cry and she hollered, 'Pa! Pa! there's a big tiger coming after me . . . !' "

"So if you could give me a little something, Harry, believe me it would help a lot," Mr. Golden said.

Pa was quiet for a little while. Then he said, "Hell, it's no use my trying to explain. The wholesalers . . . I've got bills to meet, I guess they'll have to carry me along for a while. It's their turn now," he said bitterly.

"Believe me, Harry, if I could help it, I wouldn't be after you like this," Mr. Golden said.

"Tell me the rest, Charlie, tell me the rest," Sylvie said.

"So she hollered as loud as she could and she looked back and she saw her father coming and the tiger was getting closer and closer all the time. . . . "

"Did I ever press you before, Harry, in all the years we did business together, did I ever press you before? Tell me, Harry, did I?"

"No," Pa said, "you always gave me a square deal."

"Ah!" Mr. Golden said.

"How much do you want?" Pa said in a dead voice.

"Charlie! Tell me."

"But her father was running fast before the tiger could come near her," you said quickly.

"Say, Harry," Mr. Golden said, "it's not a question how much I want, it's a question how much you can give me."

"Well," Pa said, "I owe you a hundred and sixty. I can give you sixty, and believe me, Golden, it comes hard."

"You don't have to tell me, Harry. I know," Mr. Golden said. "Whatever you could give me I'm satisfied."

Then you knew that Pa was reaching into his pants pocket and taking out the bills with the elastic around them. No, Pa, don't give it to him, the shout rose up in your throat, but you were quiet.

Sylvie pulled hard at your sleeve.

"So then her father came just when the tiger was going to jump on her and he grabbed a stick and began to hit the tiger. . . . "

"There you are," Pa said.

"Say, Harry, I appreciate it," Mr. Golden said. "Every little bit helps."

"It's not a little bit to me," Pa said.

"Excuse me, Harry, it don't sound right, but you know what I mean," Mr. Golden said.

"Yes, I know," Pa said in a flat voice.

"Finish the story, Charlie."

"So her father was fighting with the tiger, but it was a big tiger and it was beating, so then the father hollered for the little girl's brother to come help him. . . . "

"Tea'll be ready in a minute," Ma called out from the pantry. You knew she had been standing quietly there listening as you were listening.

"I'll give you a receipt," Mr. Golden said.

"So the little girl's brother came ——"

"Was his name Charlie?"

"Yes, his name was Charlie," you said, "and he came and jumped on the black tiger and helped his father to knock him down and then they cut off his head and took the little girl home to her mother and they all lived happily ever after."

"Here's your tea," Ma said.

"That's fine, Mrs. Robbins. Fine," Mr. Golden said.

"You going to fall asleep now, Sylvie?" you asked her.

"Yes. Kiss me good night, Charlie," she said.

You sat up and kissed her small warm face. "Good night, Sylvie," you said.

"Good night, Charlie," she said drowsily. She turned around and you pulled the cover up around her shoulders. Then you came out into the kitchen, blinking in the light.

"Ah, it's your boy," said Mr. Golden. "Hello, Charlie."

You couldn't look at him. "Hello, Mr. Golden," you said.

"Is Sylvie asleep?" your mother asked. You nodded. "All right now, you can say good night and go to bed, too," she said.

"Good night, Pa," you said. You couldn't look at him either. "Good night, Ma," you went to her and she kissed you. "Good night, Mr. Golden," and you went to your room.

"A fine boy," you heard Mr. Golden say.

"You fat old fool," you said under your breath. There was a hard lump in your throat. Then you lighted the gas jet over your bed and washed up in a hurry because you had remembered your book. You undressed and got into bed, and leaning on one elbow, began to read *Winning His Y*. But you couldn't read because you kept thinking of the dull heavy sound of Pa's voice when he was talking to Mr. Golden and of Ma standing silently in the pantry listening. You were close to crying, but you wouldn't give in.

After a while, you heard the scrape of chairs being pushed back in the kitchen and footsteps going toward the front door and the sound of voices and faint "good nights." Pretty soon your mother came in. She said, "Are you still up, for goodness sake, Charlie? Here give me that book. That's enough reading tonight. Pa wants you at the store good and early tomorrow morning." But Pa was coming to the door with the paper in his hand. "Now, Harry," Ma said, "it's time he was asleep."

"I'll just be a minute," Pa said. Ma went out, and he sat down on the edge of the bed.

"Pa," you said, "Pa!"

"What's the matter, Charlie?" He looked surprised.

"Pa, you know—Mr. Golden ——"

"Now what did I tell you last week?" he said. "I'll do the worrying for this family."

"But Pa—the money," you said.

"Never mind, Charlie," he told you. "Leave it to your old father."

"Aw, Pa, you're not so old," you said. No matter how bad you felt, he always made you feel better.

"Everything's going to be all right," he said.

"Yes, Pa, you bet."

"That's not what I came in for. We'll leave the discussion of our financial difficulties to a future date," he said, holding his chin in his hand and making believe he was stroking a beard, making a face at the long words.

You laughed. "Gee, Pa, you're a scream."

"Look," he said, "this is what I wanted to show you." You sat up and he unfolded the paper on the bed. "Sylvie's birthday's coming next week," he said, "and your mother and I thought we'd give her and you a time. So listen to this," and he turned the paper so that you could see, and read slowly with his finger tracing along each line:

FORGET YOUR TROUBLES!
At The Opera House August 16
One Night Only
The Great Big Theatrical Event
William Shakespeare's Immortal Creation
A MIDSUMMER NIGHT'S DREAM
Kings, Queens, Nobles, Courtiers, Elves and Fairies, Fools
Not Moving Pictures But Real People
2 Carloads of Scenery
Don't Miss Seeing This Great Big Show
And Don't Fail to Bring the Little Ones
Prices $1.50 $1.00   75c   50c   25c

"Gee, Pa, you mean it? You going to take us?" You had never been to the Opera House.

"Yup," he said, "we're all going on Sylvie's birthday party."

"Gee, that'll be dandy!" you said.

"Good night, Charlie," he said.

"Good night, Pa." He bent over and kissed you. You put your arms around his neck and held him a second.

"Good night, son," his voice floating back through the dark doorway, *his voice floating back over the years.*

The evening, don't you remember the dreamy summer evening of long ago? How can you forget the back streets of American towns falling asleep in the evening when you watched from your bed the summer moon hanging in the maples and smelled the bitter wild cherry trees in the back yard and heard the long, long whistle of a locomotive crying in the still of the summer evening? An echo of a sweet faraway song echoing in your ears while you fell asleep in the summer evening long ago?

And the summer morning? Do you. . . .

I remember.

In the morning Pa came in at six o'clock when the sun was still in the wild cherry trees. He was still in his undershirt, his suspenders hanging down. "All right, Charlie," he said, "all right, get up now, there's plenty to do." He scratched at the place on the bedstead where the iron showed beneath the white enamel, "And some day soon you can get a can of white paint and do this bed over. All right, get up now," he said, his voice floating back through the doorway and the water rushing in the washbowl.

At breakfast there was scrambled eggs and bread and butter and cocoa. "It's going to be another hot day," Ma said. "I wish we could all go to the country."

"Francis Connors went to the country yesterday with his mother," you said.

"Well," said Pa, "if we had the money the Connorses have, we'd be in the country, too. I can remember when Frank Connors used to sweep out his father's barroom down near the mills. He made a lot of money out of the Polacks. Well," he said, pushing his cup back, "I thought one day I'd be rich, too. But we'll have to leave it to Charlie, I guess, to make the money for this family." He grinned at you.

"Aw, Pa," you said, "quit your kidding."

"Well, why not?" Ma said. "There's plenty of poor boys who've made fortunes in this country."

"Sure, if you get the chance," Pa said. "But if you want to make real money, you have to go where money is—Boston, or New York maybe."

"Gramma used to say that the people in the Old Country thought the streets in America were paved with gold," Ma said.

"Well," Pa said, getting up from the table and wiping his mouth, "me and Charlie are going right out and pick up a million dollars."

"Two million!" Ma said laughing.

Outside on the brick sidewalk, you and Pa paused a minute. The warm freshness of the morning drifted over you, and you took a deep breath of the sweet air.

"I'm going down to the depot to see if that stuff I ordered from Boston is in," Pa told you. "You go over to the stable and get Pinky and pick me up down there."

"All right, Pa," you said.

As you walked over toward the stable, there was no one on the streets but a big gray in the shafts of a milk-wagon, pulling strongly against his collar, and all the cans and bottles rattling as he went by. The livery stable was white and square with a peaked gable. On the ridge of the gable gleamed a golden horse with a flying mane galloping up the wind. The inside of the stable smelled strongly and richly of fresh hay and the sweat of horses and manure. The hooves of the horses banged now and then against the stalls.

As you went toward Pinky's stall, Joe Flynn came out of one of the big box stalls at the back. His face was pale, and his eyes looked dark and tired. "Hey, Charlie," he said.

"Hello, Mr. Flynn," you said.

"You want to see something pretty nice?" he asked you.

"Sure," you told him.

"Come here then." He swung open the upper half of the door of the box stall. "Look there," he said.

You looked into the dimness of the stall. The brown mare, Bessie, stood leaning against the side of the stall, her nose deep in the feed bin. But on the floor you saw a tiny horse with long legs whose small hooves rattled on the floor as you looked at him. "Gee, Mr. Flynn, he's a dandy," you said. "When'd he come?"

"About two hours ago," Joe said. "Me and the vet had some time with Bessie there, believe me. But we got her son into the world all right. Up nearly all night we were. I just finished cleaning the place up."

You were still looking at the colt, so fragile-looking, his soft brown eyes half-closed, his thin delicate legs stirring restlessly every once in a while.

"He'll be getting up in a second. You watch," Joe said.

"All by himself?" you asked.

"Yup," said Joe, "he's guaranteed to stand and suck, that colt is. You know who served Bessie?"

"No," you asked. "Who?"

"That black trotter of Mr. Connors's—and Bessie's got good blood in her, too. I'm going to make something out of that colt," he said.

"Look, Joe, look!" you said.

The colt was making to get up. Bessie lifted her head from the feed bin and turned toward him. His legs thrashing, his hooves drumming on the floor, the colt was trying anxiously to rise. As you watched, he lurched to his feet, his legs outsprawled. For a moment he wavered, then found his balance, his legs spread away out like stilts. Bessie let out a long low whinny.

"She's proud of him all right," Joe said. "That's a real boyo she's got there."

As Bessie came closer, the colt lurched toward her, and she turned her flank to him. His head went awkwardly along the flank, nuzzling and searching. Then it dropped lower and under her flank.

"He's found the teat all right, all right," Joe said, grinning. "Guaranteed to stand and suck, by God," he said. "Look at him go at it."

Then, as you walked back toward Pinky's stall carrying his harness, Joe said, "By the way, Charlie, you can tell your Pa I had the vet take a look at Pinky while he was here."

"Why, what's the matter with Pinky?" you said startled.

"Well, he's been off his feed kind of the last few weeks," Joe said. "He ain't eaten any more than would keep a sparrow alive."

"What'd the vet say?" you asked him.

"Not much. There might be something the matter with his insides, but most likely it's just plain old age. How long you had him anyway?" he asked.

"Nearly as long as I can remember," you said. "Six or seven years, I guess."

"Yup," said Joe, "and I remember looking him over when your Pa bought him. He was about seven years old then. No wonder he's off his feed. He's a pretty old plug."

"He's no plug!" you said.

"No?" said Joe. "Well, have it your own way, sonny."

"It's funny," you told him, "I guess Pinky's the same age as me about."

"Yup, and it's a funny thing that a horse's days are just about over when a man's are just beginning," and going back to his little office, he said, grinning maliciously over his shoulder, "but I guess there's life in the old plug yet," and the door closed behind him before you could say anything.

The door closed behind him, and not many years later the big front doors closed, too. The livery stable stood empty with the gilt slowly flecking off the horse on the weathervane, the white paint peeled off, and a dead musty smell drifted around the place, and then the garage all steel and cement went up and where there had been the warm living smell of horses and their sweat, there was a cold dead stink of gasoline and damp concrete. The door closed behind Joe Flynn and his little malice, and you went into Pinky's stall and ran your hand over his thin flank while he rubbed his nose against your shoulder. "Good old Pinky," you said, and he rolled his eye back at you while you harnessed him hurriedly. You led him out into the yard and backed him between the shafts of the wagon and hitched him up. "Giddap," you said, and went ambling along down the street under the shade of the rustling maples.

At the depot Pa was waiting impatiently. "What kept you?" he said. You told him about the colt.

"It's a long time since I saw a newborn colt," he said. "I'll have to stop in at the stable tonight."

You told him what Joe had said about Pinky, and he looked worried. "I was wondering just the other day how long Pinky'd hold out. But I guess he's good for a few more years yet," he said. "I hope so."

You helped him load the boxes and crates on the wagon while the people who were waiting for the 7:58 to Boston stood and watched. Your father stopped to talk a minute with Mr. Barton and came back laughing.

"What's the joke, Pa?" you asked.

"He's a funny one, that Harve Barton," your father said. "Says he's sick and tired of paying railroad fares, so he's going to run for the Legislature and get free passes on the railroad. Says he'd make as good a grafter as any of the tinhorns now representing this fair state." He laughed again. "You ought to hear him at lodge meetings. He makes us nearly bust laughing." He climbed up on the seat beside you.

"Giddap, Pinky," you said.

AT THE STORE you opened the stuff that had come in on the train and put it away. Pa was busy getting the orders ready. You swept the store and straightened out the back room and got the fruit and vegetables out on the sidewalk. Once in a while you stopped to talk to one of the kids who was on his way downtown.

Along about eleven o'clock Pa said, "All right, Charlie. You can take these out now."

You loaded the orders into the wagon, unhitched Pinky, and started off down Water Street. You had no idea what was coming. You had been going along, delivering the orders, not worrying about Pinky at all, but wondering about the show Pa was taking you to see at the Opera House and wondering if any of the other kids were going.

All of a sudden, right in the middle of Laurel Street, Pinky stopped short. You jerked on the reins. "Giddap, Pinky," you said, "giddap." He took a couple of steps, then lurched forward slowly, his front legs folding under him, and went down between the shafts on his side, his head stretched forward along the dusty street, while the wagon tipped and hung on two side wheels. For a moment you sat terrified. Then you jumped down and ran to his head. "Pinky!" you hollered, and tugged at his bridle. His head came up off the street and then fell back again.

The street had been nearly empty, but suddenly there was a crowd. You heard a kid hollering, "Hey, Louie, hurry up. There's a horse dropped dead in the street."

Everybody began to give you advice, and a couple of men grabbed Pinky's head and tried to drag him up, but he couldn't move. A woman was saying, "It's a shame, the poor beast."

Then a big man in overalls came pushing through the crowd and said, "Mother of God, unhitch him anyway, pull the shafts away from him. Let him lie easy."

You jumped up and ran to one of the shafts and undid the buckles while the big man unhitched on the other side. Luckily, Pinky was not lying on the shaft; it had slipped up over his shoulder when he went down. "All right now," the man said, "a couple of you fellers pull this wagon back." Some of the men and the kids took hold of the wagon and pulled it away and wheeled it to the side of the street.

Then while you were tugging frantically at Pinky's head, the big man saying, "Now take it easy, sonny, take it easy," someone touched you on the shoulder and said, "What's the matter, Charlie? What happened?" It was old Rooney.

"Gee, Mr. Rooney," you said, you were half crying, "I don't know. All of a sudden he just stopped and went down." You brushed at the flies that were circling around Pinky's head. "What'll I do?" you asked him, "what'll I do?"

"Keep cool, Charlie," he said. "We'll have him up in a minute. Here," he said, he took a kid by the shoulder, "you go with Mrs. Hallett there. Will you give him a couple of pails of water, Mrs. Hallett?" he asked, turning toward one of the women.

"Of course," she said, "you come with me, young man."

"I guess the heat got him," Mr. Rooney said. He turned around. "Come on now, stand back a ways," he said to the crowd, "give the poor suffering beast some air." They all moved back a little and then began to edge forward again.

The kid came with the water and Rooney sluiced the pails over Pinky's head. His head reared back, but you could see the water made him feel better. "Get some more," Rooney said to the panting kid.

"All right, Mr. Rooney," the kid said, he was feeling pretty important, "right away."

"Hey, Julius, lemme carry one, willya?" One of the kids started running after him, but Rooney stopped him.

"Here, you," he said, "make yourself useful. Run up to Joe Flynn's livery stable and tell him to come down here with another horse. Tell him what happened, see?"

"Sure, Mr. Rooney, sure I will," the kid said. He began to run.

Rooney turned back to you. "Now take it easy, Charlie," he said, "everything'll be all right. You want to go back and tell your father what happened?"

"He won't have to," Mrs. Hallett said, "I just called up and told him, and he asked me to tell you he can't leave the store right now, but to get hold of Mr. Flynn up at the livery stable."

"That's what I thought," Rooney said.

"Here's some more water, Mr. Rooney," said the kid. "Willya let me throw one on him, huh, Mr. Rooney?"

"Get away with you," Rooney said. He took the pails and threw them over Pinky. His head came up again, and Rooney grabbed the bridle and jerked on it. "Up with ye now, you poor brute," he said. Pinky heaved his body forward, his hind legs drew up under him, his front hooves pawed the ground for a second, and then with a lurch he was on his feet again, his head hanging down low.

"Pink!" you said, and he rubbed his nose on your shoulder.

Then Joe Flynn showed up, leading a big black horse. "Oh, I see you got him up," he said. "Well, Charlie, what'd I tell you?"

"What?" you asked him.

"About him being a plug," he said, nodding at Pinky.

"Aw, leave him alone," you said.

Joe hitched the black horse into the wagon and came back with the halter and put it on Pinky. "All right," he said, and led Pinky off.

"Thanks, Mr. Rooney," you said. The crowd was already gone.

"You sure you can drive that big black?" he asked.

"Sure," you said.

"All right. Don't mention it," he said. You turned to look at Pinky going slowly up the street. "He'll be all right," he said. "Just a touch of the sun." He took off his helmet and wiped his red face. "Well, I'll be on my way."

But he watched until you had climbed up to the seat of the wagon. "Giddap," you said. The black started forward. Rooney waved to you and turned his wheel in the other direction. "Giddap," you said, the tears running down your hot cheeks.

PA WAS STANDING out on the sidewalk in front of the store waiting for you. "What happened, Charlie," he asked, "what happened? You didn't hurt yourself, did you?"

"I'm all right," you told him. "It's Pinky."

"I know," he said. "That woman who called told me about it, but I could hardly make head or tail out of what she said."

You told him what had happened.

"Went down just like that, huh?" he said. "That makes everything fine and dandy for me."

"You should've seen poor Pinky stretched out on the street. I thought he was a goner," you said.

"Don't worry about Pinky," he said. "You can worry about me. Where am I going to get the money for another horse? Tell me that." He cursed Pinky furiously. "It's just my hard luck," he said. "With the whole world sitting on my neck, this has to happen to me, too."

"Well, it isn't Pinky's fault," you told him.

He laughed shortly. "You sure take after your mother, don't you? I suppose it's my fault if the old plug drops in his tracks."

"He's not a plug," you said.

"Now listen," he said, "don't give me any back talk, or I'll slap your ears for you."

"Gee, Pa, what are you mad at me for? I didn't do anything," you said.

"All right, never mind now," he said. "Sweep up the store."

You swept up the store. "He don't have to be sore at me," you muttered to yourself, "I didn't do anything." Your heart felt like a hot stone in your chest.

He was busy behind the counter, figuring with a pencil and paper. "What are you mumbling about?" he asked.

"Nothing," you said sullenly.

He came out from behind the counter. "Now listen, Charlie, you better change your expression," he said.

"Well, Pinky is not a plug," you said. "And it wasn't my fault either," you burst out at him.

His heavy hand caught you on the side of the head.

A terrible rage welled up within you. "What you hitting me for?" you screamed at him. "What'd I do?" Your head was ringing. "What'd I do?" you said.

"Keep quiet," he said, "there's people coming in."

"I don't care," you said, "you don't have to hit me for nothing."

"Shut up, will you?" he said.

He smiled and went past you. "What can I do for you today, Mrs. Mayhew?" he asked.

I'll run away from home, you thought.

"What's the matter with Charlie?" Mrs. Mayhew asked.

"Oh, he's a little upset," Pa said. "The delivery horse just laid down on the road a little while ago and scared him."

"I wasn't scared," you wanted to holler, "I wasn't scared."

"Well, let's see," Mrs. Mayhew said, "I'll have a can of beans. And. . . ."

You swept the stuff off the floor into a box and carried it into the back room. "I'll run away," you said to yourself.

After a while he came in. "You can go home for my lunch now," he said. "You ought to be ashamed making a racket when there's customers in the store."

"I didn't start it," you mumbled.

"Well," he said, "I was kind of excited about Pinky and worrying about money and all." He came closer and put his hand on your shoulder. "Look, Charlie," he said, "you want to learn to make allowances for people." You were silent. "Take a man when he's upset about something," he said, "he don't think half the time what he's saying or doing. See?"

"Well, it wasn't my fault," you said.

"No, I know it wasn't," Pa said, "it's just plain hard luck. Here I am trying to make a living for all of us, trying to make some money so we can live in better style, and one thing after another works against me. It's discouraging to a man," he said.

"Aw, Pa, we'll make out all right," you said.

"That's the spirit, son. You bet we will," he said. "Just leave it to your father." He smiled at you and you smiled back. "Friends?" he asked, holding out his hand.

"Aw, sure, Pa," you said, grinning shamefacedly at him.

"Good!" he said. "Now hop up to the house for dinner, and tell your mother there's a hungry man waiting here for his." You started to go. "And listen, Charlie, don't say anything to Ma about Pinky. No use getting her worried. I'll tell her tonight," he said.

"All right, Pa," you said.

WHEN YOU GOT BACK with the dinner pail, Joe Flynn was in the store. ". . . at nine o'clock tomorrow morning," he was saying as you came in.

"How's Pinky?" you asked him anxiously.

"That old plug," he said.

"Now, Joe, don't tease the boy," Pa said.

"Well," Joe said, "the vet came over and took a look at him, and it looks as if Pinky'll never pull another wagon."

"What's the matter with him?" you asked.

"Just old age," Joe said, and laughed, "just old age."

"Yup, and tomorrow we get a new horse," Pa said. "A young one."

"But how about Pinky?" you said.

"Oh, we'll take care of him all right, won't we, Joe?"

"Sure, we will, sure!" Joe said. "See you at my place in the morning." He went out.

"Where you going with Joe, Pa?" you asked him. "Can I go?"

"We're going up to the auction stables," he told you, "and Joe's coming with me to see I get a good buy."

"Take me, will you, Pa? Take me," you said.

"Well, Charlie, if your mother can take care of the store by herself in the morning, I might take you. So you won't be mad at me any more," he said, grinning.

"Sure she can, she's done it before. How about when you took me to the hospital in Boston?" you said. "She can bring Sylvie down with her. Sylvie'll be tickled."

"Well, we'll see," he said.

You handed him the dinner pail. "Ma said for you to eat it right away before the soup gets cold."

"Don't worry," he told you. "Get me a bottle of beer out of the icebox."

At supper that night, Pa told Ma what happened to Pinky. "I'll have to get a new horse," he said. "Wouldn't you know I'd run into more hard luck just when I'm pinched for money."

"You mean you're going to buy a new horse?" Ma asked. It was hot in the kitchen, her face was flushed, and she wiped her hand across her forehead.

"Did Pinky die?" Sylvie asked.

"No, no, he just fell down," you said.

"I guess I'll have to," Pa said.

Ma sat down and began to eat. "I don't see how," she said, "if you haven't got the money."

"Oh, I got the money all right," Pa said.

"What money?" Ma asked. "You mean the bank money?"

"Sure," Pa said.

Ma sat up straight. "I thought you promised me after we moved into the new store and you bought new fixtures that we wouldn't touch any more of that money. Or what's left of it," she said bitterly.

Pa's voice got loud, you looked down at your plate. It made you feel ashamed when they argued, and you couldn't look at them.

"Didn't you promise me?" Ma asked. "Didn't you?"

"I know," Pa said, "I know I did. But what's a man to do?"

"Mamma's insurance money was nearly a thousand dollars," she said. "Where is it now? I bet there isn't even a hundred left."

"Yes, there is," Pa said, "there's a hundred and twelve."

"Oh," Ma said, "a hundred and twelve! And where's the rest of it? Tell me where's the rest of it?"

Pa didn't say anything.

"I'll tell you," she said. "First, you let that Albert Smithson who everybody knows is a swindler get you into that soda-bottling business, and you lost everything you put in with him. Then you started out for yourself with that cigar store in the Bank Building, and that failed. Then you got that newspaper and magazine agency, and that failed. And then after you got the little market on Geary Street and things were going along all right, you weren't satisfied—no, you had to have a big place, a big market, you had to be a big business man!"

"Do you have to shame a man in front of his children?" Pa asked.

"I don't care who I say it to," Ma said. "I'm sick and tired of it. We were better off when you were a conductor on the trolleys, and I didn't have Golden coming to my house trying to catch you in so he could collect the rent for your big market."

"That Jew," Pa said.

Ma's voice got shrill. "That Jew," she said, "yes, that Jew. Believe me he's treated you better than you deserve. If he wasn't so good to you, we'd be out on the street. Blame somebody else for your troubles!"

"It's not my fault," Pa said. "You don't want to see a man get ahead. You'd want me to keep on collecting nickels for the car company the rest of my life."

"Yes," Ma said, "yes. Better than worrying every day where the next dollar's coming from and being able to buy a ton of coal without wondering where the money's coming from to pay for it. Who paid for last winter's coal? Tell me that," she said.

Pa didn't answer.

"If it wasn't for my brother Gustave, we'd have frozen to death."

"You don't have to throw that up to me," Pa said. "You'd think your brother Gustave wasn't a rich man."

"What of it?" Ma said, "what of it? He's got his own family to take care of—why should he take away from them to give to you?"

"Well, you're his sister, aren't you?" Pa said.

"What are you saying, Harry? You're my husband, these are your children—why should another man, brother or not, have to do things for us? You make me mad when you talk like that. Like a child," she said.

"All right," said Pa, "all right. What's done is done. What can I do? What good is all this talk? You're just crying over spilled milk, that's all."

"The trouble with you is, you have to be your own boss," Ma said. "You couldn't work for someone. Oh, no. You have to be a big business man."

"Now, Martha . . ." Pa said.

"What do you have to buy a new horse for? You can hire one, can't you?"

"Sure!" Pa said. "Sure! That shows how much you know about business. Telling me what to do. Sure, I can hire a horse. Do you know what it'll cost me? It'll cost me ten dollars a month besides his feed."

"All right," Ma said, "but it's better for the time being than to lay out a hundred dollars for a new one and take our last cent out of the bank."

"Joe Flynn says I can get a good new horse for seventy, eighty dollars."

"Joe Flynn!" Ma said. "What does he care how he spends someone else's money!"

"Things are going to pick up for me," Pa said. "I feel it in my bones, things are going to get better. Look," he said, "if I hire a horse, in a year it'll cost me a hundred and twenty dollars, and I won't have a thing to show for my money. Believe me, Martha, old girl, I know what I'm doing. Trust me."

"All right, have it your own way," Ma said, "and we'll see who's right. But I warn you, it's better to take it easy for a while than to spend our last cent right away. You'll see," she said. She got up and went out into the pantry.

You looked up at Pa, and he winked. "Your mother is some woman," he said, grinning. "If she was a man, we'd have as much money as Carnegie."

"You bet we would," you said.

"You, too," he said, "hey?"

"Is Pinky dead, Charlie?" Sylvie asked. "Is Pinky dead?"

"No," you said, "of course not."

THE NEXT MORNING you were in Flynn's livery stable, and he was reading very fast to Pa and you from a paper in his hand: " '40 horses 40 at auction at the Hancock Hotel Sales Stables, 947 Garden Street Wednesday August 9 at 9 A.M. 28 head will arrive Tuesday the 8th from H. P. Wright, Decatur, Indiana. In this consignment there are four matched pairs 2400 to 3000 lbs., 15 head of express and delivery wagon horses 1000 to 1300 lbs. You will find in this consignment a horse for any purpose, a milk-wagon horse, a tip-cart horse, a family driving-horse. These horses are extra well-broken to city sights and ready for immediate use. Auction every Wednesday. J. R. Pratt, Prop. Tel. 372J Exeter.' Did you hear that, Harry?" Joe asked. "Extra well-broken to city sights. I wonder did they ever see the hoochy-coochy?"

You had gone into the stall where Pinky stood with his head drooping.

"Put a halter on him while you're there, Charlie," Joe called.

"Why?" you asked. "Is he going with us?"

"Sure, he is," Joe hollered, "what do you . . . ?" His voice stopped abruptly. Your father said something to him in a low voice.

"What do I what?" you asked.

"Nothing," he said. "Come on, we have to get a move on and get one of those hoochy-coochy horses."

Pa laughed. "Say, as long as he looks the goods, he can do the hoochy-coochy, and the turkey-trot as well, for all I care."

"Look the goods?" Joe said. "They all look the goods. What you want is for him to *be* the goods."

Slowly, you led Pinky out of his stall.

"Hurry up," Joe said.

". . . sound as a dollar and clever as a kitten," the man was saying. He had a derby pushed back on his head, it seemed to be resting on his ears. His face was long and unshaved. His Adam's apple slid up and down his long skinny neck while he hollered. "Yessir, gentlemen," he said, "sound as a dollar and clever as a kitten."

A boy was leading a horse slowly up and down the stable-yard, and the skinny man was pointing at him. "Look at those knees!" he said. "Any man says that horse is knee-sprung is a gol-durned liar. Why, President Taft would be glad to ride a horse like that."

"You mean two horses like that," Joe Flynn said, and everybody laughed.

"Yessir," the auctioneer said, "a big horse for a big man. And is there a big man in this crowd? Is there a man big enough to start the bidding on a horse like that?"

Joe Flynn turned to your father. "That's the one I was telling you about," he said. "If you want him, start right in."

"You sure he's all right, Joe?" your father asked.

"I give you my personal guarantee," Joe said. "And don't forget he knocks fifteen off for the plug if you buy. I already had a talk with him."

"All right then," Pa said. "But you do the bidding."

"Do I hear a bid, gentlemen?" the auctioneer asked. "Don't be bashful."

"Twenty dollars," Joe hollered.

"There's a man who knows horses," the auctioneer said, "even if he's only joking about the price, he knows horses."

"And women!" Joe hollered. Everybody laughed.

"And women," the auctioneer said.

"You two ought to go in Keith's vaudeville," another man said.

"Twenty-five dollars! Twenty-five," the auctioneer said, "now I'm getting some action. Twenty-five! Do I hear thirty?"

"Thirty," Joe said.

"And thirty I have," the auctioneer said, "do I hear thirty-five?"

"Thirty-five," someone hollered.

"And thirty-five I have. Do I hear forty? Forty, forty, forty—do I hear forty?" He stopped, his voice dropped. Then he began again in a quieter tone. "Why, gentlemen, there's a horse only four years old, a horse that's the best of the West, a gentle horse, a strong horse, a horse that will serve you faithfully and well, a horse that has no galls, no botts, no glanders, a horse that's sound in wind and every limb, a horse—why, as the immortal Shakespeare says in a *Midsummer Night's Dream*, I'd give a kingdom for that horse. Look him over, try him out, and put your bids in fast, gentlemen. Time is going fast, gentlemen, time is going . . ." *Time is flowing, Time is going, Time is going, flowing— Out of what deeps of Time, up through what days and nights, months and years, from what sunken riverbeds where rots the débris of past Time—twisted horseshoes, long corsets, brass bedsteads, picture-hats, chipped Billikens, burnt-leather cushions, cigar-band collections,*

*Turkish Trophies, conch shells, bead portieres, marble-top tables,
chamber-pots, whatnots—out of what rubbish sunk in the deeps of
Time, the pure memory rises soft and fragile as a shadowed bubble,
rises glittering from the murky deeps to wake the sad nostalgia of the
spirit.*

". . . time is going. Do I hear forty?"

"Forty," Joe Flynn said.

"Forty-five," said the other man, spitting out tobacco juice and giving Joe a mean look.

"Fifty," Joe said.

"Fifty-five," said the other.

"That's the way it ought to go," said the auctioneer. He pushed his
derby further back and wiped his head with a red handkerchief.
"Fifty-five, I have," he said, settling his hat back on his ears. "Fifty-five
I have. Do I hear sixty? Sixty, do I hear sixty from Mr. Flynn? Sixty?
Sixty?" he asked, nodding his head at Joe.

Joe nodded back.

"And sixty I have," he said. "Sixty. Do I hear sixty-five?"

Your father nudged Joe, but Joe said to him, "Take it easy, you
have to go slow. If that other feller gets excited, he'll sell his wife's
wedding ring to get that horse away from you. Just out of spite and
stubbornness. Let him cool off a little," he said.

The auctioneer was talking to Joe again. "Come on, Mr. Flynn,
you're buying a horse here, a real horse, not a plug."

Then you looked around with a start. Where was Pinky? You remembered Joe had tied him up inside when he and Pa had gone to
talk with the man. But you hadn't seen him since. "Pa," you said,
"where's Pinky?"

Your father made a vague motion with his hand. "Oh, he's around
here somewheres," he said.

"I don't see him anywhere," you said.

"Well, don't worry," he said, "and don't bother me. Can't you see
I'm busy?"

You started to go back to the stable, but he turned around and took
your arm. "Stay here, Charlie," he said.

"But Pa, I just want to take a look at Pinky," you said. A thought
suddenly struck you. "What you want to bring him here for anyway?"
you asked. "Huh, Pa? Why'd you bring him here?"

"What you want me to do with him?" he asked.

"Sixty-five," Joe's voice said.

"That's the word, that's the word I wanted to hear," the auctioneer said. "And now do I get seventy? Do I hear seventy?"

"What you want me to do with him? Put him in the museum?"

"No, Pa. But where is he? What they going to do with him?"

"How should I know?" he said. "He ain't mine any more," and pulled away impatiently from your hand on his arm.

Your heart leaped painfully. "Ain't yours any more?" you said after him.

"Now Charlie," he said, "will you quit bothering me? I couldn't keep him, he's no use to us any more. I couldn't afford to keep him. Be reasonable, son, and don't ask me any more questions. You can see I'm busy."

"I know," you said. "But Pinky—I didn't even say goodbye to him. Did you sell him to somebody else? Where is he now?"

"Yes, yes," he told you, "he's sold, I sold him already. The man took him away."

"Seventy-five I have," the auctioneer said.

"What man?" you asked. "Where'd he go? Did he take Pinky away with him already? Tell me, Pa," you begged him.

"I don't know," he said. "Will you quit nagging at me?" He turned back to Joe.

You stood still a minute with a dreadful feeling in your heart, as if you were going to faint away. Then you stepped back quickly from your father while he was talking to Joe. The next minute you had gone out of the yard and into the stable. You stood just inside the doorway. "Pinky," you said in a low voice. But the stable was quiet except for the stamping of hooves once in a while. "Pinky," you said again, expecting any second to hear him whinny. You went around looking in every stall. But you did not find Pinky. Your heart was swelling in your breast.

Then a long shrill whinny came from behind the stable. "Pinky!" you hollered. You saw suddenly the door in the back of the stable between the box stalls. Frantically, you pushed the door open and ran out a few steps into the yard before you saw Pinky. You stopped short as if a great hand had been laid against your chest, and your mouth opened in a formless cry of anguish that you could not utter. A short heavy man was jerking at Pinky's halter trying to pull down the wildly upreared head, while another man circled with a revolver, picking up glints from the sun. The short man suddenly ran in close and kicked Pinky rapidly in the belly, his leg swinging with a careful ferocity. Pinky reared up wildly away, and the man let the halter go. But when Pinky was free, he did not do anything. He stood quite still, trembling a little, with a line of foam showing on his mouth.

"I guess he's ready for it now," the man with the revolver said. He put the gun behind Pinky's ear and pulled the trigger. The cry came out of your throat, tearing its way, and seemed to hang for a long time in the sunlit air. Then the short man's head was turned toward you, Pinky stood with his head hanging, the other man's hand was behind Pinky's ear—you all stood unmoving in a terrible pause. Suddenly Pinky's legs folded under him, and he crashed down on the ground.

In the clear pitiless morning sunlight the old horse sprawled on the dirty ground, his gaunt neck stretched forward in the last agony of death, his legs already stiffening, the blood slowly bubbling from the hole behind his ear, and the iridescent flies circling his flanks.

Was this the first time, when you saw the blank protruding eyeballs, was this the first time you had seen how terrible is the difference between life and death, realizing how close death is to life? The tranquil summer-evening years of your boyhood lay there upon the ground, the years of joy and peace flung into the dirt with one blow. Did you not then feel the slow sad subsidence of the tranquil years running like Pinky's clotting blood into the filthy littered ground? "Pinky!" you screamed, "Pinky!" remembering, there is always only remembering, his nose rubbing against your shoulder and his mouth lipping your hand for the apple core. In vain the final stiffening of the body against corruption, the last stand of the muscles, nerves, bones, blood against the hungry suck of the summer-parched ground. They were pulling the dirty canvas over him. "Pinky!" you screamed. "Pinky!"

"Get that kid the hell out of here," the heavy man said. "How'd he get in anyway?"

"You let me alone, you murderer!" you said as the other came toward you.

"Now, kid," he said, "ain't no cause for calling names."

No cause. Of course not, no cause, realizing then for a moment the pressure of life squeezing you in its dirty hand, slowly pressing out the spirit, damming the heart's blood surge, bending the spine slowly closer to the ground till the heavy head falls forward, the thin body following, and the gaunt neck stretched forward, the eyeballs protruding before the final stiffening and the final surrender.

"He's too fresh," the heavy man said, "bat him one over the head."

"You touch me," you said, "and my father—" but you stopped with a murderous hatred for your father burning in your heart, suffocating you. . . .

"It's not my fault, Charlie. I couldn't help it," Pa said. "That's what life is, sonny, that's life."

"Liar!" you screamed at him. "Liar!"

"If it was my kid, I'd paste him one on the jaw for sassing me like that."

"Let me alone," you panted, "don't touch me. Ma!" you screamed.

His heavy hand rang against your ear. "In front of all these people," he said, "you ought to be ashamed."

"You—you! You're the one to be ashamed," you said and ran blindly out into the clear burning sunlight.

The sun was nearly directly overhead. The factory whistles were blowing. It was high noon of the summer morning, and a long time to a summer evening that would never come again.

A Note on Novellas

BY

WHIT BURNETT *and* MARTHA FOLEY

A Note on Novellas

A GOOD STORY needs no explaining. But a note of comment perhaps is not out of place as to why, without a plague in Florence or a convenient jaunt of story-telling pilgrims to Canterbury, five separate stories of such variety should be presented in a single book.

For, separate, unlinked stories these are, each, in a way, a creator's special world—from Eve's personal, fantastic realm in "Turnip's Blood" to the bitter realities of the flop-house world in Albert Maltz's story of the Bowery. And what morals and themes there are must be sought for by the reader: they are not set forth by a charming Queen of the Fifth Day or underlined by some ruminating narrator sipping cool drinks inside the framework of a porch or club.

In a country where more than 500,000 persons, according to a Book-of-the-Month Club survey, are writing short stories, the last year or so has seen the phenomenal emergence of a good number of stories which are less short than long. And, since they are long stories, there is, in general, no room for them in ordinary magazines. Five such stories, whose length and treatment have been gauged not by mechanical, commercial, or periodical publishing limitations, are included in this book. All first appeared in the magazine *Story*. Several other long stories have appeared in America during the year. With few exceptions they have been substantial and important stories, solidly fashioned, and worthy of a more than passing place in American letters. These long stories of literary value are something new on the American literary horizon and, while the form itself is not new, it is newly attracting widespread attention. The form is the "long short story," or, as it is called here, the novella.

A novella* (perfect examples of which are "The Gentleman from San Francisco" by Ivan Bunin, "Death in Venice" by Thomas Mann, "The Turn of the Screw" by Henry James, "Ethan Frome" by Edith Wharton, and "A Lost Lady" by Willa Cather) is a story whose development requires more length and leisure than the short story, and yet it is in the nature of the short story in its unity of effect. In its avoidance of various and complex centers of interest, it differs from the more discursive novel. America, unlike France, Germany, Austria, or Russia, has grossly neglected this long story form. It is not wholly the authors' fault. It is chiefly because anything longer than a short story has been mishandled by both authors and publishers alike in an effort to make it conform, by spinning it out, to the length of the standard novel.

Longer than the short story, and yet shorter than the novel, the novella has something of the spirit of both: the singleness of effect and mood of the shorter form and the richness of more ample treatment, with that play of emotional and, at times, philosophical overtones which are the special possibilities of the more leisurely novel. With no reflection on the beauty and effectiveness of the short story as a form of art, the novella, less fragmentary and concentrated, permits an au-

* The Italian word *novella*, used to designate the same literary form which the French commonly call the *nouvelle*, and the Germans the *novelle*, was first employed in the February, 1937, issue of the magazine *Story*, because, in publishing some of these newly written pieces, the editors found there existed no word to describe them. They were not, as is commonly supposed, "novelettes." A novelette is a potted novel, the skeleton of a novel; and the term, while tolerated by usage, is not a fortunate one—it smacks of all the synthesism of an age in which "ette" endings have been used for everything from farmerette to dinette. The novella is not a "little novel" either. And "long short story," "very long short story" or, as Ford Madox Ford describes one of Henry James's works—"a *longish* short story"—are all contradictions in terms. When Edward J. O'Brien reprinted in his *Best Short Stories of 1937* cited three examples of novellas produced last year, he urged American editorial encouragement of both the form and the word, and defined novellas as "stories of sustained breath which accept all the limitations of the short story unities."
Transplanted from the Italian, the term in American, must, of course, have its own modern sense. It is not here used as in Boccaccio's day when, as John Addington Symonds points out in *Renaissance in Italy*, "almost everyone wrote novellas"— usually mere anecdotes on a moral, or immoral, theme—but in the sense of the richer meanings with which the word has become associated in its progress through the centuries—modified and transmuted through the French language in which *conte* is the word for the short fiction piece, and *nouvelle* (from *novella*) is the word for a story much longer; and through the German in which a *Kurtz-Geschichte* (short story) is one thing while those great *novellen*, "Death in Venice" by Thomas Mann and "The Man Who Conquered Death" by Franz Werfel, are quite something else again.

thor longer breath and more time and space in which to evoke his people and his problem. It is no accident that it has reached high development with such full-bodied artists as Mann and James.

But—whether you call these works of fiction short stories, novellas, long short stories, or little novels, we hope you have found in each of them sustained moments of pleasure. Whether you are flying with Eric Knight's most human Mr. Sam Small, who could fly like a sea gull and could fly like a pigeon but could never quite fly like a lark—or experiencing with Albert Maltz the pathos of under-dog life in New York, there is a new and spacious treatment in these stories, a treatment, because of its length and yet unswerving singleness of idea, that permits a rich evaluation of all the elements of the story. This seems especially true in "The Song the Summer Evening Sings," in which I. J. Kapstein has recreated the colors and moods of a generation ago, and Helen Hull's delightfully detailed story of the small-town wife who is swept into New York to claim a literary prize. None of these stories can, by any stretch of the imagination, be called a novel; neither are they short stories. They are, we think, novellas, and effective ones at that.

WHIT BURNETT
MARTHA FOLEY

The Authors

PHOTOGRAPHS AND BIOGRAPHICAL NOTES

ERIC KNIGHT

Born in Yorkshire, England, on April 10, 1897, Eric Knight has lived an ideally varied life for an author of fiction. He has been an art student in America, a factory worker in his native shire, a Hollywood screen writer, a trainer of jumping horses,* a moving picture critic for the Philadelphia *Ledger*, has served in the United States Army, and was overseas with the Princess Pat regiment from Canada in the World War. He is the author of *Song on Your Bugles*, a Harper-Story Press book, one of the most moving books about the common people in England which has appeared in the last ten years. Mr. Knight has also written several short stories including "The Marne," which was reprinted from a story in the *O. Henry Memorial Award Collection, 1936*. He is married and lives in New York.

* He has been photographed innumerable times on jumpers but this photo, taken in New Mexico, is the first ever made of Mr. Knight on a wooden horse.

HELEN HULL

Helen Hull, who is the author of nine published novels and innumerable short stories, is presented here with her first novella. Although an experiment in this length, "Snow in Summer" promises not to be her last writing in the novella form, which she says she feels to be perfect for a subject between a short story and the full-length novel.

Miss Hull was born in Michigan and attended Michigan State College and the University of Michigan, and later the University of Chicago. She was instructor of English at Wellesley from 1912-15; lecturer in English at Barnard College, 1915-16, and has been at Columbia University since 1916 where, since 1923, she has been assistant professor. She was awarded a Guggenheim fellowship for creative writing in 1931.

Her first published work, written when she was only seven or eight years old, was a poem and a story in the *Advertiser Mercury* owned and edited by her grandfather, Levi Tyler Hull. She spends her summers on a farm in Maine, writing and gardening.

ALBERT MALTZ

Albert Maltz, author of "Season of Celebration," which at first glance will recall Gorki's "Creatures That Once Were Men," is divided in his literary allegiance between fiction and the theatre. His biography is as objective as his prose: "Born 1908, Brooklyn, N. Y. Public schools there; graduated Columbia College in 1930. Attended Yale School of Drama under Professor Baker for a year and a half. Left school for the New York production of 'Merry-Go-Round' written in collaboration with George Sklar. Play stopped for a week under Mayor Walker's regime because of its attack on political corruption. Editorial protest, etc., forced its re-opening. Worked a summer at Paramount Pictures. Wrote 'Peace on Earth' with George Sklar produced by Theatre Union. Wrote 'Black Pit' produced by Theatre Union. Won New Theatre League contest for one-act plays with 'Private Hicks.' At work at present on a novel. Member of Executive Committee of Theatre Union. Member of Authors' League Council."

RACHEL MADDUX

" 'Turnip's Blood' a novelette which you are about to read is the effort of a thoroughly unknown and unpublished twenty-three-year-old." With this introduction Miss Rachel Maddux's first story to be published came through the daily mails to its editorial haven. Miss Maddux was born on Main Street in Wichita, Kansas, in December, 1913, "just in time to ruin my mother's Christmas," she writes. "I began writing when I was six, due, I am sure, to the encouragement of my sister, Erma, who is indeed a joy, and 'Turnip's Blood' is the first thing to come of it. There was a novel before 'Turnip's Blood' written on brightly colored paper when I was seventeen, working nights in a newspaper office, but my pet white rat chewed it into small bits and built a house out of it for her family of six. It was a much better house than a novel. I spent three years at the University of Wichita and the next year was graduated from Kansas University. 'Rameses' in 'Turnip's Blood' is my own dog who in real life sometimes answers to the name of Phaedean."

I. J. KAPSTEIN

I. J. Kapstein says his autobiography is a plain one. He writes: "I was born in Massachusetts in 1904; public school education in Massachusetts and Rhode Island; was graduated from Brown University in 1926. On my way to and through college, I worked: newsboy, errand boy, filing clerk, shoe salesman, haberdashery clerk, door-to-door canvasser, mill-hand, soda-jerker; did a night-shift on the railroad, etc. After graduation, I worked for a year and a half in New York for A. A. Knopf as editorial assistant in the text-book department. I was glad to return to Brown as an instructor in English in the fall of 1927. With time out for graduate work—I got my Ph.D. in 1933—I've been teaching at Brown ever since. I published some verse in *Poetry* in 1928 and 1929; some critical articles about Shelley on whose philosophical ideas I wrote my dissertation (unpublished). 'The Song the Summer Evening Sings' is the first extended piece of fiction I've written. I've been so busy teaching English composition to freshmen and sophomores that I've not had time to do much writing myself. But I've always wanted to. I am married and have a three-year-old daughter."

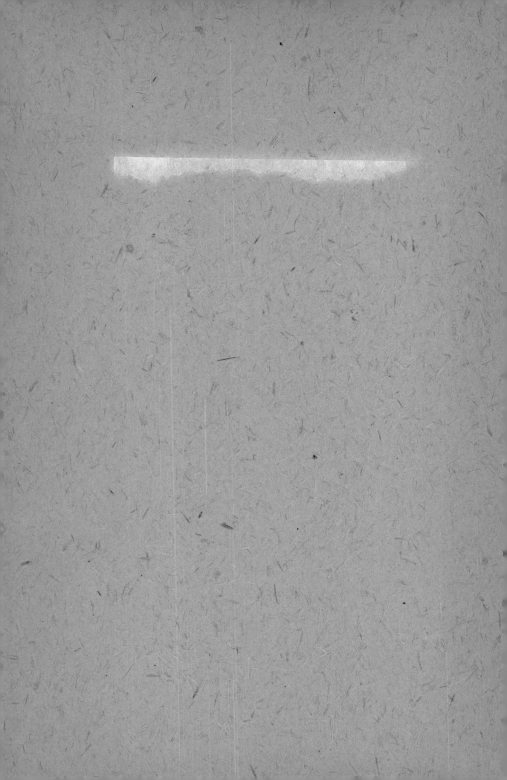